My eyes cut like a shot to my feet. There, just beyond the end of the blanket, pristinely tied around my ankles, were my pleasure-me pumps—luminescent, pink and utterly dry.

Lifting my eyes, I caught Phillip's gaze. He saw it too.

"May I?" he asked, squatting.

As he took my foot in his hand, the blood in my ears made a *wonk-wonk* like Rudolph's nose when Coach Comet pulled the fake mud one off. My host turned the shoe gently from side to side. Despite my being nearly swallowed by the sea, the shoes were dry. Not just dry, but almost glowing, like the ball of light around Tinker Bell. With his arms held loosely over his thighs, he pondered this.

"What?" I asked.

"You have very fine ankles, milady."

I blushed. Not enough men took the time to notice ankles.

The winds outside stopped abruptly, leaving a roar of eerie silence in their wake. We stared at each other for a moment, his Tom-like face sending a bolt of longing through my heart. I couldn't convince myself anymore I was going to wake up on the floor of Nine West with him hunched over me. This had nothing of the appearance of a dream.

"Where am I?" I asked at last, trying to hide the quaver in my voice.

"Off the Dalmation coast, milady. In the year 1706. You are a writer, and I"—he pulled off a nonexistent hat and bent deeply—"am your character."

Tumbling Through Time

GWYN CREADY

Pocket Books

NEW YORK   LONDON   TORONTO   SYDNEY

Pocket Books
A Division of Simon & Schuster, Inc.
1230 Avenue of the Americas
New York, NY 10020

This book is a work of fiction. Names, characters, places,
and incidents either are products of the author's imagination
or are used fictitiously. Any resemblance to actual events
or locales or persons, living or dead, is entirely coincidental.

First Pocket Books paperback edition February 2008

POCKET and colophon are registered trademarks of
Simon & Schuster, Inc.

For information about special discounts for bulk
purchases, please contact Simon & Schuster
Special Sales at 1-800-456-6798
or business@simonandschuster.com.

Cover design by Lisa Litwack
Illustration by Alan Ayers

Manufactured in the United States of America

10 9 8 7 6 5 4 3 2 1

ISBN-13: 978-1-4165-4115-8
ISBN-10:   1-4165-4115-2

For my sister, Claire,
who would have laughed

Acknowledgments

I owe a debt of thanks to many people: Leslie Reed, for giving me the book that started it all; those who always made a point to ask how the manuscript was going, for giving me more inspiration than you know; Teri Coyne, for many good things; Gretchen Wolfe Anselmo, who kindly pulled out her French and Italian dictionaries on my behalf; Gary DiBartolomeo, a master at making silk purses; Judy Steer, for some knock-out line editing; my crack marketing team: Theresa Gallick, Marie Guerra, Paul Fraioli, Richard Holme, Andrea Harkins, Janet Bednarz, De Anna Whalen, Michael Roe, Karen Schade, Camille Walton, Dawn Kosanovich, Katie Kemper, Scott DeLaney, Sharon Wible, Rich Mankovich, Joe Gitchell, Mitch Zeller, Ted Kyle, Jeremy Diamond, Alison Muir, and Jennifer Murray—what can I say? You guys ought to do this for a living; my wonderful cousins, Donna, Mary, and Lynne, who read many drafts and, more importantly, adopted me as a sister when I was bereft; Manuel Erviti—how many writers have a handsome and hilarious head of a university library at their beck and call?; Wileen Dragovan and Diane Pyle, who have always been there for me when it counted and with whom I have pulled off many, many capers; author Elaine Knighton, who generously shared with me everything she knows about this business, which is a lot, and taught me not only to be a better writer but a better person; my wonderful editor, Megan McKeever; publicists, Jean Anne Rose and Lauren Robinson; designer, James Perales; and all the professional, hard-working folks at Pocket, for treating my book like a treasure; my fabulous agent, Claudia Cross, whose confident declaration, "It's just a matter of time," kept me typing long after I wanted to throw in the towel. I owe far more than a debt of thanks to Cameron and Wyatt, whom I love a lot and like even more. Finally, all good things in my life start in one place. Lester, you're the one, babe, even if your dialogue is written by a man.

Prologue

**Adriatic Sea, somewhere between Greece
and the Italian states
1706**

The wind howled around his ears, and the blasting rain beat at his exposed skin like a cat-o'-nine-tails. The ship heaved and creaked, though he knew her fine oaken timbers would hold.

A hurricane—fifteen bloody leagues from Otranto. What next? Snow in the Azores? A sandstorm on the Thames? He rolled his eyes and brought the collar of the oiled jacket up to his ears. Today was the ninth day of this. He must bring this ridiculous mischief to an end.

Jones, the officer of the watch, pulled his way along the rope strung taut across the quarterdeck and filled his lungs to be heard above the roar. "Almost no water in the hold, Captain. And only eight men at the pump."

He nodded, unsurprised. She was a weatherly ship— one of England's finest—even in a storm only an untrained mind could have created. *Caution* was the young wench's supposed watchword. He'd heard the bloody saying so often in her thoughts he wondered if she ever acted on gut or heart or—he felt the tingle in his belly—something more primitive. Yet if one looked at the design of the world that held him and his three hundred men in its teeth, she hadn't appeared even to think before she leaped, let alone look or consider. Thank God she hadn't tried getting the science of hydraulics into her head, else he and his men would probably be bobbing toward Venice right now, rub-a-dub-dub, three men in a tub.

He opened the hatch and made his way down the steps toward his cabin, bending instinctively to avoid the low-slung beams. In the past, two of Her Majesty's marines would have clattered to their feet upon his arrival. No more.

That, at least, he couldn't blame on her. The loss of his naval commission had been his own doing, though a failure to regain it—a regaining that had seemed so close until this foolish, unnecessary business at Gibraltar—would certainly sit at her doorstep.

He dashed off a note and handed it to the ship's boy.

Before he'd even gotten his first sip of coffee, he heard the tinkle of brass coins that edged the old Gypsy's head scarf. *'Tis good she doesn't have any hopes in the way of surprise materializations.* She stared at him when she entered, eyes brown and unreadable. Among his crew, she alone had recognized the topsy-turvy world in which they were caught.

He bowed. "Thank you for coming."

"You are certain you vant to do this?" she asked in her thick Balkan accent.

"I must get those papers back." He didn't want to have to beg, but he knew that he would.

"There are reesks."

"What of it?"

"The girl may not vish to come."

"To the devil with that. She has upended my world. Look around you."

"Vorse, she may do more harm than good. You are the one who vill suffer, no one else."

Grapeshot fired at close range might do more harm than the girl had already done; he couldn't think of much else. Besides—and this he would never share with the Gypsy—there was something strangely provoking about the confection of bluster, ambition and wantonness he'd glimpsed during those moments when the wench's thoughts rang clear in his head. This vaguely glimpsed future held more promise than he expected—especially from Americans.

"I accept the risks," he said. "Proceed."

The old woman brought out two small jars from her shawl. In one of thick, clear glass sat a measure of black-speckled powder, not quite like gunpowder but not far from it, with that same sulfuric scent. The second jar was smaller and fashioned of rough clay. He could not see its contents.

She directed him to light a lantern. Normally in such a storm, no flame would be allowed. He unshipped the lantern's face carefully and touched a match to the wick. When shadows danced on the walls, she opened the clay jar and angled it over his palm, scattering into it tiny bits of pale pink fabric.

"This must come from you," she said.

He eyed the translucent wisps, thinking of the alluring young woman and all the trouble she had brought. At once, the fabric began to emit a soft, ethereal glow.

He looked up, surprised. The old woman's face betrayed no emotion. She emptied the contents of the clear jar into her own hand and leaned close to the lantern. She gestured for him to do the same.

"First I," she said, "then you."

With a *pfooo* she blew the powder into the flame. Tongues of blue, red and green flickered in the orange.

He took a deep breath and followed.

For an instant the fabric wisps sparkled in the air like diamonds, then the flame boomed like a squib, bathing the room in a dazzling display of sparkling pinpricks that faded slowly to nothing.

Heart beating strangely, he lifted his eyes to her. "Well?"

"Prepare yourself," she said.

Chapter One

Look before you leap, I always say—an important lesson when your family pet is a sheepdog the size of Chattanooga and you're doing your leaping in the backyard of your childhood home. Not that I have a sheepdog anymore—I can barely keep bread mold going, let alone care for a houseplant or pet—but I grew up with them, and my father still shares a house with one.

The lesson, however, took hold. Caution is my middle name. Actually my middle name is Jude, but only my closest friends use it and only then to wind me up. "Caution" fits a whole lot better. Persephone "Caution" Pyle. As a philosophy it's become my trademark. It has served me in business. It has served me in investments. It has served me with men. It has even served me in my divorce. I've found that without the appropriate amount of premeditation, life is too much like my childhood backyard—one moment you're having fun; the next you're digging dog do off your PF Flyers.

Which is why I ate at Campiti's, my favorite pizza joint, before leaving for the airport this afternoon and now didn't have to chance ordering off the slightly sticky "Cinco de Mayo" menu at the slightly sticky bar near my gate.

My colleague Tom Fraser sat beside me. He and I were heading to a Pilgrim Pharmaceuticals sales meeting in Venice.

Tom popped the last of his third chicken-and-corn taco into his mouth and inclined his head toward my drink. "I always say there's nothing like a gin and tonic to really capture the spirit of old Guadalajara. Are you sure you don't want a BLT to go with it? You'd at least be in the spirit of 'Mayo' if not 'Cinco.'"

"Mayonnaise? At this place?" I shuddered.

"Seph, Seph, Seph." He shook his head.

Tom bemoaned my lack of spontaneity. I bemoaned his lack of imperfection.

Surely the best-looking corporate attorney to ever come out of Fargo, North Dakota, Tom is tall with wavy chestnut hair, blue-gray eyes and a hole in his chin that looks as if my father's Craftsman drill press put it there. My girlfriend Dana claims he's the spitting image of Colin Firth, and he does possess a certain Darcy-like quality, but I'm pretty sure Colin Firth would not have spent so much time stealing surreptitious glances at my breasts.

Tom threw a twenty and a five on the table. "You ready?"

I eyed my bag with confidence and nodded. "I've got a book for the flight. My PC battery is charged and I have a spare. I have a sleeping pill, aspirin, antacids, breath mints, Jolly Ranchers, a toothbrush and a water bottle in my carry-on, and a clean pillowcase in my purse. My watch is set to Venice time—I already checked the daylight saving time conversion. Dana has the phone numbers of all my father's doctors. My passport and credit cards are strapped to my calf, and I left a copy of my passport, American Express card and itinerary with her, another set with my father, one on my desk and a fourth in my safety-deposit box."

Tom lifted a brow. "I meant are you ready to head to the gate, but I'm glad to see you've really taken that 'relax and enjoy' thing to heart."

Tom and I had become friends during a disastrous acquisition meeting a year ago. We were part of a team trying to buy a Japanese company that owned the best-selling pain reliever in Asia. I run Grant's aspirin. I'm the brand manager, which, in a world where scientists pore over steaming beakers to find the next great product improvement, advertising agencies haggle with producers to crank out heart-touching commercials, factory managers diagram every possible improvement in the manufacturing process, and attorneys like Tom tie up our competitors with lawsuits, is sort of like being the events planner at an orgy. No one pays much attention to you, but if things go well, you're a star.

Anyhow, the Japanese company had been impossible to deal with. We were at the end of our respective ropes. On the day of the final meeting, Dick Hanlon, our high-tech, low-integrity boss better known as Hairy-Eared Hanlon, had accidentally managed to record part of a particularly nationalistic diatribe he'd been spewing at me and Tom and embed it into one of the presentation slides on his PC.

If the Japanese had been hard to deal with before, hearing the head of Pilgrim Pharmaceuticals describe them as "sushi-sucking pedophiles" over the projected figures of a counter offer that did not give them a share in profits until the end of year three did not help.

Tom saved the day by standing up and launching into a karaoke version of "I Will Survive," in which he rhymed "sushi-sucking pedophiles" with "capitalists reviled" in a revisionist chorus he passed off as a frat song used to open all Pilgrim negotiation meetings.

The deal fell through, but we kept our jobs. That night Tom and I got drunk, and laughed so hard his hand slipped into my bra, and I was splayed on a Pilgrim Pharmaceuticals recycling bin cupping his finely gabardined ass before the throat-clearing of the cleaning crew brought us to our senses. I don't do frivolous, and if a drunken one-night stand with a dimple-chinned coworker does not constitute frivolity, I don't know what does.

Honor if not dignity intact, our lives returned to normal. Tom agreed, solemn-faced, to let sleeping gropes lie, though a little more quickly than I would have liked, and neither his smooth baritone nor the smoother waistband of his paisley boxers made any further appearances in my dating life. I told myself it was good to have a friend at Pilgrim, which isn't always a friend-friendly place, and since my Norwegian grandmother lives in North Dakota, we have a lot in common.

"I like the way you're wearing your hair," Tom said, picking up his overnight bag. "You're always doing something different."

I looked in the mirror behind the bar. One dark, determined lock was trying to leap to freedom from my ponytail.

"Thank you," I said. "I like to think of hair as a journey, not a destination."

Tom processed this a beat. "That's remarkably relaxed of you."

"I didn't say I didn't have a *plan*—"

"Oh, *phew.*"

"—it's just that if you do it right, the journey can be as interesting as the destination."

His eyes drifted slowly down the dangling lock to my breasts. I cleared my throat.

"Er, I'm going to check out the newsstand," he said, rising. "I need some floss."

"Oh, no. Not a Cinco de Mayo problem, I hope?"

He gave me a look. "No. I plan on donating it to your readiness kit. I understand floss can be woven into a light but waterproof sleep mask in case of an emergency."

"Ha-ha. I'll meet you at the gate."

Control is key to an orderly existence, and adherence to my rules of decorum—"Conservative Jude-ism" Dana calls it—has been a lifelong habit. My father says it's from losing my mother at an early age. I say it's the only possible reaction for a woman extravagantly named Persephone by her parents. Whatever it is, a taste for seriousness has spilled over into every aspect of my life. I drive a twelve-year-old diesel Mercedes. Pastel colors make me twitch. No thong has ever garroted my Jockey-loving flesh. Even my manicure style—French—is the plainest there is.

Which is not to say I don't like those who do frivolous. In many ways, I envy them. I've spent untold hours at the nail salon marveling not just at the polish colors, but at the catchy names and themes. It's amazing to think there is some marketing executive at a desk somewhere deciding this season will be My Galapagos Vacation and Remembering the Six-Tease. I love my job, but that's gotta be more fun than marketing low-dose aspirin, which, as we at Pilgrim like to say, is about as funny as a heart attack. In a world of white salicylic acid and orange safety coating, one finds oneself longing for What's a Gull to Do Gold and The Long and Winding Rose.

Tom loped off, his trench coat trailing from his hand. I flipped on the little recorder I carry on my key chain and said, "Sweet but unintentional imitation of Linus being stood up by the Great Pumpkin."

When a phrase hits me, I like to record it. I intend to write a sweeping love story someday, with a hero as honorable as Jamie Fraser, as brave as Jack Aubrey and as tortured by desire as Fitzwilliam Darcy. I like my heroes to be larger than life and as far from my own time as possible. Otherwise they're just guys you could meet anywhere, and where's the romance in that?

Anyway, I figured I'd need all the inspiration I could get since my plan for the flight was to finish my presentation for the sales meeting and, assuming Tom wasn't sitting close enough to see my laptop screen, actually begin drafting an outline of that love story. A number of ideas had been bouncing around my head recently. I was hoping some would feel energetic enough to pogo right down my arm and onto the page.

I grabbed my bag, stood and gave myself a quick review in the mirror, noting once again that, despite an ultrachic black sleeveless turtleneck over black linen jeans, I'd never be mistaken for a fashion model. It could have been my height—five-foot-five doesn't exactly scream "runway"—or the full-ish curve of my breasts, but it was probably the size 14 body that looked like it would always be perfectly comfortable living in double-digit territory.

The Pittsburgh airport is one of the new breed of airports—shiny, bold and stocked with shops for the captive traveler. I marched past the store selling scarves that doubled as evening pareos.

Oh, honey, not with this chest.

And as I approach anything other than a tiny sprinkle of my mother's Arpège with the self-conscious unease of a woman being offered a pair of pasties and a whip, the fragrance store offered no attractions. Nor did the bookstore, since after I read the historical romance in my bag I had a stack of at least nine more by my bed. Even the shop selling twenty-dollar wheeled totes held no temptation. Like most men, I thought. Worthless after the first unzipping.

What I was looking for was a really good present for my dad's birthday, a milestone the medical events of the last year had left me uncertain he'd reach, and I had every intention of marching past the Nine West shoe store as well when a vision in shell pink jerked me to a stop.

I am not one to salivate over shoes. My black Anne Klein flats are endlessly all-purpose. I can't even remember the last time I did anything more than reorder them online in whatever minor variation the latest season brought.

But the pink evening shoes sitting in the window were, well, magnificent. Two-and-a-half-inch modified kitten heels. Tall enough to be sexy, but not so tall I'd feel as if they'd brought back foot-binding. And in place of standard-issue leather straps were two wide swaths of delicate, translucent taffeta that I swore for an instant sparkled like the Northern Lights. The taffeta started over the toes, crisscrossed over the arch, then circled the ankle, tying with an exuberant bow in front. They were shoes that said, "Fuck me, but do it after you've fed me strawberries and maybe given me a nice pair of earrings."

The salesclerk smiled encouragingly. "Would you like to try them on? They just came in. We've only got the one pair."

"One pair!" I squeaked, afraid my hopes would be dashed. "Size eight?"

She lifted the foot-equin and checked the sole. "What do you know? Size eight it is."

The woman untied the swaths as I watched proprietarily. I kicked off the Anne Kleins and removed my socks. I wanted nothing coming between me and that taffeta.

She handed me a shoe. The fabric was cool, and it rustled like my high school prom dress. I sank into the nearest chair and inserted my foot. My toes, which usually looked like half-cooked shrimp, seemed to lengthen and tan right before my eyes. Even the spots of Sonny and Cherise the manicurist had applied while I locked down the childproof cap deal on my cell phone yesterday looked like they belonged.

I drew the ties around my ankle and gasped. I didn't even have to finish knotting the bow to know the fit was perfect. The base cradled my foot in a lover's hug. It was like a Birkenstock for women who shaved their legs, an Easy Spirit for women who hadn't signed away all hope, a Dr. Scholl's for women who wanted to exercise muscles higher than their arches. The shoe seemed to pulse with life.

I stood.

The heels held me perfectly. No pain. No pinch. Flamingo-like, I lifted my unshod foot. Flawless equilibrium. I could stand forever.

I thought of Dorothy and her ruby pumps. I thought of Cinderella and her glass slippers. I thought of Mercury and his winged heels. A gentle, living warmth rose through the sueded insole that reminded me of the wave-lapped sands of St. Barts on that first glorious getaway with my ex-husband, when sex had been like a rocket blast into space, not a half-awake commuter special at the end of a long week.

"I'll take them." I unzipped the pouch around my calf and slapped my American Express card on the counter.

The shoes didn't go with a single thing I owned. I'd have to buy an entire new wardrobe. I licked my lips, wondering how much time I had before the flight.

While the clerk was running my card through the reader, Tom appeared on the other side of the shop window. He waved. I pointed to my foot, smiling. He gave me a thumbs-up.

I sat down to put on the other shoe. When I tightened the taffeta around my ankle, I swore I could hear violins. I unfolded myself and gazed into the full-length mirror. All at once, the scent of sandalwood hit me like a wave, flashes of light appeared at the edge of my vision, and in a booming crack, the store disappeared in a cloud of Lo-Lo-Lo-Lo-Lola-civious Violet.

Violet, blue, green, orange, red: the world pinwheeled backward through the rainbow as I struggled, terrified, for a toehold. The first drop shot my stomach northward, the second nearly launched its contents into orbit, and the third dropped me hard on my ass while fist-sized water balloons exploded in my face.

I managed to find an iron bolt and clung to it, terrified. Alarms rang in my ears and chest. If it had been a bomb, I'd be dead, or at least not wet.

The world was dark and gray and steeply pitched. I had the impression of being at sea, but it was only an impression, for absolutely nothing could be made out of the buffeting sheets of stinging wet formlessness that assaulted me in every direction. I cried out, hoping someone would hear me, but if someone replied, I couldn't hear it over the mosh-pit roar of the water.

The floor dropped again, and the impact tore me from the bolt. Cold terror shot through me. I scrabbled to catch hold of something while the relentless water dragged me down the slope, but my grasping fingers found nothing.

I slid and slid, and the salty liquid filled my nose and mouth. I gasped but no air would come. The water seemed to pour in on all sides, pounding me in all directions. I thought of my father and my brother and the good-byes I'd never get to say.

All at once, a steel arm circled my waist. I struggled to anchor my hands around its ropy circumference, but a wall of spray as hard as sand flung me loose. I reached again, desperate for the hope it offered, but it was gone. My lungs screamed with wanting. The world turned silver, then sparkly, then there was nothing but Paint It Black.

"Good gad! What have you there, Captain? It looks to be a drowned mermaid."

"Take her if you please, Mr. Haverhill," a deep voice rumbled through the muscled wall at my ear. "Put her on my cot."

I was dimly aware of being heaved from one set of arms to another. Slipping in and out of the half sense my cotton-candy-filled brain was making of the world, I found myself shivering and flat on a bed in an alcove set off from the rest of a small, dark room. In truth, it reminded me quite strongly of a scene in a historical romance novel I had just finished reading, where the Duke of Silverbridge and his estranged duchess reconcile tearfully on a boat docked at Tynemouth, just as she's about to leave him forever and sail away to France. But my mind did not linger on this: the world was still pitching, my butt was on fire, and the damp, low-planked ceiling looked like it might collapse on me at any moment.

When I say a pair of appraising blue eyes appeared over me, it is not a figure of speech. In the light of the bedside lantern, appraising blue eyes were the only appearance of humanity my observer revealed. A red flannel scarf covered most of his wet, dripping hair, a canvas storm jacket was buttoned high over his mouth and nose, and the narrow swath of cheek visible was set at an ironic angle and covered by several days' growth of beard.

"Mmpf," he offered, unenthusiastic.

Across the room Mr. Haverhill asked, "Oughtn't we get her into some clothes?"

That jump-started my brain.

I cut my alarmed gaze from the swaddled beast over me just long enough to determine my state of dress. Whatever I was wearing was thin, cold and soaking, but I wasn't naked. Ready for a wet T-shirt contest but not naked.

"Mmpf," repeated the owner of the eyes, this time with a note of reluctance.

The beast withdrew. I heard the wet coat being unbuttoned, the scarf being flung across the room, and what sounded like the thrum of my neighbor's border collie after jumping from his bath. Droplets flew in every direction.

"Where do you suppose she came from, sir?" Mr. Haverhill asked.

"A stowaway, of course. Explains our run of ill luck." My savior had the voice of a slightly rough-edged BBC commentator. Russell Crowe on unfiltered Camels. "Thank you, Mr. Haverhill. Tell Jones not a wisp of cloth now, not even a stuns'l. We'll scud until the storm breaks."

I tried turning my head to protest, for the last thing I wanted was to be left alone with the beast, but my stomach did not approve of me flinging the world around with such abandon.

I heard Mr. Haverhill, gentleman that he was, hesitate. "But, sir . . ."

"That will be all," the beast said firmly.

The door shut.

"Where am I?" I demanded. Without warning, the room dropped what seemed to be the height of the Empire State Building. "Oh, God, I think I'm going to be sick."

This elicited a brief, Crowe-like chuckle. "Now there's a bit of poetic justice."

"I beg your pardon?"

"You are in the brig *Neuf Ouest*, madam." A blanket landed with a soft *plonk* on the mattress beside me. "In perhaps the only hurricane the Adriatic has ever seen."

"I'm on a boat?!" I pulled the warm, dry wool over me. Like its owner, it had the faint odor of exotic spices.

"A ship, madam, an oceangoing vessel with forty-two

guns. Second rate. That is," he added with a touch of
woe, "were she still a rated ship."

Second rate, indeed. The walls around me creaked
and moaned. If this was a ship, it was a damned small
one. The ships I usually travel on go through storms
like a Porsche through North Dakota—level, straight
and as quickly as possible.

"Wait a second," I said, trying to get my bearings.
"There are no oceans near Pittsburgh." Pittsburgh is
irredeemably landlocked. The Ohio River, on which
Pittsburgh sits, does quite a bit of barge traffic, but this
was no barge, and the harsh assault of water on the timbers beneath us was definitely not that of a river. Lake
Erie was ninety miles north of Pittsburgh, but Erie
wasn't the dangerous Great Lake, was it? I begin to sing
"The Wreck of the Edmund Fitzgerald" in my head.

"Pittsburgh?" he repeated, uncertain. "There's a
Pitsford near Northampton, I think—dreadful place—
but I am not familiar with Pittsburgh. Near Swindon,
perhaps? Er, I must recommend you shift out of those
wet linens."

I was trying to wring water out of my skirt, but with
the movement of the room, the chilly stream kept running down my arms. Freeze with cold or warm with embarrassment, I asked myself. My chattering teeth won.

"Turn your head," I insisted.

I heard an aggrieved "Harrumph" and a few shuffled
steps, which I took to indicate compliance. With a
jerking wriggle that sent the taste of Campiti's pep-
peroni pizza to my mouth, I lifted myself to my elbows
and peeled off the—what on Earth was this anyhow?

A *slip?* I haven't worn a slip since fourth grade. Besides, I'd been wearing black linen jeans at the airport. In a moment I was back under the blanket. This was very strange and getting stranger by the minute. "All right," I said.

"Come, come, Miss, er— What is your name?"

"Pyle."

"Miss Pyle. This will never do. The bedding's wet too."

Much as I hated to admit it, he was right. I gathered the blanket tightly, gave my stomach a pep talk, and stood. When my eyes met his face, I nearly passed out.

"*You?!*" I cried.

"Perhaps ways are different in Pitsford," he said as he pulled the bedclothes away, "but where I was brought up, 'tis considered unmannerly to point."

My knees buckled. Standing before me in a pair of loose-fitting, damp cotton trousers and open blue shirt was Tom! But not my Tom. This Tom was a hairy, disheveled . . . ruffian. The fundamentals were there: the strong chin, the dark hair, the rugged profile, even the cute muscled ass—though I'd never seen Tom in damp cotton anything, and the effect was breathtaking. The details, however, were slightly offset from the original, like a 3-D print when you're not wearing the glasses. Instead of close-cut locks, shaggy waves hung to his shoulders. Instead of smooth, contoured cheeks, stubble on which I could file my nails bristled. There was a tattoo on his forearm, a scar through his eyebrow, and the chin—

I blinked. "Hey! Where's your hole?"

"I beg your pardon."

"That divot in your chin. The crevasse big enough to rappel down. Where is it?"

"Oh, that." Spots appeared on his cheeks above his beard. "It's there. Haven't shaved in a week." His hand went abstractedly to the dimple. "What is it about women and this thing?"

I paled. That was the exact toe-in-the-sand response Tom had given me the first time I mentioned the dimple to him.

"Oh, God." I squeezed my eyes shut and willed myself to wake, the way you do in the middle of one of those horrible dreams where your boss is about to stick his tongue down your throat or you've shown up at a meeting naked.

I opened my lids. "Shit." Still naked, or nearly so.

He lifted his brow at my language. Another Tomism. "Who *are* you?" I demanded.

"If you mean my occupation, dear lady, I am the captain of this ship. If you mean my name, it is Drummond. Phillip"—he rolled his eyes in pure distaste—"Drummond."

"What's wrong with Phillip?" I asked, slightly irritated. As it was, this was the name I had decided upon for the hero of my theoretical novel. "It's a wonderful name. As it happens, it was the name of my first boyfriend—the one who took me to the prom," I added grudgingly when his gaze intensified.

"And one takes such pride in being the immortalization of the boy who wore his shirt studs backward and made you pay half the bill at the inn."

My chin dropped and so, too, nearly did the blanket. "How did you know . . . ?"

He grunted. "I am well versed in any number of matters, madam."

"But Tom doesn't know that. I don't know what kind of a dream this is, or who you are, but I'm not playing along."

"Not playing along?"

Sparks of anger appeared in those sapphire pools, and I found myself taking a cautionary step back, which, given the minuscule dimensions of the cabin, dropped me back on my bruised butt on the cot.

"At least you have that option," he continued. "This is not a dream. This is my life, my life envisaged by you, at least. And therein lies the problem. You have cut corners, you have mixed fish with fowl, you have,"—he gestured wildly—"taken a pinch here and a dash there until we have a bloody Merry-Andrew show on our hands."

"Me? That's impossible."

"Look here. Do you see this wall?"

Plain and white. "So?"

"Ships don't have walls. Ships have bulkheads. Bulkheads have sections that can be stripped down for battle. Walls have, well, nothing that can recommend them for battle. And this?"

He pointed to a round mahogany table in the corner that happened to have the barrel of a cannon rising from a hole that had been cut in its middle. Ingenious, I thought.

"It's a gun," he went on, "my best chaser, in fact. A

gift from the Dey Ahmoud. But you have built a dining table around it, a handsome one, I freely admit; only you have provided no hinges or bolts with which to break it down. So I am reduced to lifting it whole and rolling it into the paddock, legs wheeling like some sort of spinning jenny, catching sheets and lines and, last week, Mr. Kenney's groin, when battle is imminent. After our run-in with the *Royal Louis*, the ship's cat kitted upon it, and I had to eat in the gun room for a week."

Despite my confusion—at this point I had decided just to let the dream take its bizarre course—the thought of this grizzled hulk deferring to fluffy, slit-eyed kittens made me smile. An instantaneous glower from him froze it mid-curve.

"Even that," he added, "would be tolerable if you hadn't dropped a French agent into my midst. Christ—*pardonnez-moi*—I would have preferred yellow fever. Then at least one or two of us would come out with our honor intact." He dropped into a chair dejectedly. "Queen Anne will have me hung from the maypole at Hampton Court."

"Queen *who*?!" I squawked. "Don't tell me Princess Anne is queen!" Visions of the horse guard at Buckingham Palace running Olympic jumps and the English monarch flipping off the press blazed through my head.

"Anne ascended the throne in '02," he answered patiently, "upon the death of her sister's husband."

I felt dizzy, and this time it wasn't the room. Princess Anne doesn't have a sister, and she certainly did not ascend the throne in 2002, at least not the Princess

Anne I knew. That was the year we launched Grant's Maximum Strength Formula and I had a lot going on, but I'm pretty sure I would have noticed a change in English monarchs.

History had never been my strong point, so it was with some effort I scoured my mind for the queens I could name: two Elizabeths—the one now and the Judi Dench one with Shakespeare. Victoria—face like a boxer, Prince Albert in a can. Mary, Mary, Mary? Wasn't there a Mary? Ah, yes, of the famous William and Mary, my brother's alma mater in Virginia and a reigning king and queen. In fact, the only king and queen to rule in tandem, I remember learning on the campus tour.

What else had that cheery undergrad told us? Mary inherited the crown from her father, who'd been kicked off the throne for being Catholic, a very bad thing at the time, worse than sex with an intern. Upon William and Mary's death, the crown went to . . .

"*Eek!*"

"What?" he demanded.

"Queen Anne was Mary's younger sister!"

"Indeed, she is."

Is. My legs were shaking. "What year is this?"

"Aught-six, madam."

"Aught-six? As in s-s-seventeen-aught-six?" As in baroque music, as in the last of the Stuart monarchs, as in bitter battles with Scotland and France?

"Aye."

Despite the gradual lessening of the storm, my head was spinning faster. I felt like Dorothy in the land of Oz, thrust into a world she couldn't comprehend, with nothing but a dog and those absurd blue anklets and ruby slippers—

My eyes cut like a shot to my feet. There, just beyond the end of the blanket, pristinely tied around my ankles, were my pleasure-me pumps—luminescent, pink and utterly dry.

I swallowed.

Lifting my eyes, I caught his gaze. He saw it too. He unfolded himself from the chair and sauntered over, brows knit.

"May I?" he asked, squatting.

As he took my foot in his hand, the blood in my ears made a *wonk-wonk* like Rudolph's nose when Coach Comet pulled the fake mud one off. My host turned the shoe gently from side to side. Despite my being nearly swallowed by the sea, the shoes were dry. Not just dry, but almost glowing, like the ball of light around Tinker Bell. With his arms held loosely over his thighs, he pondered this.

"What?" I asked.

"You have very fine ankles, milady."

I blushed. Not enough men took the time to notice ankles.

The winds outside stopped abruptly, leaving a roar of eerie silence in their wake. We stared at each other for a moment, his Tom-like face sending a bolt of longing through my heart. Where was Tom now? Had he found floss? Was he missing me? I couldn't convince myself anymore I was going to wake up on the floor of Nine West with him hunched over me. I couldn't convince myself I was going to wake up at all. This had nothing of the appearance of a dream. I pinched myself. I bit the inside of my cheek. I squeezed my eyes and said, "There's no place like home." Nothing. Nothing. Nothing. Nothing but me and Phillip Drummond and the sound of the now gentle sea.

"Where am I?" I asked at last, trying to hide the quaver in my voice.

"Off the Dalmatian coast, milady. In the year 1706. You are a writer, and I"—he pulled off a nonexistent hat and bent deeply—"am your character."

Chapter Two

"*B-but* I don't have a character. I'm not a writer. At least not yet." Not unless you count thirty-second commercials in which an actor who looks like Brian Dennehy tells you an aspirin a day can save your life. I mean, I hadn't even clicked File New to start the book's outline yet. If this happened now, what would happen when I actually put fingers to keyboard? The immediate implosion of the universe? Dana had suggested writing might be cathartic for me. If this was her idea of catharsis, I'll stick with Silverbridge and his duchess.

"Not at all?" Phillip looked disappointed.

I was dressed in his linen nightshirt and drinking a mug of coffee at the cannon-barrel table. The cream and sugar swung in a little wire basket that hung from the muzzle. The coffee had the consistency of roasted mud, but the one-two-three punch of caffeine, blister-

ing heat and double shot of whiskey Phillip had added
had been enough to moderate my babbling.

"Well, I mean I have written," I said. "I was a literature major in college, after all—British literature, ironically enough. But I don't have a character, per se, no. I
don't even have a dog. I have a tree."

"A tree?" Toast had arrived with the coffee, and Phillip stopped in the middle of slathering a plank-sized slice
with orange marmalade to regard me with curiosity.

"A sequoia."

He stared blankly. Never heard of a sequoia, I suppose. They don't grow in Europe.

"A *big* tree." I racked my brain for tall things in England. "As tall as Big Ben."

"Ben who?"

Oops, too early for Big Ben. "Er, as tall as the ca-
thedral of Notre Dame." That, I was fairly certain, had
been around for at least half a millennium. "And fat at
the bottom. Like the biggest haystack you've ever seen.
But mine isn't tall or fat. Mine's a baby. Like this." I held
one palm about a foot higher than the other. I'd gotten
McCoy on my one and only trip to California, last spring.
McCoy was a very good listener. After four years with my
ex-husband, it was a quality I valued highly.

Phillip considered this. Sucking a spot of orange off
his finger, he said, "We use Scandinavian pines for the
masts, and with this war, they're blessed hard to come
by. Is this sequoia a good, hard wood?"

"Oh, no!" I thought in horror of one of those beautiful trees felled. "I mean, you couldn't use one for a
mast."

"Why not?"

"Well . . . because they're protected, I guess. They have their own park."

"And would not this gentleman be amenable to the right offer?"

"Gentleman?"

"The one within whose parkland the trees grow."

"Oh." I shook my head. "No. He wishes to preserve them."

"Odd." He handed me the piece of toast, and began to plaster two more for himself. A good fifth of the marmalade was falling over the edges.

"You don't seem like a character to me," I said. "You seem like a real person."

"I am a real person. That's the worst of it. We were sailing the North Sea one day, when the water started sloping toward land."

"Sloping?" The marmalade was wonderful, with big chunks of zest.

"Aye, a bit like a whirlpool, only without the revolving current. Just a slow, easy glide into Tynemouth port. The next thing I knew I was transporting some nobleman and his wife to France, the ship had walls, and my best cannon was wearing a mahogany necklace."

I choked on my toast. "Not a duke, perchance?" I thought of the tearful Silverbridge reconciliation. The sequel was in my flight bag.

"Indeed. A good fellow, if a trifle used to getting his own way. Insisted we were old acquaintances. I dropped them in Calais, which was in truth not far from my destination, and off they went, happy as the day is long."

"I have good news for you," I said, brightening. "You're someone else's character, not mine."

He shook his head firmly. "I am quite familiar with the story to which you refer—*Blackmuir Fires,* I believe it is called. There I was but a specter, a convenience for the writer—though I must say she captured my quiet authority with a skillful brush." A self-satisfied smile filled his face. "I could have worked for her indefinitely; the time requirement was minimal and the emoluments attractive. His Grace has numerous contacts in the government, you see. It was you, madam, who got me into the fiasco I'm in."

"What fiasco are you in?" I asked warily.

"I was given a sealed packet by Lord Dunwoody, the chief of naval affairs, to deliver to my admiral on the Mediterranean station. It was in my strongbox when we left Greenwich, and there again when I checked just before we touched at Gibraltar. Somewhere between Gibraltar and ten days ago, the packet disappeared. I'll be keelhauled if I arrive without it. More important, England's chances in this war will be ruined."

"Why?"

"The dispatch names the harbor France plans to attack. If England can beat her to it with all the naval power we can muster, we may be able to turn the tide of this war. If not, I'm afraid . . . well, I'm afraid our hopes are lost."

"So where's the harbor?" I asked.

"If I knew that, I would hardly need the dispatches, would I?"

"And how is this my responsibility?"

"Do the words 'a bosom like the breakers of Scylla and Charybdis, through which even the most confident men have sailed to their doom' spark a flash of recognition?"

I blanched. On my little key chain recorder were those exact words, inspired by a mural of a buxom Venetian woman gazing forlornly at a couple in a gondola on the wall of Campiti's.

"I thought so," Phillip exalted. "The lady with the rocky coast has been installed in a cabin abaft. Gathering her and the rest of her traveling companions was the reason we had to touch at Gibraltar." With the last of the second piece of toast still in his mouth, he picked up a third. "And for the record," he said, swallowing, "the breakers of Scylla and Charybdis are off the coast of Sicily, not Venice."

It had been a speck, only the merest speck, of an idea for a story when I recorded it, inspired, I admit, by the Silverbridge ship scene: a duty-bound sea captain and the beautiful admiral's daughter admiring him from afar—a soaring romance set against the background of exotic ports and warm, star-filled nights.

"Is there a problem with the lady?" I asked indignantly.

Curling his lip, Phillip said, "I suggest, madam, you see for yourself." He twitched his ragged sleeves back from his wrists and reached for his coffee.

"And what kind of uniform is that, anyhow?" An

image of Horatio Nelson emerged from the depths of my brain. "Aren't ship captains supposed to wear blue coats and big half-moon hats?" Not to mention shoes and unstained shirts.

His face tightened. "You are thinking of a naval captain."

"You mentioned your admiral and the chief of naval affairs."

"Oh, that. Well, Basehart was my admiral once—and will be again," he added quickly, "if I can find those bloody papers."

"Exactly what kind of a captain are you, then, traveling about capturing ships and—Oh, God, you're a pirate! I'm at sea with a pirate!"

The chair hit the floor as he rose. "I am *not* a pirate. I am a private captain with a fully executed letter of marque, and I'll thank you to remember that. I am a private captain on temporary leave from a very successful career in Her Majesty's navy, and if I can get you to get your plot in order and those imbecilic characters off my ship, perhaps that will happen slightly faster than at the glacial speed with which it appears to be occurring now." He punctuated each phrase with his finger.

"Ah, ah, ah," I warned. "Remember that upbringing."

He growled.

"Losing your temper is not going to help," I said. "And now that we've laid out your problems, let's do the same for mine, shall we? I am supposed to be en route to Venice for a sales meeting, and at this point my friend is probably—"

"The friend that doesn't pay for rooms?"

"That was fifteen years ago, and for the record he paid half. I'm talking about Tom. Tom Fraser. He's an attorney. Er, a solicitor," I said, translating into England-ese.

"Ah. Explains your fascination with pirates." He gave me an odd, knowing look. "He is your betrothed?"

"Oh, God, no. The thought's never entered my mind."

"That doesn't bode well for young Tom."

"He's not young. He's your age." *Exactly your age, in fact.* "And it's not like that anymore. Women have relationships with men without marriage or protection as a goal. And I don't mean *that* either," I added in response to the look forming on his face. "Women of my day are different."

His gaze skimmed my linen-clad form. "The fundamentals appear to be identical. You'll forgive me for observing, however, the women of my day are better fed." His tone suggested this was a significant advantage. I gazed down at my figure, wondering for the first time in my life if skipping dessert was the miracle it was cracked up to be.

"What business brings Tom the solicitor to Venice?" Phillip asked.

I stared into the sludgy depths of my mug, thinking of the pictures of the hotel overlooking the Grand Canal we'd be staying at for the week. *Hotel al Ponte dei Sospiri.* Even the name sounded wonderful, like a soft, lavender-scented breeze. Tom's obligations—a seminar on the changing global regulatory environment—were over after the first day. He was going to explore the city while I attempted to wow the international marketing managers with the advantages of launching a woman's formulation. "It is *my* business that brings us."

Phillip's brows peaked. "I see. A personal matter?"

"No. Brand management, if you must know." I searched for an eighteenth-century idiom. "Commercial interests."

"Commercial interests? What, may I inquire, is your commerce?"

"Aspirin."

Blank stare.

I laid a palm on my chest. "To help prevent heart attacks."

What did they call heart attacks here? Surely people died of them. Gout, ague, flux, apoplexy; I ran through every disease I'd ever encountered in a historical romance. Nothing. I pressed my chest tighter and made a face. "Much pain."

"I see. 'Tis strange for a woman to have commercial interests."

"So sorry. Next time I'm dragged across three centuries I'll try to forget I was born after the Age of Enlightenment."

Three *centuries*. What was I saying? I started to feel dizzy again and fanned my face.

"So I need to get to Venice," I went on. "How long will it take us to get there?" Please don't say three hundred years.

His head turned suddenly as if he'd heard a noise. "Damn that man!"

"What?"

"Can you not feel the change? Jones has run up a t'gallant." He tilted his ear toward the ceiling. "Two, upon my mother's honor. I'll flay the goddamned skin off that poxed Welsh back."

As far as I could tell, the ship's movement, blessedly smooth these last few minutes, had not changed a whit. He dashed to the stairs just outside his door and charged up them, two at a time.

"Wait! What about Venice?"

"See for yourself," he called. "We made the Strait of Otranto an hour before the storm."

I dropped my head into my palms. This was insane. I couldn't be in 1706. I had to be at some freakish masquerade party. I took another sip of my coffee-flavored whiskey, and a colorful map on Drum's desk caught my eye.

I could certainly make out the familiar shape of Europe, though the country boundaries within it looked bizarre even to my limited geographical understanding. It was a nautical map, filled with lines and numbers, and not all the country names were filled in. France looked like it covered half the continent. Of course, 1706 was back when France was the most powerful nation on Earth, not just the third country on your Europass. And what exactly was the "Spanish Netherlands," I wondered, contemplating the purple mass that sat just to the right of France's northeast shoulder. A vision of Hans Brinker munching tapas floated into my head. The name Italy was nowhere to be seen over the colorful blobs of city-states that filled the high-heeled boot.

Above me, I could hear Phillip's deep-voiced rebuke, Jones's shocked tenor protest, then a machine-gun fire of corrections and commands.

There was Venice, high on the boot, north and east of Rome, just as I had found it on the guidebook map. I touched the thick, smooth paper. Was Tom there? Had he boarded the plane thinking I was already seated? Or had he torn the airport apart when he couldn't find me? Did my father know I had disappeared? Would I see him again?

If there was a way to get home, it seemed to me it was through Venice. I wanted to get there as soon as I could. But where were we now?

What had Phillip said? The Strait of Otranto?

As a hint, it failed miserably. Phillip might as well have blindfolded me, turned me in a circle and handed me a donkey's tail. But he had mentioned the Adriatic. That was a sea, wasn't it? Not one of the big seven— Atlantic, Pacific, ah, Indian . . . and um . . . um . . . Well, it wasn't one of the big seven, I was sure of that.

Must be one of those little ones in western Asia. Black, Dead, Adriatic, Baltic. Unfortunately the map-maker had not bothered naming the bodies of water. Hmmm. Maybe I should start with something I knew.

I looked for St. Petersburg, where the sales meeting had been two years ago. I knew it was right across from Finland. Finland was the penis. That's what my friend Dana called it, anyway. She was an elementary school teacher prone to rebellion when freed from the class-room. She thought the Scandinavian landmass looked like her ex-boyfriend's testicles and penis. She had a thing about penises—either that or she had a thing about pretty weird-looking Scandinavians. But frankly, geography would be a far more popular subject if they used visual mnemonics like that.

Left ball, right ball, penis. I dragged my finger across the water. No St. Petersburg. No Adriatic either, for that matter.

Phillip's voice made me jump. "Too cold for gondolas there, milady."

"I knew that. I was looking at other things." I crossed my arms casually. "So, based on this"—I inclined my head toward the map—"it looks like it won't take us more than a few, er, weeks to get to Venice."

"*Weeks?!*"

"Months, I mean."

Phillip narrowed his eyes. "Point to Venice."

I jabbed the top of the boot.

"And now the Adriatic."

I bit my lip. I'd graduated from the University of Chicago in the era of the internet, cloning and text messaging, which is far more than Phillip the Hun had done. Granted, I'd gotten a degree in British literature, but I wasn't about to admit I didn't know where a simple old sea was. Dammit, I wish the Adriatic had looked like Dana's boyfriend's ass or something. I put my finger on something blue east of Turkey and smiled confidently.

Phillip gave me a look. "Did you study geography in Pitsford?"

Sure, ask me anything about Scandinavia.

He took my finger and drew it several hundred nautical miles to the southwest.

By God, Venice was *on* the Adriatic! I would have guessed, oh, I don't know, the Venetian Sea.

"We're so close!" I cried. "Oh, thank God."

Phillip stared at the map. His jaw flexed. "You must really care for this Tom."

"Can you get me there?" I prayed he knew the way back.

"I can," he said slowly. "But I shall require the return of the dispatches first."

Blackmailed. I was being blackmailed by a two-bit pirate who wouldn't have made a decent romantic lead in a high school play. How could any hero of mine have turned out like this?

"So, you want the dispatches," I said. "Great. How the hell am I supposed to help?"

But before he could answer, a plump man of about thirty burst in. "A sail, sir," he cried, red-faced, and I immediately recognized the voice of Mr. Haverhill. "Watson spotted it at six o'clock. She looks to be *The Constant Wake*."

"Hell." Phillip folded like a twenty-dollar wheeled tote. "Admiral Basehart's ship."

Chapter Three

Basehart was brought on board with an extraordinary amount of pomp. Drums beat, pipers piped and more swords clashed than in a Quentin Tarantino film. There may have been pageantry for the eyes as well, but I had been exiled by Phillip to his quarters.

When the ship reached signaling distance, Phillip had tossed a parcel at me and ordered me to stay below. Not bloody likely, I thought. Well, at least that's what I thought until confronted with the god-like authority of a captain at sea. Sailors Simon and Gar Funkel, brothers from Yorkshire, had been posted outside the door on stools, each as big as an ox and, more to the point, each wearing what looked to be a fully loaded pistol.

In the parcel was a white silk gown, clearly new, still wrapped in paper, as well as a confusing array of bleached linen, whalebone and lace. As a rule I decline any lingerie that must be declared as a weapon at an airport, so the whalebone bits were put aside. The corsets and shifts and drawers and Lord knows what else were too confusing to even consider, so I started with a loose-fitting minislip as my foundation garment. Between that, my taffeta pumps and the fact that the slip's hem barely covered the spreading purple bruise on my ass, I was definitely rocking a slutty schoolgirl look.

Good look for a home-based porn site; not so good for 1706.

Fortunately the gown that went over the mini-slip put me back into the realm of proper attire. It was sleeveless save for dainty puffs of white that fell just below my shoulders, and on the lustrous raw silk that fell in a swooshing wave to the floor were delicate hand-painted blossoms of lilac. It was gorgeous, low-cut and summery—not at all like anything I've ever worn before. I felt like Scarlett O'Hara on the porch with the Tarleton twins. I sashayed over to the door and peeked out.

"La-di-da," I said to the Funkels. "I do declare I've dropped my comb. My mother says a hundred strokes a day. Oh dear, I suppose a hundred strokes mean something entirely different to a sailor." I giggled in a way that half ejected my breasts from the dress and pointed to a door beyond which a small balcony overlooked the sea.

"Out there?" Gar said. "You dropped it out there? Did it not fall into the water?"

"Amazingly, no. It's stuck on something."

He made his way to the railing and leaned over. "I don't see it."

"It's sitting on that first little brown thing." I pointed to a series of vaguely ladder-like bumps growing out of the ship like a case of acne. "There, just behind the black stuff. The comb's black, too, so it's probably hard to see."

Gar took the lead, but it wasn't long before Simon was draped over the railing, too, holding Simon's hand as Simon explored the little ledge with his toes. (Poor thing, that first little brown thing was quite a distance down.) I tiptoed out, closed the door, and slipped Gar's chair under the knob.

The sky was all Blue-Footed Booby and Yellow Submarine when I crested the stairs, but Phillip's face was definitely Purple People Eater.

I must have cast a very fine figure, for two hundred pairs of eyes turned toward me in unison, though admittedly their point of focus was somewhere south of my actual face. Phillip choked back an anguished noise and said, "Admiral, allow me to name Miss Pyle."

It was my turn to purple. Admiral Basehart was the spitting image of Hairy-Eared Hanlon—balding, severe and Napoleonically short.

"Well, well," Basehart said with a slight leer. "I understand now why your voyage has been so leisurely, Drummond."

It was hard to say which of us squawked louder, but Phillip found his tongue first. "No, no, Miss Pyle is my . . . my, er—"

"—captive?" I suggested.

"—cousin," said Phillip. "My captivating American cousin. She has made a fine fourth at whist these last few weeks."

"I see." Basehart observed me with an eye growing warmer by the second. "Miss Pyle will be joining us later, I hope, after I get a chance to sit down and review—"

"The crew, aye, sir," said Phillip. "I can assure you they are ready to be reviewed. It has been many months since they have been favored with a visitor of your stature."

Stature? The tip of the man's hat came to Phillip's nostrils.

"Oh, very well," Basehart grumbled. "Let's get on with it. Join us, will you, Miss Pyle."

I could see a review would be no worry to Phillip. He might be many things, but at keeping a ship, well, shipshape, he surely had no equal. Despite a storm that had pelted me with seaweed, dead fish and a Sahara's worth of wet sand, the ship gleamed. The crew, standing in ordered rows at the far end of the deck, looked reasonably navy-like in red striped shirts and long white shorts. Phillip himself had changed into a bleached shirt, a long blue coat over a glistening sword and snug, knee-length trousers that put gabardine to shame—hell, that put the Chippendales to shame. There was no linen under there, and what was there needed no whalebone for support.

Basehart bowed deeply and gestured for me to fall in to his right as Phillip fell in to the left. I stepped cautiously, for the deck was slick, but my pumps seemed to be equipped with little treads, like tiny taffeta SUVs.

The sun emerged from a cotton-ball cloud and shone full force. It lit the silk in my gown like a spotlight. I swore I heard the crew gasp. This dress-up stuff could be addicting.

"She is an exquisite creature," the admiral said to Phillip.

By creature Basehart must have meant horse, for no more than two steps later a firm hand gripped my flank.

I squeaked, and Phillip's head swung around in time to see the look on my face grow from shock to outrage as the squeeze tightened into a pinch.

I drew a fist back to clean Basehart's hair-challenged clock, but Phillip caught it fast and swung me in a neat half circle.

"Milady," Phillip said through gritted teeth, "you nearly fell. Take care or we shall both regret it." He pulled me to the rail. "Here. There is a flock of birds to starboard I believe will excite your interest."

"That little prick pinched me!" I said in a furious whisper. A few of the closest heads turned.

Phillip grasped me by the shoulders and turned me farther around. "No, no," he called out, "no finches this far from land," then added under his breath, "That little prick is my last hope for getting back into the navy."

"Then maybe he should be groping *you*."

"Oh no, I am afraid they are not robins, Miss Pyle," he boomed. "They are what we call gulls."

"Great. Now I'm clumsy *and* stupid."

"Look, he's a lecherous old blackguard, but I need his recommendation to get my commission restored."

I narrowed my eyes. "And why exactly was your commission revoked anyway?"

Phillip shuffled his feet. "Dereliction of duty. I let a French cutter get away."

"You what?!" More heads turned, including that of Basehart, who had nearly reached the end of his review.

"Oh, aye," Phillip cried enthusiastically, "the sighting of one's first frigate bird is certainly worthy of exclaim. Feel free to hoot or yell as required. I'm sure the men will understand."

A dozen bright pink heads nodded vigorously.

"How could you do something like that in the middle of a war with France?" I whispered.

"They accused me of taking a bribe from the French captain. It was a lie, of course."

"Of course."

"It was."

"Then why did you do it?"

Phillip eyed me with careful calculation before he spoke. "Someone quite innocent would have been harmed. Not physically, but harmed nonetheless. 'Twas the honorable thing to do."

I guess it was, given that Phillip's career hit the metaphorical rocky coast soon after because of it.

"There wasn't enough evidence to convict me," he went on. "Not even with the parts that were made up. But after the next battle, the navy ordered my ship in for repairs. The repairs dragged on and on, and eventually the ship was decommissioned. I was told there were no other postings. It was either half pay on land or privateer work. Since my crew and I have a fondness for eating, I've been prowling the Atlantic and Mediterranean ever since in the *Neuf Ouest.*"

"You own your own ship?" I don't know much about sailing, but Tom owns a boat about a hundredth the size of the *Neuf Ouest,* and it cost him as much as my car.

"Someday, perhaps. I sail this on behalf of a group of investors."

"Investors?"

"We are at war with the French, Miss Pyle. Their trade ships are fair game, and any English ship that can capture one gets a share in the spoils. A captain with a record for quick, decisive action in battle can turn out more money for an investor than the best sugar plantation or the biggest cotton mill. Six weeks ago, we captured a corvette out of Toulon loaded with brandy and Dutch spice. The week before that, it was a frigate with silver, porcelain and a French minister with a particularly enlightening codebook, though to be sure there wasn't much left of the porcelain after the six enormous broadsides we gave her. We've captured or destroyed five French ships in the last three months."

The gleam in his eye was definitely piratical, but I dared not mention the *p* word.

"And you think *I'm* the person who put a French agent in your midst?" I asked. "I'd say you're lucky you and your ship haven't been blown out of the water."

"It couldn't be one of my men. I hired each of them personally—worked with most of them nigh on ten years. They hate the French as much as I do, if not more. None of them would divert a dispatch meant for our navy. The only other passengers are your Miss Quimble"—another roll of the eyes—"and her entourage."

Quimble? The name plucked at the far reaches of my memory.

"So you see, Miss Pyle, why I think you might be helpful in effecting their return."

"'Helpful.' Such a polite word to describe the actions of one being blackmailed."

His dark sapphirine eyes did not waver.

"And I'm to believe you hold the key to getting me home?" I said.

His brow arched. "Have you another choice?"

Bastard.

He said, "I can hold off Basehart for an hour. Two, if what's left of my best Spanish port holds. Please work within that time frame."

He clasped his hands behind his back and bent his head a degree, dismissing me with captain-like efficiency.

The daggers I was shooting him might as well have been flowers of admiration. He held my gaze, unmoved.

Having few other option, I picked up my skirts with a huff. "It's too bad Miss Quimble's not a man; I seem to make quite an impression in this dress."

I saw the corners of his mouth rise in a gentle curve. "Next time I would suggest adding an underskirt."

The sailmaker, Abel Kenney—he of the table-legged groin—had been quick to offer his wife for my lady's-maiding, and thank goodness he had. By the time she'd found me, I'd managed to remove my gown, but was hopelessly adrift in the sea of linen and lace they called an underskirt in 1706. Now, bracing myself Scarlett-like against a beam, I watched as Mrs. Kenney cinched the cat's cradle of ties around my waist.

A squat, fifty-something émigré from Bucharest, Mrs. Kenney gave the impression of a Balkan bomb shelter decorated Miami Beach. A jewel-toned scarf knotted behind her head hid most of her raven hair, wide silver hoops dangled at her ears, and bright spots of rouge dotted her cheeks.

It was not uncommon for a wife or two to accompany the sailors on a voyage, Mrs. Kenney explained in English as viscous and stick-in-your-throat as my grandma's turkey gravy. (My grandma upholds the proud, flavorless tradition of Norwegian cooking, where pepper is considered exotic and a clove of garlic is enough to send one's loved ones running to the medicine cabinet, clutching their tummies.) The wives, though, Mrs. Kenney added, must have skills the ship's company can use.

"And what are your skills," I asked, "apart from lady's-maiding, of course?" The wind and sea air had left me with an upsweep only Medusa could love, and when Mrs. Kenney finished my underskirt, she began brushing out my tangles.

"I'm a seamstress. Oh, unt I cobble unt I scry."

Really? Well, *I, Claudius* and *I Spy*. There's no way I could have written this woman; I had no idea what she was talking about.

"Cobble?" I repeated politely.

She pointed down to her sleek but utilitarian ankle boots and made a hammering motion with her arm.

"Oh, cobble as in cobbler!" I exclaimed. "You're a shoemaker. Gosh, maybe you can look at these when you have a chance." I shoved a sandal out from under my skirts.

Mrs. Kenney's face turned white, and she shot up like a Romanian jack-in-the-box. "Time for your gown."

Well, okay. My hair was only half done, so I looked like a punker with a commitment problem, but if Mrs. Kenney was ready to help me—

"Arms up," she barked.

I threaded myself through the bodice, and in a moment the painted silk cascaded to the floor. With the underskirt, my waist looked two sizes smaller, and the gown floated like a cloud around my legs. I felt like a princess, but I was quite curious as to how Phillip came to be in possession of such a lovely gown.

"I really must thank Miss Quimble for the loan of the dress," I said, digging not very subtly for information. "It's beautiful."

"No, no. Dis eez not Meez Qweemble's."

"Oh." I bit my lip. "One of the sailors' wives', then?"

Mrs. Kenney shook her head. "No one here has need of dis gown, Meez Pyle. You enjoy."

"But it isn't something one just keeps around for an unexpected guest, is it?" Like the solitary can of cocktail peanuts and cold bottle of chardonnay at my house? "I mean, it has to belong to *someone*."

The elder woman sighed. "Captain Drummunt has an acquaintance in Toulon."

"Toulon?"

"France."

Her face pinched into a look I associated with vinegar, Sour Patch candy, and Grandma's pumpkin pie. My affection for Mrs. Kenney grew. What was Phillip doing with a French floozy, anyway?

Mrs. Kenney finished my hair. I gave myself a once-over in Phillip's tiny shaving mirror: shoes, skirts, my dark curls pinned into a charming topknot. I looked sweet and beautiful—like a large silken petit four. Totally unlike me.

When I looked back, my companion was staring surreptitiously in the direction of my hem.

"Mrs. Kenney, do you know something about my shoes?"

She pressed her lips and shook her head. Not a very convincing show of innocence. My ex did better with the teenage neighbor's flip-flops up beside his ears.

"Mrs. Kenney . . ."

She shook her head again. I waggled a shoe in her direction. She flinched.

"What? Does a little shoe scare you? Just because it glows like a Love Canal garden gnome. What if I did this?" I tapped my toe. "Or this?" I kicked. "Or this?" I bent my knees to jump.

"*No!*" She threw herself around my waist like a crazed Balkan linebacker, and we tumbled to the floor.

Jesus, were the heels packed with dynamite?

"Dos shooz are very powerful, *ja?*"

"How powerful?" I removed her elbow from my neck.

"Powerful. Be careful vhat you vish."

Yeah, like don't wish for extra time in an airport shopping mall. I climbed to my feet with more care than you can imagine. "Here's the thing, though. I didn't wish for anything."

"*Ja, ja.*"

"Not *ja*. No. I didn't want anything. I just wanted shoes. I certainly didn't want"—I gestured to the heaving ship around us—"this."

Her eyes pinballed furtively. She gave a noncommittal shrug. "Maybe someone else had vish."

"Someone else? Like who?"

"Was that a knock?"

A second later came a *thump-thump-thump.*

"*Ja?*"

"Miss Quimble's compliments," a man called. "She's ready to see Miss Pyle now."

Mrs. Kenney looked at me. Whatever she knew she wasn't about to share.

"Mrs. Kenney, wait. Do you have any idea where the dispatches might be?"

Her eyes betrayed nothing.

"The captain says he can help me get home if I can find them. Mrs. Kenney, I need to get home. I have a sick father, and a job, and there's a man there who's very worried about me."

She narrowed her eyes. "Vhat man?"

"A friend. A friend I was traveling with."

"Hmmm." Mrs. Kenney put a plump finger on each

side of my forehead and closed her eyes. After a second, she pulled her hands away. "A friend, eez it? *Tsk-tsk.* Affection is not some medicine to be given in self-selected doses, Meez Pyle. Vhat you have done is like trying to stopper a hurricane with a cork. If I had known this, I vould not have—"

Remembering herself, she stopped.

"Would not have what?" I demanded. Clearly this chick knew something. I was going to wring it out of her.

She shrugged her shoulders.

"Mrs. Kenney, I was innocently on my way to a business gathering in Venice when I found myself, er, unstoppably drawn to this ship. Do you have any idea why?"

She stuck out her chin. "Perhaps for you eez test."

"Of my sanity?"

"To see if you can find love in story." She gave me a toothy smile. "Eez love story, no? Find love, end story. Shooz vill help."

My taffeta companions merrily gunned their engines in agreement. "My shoes will help?" I asked.

"*Ja.* Only one person can take them off, *ja?*"

"Captain Drummunt—or someone else?"

"*Ja.*"

"That's not an answer."

"*Ja,* no." She smiled.

Ah, the famous cobbler inscrutability.

"Mrs. Kenney, the captain has given me reason to believe he can get me home. Is there any chance that's true?"

For an instant, I swear, she looked surprised, and she made a quick glance to a shelf of bottles along the wall.

"Mrs. Kenney?"

"Captain Drummunt does not lie."

Right, the honorable blackmailer. "And the dispatches? Any thoughts there?"

She gave me a long, contemplative look. "A ship cannot run on desire alone," she said. "Consider that as you look."

Gee, thanks.

She nodded toward the shoes. "And be very careful with those, *ja?*"

"*Ja.*"

"*Ja?*"

"*Ja!*"

Sisterhood established, though almost nothing else, I gathered my skirts and made my way through the unbulkheaded door.

Phillip, my hero?

I hardly needed "shooz" to tell me the answer to that one.

Which is not to say he had no redeeming qualities. If Mrs. Kenney was any indication, he had clearly won the loyalty of his crew, and, of course, that story about letting the French cutter go to help a friend was pretty admirable. Still, he hardly fit the mold of hero.

It was with some trepidation I found myself in front of Miss Quimble's door. I'd already run into unnerving copies of Tom and my boss. Should I be bracing my-

self for the neighborhood dog walker? Susan Dey? My
ninth-grade geometry teacher?

Phillip insisted Miss Quimble was my character. And
it was getting hard to deny I hadn't had a hand in some
of this. If I was responsible, I'd better be prepared.

I knew any heroine of mine would be strong-willed,
smart, tenacious and, let's face it, brunette. Actually
Susan Dey would be about right. I like Marcia Brady,
but it was Marcia's cooler, feminist counterpart across
the street I really admired. Marcia got to kiss Davey
Jones. Laurie Partridge got to kiss the boys at Mul-
doon's Point, go home, take off her TV makeup and
hang out with David Cassidy.

Moreover, Laurie grew up and became a lawyer in
L.A. Empowered, sexy, independent. Are we seeing
the parallel yet? Okay, all except the lawyer and L.A.
parts. But Tom's a lawyer, and he says being a lawyer is
like owning a boat: it's always better if a friend does it
instead of you.

I raised a fist to knock when the door opened. A be-
draggled chambermaid slipped out, rolling her eyes.

"Good luck," she said, and tucked an empty liquor
bottle under her arm. "Hope you weren't thirsty."

As she took off down the hall, I caught a whiff of
the bottle's former contents. Brandy. Very expensive
brandy.

Bracing my shoulders, I peered inside. There was a
cot in the corner. My heroine was lying on her back applying rouge. To her ankles.

She wore Little Bo Peep drawers—the kind with
rows of ruffles around the length of each leg—and a

camisole so taut with its heaving contents, I not only saw London and France, but Vienna, Prague, and Gary, Indiana, as well.

For those of you wondering, I could place Miss Quimble. She was my first piano teacher, as I now recall, and the heroine of a Nancy Drew–type story I wrote in second grade. Good God, I thought. What next?

The hero and heroine I'd been handed were people from such incomprehensible and unrelated sources in my head they should have come with a warning: "Do not mix! Danger of absurdity!"

Of course, the heroine from my second-grade story didn't drink brandy or roll about in her underpants. She made her own chocolate milk, wore a calico skirt and solved the mystery of Mr. Albertson's missing dachshund, Peaches, using footprints and a purloined letter.

With a start Miss Quimble caught the cot's side rails and closed her eyes. "Uh-oh, Miss Pyle. Here comes another wave! Whoo-*hoo*!" She giggled. "That was a big one."

The ship had barely moved. She rolled off the cot onto the floor, cooing with laughter.

Now why weren't my episodes of drunkenness ever charming? My first occasion, in college, consisted of drinking a tankard of Harvey's Bristol Cream, then vomiting so long my eyeballs collapsed. To this day, even a hint of sherry makes me break into a cold sweat. Then there was the time I got into an argument at a party at my professor's house and accidentally flung a tequila sunrise over his first-edition Hemingway. And the time I whispered my phone number into the ear of a nice cardiologist at the bar of the William Penn Hotel, slipped off the stool and cracked a tooth on his cell phone. The list goes on. It's little wonder I stick to no more than beer now.

Apparently my hostess had been dining on grapes, for a handful of denuded stems lay scattered about the floor. She found one that still held a grape, dangled it over her tongue and levered it loose with enough aplomb to make even me squirm. Screwing her face into an adorable pout, she said, "So you're the reason Drummy won't play."

Drummy? "No, not me, Miss Quimble—"

"Please, call me Peaches."

"Drummy, er, Captain Drummond has his hands full right now with the admiral."

"The admiral?" Her face brightened. "There's an admiral on board?"

"Yes, and he's intent on reading his dispatches."

"Oh." The pout returned. "Those silly papers. That's all Drummy cares about."

"If he doesn't find them, he'll be in very serious trouble." And I'll be stuck forever in this floating nightmare of a plot. "He'll forfeit any chance of returning to the navy."

She sighed. "One so likes one's lovers to be officers. I was in love with Drummy's first lieutenant, Mr. Haverhill. And a few days after that I was in love with his second lieutenant, Mr. Black."

"My goodness. That's a lot for one heart to bear."

"'Tis true. Sometimes it positively aches—and the thumping! Steady like a drum, and so low in my belly.

Wa-a-a-y down. I feel like I'm going to burst. Why, I remember falling in love four times in a single night before the feeling went away. This morning I was just about to fall in love with two of Drummy's midshipmen at once when that silly storm hit and they ran off. Lord, how I long to be in love again. It makes me feel all warm and tingly inside. Have you ever been in love?"

I thought myself astride the recycling bin. But did I fall in love? Oh no, not good ol' Miss Chastity Pants. I just teetered six or seven long, wonderful inches from the edge, worried about the business impact. *Aargh!* Who thinks business impact with a guy's hand in her bra?

"Not for a very, very, very long time," I admitted.

"How sad."

Boy, howdy. "But you've never, um, been in love with Captain Drummund?"

"No! And those eyes and shoulders! He just makes the blood in my heart throb so hard I feel like I'm going to—"

"I've got the picture."

"But he says it cannot be."

Curious. I couldn't think of too many men who would refuse to put their hearts in Peaches's hands for an hour or two. "I wonder why."

"Mrs. Kenney says he's in love with a woman in Toulon."

"In love or 'in love'?"

"What?"

"Never mind. Look, Phillip needs those papers. I wonder if we really thought about it, if we could come up with a way to help him out."

She squinched her eyes closed and put three fingers to her forehead. The Thinker, in repose.

"I know!" she cried. "Let's look for them!"

"What an idea! Why don't you search up on deck with all those nice sailors, and I can search . . . Hmmm." I tapped my lip. "Why don't I search here?"

Peaches stumbled to her feet with the sort of energy one reserves for beating the meter maid to one's car or answering the call for a fresh batch of chocolate-chip cookies.

"Search here if you want," she said, "but I don't think you'll find anything. Phillip wouldn't even unbutton his breeks, let alone take off his coat."

Given my status as her inventor, I noted with some discomfort Peaches didn't exactly possess a spy's capacity for cunning. But I wouldn't expect a heroine of mine, even a drunken one, to be involved in treason anyway.

Nonetheless, I knew I should take a look around. There was always the chance someone else was using her without her knowledge.

"Say, I have an idea, Peaches—Oops, let's not go out without our gown, shall we? Why don't your friends—you are traveling with friends?—assist you in your search? They are, I think, in the rooms up near the captain?" I said, dropping again into information-gathering mode.

"Oh, no, my maids are next door, and Uncle Charles is across the hall."

Bingo.

It took a buttonhook, a washcloth and twenty minutes, but I managed to get Peaches into her frock and presentable enough to exit the room. When I heard her and her entourage heading up the stairs, I collapsed on the cot.

An hour ago I was on my way to a business meeting in Venice. Now I was stuck in a sea-bound disaster, apparently of my own making. Think, Seph. How would your story have ended if it had ever been started? The answer was straightforward: with the heroine in the hero's arms, of course, after resolving the central conflict.

Great. So now all I had to do was find the dispatches, win the war for England and fashion this unlikely hero and heroine into a pair worth turning the page for. A little overreaching for a first-time novelist, wouldn't you say? Would there have been any dishonor in a plot involving a pretty widow and her moody daughter's soccer coach?

I heaved myself to my feet.

The uncle's room seemed like a good place to start. I made my way across the hall and knocked, just to be sure. When no one answered, I let myself in.

I don't know what Charles did for a living, but he seemed to have a number of odd habits. Stuffed into the drawers of his trunk I found a handful of French broadsheets, an ivory-handled pistol and a deck of playing cards adorned with some very interesting images of knights and ladies, only the ladies were *sans* clothes and the knights wielded lances considerably shorter than the ones I'm used to seeing. Even more eye-opening, however, were a dozen hand-rolled cigarettes—or something like cigarettes—and a hose with a mouthpiece connected to a round, ceramic piece of equipment that could only be described as a bong.

Well, well, well. What was Charles "Cheech" Quimble up to? Tobacco? I sniffed the cigarettes. Nope, but the scent sure brought back college days in a rush. I sniffed the bong. Definitely not tobacco. Definitely not pot, though, either. The scent was Hawaiian Punch sweet. Hmmm. My experience beyond sherry, some occasional pot and Maximum Strength Grant's was woefully limited. Freebase, maybe? Oh, yeah, I can just see it. Charles and Richard Pryor, getting it on. ("I say, Richard, this shit of yours is bloody marvelous." "You a crazy English m*&#$ f*&^%, you know that? Pass the pipe.") Which left me with what? Of course! I slapped my forehead. The stuff of all eighteenth-century soap opera. Opium.

Nothing else of interest surfaced, but frankly that was more than enough. I slipped a doobie and the ace of spades into one of the cavernous pockets I was delighted to discover these period skirts held and shut the door behind me.

Peaches's chambermaids shared a room about the size of a commemorative Tobago postage stamp. My efforts there yielded nothing more enlightening than a note to one of their fathers begging for help in finding a different post.

Peaches's room was last. Under her cot was a box of letters. I scanned each quickly. Unless Lord Dunwoody hid his instructions in the middle of a poorly crafted love letter, there was nothing here of value. She had a half dozen gowns stuffed in her trunk, and her drawers were filled with pots of cosmetics and perfume. Only three items drew my attention: a riding crop, some coconut-scented oil and a longish, unusually shaped mahogany paperweight.

In anyone else's drawer, such items might have raised a brow, but for Peaches I knew they represented no more than that to which I myself had devoted most of my waking life for the last five years: heart medicine.

Though I finished empty-handed, I didn't give up. I may not be a writer, but if brand management taught me anything, it taught me how to work a project to its completion. If the dispatches were on this ship, I'd find them. I picked up the grape stems, threw them out the porthole and walked out.

Chapter Four

Phillip caught me in the hall. He had the wild-eyed look of a man about to be swallowed by his fate, and the odd hunching he had to do in order to stand under the low ceiling only added to an appearance of disquiet.

"Do you have the papers?" he whispered furiously. "The liquor's gone. Basehart and I have been playing One and Thirty for the last hour, and I've graciously lost my earnings for the last three months, a Turkish sword and my favorite pair of dress shoes, so unless you'd like to see me give up my shirt, coat and breeks as well, I need those bloody papers *now.*"

A vision of that last eventuality froze the words on my lips. Phillip's stock was undone, and I could see the narrow expanse of a lightly furred pectoral at the V of his shirt. He had the air of a man who would be perfectly at ease without his clothes. "Er . . ."

"Er, what?"

"No papers," I squeaked.

"Damnation! Isn't Miss Quimble your character?"

"No. Well, yes. It's a long story. She's a different character."

"She certainly is."

"I mean from another story."

"*Another* story? Good gad! Someone needs to hide your quill."

"Hey. It was a very good story. She found Mr. Albertson's dachshund."

Phillip screwed up his mouth. "I'm certain she had no trouble."

"Look, all I know is, if this is my story, I've not had a conscious hand in creating it, and I'm obviously having no impact on moving it to its conclusion."

"I had to get a novice," Phillip muttered. "The other writer had her plot well in hand."

"Let's not forget the operative word there—*writer.* I am not a writer. I am aspiring to be a writer. I am aspiring to be a writer and being tumbled through time. It's a little different from sharpening the pencils and pulling the thesaurus off the shelf. What's going on here is like the literary equivalent of speaking in tongues. I know the people, but I haven't the foggiest idea where the plot is coming from."

"People?"

Oops.

"Did you say you know the people?" he repeated. "Plural?" He narrowed his eyes. "You mentioned Miss Quimble's resemblance to someone in your life. Whom else do you know?"

"Um."

"I?"

Jesus, the man's ego was big enough to sail a ship around. I certainly wasn't going to mention he looked like Tom.

"Yes, you're a pain-in-the-ass clerk I know who made me jump through hoops to return my cell phone."

"Cell phone?"

"Forget it. All I'm saying is, Miss Quimble is a sweet if somewhat misguided girl. She is not your man, er, woman, er, spy."

"Is that so, Madame Author? Then who is?"

"Frankly Uncle Charles seems a likely suspect. He's reading French broadsheets, he's got a real taste for opium, and he appears to consider card-playing something of a spectator sport." I flashed the ace I'd palmed.

Phillip snatched the card from my hand and stuffed it into his pocket. "*Mon Dieu!* Can't people keep this kind of thing in France, where it's not so noticeable?"

I thought of his woman in Toulon. A noise behind us made us both turn, but no one appeared.

"Opium, is it?" he asked quietly.

"Yes."

Phillip nodded. "I had noticed the sunken eyes and curious lack of appetite, but I assumed he was just another of Miss Quimble's paramours."

"Her *uncle*?"

"He's not her real uncle. Her grandfather was Charles's guardian. Do you think the papers are in his room, then?"

"I searched there. No papers. Are you sure they didn't get mislaid somewhere else on the ship?"

"I've had men—men I trust—tear the place apart."

"Are you sure they're as important as you think they are?"

"I told you. We're getting our wickets knocked about by France on the continent and on sea, especially off the coast of Portugal—er, you do know where Portugal is, don't you?"

"That thingy on the side of Spain."

"Indeed. Well, frankly things haven't been looking good for our side. General Marlborough has managed some astounding victories in Europe, but even now we're getting pushed back. At sea, it's worse." All trace of youth had left his face. "France has far more ships than we do, enough to protect their ports and block our own. I fear one more significant victory on their part will change the course of the war. The official who gave me the dispatches in Portsmouth is rumored to head our intelligence efforts. What I hope—what I fervently hope—is that the admiralty has uncovered France's next move and plans to throw everything we have in her way. God help us, it may be England's last chance." He collapsed against a wooden column. "Basehart and his fleet need to be on their way, but unless we can find those papers, we'll never know to where."

"Oh, if only Tom were here!"

Phillip's face altered a degree. "Tom? Your solicitor friend? Why?"

"He was a history major. D-day, the American Revolution, Napoléon, Vietnam—you name it, he's put me to sleep talking about it. I mean, he saw *Saving Private Ryan* five times."

Phillip's eyes narrowed. "The American what?"

I slapped a hand over my mouth. "Nothing. But I'm sure Tom would know where the next big battle is going to be."

"Drummond!" a port-soaked voice called. There was a fumbling at the latch, and the door to the officers' dining room opened. Basehart, wearing a scimitar in his belt and swimming in velvet evening slippers far too long for his boyish feet, raked us with unfocused eyes. The ceiling posed no problem for him.

"Ah, cousin to cousin." A saccharine smile uncoiled on his face. "Upon my word, you two are the picture of familial bliss. Drummond, I've had enough of cards. Run along and fetch me a pot of coffee, a toasted cheese and my dispatches. I pray Miss Pyle will indulge me with a story or two of growing up in the Drummond household while we wait. I am so extraordinarily eager to hear about those long-ago days of playing in the hayloft and pulling taffy."

"Miss Pyle," Phillip said flatly, "is on her way to see the surgeon."

I clutched my stomach. "Bilious."

Basehart's mouth twisted. "The sort of thing only fresh air and nine months can remedy, I daresay."

Phillip's chin dropped. "Admiral, I must protest—"

"The dispatches, Drummond," he said. "Get them."

"I don't have them."

A quiet fell over the passageway. Basehart's cheeks flushed bright crimson. "You don't have the dispatches?

The man who hopes to wear an epaulet again in my service doesn't have the dispatches?"

"No." Phillip's face was solemn. "They've been lost or stolen. I don't know which. I've searched the ship to no avail. The last time I saw them was after we left Gibraltar, and that was the last time we weighed anchor."

"Drummond, you're either a damned cunning spy or the stupidest man I've ever known." He turned toward the hatch. "*Mr. Haverhill!*"

Phillip's first lieutenant thundered down the stairs. "Aye?"

"Search the ship," Basehart commanded, "starting with Captain Drummond's quarters. We have word Gabin has men at work in the English navy. I want every cask taken apart, every hammock shaken, every rat hole examined. Drummond, you and your cousin will stay here, in my sight, until Mr. Haverhill finishes."

"Gabin?" I whispered to Phillip.

"A Frenchman," he replied enigmatically.

We entered the officer's dining room, and I took a seat. Phillip sat across the table from me, staring grimly into the distance. Basehart poured himself something from the bottle on the table and swirled it in his glass. He laid the scimitar on the table.

"You know," he said to Phillip, "I fought like hell to get the charges against you dismissed. Letting a French ship go? Not the man I trained, I said. But this is unconscionable. If the dispatches don't turn up, the odds of your returning to the navy are about as high as someone flying to the moon."

Well, there was something.

I began to pace. How could this be happening in something that was supposedly my story? I don't know anything about military intelligence or Marlborough or letters of marque. Where was the admiral's daughter? Where were the exotic Mediterranean ports? This was like some horrible collision between *My Captain, My Darling* and Military Week on the History Channel. I longed for the time when lack of bulkheads was my only worry.

A torque-y buzz rose from my taffeta shoes, like two little Pekingese vibrating with eagerness for their master. Yeah, Pekingese with grenades in their asses. I slowly slid my heels apart.

Phillip intercepted my gaze. He gave me a weak smile and a quick roll of the eyes, as if to suggest enduring Basehart's imperiousness was his only care. But I could tell by the set of his jaw this was excruciating.

"Miss Pyle," Basehart said, "let us leave Captain Drummond here to his thoughts, eh?" He tossed down the contents of his glass. "The ship is turning—can you feel it? There'll be a breeze through the gun port of that cabin there, and I should dearly love to show you the fine, long lines of my flagship."

I knew I would accept. Any effort to flatter the admiral's vanity would help Phillip, and I'd kissed enough toads to know one more wasn't going to give me anything a mouthful of Listerine couldn't fix. Besides, I doubted Basehart possessed the imagination to try something really intriguing in the cotless, tableless room I saw before me. But if he did, I had a taffeta-covered heel that would make his instep sing "My Heart Will Go On" with more emotion than Celine Dion.

Phillip, however, clattered to his feet before I could speak.

"Miss Pyle stays."

He looked just about as stern as a man could look bent into a lower case *f*. I couldn't help but smile. "It's all right," I protested gently.

"Aye, it's all right," Basehart said. "Listen to the young lady. Girls today do not care for such interference."

Phillip bared his teeth. "I beg you to recall your manners, sir. She is my cousin."

"Aye, aye. And if I weren't acutely aware both of your parents are only children, I might be persuaded. Come, Miss Pyle."

I hesitated. The entirety of Phillip's being was focused on Basehart. It looked as if he might sprout fangs and attack.

Basehart held out his arm to me. "Miss Pyle makes her own decisions, don't you? Come. I assure you it will be for the best—for everyone." He gave his former officer a significant look.

I crossed my arms, considering Phillip's feelings. "If my cousin desires me to stay, then I must depend on his superior understanding of the situation. Thank you, Admiral, for your offer, but I decline."

Basehart's eyes darkened. "I see. Well, Drummond, I suppose consanguineal influence prevails. I am reminded of a poem I learned in my midshipman days. Perhaps you've heard it." He cleared his throat.

> *"A merry man of York am I,*
> *For cousins I have twenty,*
> *Each and every one a girl,*
> *Soft and round and plenty.*
>
> *I am the envy of my friends,*
> *So blessed by Lady Luck,*
> *As cousins are too close to marry*
> *But far enough to—"*

The last word was swallowed in a loud, bony *thunk* as Phillip's fist launched Basehart into a perfect parabolic curve. Basehart landed for a moment on the table, sending the scimitar and slippers flying, before the finely turned table legs, ever ready for battle, gave way at their prehinged joints and dropped him with a crash to the floor.

Haverhill burst into the room, and his expression went through rapid-fire changes from shock to realization to embarrassment. He shuffled his feet, trying to keep his gaze off Basehart's bloody lip and split breeches.

"What is it, Mr. Haverhill?" Phillip rubbed his fist.

Haverhill gave his captain a woeful look. "We found them."

"You did? Where?"

"Well, we started as we were commanded, and even though—"

"Goddamn it, Haverhill," Basehart bellowed as he pulled himself to sitting, "make your report. Where in the bloody hell did you find them?"

Haverhill's head dropped. "In Captain Drummond's desk, sir."

Basehart spit a large quantity of blood onto the floor, followed immediately by a tooth. He wiped his mouth on his sleeve. "Lieutenant, I'm promoting you to acting captain. Confine Captain Drummond to his quarters."

Chapter Five

I gave Simon and Gar a slightly embarrassed smile as I knocked on Phillip's door, coffeepot in hand. They were seated on their usual stools, though I couldn't help but notice they now had their pistols at the ready on their laps. Since I had seen them escort Phillip out of the dining room an hour ago with less respect than I felt he deserved, my embarrassment did not extend to regret.

"Enter," Phillip called.

"Sorry, boys," I said, lifting the latch. "No more tricks, I promise. Uh-oh, is that *gullible* written on the ceiling?"

I entered to the squeak of two chairs tipping back against the wall.

Phillip sat slumped on the stern window bench, his polished boot pressed against the edge of his desk. The sun was falling, and the purple-tinged sky lent an uncharacteristic guardedness to his features. He roused himself to stand, but I waved him off and closed the door behind me.

"Well, I believe I shall go to my grave happy," he said with a bemused smile. "I have heard the words 'I must depend on his superior understanding of the situation' emerge from your mouth. How much did that cost you?"

"More than I can afford, I'm afraid." I tried to match his tone, but I couldn't raise lightheartedness.

He nodded toward the door. "No problem getting in?"

"Oh, Basehart's not here. He's returned to his own ship, with the dispatches. Rumor has it he'll be back tomorrow—once he decides what to do with you. Mr. Haverhill's running things."

The ship jerked hard to the left, and a muffled oath cut the air. Phillip lifted a brow. "You don't say?"

I picked up his mug, but it was already full of cold coffee. Though he seemed in no mood for socializing, he automatically swept the mug from my hand and tossed its contents out the porthole. I poured and he accepted the hot mug with a bow.

"It was very kind of you to protect me," I said. "Thank you."

Phillip grunted. If my shoes were Pekingese, Phillip was a large brown Newfoundland. While I hadn't felt I needed the protection, the fact that he had given it without a word, without, it seemed, even conscious thought, affected me deeply. It struck me that a mere thank-you wasn't enough. "Men today—in my day, I mean—wouldn't do something like that."

"When is your day, exactly?" He took a polite sip of the coffee, though I could tell he wasn't really tasting it.

"Three hundred years from now. The twenty-first century."

"If that's the state of the world in the twenty-first century, perhaps I shouldn't be trying so hard to save it." He sighed. "Basehart behaved a total scrub. I'm sorry."

"I'm sorry to have gotten you into this. It seems my story—or at least the people who apparently have sprung from my story—have really screwed things up here."

"I thank you for your concern, Miss Pyle, but I'm afraid I have no one to blame for that punch but my-self."

"At this point, I think you're going to have to start calling me by my first name. It's Seph."

He gave me a quizzical look—the same quizzical look I always got when I gave my name. Damn that six-ties haze my parents cavorted in.

"It's short for Persephone," I said.

He threw back his head and laughed.

I crossed my arms. "I take it you know the story."

"Persephone. Maiden daughter of Demeter, Greek goddess of grain. Abducted by Hades to live in the underworld as his wife. Nearly escaped but made the mistake of eating four pomegranate seeds while in Hades's care, an act fraught with, shall we say, deeper symbolism. Doomed eternally to spend four months out of every year in the underworld—the season we know as winter."

I nodded my head, impressed. Most people hadn't a clue.

He gave me a look. "Mildly ironic, wouldn't you say?"

"More than mildly."

His eyes glittered blue. "I'm sorry the *Neuf Ouest* has no pomegranate seeds to offer you."

"Let us hope orange marmalade does not have the same effect." I bit my lip and said honestly, "Phillip, I hope you know I had nothing to do with the dispatches ending up in your desk."

"I or a member of my crew has been with you every moment since the time of your arrival. And I can assure you," he added matter-of-factly, "you didn't have the dispatches on you then."

Humpf. Without the slightest hint of impropriety, Phillip had a way of looking at me that suggested he could see through my clothes. I sat down behind his desk and crossed my arms.

"You weren't with me the entire time," I corrected. "You left to greet Admiral Basehart while I—"

"Lost a comb?"

"Oh." A faint warmth crawled up my cheeks. "You heard about that."

"Aye. The Funkels will be cleaning the heads for a month—or at least they would have been had I remained in command."

"I could have planted the papers when Mrs. Kenney was dressing me."

"You could have, but why do you suppose I had Mr. Kenney volunteer her? It wasn't to get you into your underskirt, which was clearly in direct opposition to my own wishes, not to mention those of the crew."

"Phillip!"

He chuckled—a full, throaty chuckle that made me smile too.

"Persephone, no man earns my full trust until after his first battle."

I liked the notion of being one of Phillip's "men." "Is this a battle?"

"'Twill become one, I think." He shifted on the cushion. "You seem to presume I didn't hide the papers in my desk myself."

"You didn't," I said flatly.

A seabird floated by the window, hovering on some invisible current above the iridescent water below. It cried a plaintive cry and flew off.

"Are you certain?" he asked.

"Yes. You are not the only one with standards, you know. You're my character."

A warm blue twinkle lit his eyes. "I am not entirely your creation, you know. I am a man wholly apart from the situation you have created for me, with hopes and hungers and faults. I have killed—"

"In war."

"I have stolen. I have lied when it suited me. I have stooped to vile flattery to regain my post in the navy. And there is a woman whose charms so compel me, I would do more than that for a chance to possess her."

My throat dried—in nearly equal measure to the dampening of other areas. No wonder there were no panties in 1706. With men spouting lines like that, the fewer the impediments the better. I uncrossed and crossed my legs, wondering if I'd ever meet the woman who inspired such feeling and, to a lesser degree, if the underskirt would hold.

"You may have other faults," I said when my voice returned, "but I would never have summoned a man capable of disloyalty."

I met his eyes, challenging him to deny it.

"No," he admitted after a moment, "disloyalty is not one of my faults."

I gazed at the neat row of inkpots and carefully shelved logs. "What's going to happen to you? I mean can Basehart really take away your command?"

"Technically no. I am not, as he has so unequivocally expressed, an officer in the navy. But he has the power to arrest me and take me to the nearest English port. As it amounts to nearly the same thing, I let him have his way. Besides," he added with a tinge of rueful pride, "the handing over of command is appropriate conduct for a naval officer under accusation."

Ah, Phillip.

He seemed to notice the coffeepot for the first time. At once he stood and reached into a cupboard high on the wall to remove a beautiful blue Chinese porcelain cup and saucer. Without a word, he handed me both, then steadied my grip with a palm as he filled the cup with coffee. *Wonk-wonk.* Rudolph was back.

"Take care." He flopped back onto the bench. "That's hot, and Haverhill's tacks are more in the nature of lurches."

I didn't trust myself to lift the cup to my lips—not

because of Haverhill, but because the spot where Phillip's hand had brushed mine still burned like a small wildfire. "So you shall be brought up on charges of stealing?"

His attention went to the long florescent wake stretching out beyond the windows. "Stealing . . . aye."

Well, thank God the nearest English port was three-quarters of a decent-sized continent away. We'd have plenty of time to get this straightened out. "Phillip, I'm so sorry. I don't know how any of it is happening. I mean, this isn't the story I would have written."

"Thank you, milady."

"Is there anything I can do?"

"There are—two things, in fact. First, you can stop calling me Phillip. Not even my mother calls me that—for the most part because she named me George. My friends, however, call me Drum. I would be honored—and relieved—if you would do the same." He held out a hand.

I took it. I could feel the warm strength of it as my fingers disappeared inside his grip. Drum, indeed. I felt the drumbeats all the way to my toes. *Wonk-wonk-wonk.*

I returned my hand to the handle of the cup, but was quaking so much the porcelain rattled. "You're right. It's too hot," I said, and set the coffee on the desk. "I can certainly call you Drum," I said, adding under my breath, "though there's nothing wrong with Phillip. What's the second thing?"

"Someone did plant those letters. I'd like to know who—and why. Anything you could find out without stirring up too much trouble would be helpful. I don't suppose Basehart revealed anything of the contents after he read them?"

"He didn't read them—at least not here. He just kept fingering the green ribbon and calling for his barge."

"*Green* ribbon?" Drum leaned forward sharply.

"The one around the packet. I dunno, maybe it was brown. It looked green when Haverhill handed it to him."

Drum shook his head. "The ribbon around the packet from Lord Dunwoody was red."

Chapter Six

"*Where* exactly are we heading, Mr. Haverhill?" I
asked.

The acting captain of the *Neuf Ouest* stood on
the quarterdeck, watching the sailors on the lines
high above us and the quickly disappearing flagship
ahead with a troubled expression. We were following
Basehart's ship on an alacritous journey into a gusting
headwind, which meant making sharp turns to the left
and right at precise, synchronous intervals, an effort,
it seemed, beyond Mr. Haverhill's fairly constrained
competence.

"I cannot tell you," he said with sincere regret.

I wondered if his response reflected a bow to secrecy
or the frank admission of a man in well over his head.

"Well, certainly south," I offered, thinking a politic
hint might help.

His face was seized with terror. "How did you know?"

I pointed to the kitschy red-orange sunset to our right.

"Oh, dear. Of course. Silly of me. It's just that the admiral . . ." The polite cough of another sailor interrupted him. "Oh, dear, oh, dear." Haverhill stared into the rigging above as if he were trying to read tea leaves. He laid a hand over his heart. "Oh . . . oh . . ." With panic in his eyes, he gave the man a single, uncertain nod.

The man's whistle screeched, and a hundred sailors began the complicated choreography of adjusting the sails, pulling ropes and tying rigging. The ship's timbers moaned as the stern slowly, slowly made its way from left of the wind to right of it. At the center, with the wind directly before us, the ship shuddered infinitesimally, as if unsure whether to complete the turn or return to its starting point. Mr. Haverhill closed his eyes.

The words *please, please, please* formed on his lips.

The wind let out a long puff, and the ship finished its turn.

"Praise God." Haverhill mopped his face with a handkerchief. "If you miss your stays, milady—stays being what sailors call the process of turning through the wind—the admiral fires his stern gun. It's supposed to be no more than a warning, but my cousin is second lieutenant on *The Revenge,* and Basehart nearly blew a hole in their quarterdeck once."

"He's that bad a shot?"

"No, best in the Med."

"I would like to ask you a question or two about the packet." I held up a hand to stop his protest. "Not about the contents, of course. About the condition of the letters when you found them."

Haverhill's face instantly pinched into an amazing variety of tics. Success at cards was not in his future.

"I don't think so." An eyelid twitched. "Admiral Basehart said—"

"Admiral Basehart can have no objection to you describing how the letters were found."

"They were in Captain Drummond's desk, just as I said."

"I know, I know. I don't question your word, not for one minute. What I'd like to know is if anyone else was around when you found them. You know, an overly curious sailor? A guest or two skulking about?"

"No one was skulking." His cheek jumped.

"You were alone?"

"The Funkel brothers"—cheek, eyelid—"were outside the door."

Guarding an empty room? I thought of the old chestnut about the barn door and the cows getting out. Or was this the cows getting in? Or the barn door being locked even though the cows were already— I shook myself. "And the letters . . . they were hidden?"

"They were in his drawer." Cheek, eyelid, cheek, cheek, nose.

"What I mean," I explained patiently, "is were they wrapped in a handkerchief or hidden in a box or something like that? Or were they just scattered about . . . loose?"

"They were in plain sight, bound with a ribbon. Just as you would expect." His face was doing the Rockettes' holiday show now. "Miss Pyle, I feel it is exceedingly improper to talk about this without the admiral's agreement."

"Fine. Let's stop." I slouched casually against the rail and began whistling Elvis Costello's "Watching the Detectives." The man beside Haverhill began his polite coughing again, and Haverhill's eyes strayed to gauge the distance to the next turn.

"Unless you want to tell me where we're heading, of course," I added.

"Miss Pyle—"

"Miss Pyle," a smoother voice called. "Allow me, if you would, to provide a layman's opinion on the matter."

I turned to find myself eye to eye with a dapper man in a long, turquoise silk jacket with wide embroidered cuffs. He sniffed twice and bowed, doffing his hat with one very skinny arm.

Cheech.

"You must be Miss Quimble's uncle," I said.

"Charles Davitch." He took my hand and kissed it. "And you, fair lady, can be none other than our captain's American cousin."

Apparently that story hadn't reached its expiration date out here.

He inclined his head toward the bow. "Would you care to take a stroll around the foredeck?"

"Indeed, I would." I didn't know what Cheech was up to, but I had a little digging of my own to do. I turned to Haverhill. "Thank you, sir."

Haverhill nodded, smiling. The man beside him,

who mistook the nod for a command, immediately piped the call for the stays, and the sailors thundered into another change of course as Haverhill shouted his protests.

The crack of a cannon preceded a long whistling screech overhead and a watery *plop* just past our bow.

"Charming man, the admiral," Charles said as he hurried me down the gangway.

"Like a toenail fungus. Only with less to recommend him."

Charles guffawed.

Well, he might have a drug habit and a fetish for porn, but he certainly had a discerning sense of humor.

"You have a very odd way of speaking, milady."

Oh, boy, gotta watch the slang. "Er, I am American, you know."

"Indeed, that is apparent. And yet, I have known other colonists whose language was not so . . ."

"Quick-witted?"

"Unrestrained." He looked at me closely.

Help me, historicals!

"Forsooth, do not mention this to my dear cuz. 'Twas his fervent wish I master my unruly tongue. Nay, but a fortnight ago his words were as much in my ear." Yeah.

Charles scratched his chin, but after a moment his face relaxed.

Those French broadsheets still occupied my thoughts (as did the pornographic playing cards, but I had no intention of going down *that* path). Were they merely innocent packing material, or did they mean something more? Obviously the first test would be to see if he understood French. My own study of French, however, ended quickly after a single year in high school.

"*Ou est Pierre?*" I asked.

Charles cocked his head. "*Pierre?*"

Okay, no go on the "Where is . . . ?" drill. It seemed not every French student learned that Pierre was "*à la piscine,*" Marie was "*au lycée,*" and Didier was "*à la disco.*" Of course, they probably didn't have pools, high schools, or discos in 1706. Their drills were probably like "Where is Elizabeth?" "At the blacksmith getting a tooth pulled"; "Where is Peg?" "Butchering the swans"; and "Where is Sir Andrew?" "Dying of consumption in debtors' prison."

"*Parlez-vous français?*" I asked, emptying the other half of my French-language barrel and clearly throwing subtlety to the wind.

He looked like a man who'd just been told tonight's special was an all-you-can-eat shrimp buffet. "*Vous parlez français? Grâce à Dieu! Je suis si heureux d'avoir trouvé quelqu'une enfin à qui je peux parler ouvertement et confidentiellement.*"

Mission accomplished. I have no idea what he said.

"*Vous avez un visage d'entendeur,*" he went on, voice growing more urgent. "*Est-ce que je peux vous dire ce qui m'avait préoccupé?*"

Oh, boy. I'd caught one word out of that.

"*Visage?*" I repeated.

He seized my arm. "*Oui! Vous avez le visage d'un ange, un ange de compréhension, et j'entends que vous avez la magie de guérir. Oooh, le charme, le charme, ma fortune trouves ce charme!"*

"Stop, er, *stoppez vous*. Please! *S'il vous plait*. In English."

His face fell. "*En anglais?*"

"*Oui.*"

He pulled me farther away from the sailors. "My affliction is love," he said, "and the language of love is French. But if English is what you desire . . ."

"English" was not a hundredth of what I desired at the moment, but it would do.

"English will not do justice to my confession," he added.

Confession? Whoa! I'd seen those cards. Cripes, I'd have to wash out my ears with soap. Although, come to think of it, from what I'd seen of the sailors around here, washing out one's ears with soap might not be a bad habit to introduce.

"Why would you confess to me?" I demanded. It seemed odd he'd make me his confidante so quickly.

"I understand you can help. You see, I am in love, and my love is not returned."

Oh, yeah. Drum was right. He definitely had the bruised Peaches look to him. Charles might be an opium addict, but he was first a man in love. "I am sorry, but how do you think I could help?"

"Mr. Haverhill told me that you can fix a broken heart."

I blinked. "Really?"

"Oh, aye, the ship's abuzz with it. With the right inducement—and I'm a very rich man, Miss Pyle—I hear you have a way to protect one's heart from pain."

"I think you're mistaken, I—" Omigod! He meant aspirin. I remembered my "much pain" explanation. Drum must have mentioned my commerce to one of his men. "Well, um . . ."

"Do recall, money is no object." He gave me a charming smile.

No, money was no object, but finding a Walgreens around here was going to be.

"Let me consider it, Mr. Davitch. It is not that I wish to withhold this from you. 'Tis true my medicine is quite powerful, and I have no doubt it will end your torment." A lie a day keeps a marketer in good practice, I always say. "'Tis just the pills are very hard to create, and, well, I find that I am quite undone by Captain Drummond's arrest." I sniffed a little. As long as we were in confession mode, I might as well make it work for me too. "I feel certain I could summon the pluck to formulate a batch for you if only I could find a way to help the captain out of his bind."

Charles fell suspiciously quiet.

That's right, Chucky baby, there are no free lunches. This is quid pro quo, my man.

"Miss Pyle, I'm as upset about our captain as anyone here."

Right. And I'm Queen Anne. Watch out for my gouty foot.

"But I don't know how I could help," he added.

Well, let's see. You could admit to taking the packet. You could cough up the real packet. You could forge a letter recommending Drum for active duty, then accidentally drop a match in the gunpowder hold of Basehart's ship. Any combination of the three would be much appreciated.

"What do you know about Basehart?" I asked.

Charles observed me for a long moment. "He's doing well. Perhaps not so much in the navy, for despite the fact that he collects an eighth of everything his captains capture, the war's been hard. There aren't many captains like Drummond, and now of course he's left the service. But Basehart prospers in other places, certainly. He has a lot of investments. Owns a great spread of land near Maide Vale—and I hear he's buying more."

"Family?"

"A wife who died."

"Children?"

"They had but one child. A daughter."

I'd planted the seed in Charles's imagination now, an imagination I had reason to know was eminently fertile. If he wanted my miracle cure, he was going to have to come up with some miracle information.

I noticed the ship had stopped making turns. Since Basehart had thankfully not repeated the whole Francis Scott Key "bombs bursting in air" stuff, it could only mean one thing.

"We're moving a lot faster," I said as a great gust of wind swept the perennially loose tendril off of my face.

"Aye. No need to tack anymore. The wind's changed direction. It's coming from just off the starboard beam."

The ship's timbers hummed as we cleaved through

the blue. "You never told me where it is you think we're going."

"Well, south, of course, as you guessed, though I suspect we will make a sharp turn west very soon. If the wind holds—and siroccos at this time of year usually do—we shall be at our destination in two to three days' time."

"And where is that?"

"I cannot be certain, but Gibraltar is my guess. It's the closest English port."

Damn. I should have known geography would come in handy someday.

Chapter Seven

"*And* you're certain Gibraltar is English?" Charles and I were hurrying down the gangway toward Drum's cabin. If Gibraltar were indeed our destination, it was my duty to let Drum know immediately.

Charles nodded sadly. "Aye. We captured her in '04."

"I had a strange sense Gibraltar was Spanish. Or was it French?" I tapped my chin. It would come to me. "Greek or Turkish or something. That's it! An island with lots of internal fighting."

He shook his head. "That's Cyprus, I'm afraid."

"Oh, of course. I was getting that confused with the Knights on Gibraltar who wear the cute red tunics."

He coughed politely. "Malta."

"Pearls?" I asked, crestfallen.

"Majorca."

"Lots of animals?"

"Madagascar—not to mention an entirely different ocean."

"But it is an island."

"Which?"

"Gibraltar."

"Unhappily, no. It's a soaring rock on the tip of Spain."

"A *rock*?" I cried as he helped me down the hatchway stairs. "What kind of strategic value is there in that? Anyway, isn't Spain rather far from England? I mean, I'm no wiz at geography or anything, but that's got to be a good, well . . . many miles from England. Why not take Ireland or Scotland or something?"

"We own Ireland and Scotland."

Yeah, like my friend Dana owns her cat.

We reached the bottom and Charles said, "I shall leave you here. Insofar as the matter you and I discussed is concerned"—he touched his heart—"I hope you will consider my need and my resources. Both are excessive." He bowed and exited.

Gar sat guard. He observed me with extreme wariness.

"Where's your brother?" I asked.

He leaned forward on his chair, as if it might tip backward without his consent. "Checking the hold."

"Gosh, do you think one guard's going to be enough? Captain Drummond's pretty dangerous, you know. I hear he's trying to tunnel out."

Gar didn't smile.

A crash came from the other side of the closed door. I reached for the latch.

Gar stopped my fist. "No more visitors."

"What's going on in there?" I demanded. The cabin had fallen silent.

"Nothing you need to be concerned about," Gar said.

Really? "Fine," I said. "I'll just go to my room." Which would be tough because as far as I knew I didn't have one. Nevertheless, it gave me an opportunity to swish away and regroup.

I slipped into an empty room and dug the doobie out of my pocket. I'd never been a smoker, but what I needed was a diversion—Jim Rockford style.

I lifted the side of the closest lantern and sucked the flame into the tip of the joint.

I'd like to tell you I didn't inhale—of course, I'd like to tell you I could still wear my favorite jeans from college—but I did. Just once. For luck. I strolled toward Gar, doing my femme fatale.

His eyes widened.

That's right, Gar. I took a puff. Want me. He clutched the back of the chair. I arched my back against the stair railing and twitched my skirt up over my calf.

He stood. "Don't . . ."

Gar, life as you know it is over. Seph the Stone Fox is here.

He took a step toward me, like a fly toward a spider. I flicked the joint over his head and reared back with my fist.

"*Fire on Board!*" Gar shouted.

Drum's door crashed open, and he and Gar dove on top of one another to get to the joint, which had rolled into a corner. A thunderous trampling of feet came from above. When I looked up, a solid wall of water rained down on me. Suddenly I was riding the pipe at Diamond Head. I flew off my feet, and the last wave flung me like a deflated jellyfish against Gar's chair.

"What in God's name are you *doing?*" Drum roared, kicking his way through the torrent. He flung the offending object of fire out the port hole.

"I was trying to get into your cabin," I said, coughing.

"With a cigar?"

"It's hard to explain."

"Let's not try. Funkel, what's the problem?"

"Orders, sir. Mr. Haverhill says no one—"

"Belay that."

"Aye, sir."

Drum bustled me inside and slammed the door. "An open flame on a wooden ship?! Tell me, has wood taken on supernatural qualities by the twenty-first century? Have the laws of the physical world relaxed? Is reason a lost art?"

"Drum, I'm soaked. Can you berate me after you've given me a blanket?"

"Oh . . . well . . . quite." He pulled open his wardrobe. "We're down to two linen shirts, a pair of trousers and a greatcoat. One more soaking, and I'll have nothing to offer you but a pair of stockings." He slid the greatcoat around my shoulders and led me to a chair.

He was coatless, but still in the fine white shirt, buff trousers and sword belt of his captain's uniform. I wrung out my skirt.

"Why did I think there was a struggle in here?" I asked.

"Oh, is that what happened? I wondered what had inspired the sudden savagery. I was looking through my logbooks when the shelf fell off the wall."

Seph the Power Ranger—ever ready to defend against faulty carpentry.

"You're quite the brawler," he said with a grin. "You remind me of my old bosun on *The Glory*. Whenever he'd get arrested for fighting in port, which was often, he'd cause so much confusion in the bailiff's office by yelling 'Plague rats!' and pointing, he just about always got away. Of course, he was usually still so drunk and contentious we had to carry him on board in chains." He gave me a long look. "And we're not even in port."

"Yeah, well. There's just something about assholes, I guess."

"A theme for the ages. I believe Sophocles commented upon it, albeit less poetically."

"I'm not a wilting flower, you know. I was suspended in high school for decking a guy who pinched me."

"In the navy you would have been lashed to the grate and given twenty strokes. But I take your point. It was damnably unjust."

"Damnably."

"Clearly there's a side to you 'twould be wise not to cross." His eyes sparked in the lantern light. He leaned forward and touched my chin. "I shouldn't like to have to resort to chains."

I fainted a little, but brought myself to. "Just try it, pal."

"Come now." He stood. "Out of that gown."

I forced my knees back together. He meant dry clothes. "Right."

"There's no point in you sitting here wet."

Tell me about it.

He stepped out onto the tiny stern balcony. With his greatcoat slung over it, the open wardrobe door served as a fine makeshift curtain, and there's nothing, I always say, like a free peek into a man's belongings. His clothes didn't fill a third of the space in the cabinet. But each item was clean, pressed and smelled of sandalwood. I began to work myself out of the wet dress.

"I guess it's a good thing you're not in the navy now," I called, "given the twenty-strokes thing and all—I mean, Basehart can't flog a private citizen, can he?"

"No. But he'll exact his revenge. He left without seeing me, you know. I suspect a bloody nose was not the sort of impression he wanted to leave with my sailors."

"Hmmm. Who's Gabin?"

"Supposedly a minor French ambassador. In reality, he runs their intelligence work. He is not a man with whom to tangle."

"Have you?"

"No, but a colleague of mine did. He was captured in La Hogue and never seen again. But there were stories . . ." He trailed off.

"Stories?"

"Come, milady. 'Tis too beautiful a night for such tales."

My eyes fell on a shaving mug with an ancient silver

brush inside, and I nearly moaned. I love to watch a man shave, especially with a hand razor. All the rhythmic scraping makes me tingle. I lifted the mug and sniffed the spicy clean scent.

"Can I tell you something honestly, Drum?"

"If you wish."

"I don't know much about sailing, but even I can tell Haverhill's not a very good sailor. Why do you keep him on board?"

"Haverhill is a tolerable sailor when he's not under pressure. But his cousins work in naval yards—one in Portsmouth, the other in Gibraltar—a fact which has served us extraordinarily well when it comes to cordage, gunpowder and supplies. Not a ha'penny nail moves in the navy without a hefty dose of larceny, you know. I like to say Haverhill's commission was printed on the back of a chandler's list."

I freed myself from the dress and looked down at the wet, overlaced underthing remaining. Okay, how was I gonna reverse-engineer that? Oh, the hell with it. I grabbed the razor and cut the ties. Seph, one; underskirt, zero. Which left only a wet minislip, and even I could wrestle that into submission.

When I was free of clothes, I toweled off and pulled on one of Drum's linen shirts. It was soft and white and hung past my knees. A breeze from the open balcony door fluttered the tails around my legs.

"Say," I called, "were you aware Gibraltar is an English possession?"

"Acutely," he said. "I was there when we took it."

I began pulling the pins from my hair. When my hair

was loose, I reached for the greatcoat, but it was wool, and I knew I'd be too warm. I spotted Drum's officer's coat laid casually over the back of his chair.

Careful, Seph. Too boyfriend-y.

I looked down. Drum's shirt covered most of me—well, except my calves and the ever-present shoes, of course. Though for all I knew, showing your calves in 1706 might be as provocative as going topless. I examined the shoes in the mirror. My mind flashed to the challenge before me not only of sunbathing or swimming fully shod, but of showering, playing tennis, scrubbing the floors and having sex—

Okay, maybe the shoes wouldn't be a *total* drag.

The heels gave a little *buzz-buzz*.

"Hey, knock it off," I whispered.

"Pardon?" Drum called.

"Not you." I shook my finger at the shoes. "Listen, God only knows what passes for birth control around here, so don't even think about it. And even if I had condoms, I have no doubt some nasty baroque form of syphilis would make it through, and there I'd be—"

"With whom are you conversing?" Drum had moved back into the cabin.

"Er, nobody. Just thinking out loud. Get back out there. I'm not done dressing."

I heard his footsteps as he retreated. I fastened the shirt at the neck and did a final mirror check.

Whoops!

In the lantern light, I looked like a page out of the folio edition of *Renaissance Penthouse,* with three suggestive spots of dark dimly visible through the thinner-than-thou linen. I checked the back view. Yikes. Like an exclamation point.

Boyfriend coat it would have to be. I slipped it on, and in my oversized shirt, oversized coat and evening pumps, I went outside looking every bit the little girl who'd spent a busy afternoon in her parents' closet.

Drum's gaze caught the coat, though he said nothing. I took a spot on the narrow balcony and clasped the railing as the tropically scented wind swirled my damp hair. Stars blazed across the blue-black sky like sequins, and when I turned east I saw the most enormous full moon just above the horizon.

"Zounds."

Drum gave me a sidelong glance. "Comes up every night."

"What? Every ni— Oh." I pursed my lips. "I get it. What can I say? I'm a romantic."

"And a consistent one. Every morning a monsoon, every afternoon blue-sky sailing on a fine t'gallant breeze and every evening this. Even those same two clouds over there, capering around the moon like lambs around a ewe."

"Not much to complain about," I said, "not even for a sailor, though, ah . . . I have to ask. What do your men think of it?"

"They don't seem to notice. Which is just as well. It's a captain's job, you see, to keep the crew from diversions. But suffice it to say"—he nodded toward the moon—"I'm glad we're not running in tidal water."

He handed me a stout glass filled with something

pale. "I thought we'd try it. It's a muscat from Alsace." He clinked his glass with mine. "To new friends."

The wine smelled of gardenias and fresh grass, and it swaddled my tongue in velvet. I felt a divine shiver as it slid down my throat. "Mmm. Good."

I hadn't eaten since Campiti's. I'd have to be careful or I was going to get good and drunk, which could very well lead to bad and drunk. I downed the rest in a single swallow.

"So," I blurted out, "who's the woman in Toulon?"

Okay, that wasn't quite the bad I was imagining.

Drum choked a little and threw back the rest of his glass. "The daughter of a man to whom I owe a great debt."

"The owner of a French cutter, perhaps?"

He sighed. "No, but your intuition is sound. The daughter was on the cutter that day."

"Rather noble of you," I admitted with a fair amount of private reluctance. I lifted my glass again. "To men who do the right thing."

The bowline spread out behind us in a sparkling 90-degree arc. While I was changing we had turned west.

"You didn't ask me what I found out," I said.

"You didn't burst into the room shouting, so I rather assumed nothing."

"Ha-ha. I found out lots of things, actually. Haverhill's been given secret orders, Uncle Charles has a broken heart, and we're—" Oops. I clamped my mouth down firmly.

"And we're what?"

I suppose there's no point in trying to hide it. "And we're heading for Gibraltar."

"Aye." His thumb worked the pattern in the glass. "For my trial."

"You knew?"

"Navigation is an unfortunate part of the requirements."

Something about his thumb on the ridges of the glass made my nipples harden.

Oh, nice compassion, Seph. Try deep-sixing the "-passion" part and sticking to the— Oh dear! Quick, quick, quick. Think of a different topic.

"Hell," he said, "I wish I'd read those dispatches. Damn my compunction." He rolled the glass in his palm, and I broke into a sweat.

"The dispatches are gone," he went on, "the correct dispatches, that is. And a dispatch with a green ribbon has taken its place. The real dispatches would have told Basehart where to go to fight the French. Instead he's committed to Gibraltar."

He took both glasses, returned inside and reappeared with them full. His glass was dripping a little, and he cleaned the overflow with the tip of a very able tongue. I clinched my butt muscles. "Perhaps Gibraltar is where the French are, or on the way to."

"Hell, if Basehart had caught the slightest whiff of a battle, he'd have left me and the *Neuf Ouest* behind and mustered every resource at his command." He tipped the glass back and drank deliberately. The long muscles in his throat moved up and down.

I clutched the railing and with considerable effort

redirected my attention to the sea. God, it had been so long since I'd had sex, throat muscles were turning me on. I thought of Tom and that wonderful, cool, hard recycling bin lid. . . .

"So he hasn't been misdirected to the wrong battle," I said. "He's been given no information about a battle at all."

"Exactly. And without Basehart and his battalion, England is likely to fall."

"You need to tell him."

"A word from the man who hid the dispatches is not going to carry much weight. And what would I tell him? 'Forget bringing me to justice. There's a battle some-where. Go find it'?

"Good point. Well, if you haven't stopped since Gi-braltar, then the dispatches are still on board. We just need to find them." Oh, if he would just stop with the glass. "What enemies do you have?" I asked. "You per-sonally, not England."

"None of whom I'm aware, though I suppose every naval captain has his share. There could be someone out there nursing a grudge."

"What about among your colleagues? Someone over whom you were promoted? Someone who wanted your command? I mean, who brought you up on charges with the French cutter? Maybe that and this are re-lated."

"The officer who pressed charges was in a squadron whose path we happened to cross. He saw the cutter, but couldn't leave his formation. He signaled for me to follow the cutter. I believed it was more important for me to stay where I was. An enemy corvette was rumored to be running those waters, which is true, though not entirely the reason I didn't obey. The officer's been promoted to commodore now, so I don't think professional jealousy would come into play anymore."

"What about the father of the girl?"

His eyes chilled to a steely gray. "No."

"No? No, what?"

"*No*," he repeated in that irritatingly male, "The subject is closed" sort of tone.

I bristled. Bristling and stiff nipples are not a good combination. "Is that 'No, I don't want to talk about it' or 'No, he's not involved'?"

"Leave it."

Ooh, wrong answer. I don't do well with commands. I've got the same problem at work. "I only ask because not many fathers take too kindly to men putting the boots to their daughter. Especially in this backward age. Especially when the man in question is supposedly in the father's debt."

His face turned to granite. Positively Rushmore-ian.

"Look," I went on, "I'm just trying to figure out if there's a connection. I'm not trying to suggest there's anything wrong with that you're doing. Lord knows, we've gotten that whole sexual mores thing ironed out by my day."

"You are not, I hope, about to hold up the twenty-first century as a model of ideal behavior. From the little I know of it, I can think of a half dozen centuries I'd rank higher, including some where I'd be rowing in a slave galley."

"I'm just saying that in my day people don't need to pretend we're not involved when we are. We've grown past that. We do what we want so long as both parties are willing."

"Everyone?"

"The enlightened, modern thinkers, certainly."

"And you count yourself among that number?"

"Of course."

"Of course. No constraints, no judgment, no hesitation, then? Just the mature, carefree manifestation of all that is natural?"

"Yes."

"I see. Are the words 'recycling bin' of any import to you?"

Eeeeeeek!

"*How did you know that?*" I cried.

"I told you before, there are certain things I know."

"But how? *How?* And don't shrug your shoulders. It's you and that damned Mrs. Kenney, isn't it?"

"No, if you must know, milady, it's you. I am your character, recall, however nascent your writing may be. It is inevitable that I see the world at least in part through your eyes."

"My eyes?! Like now?! Like always?!"

"At times. There is no rhyme or reason—quite in fitting with the way you seem to run the rest of your life, I might add."

This was so wrong! What did he know? What had I inadvertently shared with him while he was in my thoughts? I thought of the cut glass, and my cheeks went a bright shade of Otis Red-ding.

He gave me a pointed look. "You say you are thoroughly enlightened and modern, but when I think of young Tom atop that poor bin—"

"If you know what's good for you, you'll stop."

"Tom, the man for whom your feelings were never, and forgive me if I paraphrase, anything other than friendly."

"This is unbelievable!"

"'We don't have to pretend we're not when we are. Not in my day,' you said. *Ha!*"

"You know what? Maybe Miss Toulon should help you out of this mess."

"Maybe I wouldn't be in this mess if you and your bloody ideas about sailing hadn't shoved their way into my life."

"Stay out of my head!"

"Stay out of my ship!"

"If I could leave, I would!"

"Good news, milady. I have a way."

"What?!"

"Your shoes can get you home. Not by themselves," he added quickly. "At least not according to Mrs. Kenney."

"Yeah, what else have you and Mrs. Kenney been hiding from me?"

"Well, we can't all be as open as you enlightened denizens of the twenty-first century."

"Did Mrs. Kenney have a hand in bringing me here?"

"Mrs. Kenney plucked you from Pitsford like a frog with a fly. At least *she* knows her geography."

"Mrs. Kenney would have no reason to want me."

"Truer words were never spoken." He jerked open a lantern and adjusted a guttering flame.

"*You* brought me here," I said.

"Perhaps I did."

"Then send me back."

"Like a cannon shot, milady."

"What do we need?"

"You're not going to like it."

"Why should this be any different from anything else today?"

"A kiss."

"*What?!*"

"Sorry, no recycling bin in sight. We'll have to rely on simple, old-fashioned mechanics—you know, arms, lips, that sort of thing."

"I'm not going to kiss you, you imperious ass."

"Ah, but you want to. I've been in your head, re-member?"

"Bastard!"

"Aye, well, I'm afraid mature, carefree groping won't serve. It's going to have to be a kiss."

"If you think for one minute—"

He applied his mouth to mine.

I pulled myself loose. "—that I intend to allow you to—"

He caught me again, slipping his hands under my jacket and clasping my hip bones. The kiss that fol-lowed was expert enough, but it was the light touch of thumb and fingers on one of my least favorite places that gentled me as if he were the Horse Whisperer.

How could I have ever disliked those chubby, hard-to-find spots? I loved my hip bones! I wanted to write sonnets to my hip bones! I wanted to harness the electric charge that leaped from my hips and light the East Coast for a week.

"You're so small," he whispered into my neck, "if I squeezed, I'd crush you."

Holy moley! If my clitoris were a champagne bottle I could have popped a cork the size of an Airbus. A throbbing vibrato ran from my shoes up my spine.

Drum drew my shuddering hips next to his. Hello, Airbus.

"Have you slipped a tiller rope?" he asked.

"It's the shoes," I said weakly. It was like kissing Tom, I told myself—and it was—but it was different too.

"Mrs. Kenney says only one person can take them off."

"You?"

"Shall I try?" He nibbled my ear. "If so, the shoes come last."

I was pretty sure I knew what came first because it was already coming.

He tugged the coat off my shoulders and let it fall at my feet.

"Where's the respect for the office?" I managed to choke out.

"*Hmmm.* Perhaps a clashing of arms will help." He reached for the buckle of the sword belt. The clink of metal sent a bolt threw me. The sword, belt and sheath clattered to the floor. I knew what arms were going to clash, and they weren't going to be steel.

He took me by the hand and pulled me toward the cabin.

Oh, God, should a romance writer have sex with her character? Does it violate some literary code somewhere? I thought of '20s and '30s mystery writer Dorothy L. Sayers. I'd read Sayers had become so smitten with her aristocratic sleuth Lord Peter Wimsey that she'd added mystery writer Harriet Vane as his love interest so that she, Sayers, could vicariously experience falling in love with and marrying him. Of course, Lord Peter and Harriet Vane had honorably waited to consummate their love until their wedding night. I wasn't sure we'd make it until Drum got his boots off.

He guided me to a stop just before the cot.

I looked up into those gray-blue eyes and laid a hand on his bristled cheek. "You've turned out to be not at all what I was expecting."

He smiled. "Is that good or bad?"

"Good." And if the whirlpool swirling just south of the equator was any indication, very, *very* bad as well.

His eyes grew as clear and crystalline as the morning sky. He drew my chin up, plied my lips with his tongue and kissed me with a low, devastating groan.

The thick scent of blossoms billowed up my nose. I wheeled into a stomach-churning orange vortex, and the room disappeared.

Chapter Eight

With my heart in my throat, I hurtled through time. Orange, yellow, green. Then, with a change in momentum that felt like a Ray Lewis tackle, I thudded through a blue-purple fog into a sparely upholstered chair in a loud, dark room that smelled of flat beer and shellfish and positively reverberated with the present—my present, that is. I may not know my geography, but there's no mistaking the bass line of George Michael's "Faith."

Having learned priorities from my first go-around, I peered down. Off-the-shoulder black sweater and pencil-thin black jeans. Oh Lord, I had returned as Sandy in *Grease*. Well, at least I was mostly covered and in dry clothes.

As my travel blockheadedness receded, the faces of my coworkers began to materialize. Hairy-Eared Hanlon, Eve Warwick, Russell from Sales, Larry Cartwright, Richard Baum, Trish from the agency, and Tom, directly opposite, gazing at me over an untouched glass of red wine. All I wanted to do was throw my arms around him and say, "Oh my God, I thought I'd never see you again!" But what could I say?

Everyone was laughing and talking with the slightly giddy air of alcohol and success. And no one seemed to notice my remarkable entrance. Tom lowered his eyes, silent.

"To Seph," Caroline said, raising her glass, "who showed 'em how things are done."

"Hear, hear!"

"Knocked 'em out."

"The highlight of the meeting."

I lifted my glass with a shaky arm and drank. Good Christ, a whiskey! Tom cleared his throat.

"To Seph," he said quietly, "whose hard work and determination on Grant's Aspirin has helped transform Pilgrim Pharmaceuticals into a world-class operation, and whose joy and humor and spirit is an inspiration to each of us who is lucky enough to work with her."

Yowzah!

An awed "Ooh!" went around the table. Everyone clinked glasses.

"All right, kids," Hanlon boomed, "last one to the gondolas is a rotten egg."

Venice! We were in Venice, after my presentation. Jesus, who the hell gave it? Me, apparently. But how?

My team leaped to their feet, Hanlon threw a wad of euros on the table, and we were out in the night. It was early April, but the day was warm, and the brightly colored lanterns strung along the canal walkway lent a

summery feel to the air. I'd never been in Venice—well,
except for the entire day today, apparently, when I'd been
here without knowing it—and it was breathtaking.

A line of gondolas, each with its own unique colors,
fabric and smiling gondolier, were spread along the
bank.

It was obvious the group wouldn't all fit into a single
vessel, and we were starting to break into twos and
threes when a firm hand clasped mine and drew me
away.

Without a word, Tom led me to the farthermost
gondola. He murmured something to the gondolier and
handed him several bills. The gondolier smiled as Tom
stepped into the boat and lifted me down.

This gondola had a low, narrow couch backed with
dozens of red and yellow silk pillows. The couch was
surrounded on three sides and the top by a veil of
gleaming yellow curtain. Tom lowered me carefully
onto the pillows and sunk in beside me. He extended
his long legs and settled in stiffly, eyes focused ahead.

The weight of his silence unnerved me.

Our gondolier shoved off. The gentle, rhythmic motion did little to divert me from Tom's obvious distress.
In a few minutes we were gliding steadily through the
narrow canals. The muted sounds of my coworkers disappeared into the distance.

Tom sat up abruptly. "Okay, I'm just going to say
this."

Uh, boy. That's never the start to anything good.

"I told you I had a job offer," he said, "but I didn't
tell you where. It's in Paris."

"Job offer? What job offer?"

"C'mon, don't play games. I told you yesterday. You remember Kimberly Jacobs?"

"The venture capitalist with the Botox? The one who always calls me Steph?"

"She's buying a biotech company. Needs an attorney. It's only one product now, but they have a decent pipeline and—"

"No, stay! I don't want you to leave." Kim Jacobs looked like Charlize Theron and always laughed at his jokes.

"It's . . . not that easy."

"Sure it is. 'No thank you, Kimberly.' Here, give me your cell phone."

How could he do this? I hadn't wanted to take the recycling bin incident to its natural conclusion, but I didn't want him to go either. I wanted him held in some sort of suspended animation until I needed him. How hard was that for him to understand?

I hooked an ankle across my knee to position myself for a thoughtful debate when the shoulder of my sweater drooped even farther.

"Holy hell!" His voice cracked. "You have a tattoo there too?"

I sat bolt upright, grabbed my neckline and looked down. To someone who takes a dim view of body art, almost no question could be more alarming. Besides seeing that I wore no bra, something I never do, on my left breast, just northeast of the nipple, I spotted a tiny cross with flared ends, like the *X* on a treasure map.

"Oh, Lord." I clutched the sweater to my chest.

"Did it hurt?" Tom had the addled gaze of a teenage boy after his first flip through *Playboy*.

"I-I have no idea."

"Wow. I didn't know you drank that much."

"I don't," I wailed. "Why did you say 'too'? You said, 'You have a tattoo there too.' Why did you say 'too'?"

He pointed toward my ankle.

I jerked my calf toward my face so fast, I rolled off the bench and hit the floor with a clunk.

"*Va tutto bene?*" the gondolier cried.

"No problem. Sorry," Tom called. "We're fine. *Siamo molto bene.*"

Jesus, there it was! Under the taffeta strap, some elaborate string of loops and lines. I couldn't take my eyes off it. It was like rubbernecking a car wreck. My own little, decorative car wreck. "What in God's name is it?"

"You said it was Arabic.'"

"*I* told you that?"

"Yesterday on the plane."

"I didn't by any chance tell you I bought it at the gift shop right before we left? Slip into the restroom, wet a paper towel, that sort of thing?"

"You said you'd gotten it from a Rabatan tattooist," Tom replied, discouraged. "I didn't even know you'd ever been to Rabat."

Yeah, well, I'm pretty sure you need to know where a place is before you can go to it. I peeked in at the little cross. It was bright blue with intricate black edging.

Tom looked at me and frowned. "Seph, are you all right? I have to say, you've been acting a little . . . strange."

"Have I?" I tugged my sweater back into place and allowed Tom to help me back onto the bench. "How strange? I mean, for a while, not just now?"

"Since the airport, actually." He sighed and closed his eyes. "Did you mean what you said on the plane?"

Oh, dear, that had an ugly sound. He waited, silent.

"Er, did it sound like I meant it?"

"Yes."

Whatever it was, he was far from ecstatic about it. "I didn't mean it in a bad way, you know."

"Well, no, of course not. No man in his right mind would think it was bad. I just . . . Oh, Christ!" He made a wild gesture with his hands. "Look, if that's all you want of me, I'll do it."

"You'll do it?"

Dark pools of periwinkle gazed at me. "'Any time, any place' were your words."

Oh, boy. That's what I said on the plane? Me? Seph Pyle? Perma-virgin?

"Married, divorced, dating." His voice was husky. "You said just call and the next two hours were mine. Just like that. You said that's how we were meant to be."

My mouth went dry. "I-I-"

"Is that what you meant, Seph?"

"Er . . . well . . ."

"So I can just choose now? Right here, in the warm night air? We'll just get to it?"

My brain pressed the panic button. "Okay, here's the deal—"

"The deal's been cut, has it not?"

He lifted me off the bench and spread me across his hips. Whatddya know? Different centuries, same Airbus.

He wrapped a handful of my hair around his fist and pulled me to his mouth for a hard, unrepentant kiss.

My shoes made a long buzz.

Tom jerked away. "Holy shit, what was that?"

"Heaven," I said, unhearing. His Cabernet taste was still on my tongue, and the vibrato of the shoes was bringing that Airbus into exquisite relief.

The gondola shook violently, and for a second the world glowed. I looked at Tom. He stared at me, incredulous.

I felt the horizon contract and expand, and there was a weird magnetic pull on my bones.

"No!"

The *Neuf Ouest* was calling me back, and I sure didn't want to go. Not with my first Airbus ride in sight. I clutched Tom's shoulders.

"Don't let them!" I said. "Hold me!"

A series of jerks ended in a final violent yank. The wind shrieked around my ears, and then, as quickly as it began, it stopped.

I was in Tom's arms, in the gondola, in the quiet, still night.

Tom's eyes were as round as poker chips. "What the fuck was that?"

"I-I think there's something I need to tell you."

Tom didn't answer—and he didn't blink. "What?'

"I've been traveling," I whispered.

"Traveling?"

"And there's a man—a sailor, actually—who has something to do with it."

"You offered to go to bed with me while you're seeing another man?"

"No, it's not like that. He's from a long time ago."

Tom narrrowed his eyes. "Like the Battle of Midway?"

"Longer."

"Jutland? *Lusitania?* The *Monitor* and *Merrimac?* Just nod when I'm getting close."

I swung my head left and right.

"I see." Tom sharpened into the I'll-stuff-a-lie-so-far-up-your-ass-you'll-be-recanting-your-testimony-on-a-colonoscopy-screen attorney I had come to admire at Pilgrim. I swallowed.

"So," he said, "what are we talking here? Magellan? Odysseus? *Noah?*"

"What do you know about Queen Anne?"

"She wasn't much of a sailor."

"Her *time.*"

He regarded me appraisingly, but after a long moment scholarly instinct prompted him to begin. "Right. Sure. Why not? Let's see . . . last of the Stuarts. No heir. That's when the English crown went to the German Hanoverian line. Anne's legacy was uniting Scotland and England—oh, and the appointment of a damned fine general by the name of Marlborough, who kicked France's sorry ass across the Rhine and halfway to the Baltic Sea."

"Marlborough?! He mentioned him!"

"Did he? And who, might I ask, is this fount of historical information?"

Tom didn't care for anyone tramping on his intellectual territory. The gondola had moved into the pool of light from a crowded square. "Holy crap!" I cried. "That's not just stubble. You're growing a beard!"

Tom glowered. He had no patience for witnesses who ducked down side roads. Evaders, he called them. But this evader had never seen Tom with as much as a five o'clock shadow.

"I, ah . . ." It was positively bizarre. Tom with a beard; me with a tattoo. Two tattoos. Er, at least two tattoos.

Tom gave his head a prosecutorial cock. "The fount?"

"Here's the thing," I said. "His name is Phillip Drummond—"

Tom's face pinched with distaste.

"—and he's the captain of a ship in the Mediterranean." I gulped. "In Queen Anne's time."

Tom templed his fingers and rhythmically brought them together. "You're telling me that you're traveling to see a man whose idea of enjoying Jonathan Swift is splitting a pitcher with him at the local tavern?"

"I know it's hard to believe."

"Hard to *believe*?!"

"But you saw what just happened. You heard the shoes."

He stared at me, calculating.

"Remember the buzz?" I said. "It started with the shoes. So did my traveling."

His eyes traveled to my feet.

"It seems," I said slowly, "they have the power to

take me back in time. I put them on in the store, and—poof!—I was gone."

"Poof?"

"Poof."

"But you weren't gone," he protested. "Nothing happened in the store. You were on the plane with me."

Yes, apparently handing out free liaison cards and getting nailed by Tito the Mad Tattooer in the lavatory. "That I can't explain. I was there, I guess, but I was really someplace else."

He chewed on this. "Which means you didn't make that offer on the plane."

How to answer? "Um, technically no, but—"

"I see." A flash of something appeared on his face before being swallowed in lawyerly dispassion. "And how do you know it was Queen Anne's time?"

"The captain told me. But it wasn't just him telling me. I mean, I landed on a ship's deck in the middle of a hurricane."

"A hurricane?" An eyebrow shot up. "In the Mediterranean?"

"Yes, well, apparently they don't usually have them." Bit of a screwup there, okay? Will downgrade to a rainy blow for paperback edition. "But there it was. And I'm telling you, it was another time. There were cannons on board." Mum's the word on the table frill. "And sailors with long pigtails and bad teeth."

"Well, the bad teeth could put you in England in any century, frankly. But the pigtails . . ." He tapped his chin thoughtfully. "I'm not ready to say I believe you yet, Seph, but tell me about the ship."

Tom knew his sailing. I combed my mind's eye for the picture. "It was wooden—very susceptible to fire," I added with a solemn nod. "And there was a whole bunch of sails and ropes."

"Sheets," Tom said.

"They looked heavier than sheets. More like canvas, I think."

"The ropes, I mean. They're not called ropes. On a ship they're called sheets."

"Well, that doesn't make any sense. What do they call sheets then?"

"Linens, I suppose."

"But that's what they called my underclothes—" I shut my mouth. "Er, the ship, though. What else do you want to know?"

"Did it have three masts?" Tom asked, frowning. "Or just two?" I think Tom was suffering from a touch of mast envy. His sailboat had one mast. He liked to sail on the confluence of the Allegheny and Monongahela rivers, a big blue patch just west of Pittsburgh's downtown, the area known to locals as "The Golden Triangle."

"Three masts," I said, "as tall as trees. And a big steering wheel, just like the Gorton's fisherman. And bulkheads and a table that could be struck for battle—" Well, in a perfect world, at least. ". . . And they'd just had a battle with the *Royal Louis*—"

"The *Royal Louis*?" His eyes widened, then he caught himself. "What am I saying? It can't be true. But the French ship *Royal Louis*? My God, that was one of the most famous of all of Louis the Fourteenth's ships. Did you know the *Royal Louis* once battled four enemy ships alone and won?"

Tom had a jones for sailing stuff. If I was going to convince him, this was the way to do it.

"Seph, I don't know . . ."

"But how would I know this? How would I know the *Royal Louis*? I was a nineteenth-century English literature major, remember? No French warships in Thomas Hardy or Jane Austen."

He gazed into the distance, imagining again. "Well, even if it was a dream, to have felt like you sailed in the age of Marlborough . . . My God, what an experience! What was this captain like?"

"Well, there was a bit of trouble."

"Trouble?"

"The dispatches he was carrying for the navy were stolen."

"That'll be a bit of bother for him, to be sure. But the worst thing that could happen was a court-martial, though in many cases that was a mere formality. The officers who sat in judgment already had a fair idea of the measure of the man, and any naval officer who fought the *Royal Louis* and survived has to have a pretty fine reputation."

"Yeah, except he isn't a naval officer. Well, not anymore. He lost his commission for letting a French cutter escape."

"Oh?"

"But Drum said—I mean, Captain Drummond said the charge wasn't true, and in fact it didn't stick in court. But the next time his ship was sent in for repairs, the navy decommissioned it, and suddenly he was stuck on land."

"How was he fighting the *Royal Louis* then? Skipping stones at it from shore?"

"Well, no, he has a ship. It's just not a navy one. It's owned by investors and—"

"He's a *pirate*?"

"Oh, no! It's not like that. He's a privateer. He has something the government calls a letter of marque."

"Ah, a *licensed* pirate. Passed the inspections, that sort of thing?"

"Well," I said weakly, "it seemed different the way he said it."

Tom grunted. "So our privateer lost the naval dispatches. Who cares? So long as his investors are happy."

"Well, the dispatches carried crucial information about a French attack, and Captain Drummond was rather hoping safe delivery of the dispatches would win him back his position in the navy."

"Hope he likes privateering then. It sounds like he's going to be doing it for a while."

"It's worse, though. The admiral—Admiral Basehart—thinks Captain Drummond stole the dispatches. He's been arrested."

"Ouch." He gave me a long, thoughtful look. "And you think you were there? This wasn't just a dream?"

No judgment, just an objective request for confirmation. One of the reasons I liked Tom.

"Tom, I could describe their jackets, their pistols, the cannons, the clang of the bells, the way the men stood over my head on poles—"

"Yards," he said.

"—and he mentioned a city called La Hogue and a French spy named Gabin. And you saw what just happened a minute ago."

He stroked the stubble on his chin. "How did you escape? I mean, what exactly released you?"

Hmmm, probably best not to venture too far down that road. I'm not sure what the significance of Drum looking like Tom was, and really didn't want to think about it too much. "The shoes seem to have special powers."

He twisted his lips, silent for a long moment. Now was the time for the court's ruling. "Hell of a story, Seph. I don't know . . ."

All at once, the shoes began to rev with the earth-shaking roar of a Harley. I covered my ears.

The folks in a passing gondola stared. All at once the roar stopped, and the shoes started to glow red, then blue, then green, just like my grandmother's aluminum Christmas tree, filling our little walled-off space like a carnival fun house. Tom's face looked like a cross between a Toulouse-Lautrec painting and Munch's *The Scream*.

He reached for the shoes. The instant his hand neared the taffeta, the glow enveloped him too. He pulled back his hand as if he'd been shocked. The glow disappeared, and the roaring coughed to an eerie silence.

"Christ Almighty!" He looked at his hand.

"Are you hurt?"

"No. I saw it, Seph. A ship, the men, the sails—just as you described it and just for an instant." He looked at the shoes again in awe. "Where did you get those?"

"Nine West."

"Jesus, no wonder women like to shop there."

It's not easy to shock an attorney. Actually it's probably pretty easy to shock them, but practically impossible to get them to show it. Tom and I had once witnessed Hairy-Eared Hanlon ask a member of opposing counsel during a deposition if her period was making her antagonistic and might possibly be the reason this groundless lawsuit had been filed in the first place. Tom hadn't lost his game face then, and he was already returning to it now.

"For argument's sake," he said, "let's say I believe you. What can either of us do? You're here. I'm here. It may be just one of those weird things that happens to a person. It's certainly the weirdest thing that's ever happened to me." He looked at his hand.

"I don't know," I said. "I guess I just need to know how it ends. With the captain, I mean." Drum was supposed to be my hero, after all. I hoped he hadn't been found guilty of stealing. I rather hoped he had gotten back into the navy. "Maybe there's something we can look up?"

Tom stretched his legs. "Don't think we need to. It's pretty straightforward, I'd say. So long as you weren't looking for uplifting, of course. Then again, you're the Thomas Hardy fan. Ought to fit your sensibilities nicely."

"Meaning what?"

"In wartime, stealing dispatches is treason. Your captain will have been hanged."

Chapter Nine

"*I'm* only asking," Tom said as we hurried through the throngs of tourists loitering in the morning light of the Piazza di San Marco. A battalion of pigeons launched skyward at our feet. "If it is true, are you sure you really want to know?"

We were on our way to see Signor Paolo di Marvelo, a maritime historian at the Museo Correr Tom had tracked down on the internet the night before.

"Captain Drummond's my friend." Not to mention at least partially my creation. Not to mention your doppelganger, Tom, in this mondo bizzaro, cross-century version of *The Olsen Twins Take the Mediterranean*. "If he was hanged"—the word was like dry Shredded Wheat on my tongue—"I just feel like I should know what happened to him."

I had only the most passing interest in Venice's grand basilica with its onion domes or the bell tower soaring over the Grand Canal, so emblematic of the Venice of movies and guidebooks. The sky was a glorious Gimme a High Sea blue, but all I could think about was Drum and a hangman's noose. Even the gorgeous strand of fat pink pearls in the window of a chichi jewelry store only made the muscles in my throat tighten.

The Correr was located in the neoclassical Napoleonic wing of the building that constitutes the entire far end of the square. Tom was pulling me in that direction as fast as my taffeta friends would allow, which was remarkably fast given a) the height of the heels, and b) the century lag from which I was suffering.

I'd spent my first night with the shoes the night before—a bit of a letdown given the attractive alternatives for bedmates that had presented themselves during the day. But at least it had been on Tom's bed, curled under his Burberry as he'd worked his history contacts on the laptop. Showering with the shoes had been something of a trial—shades of my youth at the Mt. Lebanon Pool where the locker room signs warned of horrors beyond human imagination for those daring to shower without flip-flops.

Tom had met me at the bathroom door with hot Italian espresso and the news that, at least from what the hotel towel revealed, my body art was limited to the two places identified the day before.

He also had put to rest any worries I'd had about the impact of my time travel on the time-space continuum (I may not have taken physics, but I'd seen the *Back to the Future* trilogy a half dozen times). "The world as we know it," Tom said, perched over his laptop, "has not changed. Paris Hilton is still considered attractive, the Pirates are at the bottom of the National League Central, and Pilgrim stock is underpriced. So, if it wasn't making sense before, it's still not making sense now. Your trip back in time hasn't changed history."

Except mine.

"*Buongiorno.*" The familiar voice at a nearby café table lurched me out of my reverie. "A bit early for a tandem jog, isn't it?"

Tom slammed to a halt, and I stumbled into him. There, seated under an umbrella with a tiny glass perched at his lips, was our fearless—but not earless—leader.

"We seemed to have lost you two last night," Hanlon said, eyeing me closely. In my rush to get us to Museo Correr, I'd put on my black jeans—thank God for boot cut—and a pink button-down collar shirt from Tom's drawer. "TJF" was embroidered in black block letters on the pocket. My cheeks turned a brilliant shade of Equador-able Red.

"Have you changed your mind about that resignation, Tom?" The stiff hairs edging Hanlon's ears glinted in the morning sun like flagpoles at the United Nations.

Tom shifted his weight. "No."

I gave Tom a look. When we'd talked about Paris last night, he hadn't mentioned he'd already turned in his resignation.

Hanlon clucked. "Too bad. I thought perhaps with your fortune having taken a rather Italian turn"—his eyes cut to me—"you might have changed your mind."

"No."

"I guess Seph's given you the standard up-and-out routine then. If she'd just pull in her claws a little, we might be able to convince you to stay."

Ugh. Nothing like a Hairy-Eared Hanlon sliming to really take the polish off a Venetian morning. Rumor had it he was in negotiations with the Olympics committee to bring sliming in as an exhibition sport. But as I liked to say to my friend Dana, if work was meant to be fun, we wouldn't be getting paid for it.

Then I saw the look on Tom's face, a look I had seen the spitting image of about twenty-four hours earlier, give or take three centuries, when Basehart recited his little poem, and we all knew how that turned out. I caught Tom's hand, which was turning to a fist.

"Whoa, Sugar Ray," I whispered. "You've put in your resignation, not me."

Tom made a disgusted noise but backed off.

"I suppose I'll be seeing you two later at the breakout groups?" Hanlon called as we made our good-byes. "Unless you've broken out entirely. Ha-ha."

"Asshole," Tom muttered as we made our way toward the museum.

"Yes, but he's our asshole."

"I don't know how you can stay, Seph."

"I love my job. I love what we do at Pilgrim. One bad person doesn't make a company bad. And he could be a lot worse."

"Could he? I mean, he lies, he's rude, he's unethical, he's a racist—"

"Don't forget ugly."

"—he's ugly, people hate him, and he's sleeping with the head of the same PR agency he pays millions of dollars a year to."

"Hey, at least he understands the cost equation there."

"Here's a little-known fact—"

"Are you just saying this to keep me from asking you about your resignation?"

"—Hanlon used to be on his college swim team."

I slapped a hand over my eyes. "Oh, God, if you say 'Speedo,' I'm going to vomit."

Fortunately the immediate proximity of the doors of the Museo Correr kept me from that fate. The Museo was founded in 1830, Tom explained, and dedicated to preserving the naval, commercial and military history of the city. It occupied the building that used to house the King of Italy. Since it was before opening time, Tom and I had to give our names to a guard, who unlocked the door to let us in. He directed us past an elegant marble staircase to an elevator. I pressed the Up button repeatedly.

Tom pursed his lips. "What are you doing?"

"If you press the button five or six times, it thinks a lot of people are waiting. It comes faster."

"Really? Maybe it thinks so many people are waiting it can't hold them and just goes on by."

On the third floor we were shown to the administrative wing, and a graduate student type who looked like Lyle Lovett pointed out Professor Di Marvelo's office.

"*Buongiorno,* Signor Fraser." Di Marvelo shook Tom's

hand in that exuberantly friendly way only Europeans and insurance salesmen can manage. He was sixty or so with black-rimmed glasses and an animated shock of snow white hair that would have made Einstein's barber salivate.

"*Grazie, professore.*" Tom had spent a year studying international business law in Milan as part of his law degree. He gestured toward me. "*Ciò è Signorina Persephone Pyle, mia amica.*"

Di Marvelo started pumping my hand. "*La specie della amica che un uomo desidera portare a Venezia, figlio,*" he said to Tom, smiling. Tom cleared his throat and found something arresting on his shoes.

I gave Tom's instep a sharp poke. I may not speak Italian, but I could understand innuendo when I heard it, however sweetly avuncular it might be.

"Yes, er, Persephone's in marketing. She works with me at Pilgrim Pharmaceuticals."

Used to work with him, I added silently.

"Welcome, welcome." The professor grinned happily. "Is not so often I get an email about a maritime history emergency. Sit, sit. You must sit and tell me about it."

He led us to chairs and took a seat behind his desk.

"We would like to determine the fate of a captain in the English navy," Tom explained, "retired, it would seem, around the year 1706."

"Name?"

Tom looked at me.

"Phillip Drummond," I supplied.

Di Marvelo wrinkled his nose. "Age in 1706?"

Tom was thirty-six. "Er, thirty-five or so. Maybe a tad more."

The professor's eyebrows rose. "That's early for retirement if he was a good captain. Good captains carried on until they became admirals or went down with the ship."

"He didn't exactly retire," I explained. "He went on hiatus."

Di Marvelo gave Tom a questioning look. "Hiatus? *Che cosa è questo?*"

"A break," Tom explained. "*Pausa.*"

"Yes," I went on, "he was put on half pay after a sort of, well, incident—"

"Dereliction of duty," Tom put in firmly. "Letting a French cutter escape."

I gave Tom a look. "There was no proof. And he was found not guilty, or whatever they find you in English naval courts in 1706. They brought his ship in for repairs and decommissioned it. He went out as a privateer."

The professor clapped his hands. "Oh, a pirate!"

Tom examined the tips of his nails, whistling. *Grrrr.*

"Can you tell me anything else?" Di Marvelo asked.

Yeah, he kissed like a Greek god, with a thunderbolt to match. "Well, he was arrested for stealing naval dispatches."

"Uh-oh. Very bad. *Che cosa cattivo.*"

"And his trial was probably in Gibraltar."

At this point a soft hum interrupted us. I looked down. It wasn't my shoes.

Tom reached into his pocket and flipped open his cell phone. "Hello . . . Yes, why?" A long pause ensued in which Tom's face took on varying degrees of perturbation. I could hear the relentless squawk on the other end. "Hold on," he said at last, and handed the phone to me. "It's your friend Dana, and a strongly worded suggestion for her to switch to decaf would not go amiss."

"Where have you *been*?!" Dana cried when I said hello. My cell phone must be with the rest of my belongings, wherever the other Seph put them.

"Is something wrong with my dad?" I gestured my apology to the professor, slipped into the hall and closed the door.

"He's fine. Now tell me what's up."

"Up?"

"C'mon, girl. You're with Tom and artfully not answering your phone. Have you scaled the heights of the—oh, dear, what's the Italian word for 'recycling bin'?"

"It's a long story," I said.

"Does it involve sex?"

"Almost."

"Almost isn't good enough for two days of not answering your phone. I need a threesome with you, Tom and Gary Dourdan." Dana's an African American with an open mind and a real thing for *CSI*.

"Well, it's kind of an amazing story."

"Honey, any story that involves you within ten feet of a penis would have to be amazing."

"You know I work within ten feet of penises every

day. This is management in corporate America, after all. There isn't much else."

"I'm talking about penises in the wild. Unleashed, unmuzzled, ready to—"

"I get it, I get it." I prayed for the souls of her first graders.

"I'm assuming Tom was the 'almost'?"

"The what?"

"You 'almost' had sex. Was Tom the lucky one-in-a-billion whose key fit the chastity belt? Kind of like pulling the sword from the stone—only in reverse."

"Funny. How'd you get his number anyway?"

"It wasn't easy. I had to tell his father I thought Tom might be the father of my unborn child."

"You did not!"

"No, but I did have to call in a favor from an old boyfriend at AT&T—who was quite relieved the baby wasn't his, by the way."

Tom poked his head through the door. "We've got something," he whispered.

"Dana, I've got to go."

"Omigod," she squealed. "I just realized it's like dawn there. Are you two in bed?!"

I handed the phone to Tom. "Here. Dana wants to say hello."

The professor had several old leather volumes spread across his desk. He was chewing the stem of his glasses. I sank into the chair. I couldn't read the words. They were all in Italian. Outside I could hear Tom saying, "Yes, but you're not *my* best friend, so technically I am under no requirement to reveal anything, certainly not a requirement called the 'Right of First Night Information,' which I strongly suspect has been fabricated specifically for this situation."

Di Marvelo looked at me. "I think we may have found a ship." He pointed to an entry in a long list. "*Neuf Ouest,* c. May 16, 1694, Cap. G. A. Drummond."

"*Neuf Ouest,*" I exclaimed. "That's his ship."

"You said his name was Phillip."

"His real name was George." I touched the listing, thinking of everything that had happened. Can a life lived three centuries ago really feel as close as yesterday. I breathed deeply but the sandalwood had disappeared. "What does *Neuf Ouest* mean?" I asked.

"Nine West. Dees is not quite a compass reading—"

Sure ain't.

"—but it seems meant to suggest one. Sometimes those ship owners made odd choices. The same group of investors also owned *The Lavender Field* and *The Maide Vale.*"

Now why did that sound familiar? "Who were the investors?"

Tom slipped into the other chair and gave me a look. I noticed he had powered off his phone. With his growth of beard, light trousers and pale blue shirt open at the neck, he looked like a young Marcello Mastroianni. Too bad there was no universe in which I could pass for a young Catherine Deneuve.

Di Marvelo had flipped to another section, a few pages earlier. He ran a finger halfway down the left column. "It says the ship was owned by 'Norfolk Investments et al.' For names I will have to research more."

"It doesn't matter. What about the trial?"

They both fell silent. Oh, I didn't like that.

"Phillip's Christian name is George," Di Marvelo said to Tom.

"Oh." Tom took my hand.

My eyes started to smart. Dammit, I was not going to lose it here.

"There were charges filed in Gibraltar on April 10, 1706," Di Marvelo said.

"The charge?"

"Treason. A number of motions were filed, delaying the trial for a couple of weeks. It was a well-known case in Gibraltar and written up in the local broadsheets at the time."

"Broadsheets?" I asked, brushing the corner of an eye.

Tom squeezed harder. "Essentially newspapers," he explained, "but pandering to the lowest common denominator. The eighteenth-century equivalent of Fox News."

"What was the outcome of the trial?" I asked.

Di Marvelo sighed and opened a volume. "From a broadsheet dated 24 April 1706: 'Captain George Drummond, age thirty-six, lately of Portsmouth and formerly of Her Majesty's Royal Navy, was hanged today after being found guilty of treason.'"

Chapter Ten

I am not a crier. When other little girls scraped their knees, they'd go running to their mothers, weeping and wailing. I didn't have a mother. When I scraped my knee, I gave the offending stretch of ground the finger and fired off a choice phrase I'd heard my father say the time he dropped a canned ham on his foot.

But there was no stretch of ground to flip off, and what was scraped was my sense of order, not my knee. Tom held my hand all the way back to the hotel, which only made the not crying worse. It took Zen-like control to keep the despair at bay until I could throw the deadbolt on my hotel room door, calling to an uncertain Tom in the hall that I'd be fine; I just needed to rest.

I flopped on the bed, noting as I glanced around that the stand-in Seph, the Seph who'd given a fantastic presentation while I cannonballed Drum's life, the Seph who'd made Tom an offer I didn't have the guts to make, had unpacked her bags and added little touches like flowers and a candle that already made the room more homey than my condo.

Sigh.

I lay on the bed, counting the crystals in the tiny chandelier that lit the room, feeling like the water show at the Bellagio on the inside, but dry as my grandmother's coffee cake on the outside. I don't know exactly what my feelings about Drum were. I'd known him—what—a half a day? In some ways it seemed like I'd known him far longer. I guess there was more Tom in him than I was willing to admit.

Drum said he was my character. He wasn't strictly a character, though. Those lips on the tiny stern balcony hadn't been paper, and those eyes hadn't been ink. Drum had been a living, breathing, exasperating man (do they come in any other flavor?). And now he was gone.

But remember, I told myself, he was gone just as surely yesterday, before you knew his fate, as he is now. Three hundred years is three hundred years, after all, and even if he'd died peacefully in his sleep at age one hundred and eight, you'd never have seen him again.

Leave it to me to finally be willing to consider giving it up to a man who couldn't have called me the next day even if he'd wanted to.

I dragged myself to my feet and went out on the hotel room's little balcony, one of a handful of similar balconies above me and to the left and right. The hotel stood on the last curved arm of a canal just before the Bridge of Sighs, one of the most famous sites in Venice.

It was called the Bridge of Sighs because it offered those convicted in Venetian courts their last glimpse of freedom before prison. The bridge was beautiful, peaked and windowed, and the morning sun bathed the water and quiet, gliding gondolas below in a crisp white glow.

A gull swooped close, squawking once, before rising in the breeze to trace a lonely figure eight against the blue. Then my eyes fell upon it, round and low in the morning sky. It was a trick of time and atmosphere, I knew, to be visible during the day, but there it was, nonetheless—a fat, contemplative, full moon.

Drum was dead, and it was my fault.

I started to cry. I hugged my sides to stop it, but it rose to a hard, gasping sort of noise that shook my whole body.

Tom appeared in his balcony doorway. I hadn't realized his door had been open. I tried to stop crying but it was pointless. Tom cleared both railings in a single smooth motion and pulled me into a tight embrace.

"That's all right, Seph. That's all right."

Chapter Eleven

"*I* have to fix this for him, Tom. I have to."

"C'mon, Seph." He patted my back. "It's not your fault. If Drummond took the dispatches, it was inevitable."

"He didn't take the dispatches," I wailed. "I know he didn't. You have to help me."

"I will, I will. Anything, Seph."

Just hearing that helped. I looked at his shirt. Tears make a big stain on linen. I took a deep breath and wiped my eyes.

"Let's get you some tissues," he said.

He led me to the bed and brought tissues and a glass of water. I blew my nose.

"Tom, what can we do?"

It was almost comic—asking a Harvard-trained attorney to figure out how to keep a guy who was hanged three hundred years ago from ending up that way. If I wasn't feeling so crappy, I might have smiled.

"Well . . ." He collapsed on the bed beside me. "I suppose it might be possible to reverse-engineer the time travel."

"How, though? It's got to involve the shoes. We've got to think."

"Right. Of course." His eyes met mine. "It's actually not as easy as you'd imagine with your lip quivering like that."

Oh.

"Perhaps if I just stop the quivering for a moment," he offered.

"Y-yes. That makes sense."

His lips skimmed mine, then returned, more demanding. Every part of my body gasped. I clutched his head hungrily. He slid a hand up my sweater.

Oh, dear! "Wait."

He moaned, "Not again."

"No, no, I'm not stopping. I, um . . . just let me freshen up a little." I made a vague gesture to my teeth, though what I really needed was about six hours of spa treatments. And I needed time to think.

I flipped the light in the bathroom and looked in the mirror. My eyes looked like two hunks of raw salmon. I started the cold water.

God, I was finally doing it. It felt triumphant and terrifying, and I knew I'd better not think too much or I'd reason myself out of it. Drum could wait. Whether he was dead or not, I needed to have sex. Knowing Drum, he'd understand. Besides, with

Tom's help, I knew we'd figure out the Drum problem somehow.

I've never been good on that transition from regular date conversation to hot monkey sex. Dana tells me to screw trying to read the signals, that there isn't a man in the world who won't happily get down to business with a woman who simply walks into her apartment, whips off her blouse and lays down on the couch. I don't know. Maybe Laurie Partridge or Grace Van Owen could pull that one off. I'm always sure I'm with the one guy who'll press charges.

I looked at myself in the mirror. Laurie Anderson, maybe; Laurie Partridge, definitely not.

I splashed some of the water on my face and looked again.

Whoa! Maybe the water's supposed to be hot.

I reapplied deodorant, brushed my teeth, and touched a drop of Arpège behind each ear, all the while holding a cold washcloth over my eyes to try to tamp down the swelling. As far as bedwear, I knew what was under the jeans. It wasn't the stuff of fairy tales, and as we know, Backup Seph had not favored bras. But unless I wanted to switch to just a towel or venture out into the room to fish through my lingerie drawer, where, believe me, the alternatives were no great shakes either, there really wasn't much choice.

I picked up the dreaded pink plastic case, a winking nod to pop culture. It's hard to believe that in fifty years they haven't come up with any better birth control for women who have sex once every Olympiad than a diaphragm.

A few complex yoga moves later, and everything was in order. I washed my hands, did that thing where you flip your hair over and up, hoping for Claudia Schiffer but willing to settle for anything better than Joan Rivers, and was just about to step out when I remembered condoms.

Dammit, does everything have to rest on the shoulders of the woman? Yes, I know diaphragms aren't enough. I have managed to read the paper once or twice in the last twenty years. But it's hard to be Laurie Partridge, Claudia Schiffer and my old health teacher all at the same time.

I figured I had three choices, and, as usual, none were attractive. I could step out of the bathroom, whip off my shirt, and hope Tom carried a condom in his wallet (eeuuww, gross!). I could step out of the bathroom, turn down the cover and say in my most in-control voice, "Tom, it seems a condom or two would be in order. Would you mind slipping down to the nearest drugstore and grabbing a couple?" Or I could step out of the bathroom, slap down the two I always carry in my travel bag, collapse in an embarrassed heap, and pray that the next time I opened my eyes everything would be taken care of.

I grabbed the foil strip and buried it in my palm. Then I squinched my eyes tight and opened the door.

Tom stood silhouetted on the balcony, his lanky form slouched against the doorframe. When he heard me, he turned. He eyed me tentatively, uncertain, I'm sure, as to whether Sheila the Wonder Weeper had cashed in her chips for the evening.

I gave him a crooked smile and did a little turn to show him not only that I cleaned up okay but also that the fragile sex juju was still in the air.

"Sexy," he said with honest-to-God feeling.

Only Tom could make me feel like a centerfold, dressed in jeans, a borrowed shirt and yesterday's underpants.

He pulled me toward him and laid a hand on each side of my face. Yum. A soap opera kiss. With a gentle tug, he lifted my mouth to his. My shoes started to purr and so did something higher. When his tongue flicked mine, my flesh galvanized for action. Without breaking stride, he unsnapped my jeans, slid them slowly over my hips, and let them drop.

"Even sexier," he said, cupping my ass.

Since 'sexy' and my ass have never even occupied the same zip code, I let that wash over me a good long time.

With an outstretched arm, he guided me out of the puddle of black denim. I knew my long legs were my best feature, and columned over taffeta pumps they had to look spectacular. I watched his eyes widen.

He drew me against his chest, hugging me from behind, and kissed my neck. "Your smell is making me weak."

"It's Arpège."

"It's not just Arpège."

He palmed my belly, and I wanted to moan. The caressing was hypnotic, and the faint foresty smell coming off his skin was making me rethink my lifelong opposition to Pine-Sol. The tips of his fingers slipped just under the elastic of my panties.

Wonk, wonk, wonk, wonk.

I sucked in my breath, and not just in an effort to flatten my stomach. Whatever he was brushing down there was feeling mighty close to paradise. And I could tell he liked it, too, since the barometer shoved up against my back was giving me a pretty solid read.

I stepped away and teased Tom's shirt slowly over my head. I was just about to fling it away when my hair caught on a sleeve button.

"Ow, ow, ow, ow!"

I freed one arm and flopped over to try to ease the hair loose, but it just tangled harder.

Tom said, "Let me," and took the offending sleeve. I yanked the rest of the shirt over my breasts as he examined the mess.

"Stop jiggling," he implored. "You're making it worse."

"Should we just cut it off?"

"I wasn't talking about your hair."

He labored intently, and the effort with which his long, capable fingers worked the knot was stirring up a tropical depression on the southern part of my weather radar.

"There," he said after a moment. He brushed the strands of hair back, letting the sleeve fall free, and looked at me.

I stood in my shoes, panties and oxford cloth camouflage, and looked back nervously.

Tom wrapped his arms around mine, camouflage and all, and kissed me. "Are you going to make me sorry I lent you that shirt?" He edged me toward the bed.

"Probably."

He lifted me off my feet and placed me on the mattress. "I don't think so."

With a knee on the bed, he pulled his shirttails free of his trousers, unbuttoned his cuffs and pulled the whole thing over his head. His chest was lean and tough, and it carried a narrow diamond of chestnut hair right in the center.

"Maybe we should save this for when we get home," I offered. "You know, after a lovely dinner in the Golden Triangle."

"Looks more like copper from where I'm sitting." He leaned down to kiss the inside of my knee. "The heels stay, right?"

I nodded. "Actually they don't seem to come off at all."

"Good," he said. "Let's see what we can do to keep them aimed at the ceiling for the next half hour."

He unbuckled his belt.

A matched set of fuses burned their way down my inner thighs. Then he stripped off his pants and boxers. Oh, my God! He had an erection the size of Montana! My experience to date has been entirely mid-Atlantic: a Maryland, a Delaware, the occasional New Jersey. This Mountain Time Zone stuff was way beyond my comfort zone. I grabbed the headboard and shimmied away. It is not easy to shimmy in high-heeled shoes.

"Ah, ah, ah," he chided, catching my ankles. "I

thought we just talked about that." With a small jerk, I was beside him again. He pried open my hand, tore off one of the condoms and ripped it open. "It's about time we finished the tattoo check, don't you think? Panties first—or shirt?" He finished applying the condom with an electrifying snap. I thought of my favorite dipped cone at Dairy Queen.

"Panties," I said. Actually what I said was "Grfrrprl," but Tom seemed to understand. He hooked my panties with two practiced thumbs and removed them.

"Very, *very* sexy," he said.

The tropical depression had grown into a full-fledged tropical storm, and the storm surge was fast approaching.

He unfurled himself on the bed and drew himself over me. Oh, boy. There was only one direction I was going to move now, and that was toward the headboard, one hammering thump at a time. I wiped my palms on the shirt still bunched between us.

"I've wanted this for a long time, Seph."

He kissed me—a soft, deep kiss that made my fingers curl into his hair, my toes curl in my shoes and my shoes curl around his back. I felt a shudder, like a bump in the road, but not the kind you're thinking. For an instant the stubbled cheeks transformed into the fuller beard of Drum. I was so shocked I nearly bit Tom's tongue.

"*Ouk,*" he mumbled.

Another bump, and his face turned shimmery at the edges, all blues, purples and pinks.

He rolled off to the side and gazed at me. "Seph?"

A series of bumps overtook me, like turbulence in a prop plane, and the transformations continued: Tom as an Andy Warhol print: green and purple, turquoise and blue, black and white.

He cocked his head. In a roar only I could hear, the prop thudded hard, took a barreling nosedive, and I was gone.

Chapter Twelve

Instinct kicked in like a jolt from heart paddles. I curled into a ball as the world turned yellow then orange then red. The ride was bad, but I knew the end could be a helluva lot worse.

Thunk.

Bare ass on bare wood. Yowee! My head followed the momentum of the fall, but was spared being smashed like a ripe watermelon by a wall of sea-smelling wool and cotton, which cushioned the contact, then dropped down consecutively on top of me like the hands in Hands Down. I was in darkness dappled by an odd pattern of light.

"What was that?"

Haverhill's voice. I froze.

"Hell, the shelf in that thing's been threatening to fall ever since I had it repaired on Man," Drum replied, and my heart soared. He was alive—for now, at least. That meant I had a chance to save him.

"Cheap Irish nails," Drum explained to Haverhill. "I'll take care of it. Will that be all?"

"Er, aye."

"Then I shall let you get back to your duty. Thank you for your kind words."

I didn't dare move—not with cheap Irish nails and no pants.

Haverhill excused himself. I heard the click of the latch, followed by Drum's hesitant footsteps toward me. I must be in his wardrobe.

"Don't open the door," I warned.

"Persephone?"

"Oh, God, it's good to hear your voice." I felt my throat tighten with joy.

The wardrobe door panels were tight latticework bamboo. I could see him kneel and try to peer inside.

"And don't look either," I added. "What day is it?"

He averted his gaze. "Friday, madam."

"I mean, what day in relation to the last day I was here, whenever that was?"

"The day after. You disappeared yesterday."

Oh, thank God! We still had time.

"Is there a reason we can't open the wardrobe?" he asked. "Have you turned into a sea serpent?"

"I have nothing on but my shoes."

The corner of his mouth curled. "It is exceedingly temperate within my cabin. I myself do not require even a coat."

"You're a real comedian. Why didn't you tell me you were being charged with treason?"

The playfulness vanished. He said, "I didn't know if I'd ever see you again. It's not how I wanted to be remembered."

"Sweet. Except you didn't know I was leaving."

A slight tremor passed over his features.

"You bastard!" I cried. "You knew I was leaving!"

He held up his hands, smile in place. "Of course I knew you were leaving. We kissed, remember? The magical kiss to help the shoes along?"

"We kissed and nothing happened. And wipe that smirk off your face. What I meant was, nothing happened that made me leave terra firma."

"No," he muttered, standing. "That was still a good quarter hour away."

"Ooh, Mr. Big Talk." Of course, I had just seen his twenty-first century counterpart. All things being equal—and the evidence so far suggested they were twins in all but the most superficial grooming habits—Drum had the goods to back up a lot of talk, big or otherwise.

With regret, I thought of Tom and that last, wonderful kiss. Twice now in the last two days I'd managed to snatch chastity from the jaws of my ruin. Or was it chasing ruin from the jaws of my—

"Do you intend to venture out at some point," Drum asked, "or shall I ask cook to matchstick tonight's supper for delivery through the latticework?"

"Where's the dress?"

"A sodden wreck, I'm afraid."

"Rather a shame for Miss Toulon, eh?"

"I'd pass along your concern, but the possibility of ever seeing the lady in question again strikes me as remote at best."

I opened my mouth to let another jibe fly, but glimpsed the cool reserve that had descended over his face. And you know what? He was right to be pissed. Why was I being so childish about something that was none of my business? Even if I'd slept with him, which I hadn't, it wasn't like we were engaged or anything, God forbid.

Resolution to self: no more cracks about the sluts Drum chooses to screw.

I shoved the coats and blankets out of the way and found Tom's shirt in my hands, balled but serviceable—which was a damned sight more than could be said of me.

"Drum, dig me up a pair of trousers, will you?"

I heard the sound of a chest opening and the contents being rifled.

"There," he said. A soft thud sounded outside the wardrobe. "They're right next to you. Open the door and you'll see them."

"You're going to have to step outside first."

"I hope the balcony will do. Basehart takes a dim view of things otherwise."

"Is he back on board?" I slid a hesitant leg out and snagged the garment with my toes.

"He is," Drum answered. "And sent a note asking for you. I told him you were *enceinte*."

I worked the shirt over my head and the pants over

my shoes and hips. The double-barreled mix of sandalwood and pine was making me woozy. "*Enceinte?* What does that mean? Under the weather?"

Drum considered. "That's a fair translation."

Heaving myself free of cheap Irish nails, I stepped out of the wardrobe and buttoned myself into decency. The trousers were Drum's loose-fitting work trousers. I cuffed them to my ankle to keep from tripping over the ends.

As I closed the wardrobe, I caught a glimpse of Drum staring out to sea. The lines on his forehead had tightened in the last day, and for an instant before he buried it under wry detachment, I saw the raw relief that came over his face as he laid eyes on me.

For myself, I felt such a stab of joy at seeing him whole again I nearly cried out. In three steps I was in his arms. His chest felt like hardened steel under my palms.

"I did a little research," I said when we finally let go. "About Gibraltar."

"I assumed you would." His eyes turned toward the water, and he said lightly. "Guilty?"

"Yes."

He seemed to sway a little. He didn't ask about the sentence. He wouldn't need to.

"And the battle?" he said.

"What battle?"

"With the French. I'm sure you looked into that too."

"No. I didn't even think about it."

"Didn't think about it?" He dropped his arms and

stared at me, incredulous. "The battle that could very well determine the outcome of the war?"

"No," I said, feeling mildly incensed. "I found out what happened to you, and that pretty much killed my curiosity."

"But that's the reason I sent you back!"

"I *knew* it! I knew you wanted me to go back! What do you think I am, some cross-century paddle ball?"

"Of course I wanted you to go back," he howled. "You were our only hope for straightening out this god-forsaken mess—the mess, I might add, you created!" He put his fingers on his temples. "This is beyond belief. What about that sweetheart of yours? The one with the historical bent?"

I narrowed my eyes. "What about him?" I asked slowly.

"Surely you thought to mention the battle to him. What did he have to say?"

"Nothing," I said, lying promptly. It was my standard defense against infuriating cross-examination. "He had nothing to say. I didn't see him. I was too busy running around, trying to get to the bottom of what happened to you."

"Oh." He cleared his throat self-consciously. "I guess that's understandable. Bit of a shock, I suppose."

"It was. I was devastated."

He tapped his lip. "What was young Tom's name again?"

"Fraser. Why?"

"Middle name, what? James? John?"

"James. But how did you—" Shit! The monogram.

Hot red embarrassment shot up my neck and face like a thermometer in a Bugs Bunny cartoon. I put my hands up to keep the mercury from blowing out my ears.

"Clearly," he said, "your devastation was immense."

The mercury turned to fire. "You know what? Fuck you."

"My, what elegant imagery you Americans employ." He wandered toward the wardrobe. "Tell me, how long before America sets the literary world on its ear? A millennium or so?"

"American writers dominate in my time."

"And what did you tell me your course of study at university was?" He crouched to snag something off the floor.

"Look, is this helping? What's that— Oh, Christ!" Drum was pondering a small foil square in his hand marked "Trojan." My heart skipped. It was the other half of the strip of condoms I'd been clutching when I disappeared! I snatched it away.

Drum unfolded himself. "Yours, I take it."

"Yes. It's . . . a napkin ring."

He frowned. "You carry your own napkin ring?"

"Yes."

"From Troy?"

"*Yes.* Look, what's up with this stuff anyway? Last time I came I didn't come with anything."

Drum pursed his lips. "Were you about to eat? I imagine whatever is in your hands comes with you. Was anything in your hands the first time you traveled? Apart from a wet chemise I recall with great clarity, you held nothing in your hands."

I thought of that day in the shoe store. My purse, laptop and suitcase were beside me on the floor. "Nothing."

"The theory holds." He gave me a pointed look. "Seph, you must go back."

"Jesus Christ, Drum. I've come to save you."

"I can take care of myself. What I can't do is help the navy. You need to find out about that battle."

"Drum . . ."

"Where does our shirtless friend Tom think you are right now?"

I froze, waiting for some further allusion to reveal Drum had been inside my head on that bed in Venice. None came—sort of a theme for the day.

"Tom knows where I am," I said. "I told him about you."

This surprised Drum. I was glad to see some of the wind drop from his overconfident sails.

He examined his cuff. "Was he, er, upset?"

"Upset? No. Surprised, certainly."

A knock clattered at the door. "Admiral Basehart is here to see you, sir." It was Gar's voice.

Drum whispered, "Kiss me."

"No."

"Think of Tom."

"Kiss you and think of Tom? That's a little weird."

"Sir," the sailor whispered loudly, "please may I open the door? Admiral Basehart wishes to see you, and he's on his way down."

"*One moment!*" Drum called, and then said to me, "I pride myself on believing it would be impossible for you to think of Tom when kissing me, so let's settle on you kissing me and thinking of the battle."

"Goddammit, Drummond!" Basehart shouted. "Declining my summons? Bloody flux, my arse. Open this goddamned door before I shove my bloody boot up so far up your bloody arse, you really *will* have the bloody flux."

"Omigod!" I whispered. "Is this the first time he's seen you since you punched him?"

"It is, but let's not let some juvenile desire to witness an unpleasant scene—"

"Will there be more punching?"

"—between a man and his former commander keep you from doing what I know you know is right. We need to find out about the battle."

"*Drummond!*"

"One moment, please!" Then to me: "Persephone, you must do this. Things are already starting to change. Look outside."

I gazed out the open porthole. "What of it? It's beautiful."

"Exactly. No monsoon. This is the first sunny morning we've had in weeks."

I swallowed. He was right. No more misplaced hurricane. It seemed like I should crack a joke, but suddenly it didn't seem very funny.

"We've begun the inexorable march to the end of the story," he said. "No matter what happens to me, I don't want this to be a defeat for England. Please." He took my hand. Basehart's first kick shook the door.

"Oh, Christ, all right," I said.

He moved the lantern hanging near the door to the table and pulled me up against the wall.

"Oh, and, ah, unless you want Basehart to get really mad," I said, "I suggest you unlatch the door. Walls hold out a lot longer than bulkheads."

Drum bent me, kissed me hard, and in a roar even louder than Basehart's I disappeared.

Chapter Thirteen

Ever have a rock tumbler as a kid? This trip through time spun me in loud, violent circles, rounding even more edges off my already bruised ass. It struck me for the first time I didn't exactly know how to aim for a landing, but then I remembered the present had a cool bluey-purple feel to it while Drum's time was definitely hot red-orange.

I managed to right myself as the world changed to the color of a clear afternoon sky, then pointed my toes down and let them drag over the gravelly wind tunnel of time. Sure enough, the world made some alarming lurches, stirring up a nauseating ball in the pit of my stomach, and, like an obedient retriever, dropped me at once. I landed hard on something firm and padded.

Buy a lottery ticket, I thought. I'd landed in a chair.

I ran through the standard checklist.

Clothes? Yes.

Reasonable clothes? I peeked. Well, only if you consider a plum satin camisole with no bra reasonable. At least I had on a reasonable skirt and—

Oh, God! No underwear. I slammed my knees together.

This other Seph was a real high flyer.

Which left me with the all-important question of place.

Gazing down, I opened my eyes slowly. Okay, I was someplace well lit, with a carpet. That meant I was inside. And in the year . . . ? Well, sometime after they discovered electricity. Whoa. Stand back, Sherlock Holmes.

No, no, I actually knew where I was! I was in the lobby of the hotel in Venice. I recognized the green and gold carpeting. I lifted my eyes—and looked right into the concerned stare of a stout middle-aged man in black socks, hiking shorts and a Peyton Manning jersey. I'm pretty sure it wasn't Peyton Manning. I remember him being taller.

"Hey." I gave the guy a nonchalant wave and accidentally flung my favorite napkin ring in front of his feet. Peyton pretended not to notice.

"Are you okay?" he asked.

"Yeah. Why?"

"I dunno. You were just sitting there, then all of a sudden you made a sorta . . . *whoop.*"

"A *whoop?*"

"Yep. Then you grabbed the arms of the chair, closed your eyes and started breathing funny. It reminded me of my wife, right before her water broke."

"Yeah . . . um, just a bit of indigestion for me. Bad scallops."

"You had scallops for breakfast?"

Breakfast? Cripes, it was getting hard to keep a schedule straight with all this back-and-forth. "Oh, sure. Scallops and gravy on toast. Mmmm."

"Yeah . . ." He took a step backward. "Well, as long as you're all right . . ."

"Completely, thank you. Say, ah, what day is it?"

He gazed at me with increasing worry. "Friday."

"Friday, right. Just after breakfast." Shit. It was a day after I'd left Tom. I smiled at Peyton like we had just shared one of life's truisms.

"Lady, do you need me to call someone for you?"

"Um, can I just borrow your cell phone for a minute?"

He shrugged and handed me a tiny Nokia. Have you ever noticed the larger the man, the smaller the phone? "Thanks," I said. "I'll just be a minute."

"Take your time. My wife's checking out the glass shops across the street. I've probably got all morning."

I flipped it open and dialed Tom's number. On the fourth ring he answered.

"Hello?" I could hear people in the background.

"You in a meeting?"

"I was running a meeting."

"Oops."

"That's all right. It was time for a break anyway. How's sightseeing?"

It dawned on me that Tom didn't realize I'd been gone. And then I remembered why. The other Seph.

It was kind of interesting when you thought about it. With a living, breathing body double that appeared whenever I left, I could zip around time doing whatever needed to be done and leave all my problems in the hands of—

Holy crap! I hadn't left her hands full of problems! When I winked out, I'd left her hands full of . . . Tom! I suddenly felt like I *had* eaten scallops and gravy for breakfast.

"Yeah, um, I'm feeling a little funny about what happened with us," I choked out.

Peyton Manning's eyes widened. He took a step back and buried his nose in a guidebook.

Oh, God, please let them have stopped. Let my hair have caught on fire or a plague of locusts have descended on the hotel or Tom have remembered he'd promised to remain a virgin until marriage. Something—anything—so that my first sex in three years hadn't happened without me.

"Feeling funny?" Tom said. "About what in particular?"

Oh, dear. He definitely had that satisfied I'm-the-big-man sound to his voice. "Er . . ."

"Not the silk wrist ties, I hope."

I leaped to my feet.

"Maybe it was the unusual tableaux on the balcony?"

Lord, take me now. My body went to Heaven and all I got was a lousy T-shirt. I thought of that long and oh-so-expansive effort Tom had been embarking on and how I'd squandered my time in an English wardrobe held together with cheap Irish nails. *Aargh.*

"Did you just make a noise?"

Yes, just swallowing my tongue. "No, just reliving it all in my head."

"Really?"

"Really."

He chuckled. "Nothing happened after you left, Seph. I excused myself and went back to my room."

Rat bastard. "How did you know it wasn't me—the real me, I mean?"

Poor Peyton had given up all pretense of disinterest.

"You really want to know?" Tom asked.

"Yes."

"You have a certain—er, how shall I put this?— charming gracelessness in bed. Your twin, however, is a different story. She's very . . . confident. Scarily confident. Like Pamela Anderson on testosterone. I was pretty sure only one of us could come out on top, and I didn't think I was man enough to be the one. God, I'm relieved to get your call. It's been almost a day. I was getting pretty worried. Where did you go?"

"Back to the ship."

"Anything new?" he asked cautiously.

"Yes, Drummond's alive," I said before remembering Peyton. "Of course, it was before he was scheduled to be . . . well, you know. But I was so relieved. It was like just seeing him convinced me there's something we've got to be able to do to fix things. He's still under house arrest, or ship arrest, or whatever they call it. I need to find out more about the battle."

"Battle?"

"With the French." Peyton's guidebook dropped lifelessly to his side. "Where the English fleet is supposed to go. The place the missing dispatches supposedly mention. If there's a chance the fleet not being there changes . . . *things*—"

"Things?"

I lowered my voice. "The uture-fay."

"Ah, the uture-fay."

"Then Drummond needs to know. This is really important. The future of the British empire may depend on it."

Peyton's mouth fell open.

Tom said, "All hail Britannia, then."

"So what battles happened in 1706?"

"Blenheim?"

I covered the phone and turned around. Peyton, not Tom, had offered this suggestion.

"My wife and I were in England last year," Peyton went on eagerly. "We visited the Duke of Marlborough's house near Oxford. Huge old place called Blenheim Palace. It was named after a big battle at the start of the 1700s."

Hey, anything's possible. I put the phone back to my ear. "Blenheim?" I said to Tom.

"Too early. Blenheim was 1704, not to mention on land."

"1704," I whispered to Peyton. "Too early." His face fell.

"That's the trouble," Tom went on. "All the battles I know around that time—Blenheim, Ramillies, Oudenaarde—were Marlborough's and, by necessity, on land since he ran the army. The British navy, industrious as

it may have been, had not reached its zenith as a fighting power. They were still lagging behind the French in
tonnage and experience."

"They captured Gibraltar," I put in defensively.

"Oh, don't get me wrong. There were a few victories
here and there, including a lovely win at La Hogue a de-
cade earlier. And they definitely helped saved the allies'
bacon in the peninsular campaign."

"Peninsular?"

"Spain and Portugal."

"Drummond mentioned Portugal! He said the
French were haranguing the British navy there."

"Could be it."

"But you don't know the battle?"

"I was a history major, Seph, not the military studies
equivalent of a Trekkie. A few details escaped me."

"Tom, what would have happened if France had won
back then? I mean, they didn't win, did they?"

"No, it ended in a sort of draw, which in itself was a
big surprise. You have to understand, France was like
the USSR and the United States rolled into one at the
time, and England was like . . . well, England today—
semi-important but kind of small. Your captain, along
with his countrymen, lived in constant fear of a France
grown so strong she'd swallow England whole. The battles in 1706 were part of a broader war over who would
take over the throne of Spain when the heirless king
there died. England's hoped-for heir for Spain was the
son of the emperor of the Holy Roman Empire—"

"Rome still had an empire in 1706?"

"No, it was just a name they used. The Empire covered pretty much everything north of Italy and south of Holland, minus France, of course."

"Got it."

"But Louis the Fourteenth, the king of France, wanted his grandson to have Spain's throne, which would have put Spain neatly into France's pocket when the grandson eventually inherited Louis's throne as well. Through a series of incredibly Byzantine events which I will not bother even trying to explain, the grandson did end up getting the Spanish throne. But to end the war with Marlborough, a war France seemed surprisingly incapable of winning, Louis had to sign a treaty that removed the grandson from the line of succession to the French throne. England's ability to keep France from victory and therefore to negotiate that settlement was the start of her ascendancy to a position of world power equal to France's in the nineteenth century."

"Wow. Kinda like when Britney Spears started wearing Madonna T-shirts. And if France had won?"

"Well, clearly France wouldn't have signed the treaty. The grandson would have inherited both thrones, France would have become an even greater power, and England's fortunes would have fallen. After that is anyone's guess. But remember, France only became America's ally seventy years later in the War of Independence because England was such a threat. If England hadn't matured into the world power it became after this war . . . well, let's just say I doubt France would have been as generous as she was to America's forefathers. In fact, with the French history of imperialistic appetite, I suspect they would have tried to take control of the colonies themselves. After all, they'd nearly succeeded in that very venture a few years before the American Revolution as you, being a native Pittsburgher, are undoubtedly aware."

"I am?"

"For heaven's sake, Seph, were there requirements at the University of Chicago apart from literature courses? Google the French and Indian War next time you're on a conference call. Man cannot live by Thomas Hardy alone."

"No, one requires Austen, Sayers, Gabaldon and Evanovich as well."

"Well, suffice to say, one could easily hypothesize that had Marlborough not held back the French in the War of Spanish Succession, we might all be saying *bonjour* to rich sauces, hairy underarms and cranky waiters."

"I've always hated Jerry Lewis."

"Hey, at least it would shut Quebec up."

"I'm going back to Di Marvelo. That battle might be important."

"Seph"—the lightness had left Tom's voice—"I'm really concerned about you leaving."

Well, there it was, just dropped out there like a semen-stained dress on the desk of a *Washington Post* reporter. "I, er—"

"We don't know what takes you or what brings you back," he added. "We don't know how dangerous the travel is—and frankly 1706 on its own is no bed of roses. We don't know why it's happening. But most of all, I'm not prepared for the possibility that this flip-flopping will end unexpectedly with you on the wrong end of things."

I dry swallowed. Everything Tom had said had gone through my own mind in various bits and pieces, but I hadn't faced it all laid out in one lawyerly summation, especially with the weighty added argument that Tom's feelings were at risk.

"A man's life is at stake," I said at last. Tom would do exactly the same thing if he were me, and we both knew it.

He gave a long sigh. "Be careful."

"I will."

"Oh, and Seph?"

"Yes?"

"Try to be back by bedtime."

I smiled, snapped the phone shut and handed it to Peyton. "Thanks."

"Hey," he said, catching my sleeve, "my wife and I spent five hours in a train station in Paris last week trying to get someone to help us find a train to Nice after ours was canceled. We ended up in Copenhagen. Kick their freakin' asses."

Yo, Peyton.

Chapter Fourteen

Charming gracelessness.

Okay, it probably wasn't the way Richard Burton described Elizabeth Taylor or even the way Ben Affleck described Jennifer Garner—okay, maybe it was the way Jennifer Garner described Ben Affleck—but heck, every time I thought about it, I grinned.

I was on my way to the Correr again to see Di Marvelo. I had convinced the hotel manager to let me into my room, where I added a chocolate-colored bra, matching lace tap pants and a cream blazer to the scant camisole and skirt. Unlike yours truly, whose underclothes could best be described as "journeyman-like," Backup Seph had half a dozen sets of matching bras and panties in varying combinations of fabric weight (thin, thinner and see-through), decorative appointments (pearls, bows and lace) and coverage (demi, plunging and meet-my-aureoles). What's worse, the bra straps all looked like they were made of sugar piping. Were her breasts filled with helium? All my bra straps needed the strength of ten Grinches plus two.

I picked the least provocative and most reinforcing choices available, and now hurried across the piazza, safe from unchecked sensuality, not to mention a sharp gust of wind. Slipping through a throng of Japanese tourists, I skipped the elevator, ascended the Correr's grand staircase, and was directed around the corner by a museum staffer. I found Di Marvelo hunched over a file cabinet in the hallway outside an open door.

"Are you feeling better today, *signorina*?" He gave me a fatherly hug.

"A little. Thank you for agreeing to see me again."

"Two emergencies in two days. Sometimes the past has a powerful pull on us, no?"

"I came to talk to you about a battle."

"A battle?"

He directed me through the door. Before me stood an awe-inspiring hodgepodge of items. Against the wall leaned dozens of paintings draped in cloth, some as tall and wide as a garage door. Three poleaxes stood at rakish angles next to an umbrella stand filled with jewel-handled swords. A soup tureen shaped like a narwhal resting on four ceramic waves sat on a bookcase that also held an impressive array of silver plates and chalices, a stuffed penguin missing a wing, several peacock feathers, two leather chests, a ship's wheel, three small anchors, a jar full of rusted nails and twenty or so red leather volumes, each with a square manila tag attached to it.

Behind that bookcase stood a half dozen more, full of similar wonders. At the front of the room a gooseneck lamp lit a little drafting table. The table's surface was covered with several brass compasses and a handful of other oddities.

"Hell of a Lost and Found Department here, *professore*. I'd hate to see the tourist who lost this." I held up what looked like a foot-long bread knife and pretended to pick my teeth with it.

"That was used for amputations."

Gak! I placed it back on the table.

"Actually," he went on, "most of this is storage, but it's also where we do a little restoration work. Some of these items are in need of repair."

He picked up a small statue of a naked Greek archer missing not only the length of his arrow but the length of something more important as well. Nock, nock. Who's there? Not my willy.

"Almost everything here came from ships," he said, smiling.

I tilted a canvas forward. "Paintings? On a ship? C'mon, *professore*, everyone knows you'd need a wall to hang one of those, and ships only have bulkheads."

"Not from on a ship. From in one. This is pirate treasure, privateer prizes, naval captures—whatever you want to call it."

"Wow."

"Historian was my second choice—after pirate."

His green eyes glittered. "What battle can I help you with?"

"I don't know."

"That will make the assignment more challenging."

"I know the year and month."

He met my eye. "1706?"

"Yes. April."

"English navy? Captain Drummond?"

I nodded. He sank into the chair at the drafting table, absently fingering the largest compass. "There was nothing in the Med. . . . The North Sea was quiet except for the usual harassment of French trade and blockades."

"What about the peninsula?" I slipped into the chair to his right. I'd never get used to thinking of Spain as a peninsula. Florida was a peninsula. Baja California was a peninsula. Spain was like a junior version of South America. It made no more sense than calling Australia an island.

"Ah, yes. Spain," Di Marvelo mused. "In the spring of '06, the English army held Barcelona."

"Barcelona's no good. If it's the army, it must be on land."

"Ah, but it's also on the sea."

I lifted my brows. Perhaps we were on to something.

"They were in over their heads, though," Di Marvelo continued, "and were about to abandon the city when the English navy sailed in to save the day. Their admiral got word while refitting in Portugal, an admiral by the name of—"

"Basehart!"

"Who? No. Leake, it was. I've heard of Basehart, though. There was a mention of his daughter and a silk merchant of the time—"

"That's got to be it, though—I mean about Leake. That's got to be it."

"What?" Di Marvelo gave me a curious look.

I shifted. "The battle I was trying to think of."

The gears were turning. I could see it on his face.

"You have an uncommon interest in the early eighteenth century, *signorina*. First the captain, now the battle."

"I'm researching a book."

He nodded, unconvinced. "Your young man seems quite concerned about you."

"Oh, he's not my young man. I mean, he's a great guy and I really like him and all, but, you know, he and I, well, we're not, um . . ."

"May I tell you a story?"

I bit my lip and dipped my chin.

"When I was your age I was at the top of my field. My specialty was the Spanish Armada. I lived and breathed the ships, the guns, the men. Oh, God, I loved the details." He turned the compass slowly, aligning the delicate, wavering needle with the ornate *N* inscribed on its dial. "There was a young woman, but I was so involved in my history and my books, I didn't pay attention to what was happening right before my eyes. She married someone else. It took a lifetime—thirty-three years—before the mistake was set to right."

I lifted a brow.

He held up a hand on which shone a thin gold ring. "We finally married two years ago, a year after her husband died." He stood and brushed the dust from his hands. "The past deserves our respect and attention, but what happens there can never take the place of what we make of today. You have to let go of things you can't change. Take care to keep your priorities in order."

He led me down to the end of the administrative wing and held the door for me.

"Thank you for your help, *professore*."

"If I can be of further assistance," he said with a kind, nostalgic smile, "I presume you'll let me know."

I kissed his cheek. "You're wrong about the past, you know. You didn't let go of it. If you had, you'd never be wearing this." I tapped the gold band, gave his hand an affectionate squeeze and hurried toward the grand staircase.

Chapter Fifteen

I hadn't gotten lost in the past, I told myself as I hurried back through the piazza. It was more like I'd gotten my heel caught in a crack—a big, tar-filled 1706 crack. It wasn't like I *wanted* to go back. It wasn't like I *wanted* this kind of excitement in my life. Let's not forget, I had an exciting, high-powered life right here—

"Seph, you missed the IT open house! They had free mouse pads!"

That unmistakable bray belonged to Rita Ellenbogen, the brand manager on Gutter's Chewable Antacid (Poor Beethoven; I'm sure he never imagined the thematic climax of his Fifth Symphony going down in history as "Gas, gas, gas, gone"). Free gifts were as much a part of corporate life as skyrocketing health premiums, oddly enthusiastic HR initiatives ("Cleanup Day!" and "Risk-Free Health Assessments!") and sinister maintenance men. Rita lived for the corporate swag.

When I turned around, I could see she was wearing a red Pilgrim Pharmaceuticals T-shirt, carrying a Team Pilgrim tote bag and waving a "Don't be a Turkey, Catch the Pilgrim Spirit" baseball hat.

"Let me guess," I said. "You work for Pilgrim Pharmaceuticals?"

"Seph, where have you been? Not only did you miss the open house, but Hanlon's been looking all over for you."

"Yeah, I had an upset stomach last night."

"I suppose you heard"—she spoke in a conspiratorial whisper that brought the souvenir vendor fifteen feet away into our confidence—"Tom Fraser's leaving for a job in Paris. Apparently a woman who runs some venture capital firm thinks very highly of him. Enough to offer him half the company—"

"What?!"

"Oh, yeah. Wants his 'brain power' on all sorts of big-time deals. Paris and a partnership. Hard to beat that. Are you going to lunch? It's a seafood buffet."

I'm thinking Pilgrim Pharmaceutical lobster bibs. "No, my stomach's still a little sensitive. In fact, I was just on my way to find a drugstore."

"But we'll certainly see you tonight at the awards dinner?"

I patted my belly. "Depends on the tum-tum."

She pointed a knowing finger at me. "Gas, gas, gas, gone!"

I gave her an energetic thumbs-up. There's nothing scarier than a brand manager who recites her own tagline.

As I sped back to the hotel, I made up the tagline to my own sad little commercial: "Seph Pyle . . . sure ain't Paris and a partnership."

It quickly became clear that having critical information and having a way to deliver critical information to the intended recipient are two very different things. I had no idea how to initiate time travel on my own. Of the two times I'd gone back, once I'd been admiring shoes, and the second time, on the bed in my hotel room, I'd been admiring Tom.

I stared at my shoes. Mrs. Kenney certainly believed they packed a wallop, but was it enough to power trans-century travel? And would I be brave enough to find out? So far, neither walking, nor a shower, nor even sex—well, at least not a vigorous round of preliminaries—had been enough to launch me into anything more than a painful case of blue ovaries.

"Whattdya say, fellows?" I asked. "Promise not to blow me up?"

They were uncharacteristically quiet.

What the hell. I tapped the toes together.

No explosions, no time travel, not even a satisfying Gregory Hines–type tap shoe clack.

I tapped the heels together. Nothing.

I stood, tapped my heels and turned in a circle, saying, "There's no place like home, there's no place like home." Apart from making me feel like an idiot, it had no apparent effect.

I collapsed on the bed. What was the use of knowing about Leake and Barcelona if I couldn't get word to Drum? Fantastical or not, I didn't want him to die. I wanted him to beat the rap, live, help save Barcelona, regain his commission, discover the woman in Toulon was harboring a virulent form of venereal disease, then stand on that balcony again, filling me with wine and unbuckling his belt.

The shoes *zinga-zinga'd*.

Fair-weather friends.

I decided to surf the Net while I waited to be called back, but my laptop was gone, so I scrambled over the balcony railings—not as gracefully in my skirt and shoes as Tom, but hey, let's not forget whose middle name was James and whose was "charming graceless-ness"—then slipped inside the French doors that led to his room.

Bingo. Tom's laptop was sitting on his desk.

I should have jumped right into surfing, but the place exuded Tom the way Borkum Riff pipe tobacco exuded my father. The room was neat, but not too neat. A hand-ful of legal files sat in a heap next to the laptop. A paper-back copy of Patrick O'Brian's *Master and Commander* lay open on the bedside table, which made me smile. It had been my father's suggestion for a birthday present for Tom. Tom's Burberry hung in the open closet.

I sat on the bed and took a deep breath. Tom used forest-scented shampoo. I know because I smelled it every time I sat next to him in a meeting. Even now the barely detectable scent made me think of him. I always imagined it to be the way a North Dakota tree claim smells in December.

Across from me sat a low, wide chest of drawers. I'd

had no scruples about poking through Drum's stuff, but I knew I would not do the same here. Maybe it was because Tom seemed to have more boundaries. Maybe it was because Tom was a degree more formal (A degree? Who am I kidding? A chimpanzee was a degree more formal than Drum; Tom was light-years ahead). But I think the truth was, Tom was simply more . . . real.

Tom was flesh and blood and *The Bridge on the River Kwai* and jokes about Arnold Schwarzenegger and allergies to dust not mold and a weakness for pad Thai. Drum was . . . well, something else. Flesh and blood? Yes. I'd felt them both under my fingers when we kissed. But a man who traces a large part of his DNA to your imagination is, by definition, more superhero than human.

Which is why the notion of sex with Drum scared the hell out of me. If the time ever came, Drum was going to be large, directive and thorough—the culmination of every fantasy I'd had since seeing Katharine Ross and Robert Redford in *Butch Cassidy and the Sundance Kid* when I was thirteen. I'd probably be yodeling myself hoarse.

Which left Tom for of-this-world intercourse.

The trouble was, that scared me even more.

I got off the bed and moved to the chair.

Nope, I just didn't know what was behind Tom's crinkly eyes and warm smile, the way I thought I did with Drum. I didn't know what was going to boil up or cool down or spill over or slip away when we stepped over that scary Maginot Line. I didn't know nothin'. *Nothing. Nada.* And that's no way to run a relationship, now is it? What's the point of getting an MBA if you couldn't work the uncontrollable events out of your life one by one, like wrinkles out of a wool skirt? Sex with men in the real world was like being led through an amusement park with a silk tie around your eyes. Could be the line for the roller coaster; could be the line for the carousel; could be the line for slightly rancid nachos and cheese.

No, thank you. I'll keep my eyes open and take my silk ties where they belong—around my wrists. Okay, only around one wrist and none too tight at that.

As a reward for my incisive personal analysis, I picked up the phone to order lunch, said *sì* to chilled mussels with lemon basil mayonnaise and grinned when they said, "Thirty minutes, Signorina Fraser." Then I snapped on Tom's laptop, entered his password ("Biscuit," the name of his childhood dog, a tidbit he'd shared with me during that same drunken night that ended with us atop the recycling bin) and brought up Google.

The first thing I searched was "Captain George Drummund 1706." Tom had done the same last night, but I wanted to be sure. As before, there was nothing helpful. I tried "Phillip Drummond 1706," "Neuf Ouest 1706," and even "Naval Hanging 1706." I got thousands of hits, none more relevant than a photo of Portsmouth Naval Base, sold by Carol's Gift Shop at 1706 Elmspring Lane, Portsmouth, Virginia.

Next I searched "Admiral Leake," sniggering impolitely over the unfortunate name. It reminded me of my sister-in-law's obstetrician, Dr. Grunt.

There wasn't a lot on John Leake. In 1706, he was

commander of the "White," a large division of the English navy based in the Mediterranean. His ninety-gun ship was called the *Prince George*. And by 1708 he'd been promoted to the high-powered naval board at a salary of one thousand pounds per annum.

So I searched "Leake Barcelona." A few more hits surfaced, most for the Leake Cottage Bed and Breakfast in that city, but one was titled "Mediterranean Tactics, 1706." I double-clicked and found a short narrative of the action Di Marvelo had related. With the Spanish navy gathering outside the Barcelona harbor, the English army had been ready to abandon the city they'd captured only a few months earlier. Leake and his squadron, who had been refueling in nearby Portugal, received word Spanish ships were closing in on their fellow countrymen and sailed in to save the day.

For good measure, I searched "Admiral Basehart 1706" and "Charles Davitch 1706," neither of which yielded anything. It pleased me to see Basehart had left a big, fat blank mark on history.

I'd gotten everything there was to be got, it seemed. For a laugh I put in "Pornographic Playing Cards 1706" and was rewarded with Pilgrim's "Naughty, naughty associate" screen. Poor Tom was going to go on someone's list. No mouse pad for him.

Not that it mattered much with him leaving. I laid my head on my hand, absently tapping the desktop.

Tom.

He was such fun . . . and so damned smart, always revealing some new vein of knowledge that would inevitably amuse, fascinate or educate me—the reason for the infield fly rule, how cod fishing changed the world, why Martha Stewart's defense failed, how the ancient Romans could tell the direction a distant army was traveling by the flickering of the sun off their shields, properties of inert gases, Napoléon in St. Helena, vulcanology, the simple perfection of the toggle bolt, the seminality of the Ramones, the philosophy of Lemony Snicket.

I typed in "French and Indian War" and hit enter.

I'll be damned! A war practically in my own backyard. It seems good ol' France, unhappy with owning only Ontario, Quebec and a few other freezer-burned slices of North America, developed a hankering for a large swath of upmarket real estate around western Pennsylvania in 1755.

Who knew?

I shoved the chair back. Now what? I'd searched everything I could think of, I certainly didn't want to show up downstairs at the Pilgrim meeting, and there was no way I was going to read *Master and Commander.* Waiting to be transported was a bit like lying on your back in the middle of Australia and waiting for a kangaroo to come by. It happens, but you'd better bring several issues of *The New Yorker* with you.

I flicked on the TV and clicked through the channels. Soccer highlights, news or *SpongeBob* in Italian? That was an easy choice. I tromped into the bathroom to the sounds of Roberto La Spugna admonishing Patrizio. After a quick bio break, during which I eyed the zippered dop kit with appropriately restrained curiosity, my eyes fell on Tom's shampoo. It sat on the edge of the shower stall. The afternoon sun streamed through the balcony doors, lighting the green bottle like an apparition from heaven.

I picked it up and put it down.

I picked it up and almost put it down.

Holding shampoo is not an intrusion, I assured myself. If Tom had said, "Here, use my room while I'm gone," he'd certainly have wanted me to enjoy his shampoo. Holding shampoo was like answering the phone. Shampoo, phone. Public, public. See?

Of course, Tom hadn't actually asked me to use his room. But I felt that was a technicality. He would have if he'd known I didn't have my laptop.

The designer bottle was long and smooth with a heft that sent a lascivious shiver down my back. I leaned against the shower door and turned it slowly in my hand. Oh, God. It wasn't just shampoo. It was shampoo and *body* wash! The blood rushed from my head, mostly in a big fat hurry to get between my legs. I emitted a loud, primitive moan and curled my toes into the shag rug. Do you suppose he poured it in his hands and then rubbed it—

A knock at the hotel room door interrupted my rapture. Lunch. "*Un momento,*" I called.

I cracked the flip-top and took a whiff.

Visions of Scandinavia filled my head. Tom in a Nordic sweater, me in a white quilted parka with faux rabbit cuffs, neither of us in pants, alone on an evergreen-covered mountain, snow stinging my lower back, Tom stinging my lower front, making our own little bonfire in the cold . . .

Oh, God, oh, God!

"Seph?"

I was so startled I almost dropped the bottle. Tom, looking almost as surprised, stood before me, room key in hand.

"I'm sorry," he said. "I didn't mean to scare you. I was just about to come in when I heard something—you, apparently—so I knocked, just to be safe. You said '*Un momento,*' but I thought maybe you were in the bathtub or something, so I let myself in."

"I was about to take a shower," I announced decisively, and waved the open shampoo. "I feel a little grimy." Like I had pine sap on my ass.

He looked at my glossy hair and pristine clothes. "O-kay."

"So, I'll just take one."

He held up his hands and returned to the bedroom. I put the shampoo back in the shower and turned on the water.

"Did you travel?" he called.

"No."

"What did you find out from Di Marvelo?" he called.

The bathroom door was still half open. According to my peripheral vision, Tom was out of sight, but since I was in my ultracool-Lara-Croft-I'm-totally-blasé-about-getting-naked mode, I couldn't bring myself to really check. I hung my blazer and skirt on the knob. Next I pulled off the camisole and dropped it carefully on the floor right next to the shower door. I was nothing if not a firm believer in a good exit strategy.

"The English navy needs to save Barcelona," I shouted back. "There's an Admiral Leake who needs to get word."

Nothing but chocolate bra, tap pant and shoes now—and don't think I didn't find it irritating that Perfect Seph's panties were too snug on me. I looked in the mirror. Totally cool. Totally together. Tyra Banks in a Victoria's Secret commercial. I could get my oil changed in this.

"Leake?" he repeated. "Hmmm. Sounds vaguely familiar."

Bra or panties next? After a moment's debate, I turned my back toward the door, unhooked the bra and dropped it on the camisole.

Tom approached the door. "Seph, I was just thinking . . ."

Eek! I slapped my hands over my breasts, leaped into the water and slammed the shower door.

Silence. Had he come in? Had he walked by? The hot water streamed down my chest, soaking my panties and shoes.

"Thinking what?" I called nonchalantly.

"Seph, did you just get in the shower with your underwear on?"

"No. . . . Okay, yes."

"Any particular reason?" His tall out-of-focus form appeared through the ridged glass—dark head, pale blue torso, light trousered legs.

"I was shy."

"Shy?"

"Yes. Can you see anything?"

"No. . . . Okay, yes. But not in much detail."

"How much is 'not much'?"

"I'd prefer not to answer that."

There was something rather freeing about the wall of blurry glass between us. No cellulite, no spider veins, no gravity. Just outline. I give good outline.

"Are you planning to leave?" I asked.

"Are you planning to take off your panties?"

"Yes."

"Then no, I don't think I will."

"But you can't see any detail."

"'Any' is very broad."

"Let me be more specific. Can you see my nipples?"

"Do you need a washcloth in there?"

"Tom . . ."

"It's more the suggestion of your nipples."

"The suggestion?"

"Yes. And might I add it's the best suggestion I've gotten since my roommate in college advised me to drop accounting my second year."

"So if I did something like this"—I twirled them slowly—"you couldn't see it?"

Stunned silence.

"Tom?"

"No." His voice cracked. "No, I couldn't see that."

"Or this?"

I hooked the panties with my thumbs and drew them down my hips and dropped them on the floor of the shower.

A faint choking noise was the only response.

"What was that?" I called. "You'll have to speak up."

"I said no."

"So I could do this"—I poured the shampoo into my hand and lathered large indulgent circles on my body—"without fear of inciting you?"

No response.

"Tom?"

No response.

I looked over. The light blue blur below his head was still there, but there was definitely something flesh tone about the legs below it.

"I thought," Tom said, "a demonstration of the level of detail visible would help."

Wood being the operative word. In fact, the level of detail was breathtaking—long and pale against a hazy halo of dark. Tom lifted the shirt over his head with a stretch. The body wash I was holding crashed to the tiles.

"Does that give you an idea?" he asked.

"Yes." Now that's what I call perspective.

"So you see, you can't see anything, really."

"No."

"Are you going to finish?"

"Finish what?" I could think of several options and all of them terrified me.

"Washing."

"Um . . ."

"Do it slowly," he added. "Very slowly."

The first "slowly" set me on "Ignite." The second dropped a match the size of the Sears Tower on the fuel. It was like having a Kenmore gas range in my pants.

"I'm d-done," I said.

"Excellent. Come on out."

"On the other hand, cleanliness is next to godliness." I attacked my neck, elbows and hands with renewed vigor.

"Seph," he chided. "You know what I mean. Slowly."

"I can't," I wailed.

"Then stand still and let the water wash over you."

That I can do. I lifted my arms over my head—never hurts to give nature a bit of a helping hand. I grabbed the shampoo shelf for support and prayed.

The door burst open. Tom lifted me out into his arms and carried me out. With the water still thundering in the stall behind us, he installed me firmly on the counter next to the sink, kissing me hard. I was still soaking wet and slightly soapy, so my ass slipped around like crazy. The dop kit went flying. My toe caught the complimentary toiletry basket, and several bottles of mouthwash hit the toilet. Tom took firm grasp of my hips and brought me back to vertical.

"Put your feet on my shoulder," he commanded, "and grab the towel rack."

"We're going to need a condom!"

But we didn't. Not for what Tom had been planning. He dropped to his knees.

All I can say is, Thank God they didn't use cheap Irish nails in Venetian towel racks.

In six exquisite minutes, all the stifling tension of the day left my body, not to mention most of my skeletal form. Tom poured me into bed and turned off the shower.

"Wow," I said after several long moments.

"You're welcome."

A knock sounded. Tom gave me a questioning glance.

"Mussels," I purred.

He flipped the comforter over me and jerked on his pants. "Don't move."

Like he had to worry.

"*Grazie.*" He took the tray from the woman's hands and signed the slip. "*E una bottiglia del vostro champagne migliore, per favore,*" he added, slipping a bill into her hand before she disappeared.

"I hope you didn't just tell her what we did."

"I didn't need to. The ten was to apologize for the noise."

He put the tray on the bed. The mussels were laid out on a bed of sea salt. I could smell the luscious twin tangs of lemon and basil. Sex famished me. I hadn't been famished in so long. I sat up and tipped the contents of a shell into my mouth.

Tom watched me, smiling. "You're beautiful when you eat."

"You should see me with chocolate fondue."

He slouched against the wall. "You were incredible in there."

"Are you sure it was me?"

He tilted his head toward the toiletry-strewn bathroom floor. "Perfectly."

With a loud slurp, I sucked down another mussel. The cool, savory cream was like heaven. "Sorry about you."

"Don't be." He reached for his fly.

A cell phone rang. His.

"Shit." He pulled it out of his pocket and looked at me. I shrugged. He flipped it open. "Hello."

An instant later his entire body language changed. I could hear a woman's voice on the other end.

He said, "No, I haven't looked at them yet. . . . In a day or so, probably. I have to finish up here."

Kimberly in Paris. *Grrrr.*

I gave Tom credit. He carried on in as business-like a way as possible, which is not always easy with your fly down and a put-out woman in your bed. I was pretty sure their relationship was strictly financial statements and balance sheets. Tom struck me as a single-minded man when it came to women. Nonetheless, the mussels lost their taste.

The call was mundane—the lease on the new apartment, a lead on a company in Holland, an odd turn in a stock price. After a moment, he snapped the phone closed and looked at me.

Nope, the sex *juju* had not survived the sudden change in velocity. He rezipped his pants with a sigh.

"Where will you live?" I asked lightly.

He sank into the chair. "A quiet neighborhood. I don't know, I'm going to be spending a lot of time at work."

"I hear you're going to be her partner."

"Yeah. Imagine me owning part of a company."

"You'll be great." I wrapped my arms around my knees. "I'll miss you."

"We'll still see each other, I hope."

Sex in Paris twice a year? Okay, maybe I could stand it.

His cell rang again. He opened it and looked at the display.

"How many times a day do you two talk?" I asked.

He handed the phone to me. It was Dana.

"Now where's your phone, Seph?" she demanded.

"Er, it's dead," I lied. Sorry, cross-century roaming's a bitch on batteries.

"What is going on?"

I pulled the sheet around me, gave Tom an embarrassed shrug and ducked out on the balcony. "Yeah. I'm fine. Listen, can I call you back in a little bit? Tom and I are kinda in the middle of something."

"Oh, baby," she sang, "I smell funky sheets."

I grinned. "Not on me. I just showered."

Dana hooted. "With Tom? Woo-hoo!"

"Look, it's not as clear-cut as you think. He's taken a job somewhere else. In fact, he's going to *Paris.*"

"Yeah, with the feel of you on the head of his—"

"Whoa. Tell me you're not in school."

"Tell me you're not going to let it slip away."

"We're talking the relationship, I hope?"

"Seph."

Tom's phone made a call-waiting noise in my ear. I looked at the number. It was one of those free-form European phone numbers. Kimberly. Jeez, if she was going to call this often, he'd have to get an earbud stapled to his head. I let it go to voice mail. "Yeah, well, Tom's not the only issue."

Dana has been my best friend since junior high. She could smell more than funky sheets at work here. "What?" she demanded. "What's up?"

"There's another man too."

"Cripes, Seph, when you go, you go whole hog. Who's he? Some young Italian waiter with a motorcycle, unflagging energy and a digital video camera?"

I stared at the phone. "You have an untapped career in erotica. English. He's English." The landline phone in the hotel room started to ring.

"And?" Dana demanded. "What does he look like?"

"Er, rather like Colin Firth, actually."

"*Another* one?" she shrieked. "You have *two* boyfriends that look like Colin Firth? Good God! Is there enough diaphragm jelly in the world?"

Tom had answered the inside phone. I could tell by the look on his face something was up.

"Look, I gotta run," I said. "I'll call you tomorrow. Give my dad a hug for me."

I snapped the phone shut and caught Tom saying, "*Sì, professore.*"

My ears pricked up. Tom gestured me over.

"Uh-huh," he said. "Uh-huh. . . . Really? . . . No, I'll tell her. Thank you." He laid the phone in the cradle. "Do you remember asking who the investors behind the *Neuf Ouest* were?"

I nodded.

"Di Marvelo couldn't find anything in the incorporation records in his collection, so he left a message with a friend in the British Library."

"And?"

"There are three men listed on the record for the *Neuf Ouest*. One Henry Lattimore, one Charles Davitch—"

I gasped. Davitch was Peaches's uncle.

"—and one Herman Aloysius Basehart."

Chapter Sixteen

"*No*, Seph," Tom said sharply, "I don't see it that way at all."

I was back in the cute flirty skirt, another of Tom's shirts, and, of course, no underwear or bra, as mine now hung dripping on the shower nozzle in the bathroom. At some point in the last fifteen minutes, Tom had declared himself in need of some air, so we were walking briskly along the Grand Canal waterfront in the afternoon sun and continuing the cracking argument that had begun upstairs.

"But it's no more dangerous than it was before," I insisted.

"It *is*. Basehart is hiding information. Did Drummond know Basehart was one of the investors in the *Neuf Ouest*?"

"I don't think so. I'm sure he would have mentioned it."

"Basehart brought your captain up on spying charges, charges you think are false. Basehart could very well be a French spy himself, set on sabotaging the English navy. If he gets wind of your interference, no one can guess what sort of danger you'll be in."

"He's a short, ugly old lech— Tom, I can't walk this fast. . . . The worst danger I could be in is of catching cooties."

"Seph," he said, stopping abruptly. "This is not just some fairy tale you're playing around in. You said Drummond mentioned a French spy named Gabin. I spent some time looking him up when you were gone. Do you know who he is?"

I shook my head.

"Claude Gabin was the head of French intelligence under Louis the Fourteenth. He used to interrogate women by flogging their children in front of them. Spies had their eyes and tongues cut out."

I felt sick. I hadn't thought of 1706 as being dangerous—only dirty, smelly and unenlightened. Sort of like a week of camping with Ted Nugent.

"I don't want you to go there again." He started walking. It was early afternoon, and the crowds were thick as we approached the Doge's beautiful Moorish palace and the dramatic seaside entrance to the city.

"It isn't like I can stop it. It just happens."

His mouth flattened. "Try telling your captain to stop it."

I caught his arm. "What are you saying? Are you saying you think he makes it happen?"

"Think of it, Seph. You're from the future. That

makes you a very valuable commodity. Has he asked you about potential investments, upcoming inventions, the outcomes of future battles?"

"Me? The outcomes of future battles?"

"All right. Did he ask you to ask me?"

I stammered.

"Aha!" he cried. "You see, he's an operator. He'd do anything to stack the odds in his favor. First he's digging around for a battle outcome; pretty soon it will be when to invest in the East India Company, or whether or not to buy land in South America. For all we know he did take those papers for a chance to sell them to the highest bidder."

"No. He's not like that."

"Really? Do you know him that well?"

"Yes."

With a stutter step he came to a halt. "Oh."

For an instant the crowds seemed to part, and a bright red silence curled around our feet like a weird, stretched-out-of-proportion cloud. Then it was gone, and the crowds were back just as they had always been.

Whoa. I put my hands on my temples.

"What is it?" Tom asked.

"Something funky just happened. It seemed like the start of travel."

He stared at me for a second, then leaned over to whisper in my ear. "Shall we take the elevator to the top of the bell tower there and try for the quarter-mile-high club?"

"Are you *insane*?"

"Good news," he said, drawing back, "it's still you. Your twin would have been pulling me inside out through my fly at that." He led me to the long, low plinth under the lion-topped column, the symbol of the city, and gestured for me to sit.

The granite was cool, and I leaned back on my palms. The water sparkled like a field of emeralds and aquamarines, barely touched by the vessels crossing its surface. Tom's hand settled over mine.

"What else did my twin say to you?" I asked. "On the plane, I mean?"

"Oh, that." He waved it away.

"It hurt you."

He turned his gaze from me to the vast bay before us. A gondolier unloaded his fare, an older couple holding hands.

"How much of the other Seph is you?" he asked.

"Well, I'd try the bell tower in the dark if that's what you're asking."

"Seph . . ."

"I don't know. I haven't met her. She seems very good at what she does."

"Yes."

"But I get the impression," I added, "I wouldn't really like her that much."

"How so?"

"She wears thong underwear."

"Ouch," he agreed.

"Whoever decided cloven asses were attractive anyhow?"

"Beats me. Couldn't have been any man over the

emotional age of fifteen. Of course that still leaves a good many of us."

"I don't know what it is, but to me thong underwear just says something about a woman that shouldn't be said."

"Pass me the Extra-Strength Woolite?" he suggested.

I laughed. "So what do you like?"

"I pride myself on being fairly nondiscriminatory as far as women's underclothes are concerned. I can't think of too much I've seen that I haven't enjoyed."

"But if pressed?"

"If pressed . . ." He drew a thumb along his chin stubble. "If pressed I would say that plain white cotton bikinis with a tiny pink bow in the center, right under the curve of the belly, is pretty damned close to perfection."

"Gee. You sound like a man who's given this some thought."

"The subject has occupied my thoughts from time to time. But—and this is a very important *but*—there is nothing sexier on earth right now than you wearing my shirt and no underwear at all."

Wow.

He kissed me slowly and very softly.

For a time we said nothing, just sat side by side and stared out at the sparkling water.

"So she's really not like me, this other Seph?"

"She is a two-dimensional, hormone-pumped version of you." He tucked a strand of hair behind my ear. "She is not the Persephone Pyle I've come to know and love."

"If so," I said, slipping my hand under his, "it doesn't matter if you tell me what else she said."

His fingers stilled.

"Please," I said.

For a long moment I wasn't sure he'd answer.

"I told her," he said finally, "that I had a job offer and was probably going to leave Pilgrim."

"And she said?"

"And she said she couldn't think of a better way for us to say good-bye than a three-day tryst in Venice." He met my eyes. "Is that what you would have said if you'd been on the plane?"

I didn't know what to say. I certainly wouldn't have said that. I probably would have been too scared to say anything—kind of like now. "I-I don't know, Tom."

His hand slipped away. "I think," he said, rising, "I'm going to give the bell tower a try. Will you be all right here?"

"May I come with you?"

He didn't reply, just shoved his hands in his pockets and nodded.

We walked to the tower in silence and stood in line outside the beautiful carved façade of the *loggietta* at the base of the tower's elevator. We were in line with a bunch of businessmen, each toting large blue bags that read "AAG." The third belch of tourists returning from the top finally brought us close enough to enter. The elevator was crowded, and I had to press against Tom to make room while we went up. Neither of us acknowledged the contact.

I emerged with a gasp. As beautiful as Venice was from the ground, it was even lovelier from above. Orange and brown tile roofs lined the meandering blue canals. Across the bay I could see what Tom said was the domed tower of Santa Maria della Salute and beyond that the narrow island of Lido. Sunshine twinkled on the water as the boats and gondolas and *vaporetti* water taxis glided quietly below and anthills of tourists moved in rapid confusion. It was hard to believe Venice was a working city filled with real people with real jobs. It seemed more like something from a fairy tale. Renaissance Disney World without the mouse ears. Tom drew up behind me.

"Stunning," he said.

"Oh, the view's incredible."

"That too." He circled my waist and kissed my neck. Dana once dated an acupuncturist who told her happiness can only flow through well-aligned chi points. At that instant, my chi points must have looked like a Super Bowl marching band.

"If three days is all we have," he whispered, "I'm not going to waste it." He covered my eyes and pressed me against the railing. "How dark does it have to be?"

My shoes began to vibrate. Not the great-sex-gotta-have-it sort of vibrate, the grab-your-ass-we're-taking-off vibrate. I clutched Tom for support. But the world did not dissolve, and I did not catch other-century glimpses of Drum or the ship. It was like I was stuck in a time machine with a bad case of connectile dysfunction. But the vibrating continued, and Tom felt it too.

"Wow," he exclaimed. "Imagine what this would feel like if we were—"

"Tom, please, I need your help."

"Just lift a leg over my arm," he said, reaching for his buckle, "I've seen it in movies—"

"Not for that. It's time to travel, and I'm stuck. I need you to kiss me."

"What?"

"My traveling, um, well, it seems to be aided by a kiss."

His eyes narrowed. "And how exactly would you know that?"

"Tom, please! I need it now."

A number of AAG heads turned. Even businessmen on holiday have their limits, it seems.

Tom pulled me behind a sign providing exit directions in Italian, English, French, Spanish, German and something that looked a little bit like my ankle tattoo.

"You're going to owe me for this, Seph—big-time."

"Owe you?"

"An explanation and twenty uninterrupted minutes—and not necessarily in that order."

He seized me by the hips and drew me up the north face of Mt. Thomas. My shoes were buzzing so hard now I thought the bricks in the tower were going to shake loose, but I discovered something fascinating. When I tightened my ankles behind Tom's back, the vibrations shuddered right through his hips into my favorite chi point of all. My eyes fluttered shut, and I made a little sound in my throat.

"Well, there's an interesting look." He adjusted his hips a fraction. "Thirsty?"

It was like riding a six-foot-two vibrator. Apparently the incident in Tom's bathroom had been a helluva warm-up. I'd never gotten this close this fast. "Oh, dear God!"

"Right here?" The corner of his mouth rose. "In the bell tower?"

My face was buried in his neck, and I was hanging on for dear life as the shoes shook me into a mind-bending, knee-pureeing fervor. I felt like Debra Winger in *Urban Cowboy.* "Oh, God. Oh, God!"

Tom rimmed my ear with his tongue. "If a kiss packs a three-hundred-year wallop," he said, "aren't you afraid this is going to launch you into the Pleistocene era? Can you outrun a tyrannosaurus?"

Then I remembered what happened the last time I went back. If I was going, I wasn't going empty-handed. I looked around frantically. "Tom, help me! Get me close to that man."

"Pardon?"

"That man!" I cried, pointing to the closest AAG-er.

Tom heard the panic in my voice and didn't ask questions. He wheeled me into the cool stucco wall next to the man in a single move. Immediately the vibrato turned to one glorious, whip-cracking wave, and the thumb Tom had slipped under my skirt was teeing me up for the big one. I yanked the AAG bag off the startled man's shoulder and brought it firmly to my side. The noises that were coming out of me were so, well, primitive, the poor fellow didn't know where to look.

"Now, now, now!" I gasped.

"Another man?" Tom asked, confused.

"The kiss!"

Tom married his hard, warm mouth to mine, heroically containing a moan that would have gotten me banned from the bell tower for life. If there was a *Tyrannosaurus rex* in my future, I was going to die happy. The world turned to a shimmery, jiggly bowl of orange Day-Glo Jell-O.

"Tell that captain of yours," Tom called as I faded into the undulating haze, "we have something to settle."

Chapter Seventeen

I groaned happily as my trans-century travel agent poured me into a gelatinous but upright mass against a wall. There was nothing like two orgasms in a row to really put the world in a happy place. I didn't care if I was tied to the mast naked. Okay, I would in a minute. But for sixty wonderful seconds, I was tranquilly trouble-free.

The blood began returning to my brain, and I clutched my sides. No nausea, no turbulence, no water landing. And clothes—not the ones I'd left wearing, of course, but a crimson silk gown with black fringe that thrust my breasts so far up and out it looked like I was carrying a window box full of water balloons.

I was sitting on Drum's bed; of that I was sure. I could smell the salt-laced sea air, feel the warm wind on my face and hear the ungodly noise of sailors scrubbing the deck above me.

The room was still, though. No Drum. I didn't like that.

And the ship wasn't moving. I didn't like that either.

I opened my eyes.

Oh, shit.

Not Drum's quarters. If the abundance of velvet and silver plate weren't clear indications, the bulkheaded walls left me no doubt.

I made my way to the stern windows, grabbing chair backs and desktops to support my wobbly legs. We were in a teaming dockyard at the edge of a bustling town, a town completely overshadowed by the huge mountain towering over it like a slightly bent pyramid.

City on a rock? Oh, Lord, we were in Gibraltar!

Flinging open the stern balcony door, I let loose my best taxi whistle. A red-headed sailor on the dock below turned around.

"What day is it?" I called. "Day and month?"

"Twenty-third of April, ma'am."

Holy crap! More than two weeks had elapsed! Had more than two weeks elapsed at home? Drum's trial was on April 24. Barcelona was saved April 27.

The height of the stern balcony made it too far to jump, though from the way the sailor was admiring the cut of my gown, I suspect he would have offered me whatever assistance I needed. I opted to make a run for the ship's main gangway, which was visible halfway down the length of the ship. I hurried back through the room and had just about reached the door when voices rose beyond it.

"The last of the cargo has been transferred," one voice said. "What shall we do with the *Neuf Ouest,* sir?"

"Return it to its owner, and give me the inventory."

The voice of Herman Aloysius Basehart, bastard at sea.

"The owner? Any idea who that might be?" the admiral's companion asked.

"Not in the slightest."

It was all I could do to keep from yelling, "Liar, liar, pants on fire."

Basehart opened the door, still issuing instructions. He spotted me and without missing a beat held the door tight to keep the other man from doing the same.

"On second thought, Jenkins," he said, "let's cover this later. I'll be reviewing my log now. See that I'm not disturbed." Basehart took a sheet from the man, folded it and tucked it into his jacket.

He closed the door and gave me a smile that sent a Red Riding Hood chill down my spine. He didn't bother bowing

"Miss Pyle, I expected you would come eventually. I don't know how he slipped you off the ship before, but I knew you'd be back."

"Did you?"

"How did you get past my guards?"

"I didn't. Five sovereigns buys a lot of access." I hoped five sovereigns wasn't enough to buy a house or anything. I wanted it to sound like a realistic bribe.

He went to the cabinet, removed a crystal decanter brimming with amber liquid and filled two glasses.

Then he took off his coat and loosened his cravat. With a look in my direction, he threw it on the table. I had an idea this was not normal procedure for a meeting with a lady.

"Should it please you to know," he said, taking a long draught, "I rather hoped you would return."

Oh, puke.

"If you've come to bargain for your cousin's life," he went on, "I think you'll know what I require."

I wanted to deck him. On the other hand, I wanted to deck him after I'd gathered what I needed to clear Drum. "Have you the power to save him?"

"My evidence will make or break him. Which would you like?"

"You're insane to think he's done anything. If you were smart, you'd get him out of there instantly."

"I don't think so."

He placed the other glass in my hand and kissed me.

I waited until he finished, drank from the glass, and slapped him.

Eeee-awwww! He'd given me sherry! I was going to barf.

Basehart rubbed his cheek. "You can make this easy or hard. Though as I think about it"—his eyes did a circuit on me that would have made a NASCAR driver proud—"I might prefer hard."

Does a taffeta-covered toe to the nuts sound hard enough for you?

He lowered himself into a chair at the dining table and stretched his legs. "I think I'd like you to start by taking off my boots."

What kind of a kinky-assed shit was this? "I think I'd like you to start by explaining how you came to be a silent partner on the *Neuf Ouest*."

That gave him pause—briefly.

"You have no proof."

"Peaches's uncle Charles Davitch does."

"Davitch wouldn't say a word."

"Wouldn't he?" I said, lifting a knowing brow. *Wouldn't he?* Cripes, I hadn't even thought about that possibility.

"No. And even if he did, what of it? It is not a crime to invest in a privateer."

"Isn't it?"

"No, it is not. And I'd advise you to cease the threat-laced rhetorical questions. They're starting to annoy me."

Are they? "Drum didn't know you were an investor in his ship."

"'Drum,' is it? Not 'Captain Drummond' or 'cousin George'? No, Miss Pyle, he did not." He downed the rest of the sherry.

"Where is he?"

"You know where he is as well as I do. He's being confined in the Admiralty jail until his trial, which I'm sorry to say is tomorrow. I keep expecting him to ask for you. Very noble of him to hold his silence, don't you think?"

"I'm surprised you can recognize nobility at all." I put my glass on the table.

"You know, Miss Pyle, I think I'd like for you to beg. Yes, that would be a salve to this old soul. And as you beg, I'd like you to think of all the things a woman could possibly do for a man in my position."

How about shoving two fingers up your nose and pulling?

At that moment, a tall, soaking-wet sailor in duck trousers and nothing else heaved himself quietly over the stern balcony railing. It was Drum. He looked paler than I remembered, and his hair was much shorter, but other than that he looked fine. He held a finger to his lips.

I don't know how he got out, and I didn't care. I was so shocked and relieved to see him, I didn't know what to do. Basehart was facing me, with his back to the rest of the room and the balcony. If he turned his head even slightly, he'd see Drum. The admiral's quarters were triple the size of Drum's, but it was still an eighteenth-century ship; I could heave a bowling ball from one end of the room to the other.

All I can say is, it's a good thing my response to Basehart at this point was supposed to be shame and horror. A gaping mouth covers many emotions.

"Er, pardon me, Admiral?" I said. "The scrubbing upstairs is so loud, I couldn't hear you."

Drum held up three fingers. *Three minutes,* he mouthed.

"Beg, Miss Pyle," Basehart said.

Three minutes *what*? Three minutes till the ship blows up? Three minutes until the coach and four pull up quayside for our escape? Drum began tiptoeing toward the desk. Oh, *shit.* He meant three minutes to keep Basehart amused while he searched Basehart's papers.

I dropped to my knees.

Thank God for the thunderous scrubbing on the deck above. Even Basehart would have blushed at my mutterings as I heaved off his skanky boots. His feet smelled like a fish market three days after the air conditioning fails.

"That's better," Basehart purred.

Drum made it to the desk and began rifling through the papers spread across the surface. He had a large cutlass tucked in the back of his trousers. Oh, boy. It was bad enough he'd escaped—if they caught him in here with a weapon, they'd kill him in an instant.

Basehart wiggled his toes. "Now tell me what I can do for you."

I gazed down in as demeaned a way as I could muster, which really was more of a "Go fuck yourself" with my eyes closed. "I wish to bargain for Captain Drummond's life." You disgusting prick.

"And what do you have to bargain with? You know, this might be easier if you loosened your gown."

Drum straightened instantly and turned around.

Idiot. "*I will be fine* with my gown loosened," I said. "*Do your job* and help me, will you, Admiral? *Quickly, please.*"

Basehart was happy to oblige. I wedged my back in between his knees, and he went to work on the buttons. Whatever the hell Drum was after, it had better be like the Rosetta Stone of this friggin' war. Basehart's hands began to roam forward.

"Ah-ah-ah. No buttons there." I slipped out of his reach and stood. Drum had a drawer of files open and was going through each one methodically. I could see his face reflected in the mirror over the desk. He wore a look of concentration that suggested three minutes were not going to be enough.

I had to clutch my gown to keep it up, and a foul grin spread across Basehart's face. He also had a hard-on under his breeks the size of a ChapStick.

"Tell me about you and Drum as you take off your dress."

I beg your pardon?

The look on my face must have said it all, for Basehart opened a small box to his left, lifted out a pistol and pointed it directly at me. My heart thumped in my chest like an unbalanced washer on spin dry. The Sundance Kid/Emma undressing sequence in *Butch Cassidy* lost all of its luster.

Unfortunately the cacophony of deck cleaning above us covered not only the crackle of paper as Drum flipped pages but also the click of Basehart cocking the gun. Which meant Drum did not look up. He did not know Basehart had moved from sadism to rape.

"Is he your cousin?" Basehart asked.

"N-no."

"No, I didn't think so. So you lied to me?"

"Yes."

Basehart pointed the pistol at the hand clutching my gown and signaled. I opened my fingers. The silk fell to the ground, leaving me in a thin cotton chemise. Basehart was loving this. The ChapStick had grown into a full-size Revlon lipstick—Color Me Gross.

"Naughty, naughty girl. Have you ever been spanked?"

This woke Drum from his reverie. He looked at me in the mirror. Unfortunately Basehart's back blocked the gun from his view.

"*Focus* your attention, Admiral. *We don't have all day*. That *gun* could go off at any time."

Drum blanched.

"So true," Basehart said, and reached for his glass. It was empty. The decanter was behind him. He'd have to turn in Drum's direction to fill it. Drum and I both froze.

"Wait a second, Admiral!" I held up a hand. "I haven't finished mine yet."

Fuck me. I picked up the sherry and took a dainty pretend sip. My gut began to roil.

"More, Miss Pyle. You have a lovely large mouth. Let me see what you can do with it."

I gave Drum a stern I'll-take-care-of-this look, and he swung back to the file.

Cringing, I swallowed. The great thing about the mind: fifteen years had gone by and it still hadn't lost an iota of its sense memory. The sherry tasted like barrel-aged vomit. I gagged.

"Sorry." I said, wiping my mouth. "I'm not much of a drinker."

Drum raised a dubious brow.

Basehart leaned back in his chair. "Are you in love with him?"

What is this, *Oprah*? Drum paused.

"It's not as easy as that." Get back to work, dammit. If you think I'm going to confess anything to a lech with a two-inch penis, you're sadly mistaken.

"Come now, Miss Pyle."

Drum's eyes met mine in the mirror.

"He's a good man," I said honestly. "Loyal, brave, true. I have the highest regard for him."

Basehart rose to his feet, took the glass from my hand, downed what remained and kissed me again. All in all, I would have preferred the sherry.

"I wasn't quite truthful when I said Drum hadn't mentioned you in jail." Basehart ran a jagged-nailed thumb over my nipple. "I told Drum you'd been found with more Admiralty papers on you. I told him you were a spy who'd used him to help France. Interestingly that didn't seem to bother the poor sod at all."

It wouldn't. Drum knew only too well who I was and where I came from. All in all, I think he would have preferred the French spy. But this story, vile and mean-spirited as it was, did tell me something important: Basehart truly believed Drum was the one who'd taken the papers. Which meant Basehart hadn't taken them himself.

"But then"—Basehart touched the hollow of my neck—"I told him you what you were willing to do to bargain for his life. Rather prescient of me, aye? He struggled so hard in his chains the guard had to knock him on the head to keep him from scraping his wrists to the bone."

Drum held up a sheet of paper victoriously. What-ever he'd been looking for, he'd found. He creased it and slipped it into his waistband next to the knife. Then he picked up a large round glass paperweight and advanced toward Basehart.

A frenzied pounding on the door stopped all of us.

"Sir, sir! Are you all right?"

"Of course I am. What is it?"

"Sir, thank God. The officer of the watch on *The Swift* reported someone with a knife scaling the side of the ship."

Drum's gaze locked mine. I began to feel sick, and this time it wasn't the sherry.

"Shall we search the room, sir?"

Basehart's eyes flickered left, flickered right.

The time for scruples was over. I closed my eyes and reached for Revlon.

"Sir, shall we search the room?"

"N-no," Basehart croaked. "*No!*"

Oh, God, I'll never wear lipstick again. Or use my right hand. Or think about wool.

Drum crept forward again, paperweight in hand.

"Sir," the officer called, "shall I send a party out to search the docks?"

"If you *insist,* Mr. Fairley!" Basehart snorted, trembling. "Just go!"

Go, I mouthed to Drum. Basehart was wiggling under my hand like a beached goldfish.

Drum stood, uncertain.

Basehart muffled an anguished cry into my neck and jerked. God, oh, God! I yanked my hand away.

"I'm sorry, I'm sorry." Basehart blubbered. "I couldn't stop it."

My kingdom for a pot of boiling antiseptic.

He hung on me, still crying. "I'm so sorry. I tried everything to stop it, even thinking about you being with child."

With *child*?!

Drum fumbled the paperweight and only a series of abrupt lurches saved it from hitting the floor.

Get out, I mouthed. *I'll be fine.*

Still looking shell-shocked, Drum replaced the paperweight. He padded out to the railing and looked up and down. After a hesitant glance, he put the folded paper in his mouth and slipped over the side.

"Momma's here." I wiped my hand on Basehart's back. "Momma's here."

Chapter Eighteen

Basehart was completely docile now. I always say there is nothing like an ill-timed ejaculation to really take the stuffing out of a man. And nothing like the suggestion of being pregnant to really make a three-year run of chastity seem like a darned fine idea.

I tucked Basehart into his cot, then listened to a long, rambling and, to my way of thinking, barely stomachable explanation for his performance that involved not only his mother dressing him in skirts until the age of nine, but the demanding sexual requirements of his now-deceased wife and a latent inclination toward self-abuse.

I told him we'd talk again later, and he fell asleep with his thumb in his mouth—a far cry from where I thought it might end up only a short time earlier.

I picked my gown off the floor and looked at my stomach. Was that a bulge, or rather a bigger bulge than usual? No, it simply wasn't possible. Even if I lost a few weeks somewhere it was too cruel to believe I could be pregnant without remembering *some*thing about the conception. Where Basehart had gotten the idea was beyond me.

I spent several frustrating minutes trying to get the gown buttoned again. What imbecile would invent a dress that requires two people to get on? I finally gave up and tied one of Basehart's sashes around my waist, just beneath my breasts, crossed the straps in back and pulled them up over my shoulders, finishing them off in a large bow right beneath my chin. It choked me a little, and I looked like an idiot, but it held the dress up and mostly closed and would do until I got the hell out of there.

Which brought me to Drum. Basehart's story about Drum in his chains touched me deeply. Probably the only scrap of comfort the poor guy had in all this was the knowledge I was out of harm's way somewhere in the future. Hearing I was under Basehart's thumb— there was that image again—had undoubtedly driven him to the edge. I don't know how he got out of jail, but I was damned glad of it. Now we just needed to commandeer a ship, find Admiral Leake and get the charges against Drum dropped—all in less than a week. I'm glad Drum was part fiction. I was pretty sure we were going to need a major infusion of poetic license to get the job done.

I suddenly remembered the bag I'd boosted from the AAG guy. Where had it gone? I looked around the room. There it was, at the foot of the cot. It must have fallen when I landed. I unzipped it, praying there was something in it more worthwhile than a camera and a round-trip train ticket to Florence. I'm not exactly sure what I thought I'd find, but a gun, ten thousand pounds in Queen Anne–era currency and Admiral Leake's cell phone number would have been helpful.

What I found instead was a bottle of water—gosh, just what I needed in Gibraltar: more water—a foldout map of Venice, breath mints, a balled-up rain poncho, an Italian phrase book opened to the "Making *Amore*" page, two ketchup-smeared McDonald's Mac Grande wrappers and a half-written postcard addressed to "My dearest wife."

Perfect.

Then I saw the container of pills. It was plastic, the kind one carries for travel, and it was filled with drugs of several shapes and colors.

I had a small twinge of guilt. Any man who ate two Big Macs for lunch probably needed medication to keep his heart from blowing, but I also knew there was a *farmacia* on every corner in Venice, so I figured he could work it out.

I flipped open the container and dumped the pills into my hand. The orange ones were easy to identify. They were Grant's Low-Dose aspirin—the perfect antidote to a diet of McDonald's.

I was less certain of the identity of the others. The pink ones looked a little like an antibiotic I'd taken once for a sinus infection, and the green ones had the general appearance of a constipation remedy Pilgrim sold. Consumers knew it as Stanelux. But it was so strong, we in the company referred to it as Morning Liftoff.

Mixed into this rainbow selection were several diamond-shaped blue ones engraved with a V. These I had seen before—in TV ads with athletic old guys throwing footballs through tire swings and satisfied wives extolling the virtues of "private moments" and "erection quality." Apparently Mr. Mac Grande had had extravagant plans for the trip, which could also explain the breath mints and phrase book. Nothing like a business trip to really bring out the best in a man.

My uncertainty concerning the other pills' exact uses made them somewhat less helpful. An antibiotic wouldn't be so bad if you were constipated, I reasoned, but getting your bowels to move ain't gonna do zip for an infected bullet wound no matter how much rocket fuel it puts into your morning routine.

I picked up the balled-up poncho to check the pockets and was surprised to find it was wrapped around another object. I unrolled it, hoping for something in the weapons line—at this point even a San Marco Square snow globe would have been a step in the right direction—but instead nearly dropped the entire bag.

Sitting in the poncho was a gleaming new plastic speculum, still in its sterile plastic wrapper.

Jeez, what sort of evening did this guy have planned? Then I saw the tag on the plastic wrapper— "A special welcome from Tyler Gynecological Devices to the 47th annual American Association of Gynecologists convention attendees. Enjoy a sample of our newest speculum, the T190, with unique no-pinch safety features. Tyler

Gynecological Devices—Always at Your Cervix!" I crossed my legs hurriedly and decided lobster bibs were looking better and better.

I loaded the pills into my pockets. The pills weren't exactly the crown jewels, but, hey, a good time traveler works with what she's given. And while the *click, click, click* of the speculum has struck fear in many twenty-first-century women's hearts, unless the bad guys were in urgent need of an anal probe, I think I was at a dead end on that as a resource. Nonetheless I stuck it in a pocket too. Everything else I tossed overboard except the breath mints. Sherry and Basehart's tongue were not a good combination.

Then I looked up and what I saw made me smile.

Despite his flaws, the good admiral had been kind enough to fill the hole in my lineup (again, unfortunate choice of words). Lying before me on the desk was his pistol, which I slipped in with everything else.

A loud snore from Basehart reminded me I had a job to do. Drum wasn't the only treasure hunter here. I snagged the inventory list out of Basehart's coat pocket as well as three sovereigns, four shillings, nine pence and a particularly dirty limerick about a blacksmith from Kent—Basehart clearly had a deep-seated love of poetry. In the event posthypnotic suggestion had any effect, I whispered, "Go to Barcelona" three times in his ear. Alas, he gave no sign of understanding, though his hands did settle into their familiar haunts with a certain eager vigor as I drew back my besashed shoulders and left.

I had overestimated the price of entry; all it cost me to bribe my way off the ship was four shillings. I hurried through the docks area, wondering where to find Drum. Gibraltar was not exactly Manhattan, though the sheer-faced mountain perched over the quaint little town did give it a sort of metropolitan skyline appearance. Nevertheless, there were still a hell of a lot of places to hide. Where does one find a man who has escaped from jail, is known by fellow sailors all over the city, is being hunted by his former admiral's men, is hoping to avert a battle for which he does not know the location and is, one hopes, intent on meeting me? A tailor shop? A tavern? A travel agent?

As it turns out, one finds such a man standing in the shadows of a large elm at the edge of the commercial district, for I looked up and there he was, waving discreetly in my direction. He now wore a dark blue shirt over his sailor trousers.

Drum, what are you doing standing there in plain—

"George Drummond, as I live and breathe." A gaunt old officer with a droopy mustache walking not ten feet to Drum's right stopped dead in his tracks and stared at him in shock. "Is the court-martial over?"

Drum did not answer. In fact, Drum did not even seem to hear.

Behind me, a hubbub of hurrying feet rose. I turned. A dozen of Basehart's men were fanning the street, taking long careful looks in shop windows and down alleyways.

When I turned back, Drum was gone, but standing beside me was Peaches's "uncle," Charles Davitch—

speaker of French, lover of pornography and wearer of a turquoise silk coat with bright vio-Let's Sail Away cuffs.

"Good day, Miss Pyle."

"My goodness, I didn't see you there."

"Aye, well, I have some business in port."

Yeah, cashing in on Drum's hard work as a privateer.

One of the more eager sailors spotted me. He started to walk casually in my direction.

I grabbed Charles's arm. "Shall we take a quick stroll?"

I led as we slipped through a gathering of prostitutes, down a narrow alley, and in and out a dry goods shop.

"*Mon Dieu*, Miss Pyle, you have a very unusual way of strolling."

My pursuer seemed to have fallen by the wayside. Nonetheless, I wasn't going to take any chances.

"I want to talk to you," I said, "but I don't have much time. We'll need the *Neuf Ouest* to be readied for sailing. Who's captaining it now?"

"Mr. Haverhill. Why do you need it?"

"It's not for me. It's for Drum."

His eyebrows lifted. "Have you found a way to get him released?"

"In a matter of speaking, yes."

He grabbed my arm. "*C'est vrai?*"

"*C'est vrai.*"

Davitch halted, eyes closed, and put a hand to his heart.

Then it struck me like a two-by-four. His heart's desire wasn't Peaches. Hell, it wasn't even Peach-flavored.

He was in love with Drum. I put my hand on his arm, and my shoes gave off a long, empathetic sigh, like the sound of a car turning over once before dying.

A horrible thought struck me, and I said, "You aren't from Toulon, are you?"

"Toulon? No. My home is outside London, in Buckinghamshire. Why do you ask?"

"Never been a visitor, never had a second home, never went through on a ten-day if-it's-Thursday-it-must-be-Toulon sort of thing?"

"No. Why?"

"No reason."

We stared at our toes. Charles drew a surreptitious sleeve across his eye. He wore the same look I'd seen in the mirror all through the spring of my senior year after Michael LePore asked Trish Mucha to the prom.

"By the way," I said lightly, "how is that broken heart of yours?"

"Choking me."

Basehart's sailor appeared in the distance in front of us, head gyrating in every direction. I pulled Charles back into the shop.

"Have you told the lady in question?" I dragged Charles by bolts of cloth and barrels of buckles and buttons.

"I cannot. It . . . well, it would not do."

Now I have no beef with love of any flavor, shape or size, but the one variety that can never bring anyone joy is unrequited. Charles needed to move on. Trust me. I'd thrown my last Michael LePore picture away two years ago.

"May I make a guess?" I shoved him through the door and back onto the street. "May I guess that the woman in question is married, which is why your regard is not returned?" I took his arm and began jogging toward the same grove of elms under which Drum had stood. "Mr. Davitch, is your love a love that can never be?"

The look in his eyes told me I was spot on, and for a moment I feared another torrent of French.

"*Oui,* Miss Pyle," he said between gulps of air. "That is the situation. You are very intuitive."

Yep, that's me, the woman who would have stranded you on a deserted island with Peaches.

We stopped beside a couple of parked horses, which hid us from the street.

"Do you remember my medicine to fix a broken heart?" I asked.

His face flooded with hope. "I do."

I dug in my pocket and pulled out the cache of pills. "Here." I selected the two Grant's aspirins. "Take these. They're very powerful. Then within the hour I want you to find others suffering like you. Do you know where in Gibraltar to find men in your, er, particular circumstance, Mr. Davitch?"

He bit his lip. "*Oui.* I think so."

"Good. Find them. Share a large carafe of wine. Confess your unhappiness." Talk Barbra Streisand. Share decorating plans.

"That's all?"

"Er, take these too." I handed him the blue pills with a V on them. "But save them for later. The combination will release you from this prison of woe." And the orange ones work wonders for a tension headache as well. Just ask the Grant's brand manager.

"But the, er, woman—"

"You won't forget her, but your feelings will resolve into a painless regard."

"Bless you, Miss Pyle." He tossed the aspirins in his mouth and began chewing.

"Oh, no, it's best—"

His face pinched tight.

"—to take them with water. Oh, well."

"One must suffer for one's love." He swallowed with a shudder. "Good God, I can feel it already."

Ah, the esophageal burn of salicylic acid—often mistaken for efficacy.

I turned to look him straight in the eye. Seph Pyle, seer of truth. "Mr. Davitch, I don't have much time. I've helped you, and now I need you to help me."

"With your buttons?" He looked askance at my unorthodox dress.

"What? No. Well, okay, I guess. But that's not what I meant."

Charles began to rearrange me. "What did you mean?"

"You are an investor in the *Neuf Ouest*."

His face flushed. I hoped it wasn't the pills. "I-I . . ."

"I know you are, Mr. Davitch, and in return for the help I just gave you, I expect the truth."

He shifted. "Aye, Miss Pyle, I am an investor."

"You *and* Admiral Basehart."

"Aye."

"But you hid it from Captain Drummond."

His fingers fumbled. I peeked over my shoulder. His face was filled with shame.

"Basehart," he explained with regret, "wanted quick capital. The best captain for taking enemy ships is Captain Drummond."

"So Basehart arranged for Drummond to get kicked out of the navy?"

"It was only meant to be for a short time," Charles said, taking up the buttons again. "Until the partnership recouped its investment and turned some profit."

"Has it been profitable?"

He hung his head. "Enormously. Miss Pyle, please believe me. We had nothing to do with the missing dispatches. Even if I didn't find the idea of treason appalling, which I do, why would we want to lose the man who was making us rich?"

It was the same conclusion to which I had come after learning of Basehart's and Charles's involvement in the privateer. Basehart's apparent presumption of Drum's guilt could have been a ruse, but greed doesn't lie. For those who suffer from it, money's a primary need, like water or air. There's no way Basehart would let a moneymaker like Drum be hanged unless he really believed him to be guilty of aiding France. My God, what was I saying? Basehart with morals? The sun in Gibraltar must be stronger than I realized.

Charles, on the other hand, I had pegged as an opium importer, perhaps unbeknownst to his partners. An importer with his own drug habit would probably be more than willing to sacrifice a captain or two to keep his operation running smoothly. But now, with that hangdog look on his face, Charles as betrayer of Drum seemed a longshot at best.

Nonetheless, this whole privateer operation had the distinct smell of fraud to it, and I was determined to sniff out whatever I could.

Charles finished the dress, and I reknotted the sash around my waist.

"Perhaps Captain Drummond found out your dirty little secret?" I suggested. "Perhaps you're dabbling in trade the English government would frown on—opium from the Orient, say, or any number of other items upon which you may be forgetting to pay governmental tariffs?"

This was all wild-ass speculation on my part, but it sure sounded good—a sort of weapons-of-mass-destruction approach to detecting.

"No, Miss Pyle. The partnership may have treated Captain Drummond unfairly, but we don't fool around with Her Majesty's coffers. You could go over our books with the finest Chancery Court clerk and you'll not find a single figure amiss."

On this I was going to have to take his word. I practically had to go to bed with my college professor to get a passing grade in accounting.

I pointed a threatening finger in Charles's direction. "Those pills will burn a hole through your stomach if you're lying." Of course they might anyhow, but he didn't need to know that.

Charles blanched.

Damn. Being a detective in the days of superstition and curses was a snap.

"I swear to you," he croaked, "it's the truth."

It probably was—but that didn't mean I was done with him.

"Tell me what you know about Admiral Leake."

"Leake?" Charles stared at me blankly. "I've heard of him, of course. He's one of the navy's old stalwarts. But I don't know any more than that."

I don't know where I was going with this cross-examination. Charles hadn't taken the dispatches. He might smoke a doobie or two, or toss off a *je ne sais quoi* now and again, but it was obvious to me his heart belonged to *le capitaine*. If Charles had taken the dispatches, he'd have gladly returned them by now, if only for a shot at getting a grateful hug at their return.

"Look at this." I dug the inventory out of my pocket.

He eyed it warily. "What about it?"

"Don't you see something rather unusual there?" I was co-opting my ninth-grade study hall teacher's favorite trick: when you think something funny's going on, but you don't know who's doing it, yell "Hey!" and see who looks up.

Charles did not look up.

"Has every appearance of a standard ship's inventory," he said. "The *Neuf Ouest*'s, by the look of it."

Damn. Worked better for my study hall teacher. Caught me passing notes every time. "Don't you think some of that stuff's a little suspicious. Like, what's twenty-three bubbles of molasses?"

"That's 'barrels,' Miss Pyle. 'Bbls' is barrels, not bubbles."

"Oh." I couldn't think of anything more to pump him for. Or could I?

I shifted a bit. "The woman in Toulon, Mr. Davitch. Where does she fit in?"

Charles's head whipped around like a dog who heard a hot dog hitting the floor. "What do you know about the woman in Toulon?"

Well, if there could have been anything more pathetic than the two of us panting for more information on this chick, I don't know what it was. I was nearly too embarrassed to go on.

I said, "She may very well be involved with the dispatches." Lie number 678. This was getting to be a habit. I hardened my gaze with detectivelike scrutiny.

Charles wasn't quite sure whether to buy it. I templed my fingers like the old guy on *Law & Order.* *Ka-ching.* Purchase complete.

"I don't think she'd be involved, Miss Pyle. The last time I saw her, she was *enceinte*—quite so—and dependent on Captain Drummond for support."

That's twice that effing word's come up. It was how Drum said he'd described me when explaining my absence to Basehart. "Under the weather," I think Drum had said. Who knew that second year of French might actually have come in handy.

"She wasn't well then?"

Charles gave me a look. "Not as well as she could have been. You know, Miss Pyle, I do believe that sash would be far more flattering as a shawl."

Leave it to importers to know what would make a girl look good. I pulled it off my waist and tied it in a loose circle around my shoulders.

"Do you think she'll get better?" I didn't want her to die, but a nice, long spell of genital herpes would really hit the spot. I wondered if they had sanitariums in 1706?

"I believe she will be soon. It is good and right for Captain Drummond to do what he can for her, and I respect him for seeing to it. In fact, that was what I told him just a few minutes ago when he asked me to have his will amended."

Huh? I felt like I'd been sucker punched. "You saw Captain Drummond a few minutes ago? Right before I ran into you?"

"No, it was a quarter hour before that."

A quarter hour? Impossible. That would have been exactly when he was in Basehart's quarters with me.

"Where did you see him?" I demanded.

"The same place he's been for the last month, of course. Locked in the Admiralty jail."

Chapter Nineteen

With my heart in my throat, I followed the path Charles had outlined—through the square and left past the inn with red shingles. My shoes crackled with a terrible foreboding. Until this moment, everything in 1706 had transpired under a glow of make-believe, as if I'd been walking in a dream. But there was nothing make-believe now about the cobblestones threatening to twist my ankle or the stench of fish and filth assaulting my nose or the yelping of the dog being thrashed by its owner. I needed to see Drum. And if he had been recaptured, I needed to get him out—quickly.

At the inn, I swung around a wagon full of pans and cauldrons and steamed down a street lined with large, stately oaks. At the end, on a narrow expanse of green situated on what must be the southernmost point of Gibraltar, I saw the long, cheerless brick building of the Admiralty.

I cleared the last tree and gasped. Against the tranquil blue of the sea stood a shiny new gallows. The scent of freshly cut lumber wafted toward me on the breeze.

A vise gripped my chest, squeezing my breath into a tiny, jagged ball that pierced my heart.

On the structure's bottom step a solitary workman wearing a tool-filled apron sat, pulling something from a basket. I ran toward him.

"Who?" I begged, breathing heavily. "Who is the gallows for?"

The man opened a napkin to reveal two rolls and a bowl of—*yeeck!*—sliced beets, the bane of a Norwegian childhood.

"Who *was* this for, you mean," the man said. "You just missed the show."

Ten thousand volts arced through my bowels. "What show? What do you mean?"

"I mean some yellow-bellied sailor just met his maker, m'um. Hope God has more appreciation for the wretch than we did. Bugger broke the bloody beam."

"Who? Not Captain Drummond?"

"No, m'um. His hanging's tomorrow." The man split the roll and began layering beets over it. "That is, should the judge find him guilty, which seems pretty likely. It's not often the hangings are strung together so close—so to speak." He guffawed loudly at this play on words and sucked some juice off his finger.

"Where are they holding the captain?"

The man jabbed a thumb down the rise, toward a small one-story structure set apart from the main building. It was built of stone and sat in the shade of a gloomy beech, with a narrow slit on each side of its wide, barred door. Two armed soldiers stood in front, and a large key hung on a nail in the center of the door. It was a cruel place to hold a sailor. The windows faced the sea, reminding a man every day of what he'd lost.

"'Tis a bit odd for 'im to be put in the Admiralty's jail, I suppose, but it were a crime against England—a heinous one at that for a former captain—so it makes a certain sense."

"I take it you think he's guilty?"

The man clapped the roll shut and gazed thoughtfully at it. "Admiralty says so. Course that only makes it true if you're a sailor. Me being only an honest, God-fearing joiner, I like to draw my own conclusions."

"And your conclusion is?"

He took a large bite and chewed. "Admiralty's in a hellfire hurry to hang a man that used to be one of their own," he said, swallowing. "Either this Drummond's the worst blackguard that ever sailed the seas, or there's more to this than we know."

"Who's pushing on the Admiralty side of things? Someone named Basehart?"

"That old muttonmonger? I doubt it. But the judge is moving faster than rum through a sailor. Why, he set the trial not two days after the man finally got a decent solicitor. And the talk is if the captain's found guilty he'll be hung within the hour. *Quick*'s the word here, and it seems blessed obvious to me that someone with a pocketful of persuasion is encouraging the judge to make it so."

"I want to see the captain."

The man gave me a look that stretched from the top of my window box bodice to the tips of my open-toed shoes. "Man's last day. Normally they wouldn't deny it. But as I said, the Admiralty's all ahoo about this one. Told me the beam had to be fixed if it took all night—not that they offered to pay any more for the hurry, mind ye."

I gazed at the guards in front of the jail. They didn't look like they'd fall for the old "'gullible'-on-the-ceiling" approach.

"You a bettin' man?" I asked.

The joiner cocked his head. "At times."

"I've got a crown that says the soldiers over there won't come to your rescue if you fall off these steps."

A beat or two passed before a big grin spread across his face. "I'll take that wager. But"—he held up a hand—"I'd advise you to wait an hour more."

"Why?"

"One of the guards takes his dinner then—at his mistress's house in town. His wife wonders why he's always so hungry when he gets home. He's usually gone for the rest of the watch. One's easier to distract than two."

I thanked him and gave him the biggest coin in my pocket. Then I strolled toward the seafront, changing direction and galloping around the back of the jail the minute I was out of the guards' view. As I began tiptoeing to the door someone put a hand over my mouth and twisted me up against the wall.

It was Drum.

I threw my arms around him, giddy with relief. "God, you scared me to death." He felt like heaven.

"I spotted you entering the grounds over there." He gestured toward the wall behind me. "Is this where they're holding Drummond?"

It was as if a bomb had gone off in my head. There are few things for which a North Dakotan accent can be mistaken, and an English accent in Queen Anne's day is not one of them.

"*Tom?!*" I yelped. "What in God's name are you doing here?!" We'd swerved into *Back to the Future,* and I was still working my way through *Pirates of the Caribbean.*

His brow furrowed. "You saw me in the admiral's cabin, didn't you?"

My God! That was Tom too?! I began to sink.

He pulled me up. "It seems I came with you."

"H-how?"

"I'm guessing a liberal carry-on policy."

I slapped a hand over my mouth, realizing what had happened. "You were in my arms at the top of the bell tower when I left Venice. Drum thinks that whatever's in my possession when I travel goes with me. Or it could just be one more thing my crazy story has screwed up."

Tom narrowed his eyes. "Crazy story?"

"Nothing," I squeaked. I hadn't mentioned the book to Tom because it was irrelevant. But that's not what I was worried about. I hadn't mentioned Drum to Tom either, and not because it was irrelevant—because it was too relevant! Tom wouldn't need a degree in psychology to figure out why the hero of my story looked like him, and I certainly wasn't ready to deal with that.

Holy hell!

If only I were the type of girl who faints or swoons or even storms off in a snit. But, no, not me. Too pragmatic for any of that. I just stood frozen, gaping at Tom, while the machine gun of panic rat-a-tat-tatted through me and I waited for my head to explode.

If I had wings I could fly away. If I had wings and my head exploded, I'd look like Winged Victory.

"How was the trip?" I asked, smiling.

"Better than the landing. The Clean Water Act wasn't even a gleam in anyone's eye in 1706, was it?"

"You haven't been here for two weeks, have you?!" I imagined Tom wandering the streets of Gibraltar while I'd taken the slow boat to the past. What if he'd already met Drum?! I braced myself for the inevitable question while my ears sizzled like two Fourth of July firecrackers. There may actually have been sparks flying from them. My head was definitely going to blow.

"Oh, no," he assured. "Only an hour or two. I landed in the water next to the admiral's ship. I was treading, trying to figure out what had just happened, when I heard you call to the sailor on the dock to ask what day it was."

Water again. What is it with the folks in charge of time travel? Do they have some kind of copromotion going with the Dry Cleaners Guild?

"Fortunately," Tom went on, "a bunch of sailors were being loaded onto a boat at the dock. I stole one of their ditty bags, ditched my clothes for dry sailor togs and scaled the side of Basehart's ship. At first I thought the man with you was Drummond, but he wasn't at all what I expected. Of course I only saw him from the back, but doesn't Basehart strike you as looking an awful lot like Hairy-Eared Hanlon?"

Blasting alert. Clear the area. "Er, a smidgen, maybe."

"Anyway, when you called him 'Admiral,' that pretty much cleared things up. Once I figured out who he was and where we were, I knew it was too good an opportunity to pass up, so I decided to do a little snooping while you, er . . ." He cleared his throat and the corner of his mouth rose. "Well, while you did whatever it was you were doing over there to solve Basehart's problem."

"'Doing the nasty' doesn't half describe it—and, believe me, half describing is about all you can do when it comes to Basehart's problem. I'll never roll dimes again."

Tom blew out a silent whistle. "Not even nickels, eh?"

"No. And a premature change-maker to boot."

"What can we men say?" He chucked me under the chin. "You're just a woman who inspires a speedy transaction."

"Funny, you've managed to keep your nest egg intact—in cash and hidden under your mattress."

He smiled. "I'm waiting for the free toaster before I open an account."

Hell, I'd give a lot more than a toaster to see that deposit slip again. "Well, you'd better have found something good in Basehart's desk. I deserve battle pay for that bit of hand-to- . . . whatever combat."

"Oh, I found a number of interesting things, but I'm

far more curious about something else." He pinned my shoulders to the wall and brought the laser sights of those blue orbs down on me. The frivolity had left his face. "Why," he asked carefully, "does Basehart think you're pregnant?"

Oh, I did not want to go there. "I'm not pregnant. Don't be silly."

"That's not what I asked." Tom's voice was low and steady, but his eyes betrayed how much sway the answer would have over him. "Basehart's a smart man, and I know you didn't sleep with *him*. Yet he thinks you're pregnant. Why?"

I tried, but I couldn't quite keep my gaze on his. When my eyes dropped, so did Tom's arms. A chill descended over us.

"I see." Tom took a step backward. "I assume we can return together the same way we arrived?"

My throat felt like the Sahara. "Tom, it's not what you think."

"The return, Seph? Will it work the same way?"

"Probably. Tom, please—"

"Have you told Drummond about Barcelona?"

"No, I couldn't. I thought you were—" Oopsie.

"You thought I was what?"

I thought you were Drum. Uh boy, lying to a wronged man is not exactly the way to buy yourself into heaven. "I thought you were going to tell me what was in Basehart's letters. That might make a difference."

"Basehart's in partnership with the privateer owners, which we knew. What we didn't know is that the *Neuf Ouest* is smuggling a cache of rubies into France."

"Rubies?"

"We didn't know it, and apparently neither did Basehart." He shoved a letter into my hand. "There's a cutter heading for Barcelona in the bay. With any luck I can sneak on board. You give the letter to Drummond. I suspect he'll know exactly what it means."

"You're not implying he had something to do with the rubies, are you?"

"I don't have the perspective on his character you do."

"He didn't."

"If you say so."

"Do you honestly think I could care for any man who was a traitor to his own country?"

Tom's face fell. "No," he said quietly, "I don't. He's obviously a man worth traveling the ends of the universe for. That's what hurts."

Tom looked as bad as I felt, which was pretty damned awful. "Listen to me," I said. "Drum's more than just a good man. He's like you."

"God, stop." Tom held up his hands. "You shouldn't have to do this. Seph, you're an incredible person. You deserve to be happy with whomever you choose. Let me get to Barcelona."

"Getting to Barcelona isn't enough. The admiral who saves Barcelona—Leake—is refueling somewhere in Portugal."

"Then I'll go to Portugal."

Anything to leave here, he might have said, for the wish was apparent in his eyes.

"Tom—"

"There's two of us. One has to save Barcelona; one has to rescue Drummond."

"It's not safe for you." Not looking like the most wanted man in Europe.

"Or you," he said. "What choice do we have?"

He was right. I could no more stop him from getting on that ship than he could get me to leave with him. But that didn't make it any easier.

"Take this." I dug Basehart's pistol out of my pocket.

Tom had some pretty clear ideas about guns, but he took it without a second thought and slid the barrel into his belt, hiding the whole thing under his shirttails.

He met my eyes. It was time to say good-bye. We both knew what we had to do.

"I can't let him be hanged, Tom."

He ran a gentle thumb under my eye. Apparently I'd begun to cry.

"Then get in there," he said, "put your arms around him and take him back to Venice with you."

Chapter Twenty

I spent the next hour wrestling with self-loathing and self-doubt, a one-two combo that would have left "Stone Cold" Steve Austin begging for mercy. Only the hasty retreat of Mr. Something on the Side aroused me. A minute later I heard a thump followed by the joiner's horrified "God help me! I'm hurt!" The guard that remained rushed off to his side. The joiner gave me a theatrical wink.

The plan had been for the joiner to beg to be carried to his sister's home for treatment. In a few moments, I heard their footsteps—punctuated by occasional dramatic groans—disappear over the rise.

I swung around the corner, ready to fling myself on the key, only to discover the door partly open.

"Drum," I called, flinging the door the rest of the way open, "let's go—"

He was slouched at a table with a tin cup in his hand,

thinner than before, with dark circles under his eyes. A gorgeous young blonde in a shawl, looking slightly desheveled, sat beside him, with a hand over his. The cot looked like it had been recently used. He saw me and snatched his hand away.

"Persephone!"

"Get up," I demanded. I had just hurt a perfectly wonderful man and for what? An asshole with a chippy in his cell.

He lumbered to his feet. "This is Miss Pyle," he explained to his companion. "Persephone, allow me to present Miss, er . . ." A deer-in-the-headlights look came over his face.

"You can't even remember her name?"

"Please call me Elettra." The woman thrust her hand forward. "Drum hesitated over my family name because I don't use it anymore. My situation would make me an embarrassment to my father."

The shawl dropped away, and for the first time I saw it. She had a firm profile, full lips, rueful gray eyes and a belly heavy with child.

"You're from Toulon," I said, taking her hand. My legs felt like tinder. If I moved I might snap into bits.

"Yes, at present." She bit her lip. "My family lives in England."

"And the child is Drum's."

"No," she said.

"*Yes*," he said.

"Drum tells me you know my father," the young woman said, "so perhaps you'll understand."

"Will I?"

"My father is Admiral Basehart."

I cut my furious gaze to Drum. Through gritted teeth I said, "I need to speak to you—alone."

He gave the woman an apologetic look. "Will you excuse us?"

She nodded and, catching her skirt, disappeared through the door.

I shook my arm loose from Drum's grip. I felt like I'd been slapped, but I'd die before I let him see the effect this revelation had on me. For what sort of man had I hurt Tom? For what sort of man had I risked my own life to return? "Nice of you to let me know."

"It was—and remains—none of your business."

I drew back my hands and shoved him. "Bastard!"

For a long moment we were silent. "I am sorry it displeases you," he said stiffly, "but she has run away and hidden her situation from her father. If it remains a private matter, there is a small chance she may—some-day—be reunited with him."

"And, let's face it, if it doesn't remain a private matter, there's no chance Basehart would support your reinstatement in the navy."

His eyes flashed white-hot lightning. "Incisive as always, milady. Unfortunately for all of us, the point is moot. Now tell me what, if anything, you have discovered about the battle."

"It's in Barcelona," I said flatly.

"Barcelona, eh?" He considered the French strategy with grudging admiration.

"Tom came with me."

Drum's jaw muscle flexed. "Oh?"

"He's sneaking on board a ship heading for Portugal. That's where Leake is. He'll alert the English army." Doing the job *you* should be doing, I wanted to add.

"Oh, thank God." Drum hesitated. "But do you think he's capable of—"

"He's entirely capable of it," I said severely. "And more."

"Tell him to speak to a Major Rooney when he gets there."

"It's too late for me to tell him anything. He's gone."

Drum's face tightened, and his eyes went straight to the narrow window. "What else? Come, come, we don't have much time. What else have you found out?"

I itched to shake that imperious dispassion from him. "Charles Davitch is in love with you."

That did it. Drum dropped his gaze. "I thought he might be," he said after a beat. "He was here a little while ago."

"Does that bother you?"

"No."

"Does it interest you?"

"I regret . . . his pain. There's nothing for me to do about it."

"Are you rewriting your will for her?"

"Her name is Elettra. And yes, I am. What else have you learned?"

"Basehart is an investor in the *Neuf Ouest*."

Drum's eyes widened. Yes, that's right, boyo. There's more going on than even you know.

"I take it you didn't know," I said.

"No, I . . ." Drum stared away, his mind racing.

"And so is Davitch."

"Davitch?" he said.

"Yes. Strange, that. I don't suppose he's the one smuggling rubies into France, though."

"What?"

I handed him the letter. "Tom found this in Basehart's desk."

Drum scanned it once, then again. "Basehart says he doesn't know who's doing it."

"But the rubies made their way into Paris, to fund the French intelligence ranks—and they were traced back to Toulon, the same time the *Neuf Ouest* was in port."

His eyes turned hard again. "Are you accusing me?"

"I would, but Basehart points out in the letter you were laid up with fever at the time and never saw anyone or left the ship. To me that only leaves one person. Does he know his daughter lives in Toulon?"

"No." Drum handed the letter back. "She's not involved. Move on."

"You in a hurry?"

"I'm being hanged tomorrow. Is that motivation enough?"

"Do the guards let your visitors just come and go?"

"For a price."

"Rubies?"

Elettra stuck her head in the door. "Drum, I'm leaving."

"Davitch will come to the inn tonight with the papers," he told her.

"I'm going to find my father. I know he can help."

"Don't," Drum said sharply. "Don't do it."

"I appreciate your concern, but I must decide this on my own. A pleasure to meet you, Miss Pyle." She gave me a warm smile and withdrew.

"Can she save you?" I asked.

"No. She can only hurt herself."

"Oh, but people like doing that for you."

"Christ," he snorted. "Have you been hurt?"

"Yes."

He stopped, surprised. "If that's true," he said softly, "I'm sorry. But what must be done must be done."

"Yes." I straightened my skirt and let my eyes trail to the open door. "Apparently the guards are both bribable and stupid. Why don't you leave?" I was afraid I knew the answer, but if I was going to risk everything with Tom to bring Drum back to Venice, I was determined to know the truth.

"I can't."

"Don't say it's for honor's sake. You've certainly shown that's not a critical issue."

"How you flatter. I wish I could say it is honor that compels me, but it is not."

"So, go. Run. Hide. Let the English navy find another patsy."

"I told you, I can't."

Shit, Seph, say it. "Look, I'm sure Elettra would rather have a live criminal than a dead sea captain. And if you're worried about her not following you, don't. Any woman worth her salt would follow you, wherever you go, whatever your situation."

His eyes shone a beautiful I've Got Blue, Babe. "Would you?"

"Am I here?"

He held out a tentative hand. Against all will, I laid my fingertips over his. The seismic pulse of that tiny contact shook me. He took half a step and waited. After a long pause, I took the other half. He covered my hands with his and touched his forehead to mine.

"I can't go," he said softly, "because I am chained in place. If I could go with you, I would. Elettra is my responsibility, not my heart's desire."

For the first time, I looked down. Below his knee the pant leg had been ripped away, and a heavy iron cuff encircled his ankle. The cuff was tight—too tight—and I could see the swollen black flesh above it as well as streaks of dried blood on his skin and clothes. The table, the chairs, the open door—only the appearance of freedom.

"Oh, Drum."

His hands squeezed mine.

"But the child," I said. "It's yours?"

"No. In the absence of the actual father, however, I claim it."

I felt such a cocktail of relief and admiration I could barely speak. "Why?"

He sighed. "Elettra loved me once. She was but a child, and 'twas a child's notion, but I knew of it and did nothing to dissuade her. When I did not answer her letters or call upon her, she fell in with a charming French fortune hunter here in Gibraltar—charming, that is, until she found herself carrying his child. He

took her to his family in Toulon and there he abandoned her. She wrote to me, and I came to her—as I
should have at the start. Her father believes she ran
away to America to marry a wealthy Boston merchant.
Bad enough, but not as bad as carrying the illegitimate
child of a Frenchman. When I let the French cutter go,
it was because she was on it, and with child—and her
father was a quarter mile off my starboard bow, about
to board it."

We were still forehead to forehead. I smoothed a
lock at his temple. "Foolish, foolish man."

I could feel him smile.

"I think," I said slowly, "you must marry her."

"She refuses. Says she will not drag me down to her
level."

"She is overly scrupulous, I think, given the present
state of your reputation."

He chuckled. "It was a somewhat more attractive
offer when I made it three months ago."

"But your fortune, such as it is, will go to her?"

"My fortune is rather more than even I expected.
And Davitch assures me my share of the *Neuf Ouest*'s
earnings these past months is beyond the law's reach,
no matter what happens tomorrow. Elettra will be well
provided for. Persephone, may I kiss you?"

Our mouths came together before I had time to
answer—in truth, before I had time to think. In Drum's
kiss lived the desperation of farewell. In mine, the
uncomfortable knowledge that saving one man would
estrange me from the other. I would not leave Tom in
1706; make no mistake about that. But my choice to

save Drum, necessary as it was, would leave a chasm between Tom and me that I feared neither time nor effort would erase.

Drum reached to draw me closer, and I pulled away. I needed to mark—and I needed Drum to mark—the import of the line I was about to cross.

"I can save you," I said quietly. "I have *chosen* to save you. Whatever I take into my arms when I travel will travel with me. Which," I added pointedly, "is how Tom ended up here."

Drum met my eyes.

"I was pulled away from Tom to come to you," I said. "And now Tom is braving Lord only knows what in order to get word to Portugal. I will put my arms around you, and kiss you, and take you back to Venice with me, but I will not give up Tom. Not here. Not in the future. And if anything happens to him, so help me, I will never forgive either of us. Do you understand?"

Drum chewed his lip. "If you're asking if I will kiss you without first receiving a promise of marriage, I am willing to take the risk. But if I end up with child, you can expect to hear from my solicitor."

Bastard.

He pulled me into his arms, and my back arched into a graceful, receptive curve under his fingers. His lips brushed my neck and a palm slipped expertly over my breast.

"What exactly," he murmured into the hollow behind my ear, "is your plan once you have us both in Venice? Will we split the favor of your attentions"—the gasp he elicited with the gentle roll of a nipple interrupted him briefly—"or will we serve you in tandem?"

The shoes started to buzz, and so did I. Four insistent hands. Two hungry mouths. And the logging rights to a pair of national park-sized redwoods. All for one tiny size 14 body. Okay, maybe not tiny, but thoroughly and mind-blowingly responsive, which is far more important. I was dizzy with the scene that had already sprung to life in my head. Sheets warmed by the afternoon Venice sun. The earthy scents of pine, sandalwood and lust. The quiet sound of poles plying water. The less quiet sound of poles plying me . . .

"No," I said sharply, and leaped away. Frivolity, a slippery slope—and particularly slippery just now.

"No?" The smile reappeared. "No to splitting—or no to tandem."

"No to both. Let's try to keep ourselves focused here. A kiss—nothing more—with my arms around you, and we'll be transported back."

"But a kiss with your arms out of play"—he laced his fingers around my wrists and began backing me toward the bed—"and we can probably go on like this all night."

The chain reached as far as the cot, I discovered as I barked my shin and we both toppled onto the mattress. Talk about rattling the bed frame. This was going to be like some hardcore version of *Mr. Magoo's Christmas Carol,* with Tom as the ghost of Jacob Marley and me as a very randy ghost of Christmas past.

"This doesn't seem like a good idea," I said. "Doesn't the guard ever come back?"

"It's my last night on Earth. He's hardly going to in-terfere." Drum began unbuttoning his shirt. "Prisoner tradition since time immemorial."

"Hold up there, Mr. Immemorial." I blocked him as he attempted to roll onto me. "I think I'd be more comfortable focusing our efforts on a first night back in my time, eh?" Surely even Laurie Partridge prefers a door with locks.

"You don't want to say our last good-byes here in Gibraltar?"

"No. So kiss me and let's be off."

Drum heaved himself to sitting. His shoulders slumped. "It's not that easy."

And what would be today? "Why?"

"A kiss isn't enough. Every time you came or went, it was because I blew a scrap or two of magic fabric into a flame."

"Magic fabric?" I was thoroughly confused.

"Aye, pink silk or something near to it; I'd never seen the likes of it before—till I saw it there." He pointed to my shoes.

I stared down, aghast. "Let me get this straight. You took fabric from my shoes to make me travel?"

"You have it backward. The fabric made the shoes, which brought you here."

I shook my head. "I don't understand."

"I'd had enough of cabins with walls and monsoons and full moons every night. It was time to get back to my proper job. I told Mrs. Kenney to bring you here to fix things. She poured bits of pink silk into my hand. Then she blew some powder into a lantern and told me to do the same with the silk. Whatever it was cast a spell, a spell which conjured those shoes in your time for you, and brought you here to the *Neuf Ouest*."

"She *conjured* the shoes?" Time travel, yes, but conjuring the world's most perfect sandals in the window of Nine West and stocking them in my size? Even Dumbledore couldn't do that.

"She's a Gypsy, Persephone. I know it's hard to tell since she dresses so plainly, but try to use your imagination."

"But—"

"Only Mrs. Kenney didn't know I'd held a few pieces back, slipped them into my pocket. I wasn't sure they'd work without the powder, but they did. Perhaps not as well . . ."

I snorted.

"Whenever I needed you to come or go, it was a simple matter of surreptitiously blowing a snippet or two into the closest lantern."

"So the time I came back naked? When I left a minute later with Basehart hammering on the door?"

"Lantern." He gazed at me, only marginally contrite. "Lantern in, lantern out."

"But what about the first time I went back, when I was on the balcony of your cabin and you and I almost . . . ?" That one just didn't make any sense. Why on earth would Drum have wanted to get rid of me then?

"Bit of a hasty decision there, I'll admit. Lantern in the middle of the argument which preceded the, er, latter campaign. Kicked myself later, let me tell you."

"But you still kissed me. I mean, you could have stopped me from leaving even after you'd blown the silk in the lantern by somehow avoiding that."

He shrugged. "I couldn't help myself."

Charming devil. "So cough up some more fabric. Let's go."

He shook his head sadly. "I don't have any more."

I felt my heart seizing. "Then why in God's name did you call me back?" If he had stranded me and Tom here, I was going to kill him.

"I didn't. That's why I was so surprised to see you. I had four pieces left, which I thought I could use for at least one more trip for you, here and back. But when they brought me here, they stripped me and searched my clothes. When I got them back, the bits were gone. Someone else called you back." He hung his head. "I'm sorry, Persephone. I feel certain Mrs. Kenney can help."

"Where is she?"

"On the *Neuf Ouest*."

"Is it still here?"

"Aye. The ship's due to weigh anchor when the tide turns tonight, just after the first watch."

"Cripes, give it to me in English, will you!"

He gave me a look. "She sails at midnight would be the Pitsfordian way to put things, I believe."

"Then I'll find her—and be back."

Chapter Twenty-one

I hurried past the gallows and had nearly crested the rise near Drum's cell when I heard the faint "*Pssst.*"

My breath caught. I hoped it was Tom, but it was the joiner, hidden behind the drooping boughs of a massive pine. He had a finger to his lips.

Without a word, I slowed my pace and leaned down casually to pluck a stray bloom in the lawn. A few sailors sharing a story on the walk along the seafront, fifty yards away, were the closest observers.

"Walk around the tree as if you're heading back into town," he whispered.

Whatever concerned him was behind me, then, not in front. I did as he said, and in a moment, when the tree completely blocked me, drew myself up under the boughs.

The joiner leaned against the gnarled, wide trunk. His hand was bandaged tightly, and even in the darkness I could see the bright red that drenched the front of his smock. I swallowed a gasp.

"'Tis nothing, m'um." He brought a crimson finger to his mouth and sucked. "Beet juice."

Suddenly he grew very still. A hand lifted in warning. Over the hill came the voices of two men—one English, one French.

". . . there have been several today," the Englishman said. "Davitch, of course, and a woman fat with child, doubtless trying to lay the little bastard at his doorstep."

"Eez he alone now?"

"Aye."

The men stopped. The nearer of the two was no more than a couple feet from me. Through gaps in the branches, I could see glimpses of their bodies and faces. The Englishman wore a red uniform. He was clearly a soldier of some sort. Despite the warm weather, the Frenchman wore a long gray cloak and had hidden his face under its hood. I held my breath.

The Frenchman asked, "Has he been searched?"

"Aye."

"Will anyone hear him? I won't be long, but I intend to discover what I need to know."

Fear shot through me.

"Only me," the Englishman replied.

Coins jingled out of a pouch.

"But you," the Frenchman purred, handing him the money, "will be far, far away."

"Indeed I will," the Englishman agreed eagerly.

"And you're sure no one else will be coming?"

"He gets his dinner at eight. That gives you at least an hour. No one else will check him until then. But remember, he has to be well enough to stand for his hanging tomorrow."

"I'll remember. *Au revoir.*"

The Englishman turned to go.

"*Pardonnez-moi,*" the Frenchman called.

"What?"

I heard a quick sound like curtains on a runner. *Shoose. Shoose.* The Englishman made a wheezy, wet noise. Then he dropped to his knees, clutching his chest. My veins turned to ice. Rivulets of red ran through his searching fingers.

A bloody knife lay in the Frenchman's leather-clad hand. "Tiresome English curs," he muttered. He wiped the knife on the fallen man's coat and booted him onto his back.

Whistling, the Frenchman grabbed the man's ankles and began backing toward the tree.

The joiner caught me by the elbow and pulled me to the other side of the trunk just as the Frenchman shoved his way through the boughs.

The soldier was still making a vain, whispery attempt to speak. The Frenchman placed a boot on the man's throat and pressed until I heard a nauseating crack. He dug his hand in the man's pocket and removed the coins. Parting the branches, he emerged into the fading light and started toward Drum's cell.

I tried to swallow, tried to speak. Nothing came. I knew I had to save Drum, but my legs felt like boulders. The dead man made a convulsive jerk. Suddenly

my feet could move—in fact, suddenly I couldn't get
out of there fast enough. The joiner caught me. "You're
not going after him, are you?"

"Y-yes."

"He has two pistols. There's nothing you can do,
nothing either of us can do. This is not a matter for
beets."

I couldn't have agreed more.

"You know me, *monsieur.* I can see it in your eyes."

"Your face is unknown to me. Nonetheless, I think
I'd recognize you anywhere. Your stench precedes
you."

Drum was doing a damned fine imitation of a
man without fear, but in his voice I could hear a quaver. Unfortunately hearing was all I could do. I was
pressed against the outside wall of his cell, under the
window.

"Monsieur Davitch sent me. He tells me you've been
extraordinarily successful of late with the *Neuf Ouest*."

"You wouldn't need Davitch to tell you that. You
could have read that in any French broadsheet for the
last three months."

The Frenchman chuckled. "You have a high opinion of yourself, Captain. It's a shame the English navy
doesn't share it."

"What the hell do you want?"

I heard the sound of the slap of leather connecting
with flesh and then immediately the sound of Drum's
groan and a chain being jerked to its full length.

"The beast has spirit. You would have been a favorite of the crowd tomorrow, I have little doubt. In my day, we used to put a noose around a man's neck and pull the rope over the branch of a tree. Doing away with the trapdoor lengthens the show considerably."

"Leave it to the French to overdo everything—including death."

"I want to talk to you about the rubies. Monsieur Davitch says you have them. We've searched your ship. I want to know where they are."

"Why don't you ask Davitch?"

"That would be difficult. Monsieur Davitch is dead."

My stomach knotted. Charles dead?

"You're a liar," Drum said.

"I'm afraid you'll have to take my word on it. Just this afternoon. They found his body in the street. And your cousin has been arrested for his murder."

"My *cousin*?"

My heart stilled under an icy plaster of pain, then broke into a thousand pieces.

"*Oui.* The gendarmes dragged him away. They were talking about . . . er, how does one say, dispatching him tonight. Not much need for a trial after all, not with an upstanding eyewitness."

"An eyewitness? You mean someone you paid to clean up your mess with a few well-placed lies."

"This eyewitness is sterling. In fact, he's a colleague of yours. One of your men."

Tom hanged? I was going to be ill. My vision started to swim, and I sank to the ground.

"You do not mind, then, if I search you, *monsieur?*"

"Dare you get that close? You look like you fight like a girl."

"Perhaps there are things you shall do like a girl as well. Remove your shirt before I put a ball through your heart."

"Look to your heart's content. You'll find no rubies here."

I heard the sound of a shirt being thrown.

"What is that?" the Frenchman yelped.

"The tattoo of a hawk. Are your eyes failing you?"

"With a fish in its talons?"

"Indeed."

"My youngest brother was shot in the Battle of Gibraltar, when the English navy stormed his ship. The men surrendered. The flag was lowered. My brother should have received medical attention. But an officer, a man with the tattoo of a hawk on his shoulder, ran a cutlass through his heart, dragged him to the side and tossed him into the sea."

"That's a lie. There were no shots fired after the French flag was lowered—except your brother's. He hit one of my midshipmen. I told him to give up his pistols. Told him twice. He refused. He took aim. I killed him. He did not suffer."

"Well, I did. And now so shall you."

The rock I'd been resting on tipped over, scraping the wall of the cell.

"*Qu'est-ce que c'est?* Did you hear that?"

I scrambled out of sight just as the jail's door swung open.

I held my breath so hard I thought I'd swallow my tongue.

I heard the Frenchman's footsteps move to the left and right. A half minute passed. If he decided to check around the corner, I was a goner. The footsteps retreated.

Davitch was dead, Tom might be too, and Drum's life was hanging by a thread. I needed to think of something fast.

I heard the boom of a pistol followed instantly by Drum's sudden, anguished cry. All rational thought flew from my head. I leaped to my feet and stared directly in the window. I could see the Frenchman's back. The pistol in his hand was pointed at Drum, and Drum was hunched over his ankle cuff. Blood was pouring down his foot and over the floor.

"The iron absorbs a good deal of the force of the pistol ball, Captain, but there's still enough to exert some fine punishment, wouldn't you say?"

Drum did not lift his head, but I could see the faint tremble of his back. "Go to hell, Gabin," he groaned.

Gabin?! The French head of intelligence who would flog a woman's children to gain her confession?

The Frenchman laughed and began to reload. "I've got a dozen pistol balls here, Captain. By the fourth, the arteries supplying your foot will be crushed. By the eighth, I'll be plinking off bone. By the twelfth . . . Well, by twelfth I'll know where those rubies are or you'll be offering me your mother's life for a chance to turn the last ball on yourself."

He lifted the pistol, cocked it, then steadied it to aim. Drum didn't bother looking up. Gabin was going to shoot right through Drum's fingers to the cuff.

My brain exploded into autopilot.

I burst through the door screaming and launched myself into him. We fell to the ground and the pistol fired into the wall, sending up a spray of chips. Drum lunged for Gabin's neck, but Gabin was too quick. He rolled just out of reach and onto his feet. The spent pistol was useless; Gabin flung it aside and pulled the second from his belt. A shiver went through me as the barrel brushed my temple.

"Acquaintance of yours, Drummond?" Gabin caught me by the hair and pulled me to my feet.

"I've never seen her before."

"I don't believe you." With a bile-liquefying moan, he brought a handful of my hair to his face and inhaled. He reeked of garlic and sour wine. Then, with the steel drilling tighter into my head, he spun me around and pulled my back up against him.

Drum was crouched like a panther, eyes daggered on his subject. Only for an instant, when his gaze traveled to mine, did I see the terror there, under the cold, icy murder he wished for his tormentor.

Gabin rocked me against his hips. "*Très belle.*" He jerked a hand deep into my bodice and I gasped.

Drum flew in the air but the chain snapped and felled him.

"Fool." Gabin laughed.

The barrel was cutting into my flesh, and I could feel the sweat welling under my shaking shoulder blades.

Gabin's hot palm cradled my breast. The ice in Drum's eyes had turned to absolute zero.

"I'll kill you," Drum said. "I'll tear out your heart and shove it down your throat. Let her go."

Gabin snorted. "You'll do no such thing." He reached into his pocket and tossed a wad of burlap in Drum's direction. "Put that over your head."

Drum didn't move. Fury lit every angle of his face.

"Put it on and she might live." Gabin drew his palm over my hip. My knees started to give way.

"No," Drum said.

I don't know if he was warning Gabin or encouraging me.

"Have you heard a woman beg for her lover's life?" Gabin cocked the pistol.

"*Don't!*"

Gabin paused, grinning at Drum's long-awaited panic. Gabin pointed to the floor. He had thrown a sack. With a look of dead despair, Drum picked it up and pulled it slowly over his head.

"Now tie it around your neck," Gabin instructed. "That's right. With a strong knot. Now knot it again. And again." Gabin lowered his lips to my shoulder and kissed me. "I've tried it many ways, but I think it's best when the man can hear but not see."

He turned me and brought his mouth to mine, thrusting with a scaly tongue. I shoved my knee into his testicles—or would have if he hadn't turned at the last minute. He whipped the pistol across my cheek. I yelped, and Drum clattered to his feet, clawing at the sack.

"Leave it on! Leave it on!" Gabin cried. "If the hood comes off, the first sight you'll see is her blood being splattered against the wall."

A long moment passed.

"Persephone?" A sea of sorrow lay in Drum's question.

I raised my hand to my face and brought away blood. "I'm okay. It'll be okay." I wondered if I might faint. I wondered if I'd die.

Drum breathed like a boxer. He stood and wiped his palms slowly on his trousers. "I know where the rubies are. Let her go. I'll tell you."

"Oh, I imagine you do," Gabin replied. "And I imagine I'll know too before this is all over. Now lie down, *ma petite*."

I knew if I lay down, Drum and I would be dead. We might both be dead in any case, but I wasn't going out without a struggle, or at least the pretense of one.

I lifted my heel and drove it directly onto Gabin's foot.

He squealed. I wrenched myself out of his hold, and stuck my hand in my pocket.

"I've got a pistol too."

Gabin looked down at the protrusion. How much did a silk-covered speculum look like an eighteenth-century pistol? Enough, I hoped, to buy me a moment or two to regroup.

I angled myself slowly, keeping the speculum aimed directly at Gabin's heart. Each step I took forced him to readjust his stance to keep me in view. If I could keep his eyes on me, and keep him unaware of how close he was getting to Drum, it might just be possible for Drum to leap. I hoped Drum could sense what I was doing.

"I think you're lying." Gabin was a good poker player.

"Then I guess I'm just going to have to shoot you."

I raised the "barrel." One more step. One more. He was almost directly in front of Drum. All at once Gabin caught on. He stopped moving, and a large smile spread across his face.

"*Oui*," he said. "Shoot me."

My idea bank was overdrawn. I did the only thing I could think of. I pulled the speculum out of my pocket, took aim and—

The explosion rattled my ears and a small hole appeared on Gabin's chest.

Jesus, no wonder gynecologists made me nervous. Gabin folded to the floor. In my peripheral vision I caught a large form.

"Let's move, folks." Tom stood in the doorway, holding a smoking pistol. "I've got a carriage waiting on the greens and we've got about two minutes before a very angry welcome party arrives."

A carefully aimed shot from Tom's pistol had been enough to break Drum's leg chain. Now Tom was like a border collie on caffeine, herding us at top speed toward the waiting carriage. Drum hung onto Tom's side, shirttails flying, using Tom's shoulder for support, and I was on Tom's other side, holding his hand. I was so happy he hadn't been dispatched. I squeezed his hand. He squeezed back.

Drum's foot could support him but not well. I knew that ankle required medical attention, but for now we just needed to get him to the carriage. Tom shoved us bodily in through the open door and leaped in behind just as the horses jerked to a violent start.

"The sack, the sack," Drum called. "Get it off me."

I dropped to my knees as Tom drew a blade from his belt. As he cut, I used the light of carriage lanterns to take a closer look at Drum's leg. "He needs to have the iron cut off. It was biting into his ankle before, but now it's worse. Much worse." The flesh looked like hamburger, and blood poured freely from the wound. Where the pistol ball had hit it, the iron was dimpled deeply into the meaty mess. The ankle was already starting to swell. Note to self: no more cannibal burgers at Eat'n Park.

"Did you hear me?" I repeated. "He needs to have the iron cut off."

Tom didn't answer. An eerie silence had fallen over the confined box.

All at once my heart did a high jump into my throat. I lifted my head.

My companions stared at one another in fascinated shock.

"Seph?" Tom gestured weakly in Drum's direction. "He . . . he . . ."

For his part, Drum snorted, shaking his head.

"He looks like *me*," Tom finally exclaimed.

"Correction, sir." Drum buttoned his shirt and

crossed his arms. "You look like *me*. I believe I have the advantage of age and experience."

"At three-hundred-some-odd, I'm going to have to give you that. Seph, would you care to introduce us?"

About as much as I'd care to have a fondue fork shoved through my cheek. "Of course," I said cheerily. "Tom, this is Phillip, er, George Drummond, captain of the *Neuf Ouest*. Drum, this is Tom Fraser, an attorney at my company. He is my colleague in commerce."

Have you ever seen two lions circle? Tom gave his best ferocious-officer-of-the-court impression, and Drum looked as if he were standing on his quarterdeck, leading troops into the Battle of Trafalgar.

I cleared my throat. "Acknowledgments, gentlemen?"

Twin jutting of hole-punched chins.

"Captain," Tom managed, teeth bared.

"Counselor," Drum returned sourly.

Neither extended a hand.

The next instant the carriage veered down a cobbled path, slowed and stopped.

I looked at Tom. "What the . . . ?"

"An empty carriage house," he said, and jumped from the box.

In a moment we were inside. Tom paid off the driver and for the first time since I returned, I felt I was safe. Drum stood at a window, staring out toward the harbor. Tom pulled me firmly to the side.

"Who is he, Seph?" Tom whispered, irritated. "Or perhaps I should say, *how* is he? How in the hell did he come to look just like me, and, more important, why hasn't this come up before?"

"Tom—" I tilted my head in Drum's direction. "Perhaps this is best discussed another time. We need to get him to a doctor."

"Oh, no." Drum, who had been listening, gave a large, permissive wave. "Pray continue."

Tom caught the look on Drum's face and locked eyes with him. "You knew about this?"

"I did not." Drum flicked a bit of lint off his coat. "But in truth it does not surprise me. I am, after all, the culmination of her ideal."

"Her *what*?" Tom's head swung back and forth.

Shit.

"Oh, aye," Drum continued. "I can see you provided the raw materials—a sort of supply yard from which she chose features, height, hair color and so on. I am the finished vessel."

The veins in Tom's neck bulged dangerously. "That man is . . . *me*?"

"Only better." Drum smiled.

"*Seph!*"

"Look," I said, "can we talk about this calmly?"

Four sharp blue eyes bore down on me.

I laid out an approach in my head. "Okay, it seems there's a book—"

"Of which Persephone is the author," Drum said.

Tom blinked. "You've written a book?"

I held up a corrective finger. "I haven't written it yet. But it involves a hero—"

"I," Drum stated.

"—and a heroine— *Oh!*"

Suddenly it hit me. *I* was the heroine. Drum grinned

as he watched the understanding bury me like a tidal wave.

"A heroine," Drum said, "who just happens to be—"

"—an admiral's daughter," I put in quickly. "A sea captain and an admiral's daughter. On the beautiful Mediterranean. They meet. They fall in love. They marry. It's a romance."

"That is not how it goes," Drum said.

"How *does* it go, Captain?" Tom's eyes were growing flintier by the second.

"Time out, everyone." I made my hands into a *T*. "Tom, there's more to my traveling than . . . well, just being here."

Drum muttered, "Bloody understatement."

"Apparently there's a book in me," I said, "and, well, frankly, a lot of the characters around here seem to have popped right out of my head."

"Out of your *head*?" The flint exploded into prosecutorial fire. "Like Athena out of Zeus's headache?"

Clapping his thigh, Drum whooped. "My friend, you have brought your metaphorical shot home."

"Popped out of my head," I repeated louder, "and took shape here."

"If one considers chaos to be a shape," Drum said.

"I had some, well, I guess you'd have to call them underdeveloped ideas on how a ship would run, how the weather works—"

"And how to control a cursed character." Drum's eyes blazed. "The fact of the matter is, one of her particularly ridiculous creations caused me to lose my commission."

"Did you not lose your commission letting a French cutter escape?" Tom asked. If he had had a legal pad in front of him he would have referred to it in a show of feigned confusion.

Drum shifted into a superb show of eighteenth-century backpedaling. "Er, perhaps I should have said this creation kept me from *regaining* my commission. I was forced to touch at Gibraltar to take her on, this most improbable sort of woman. She and her companions swarmed the ship, and in fairly short order the dispatches were stolen."

"Stolen, you say." Tom tapped his chin. "Yet found later in your desk?"

"The point is," I interrupted, "some of the people on the *Neuf Ouest* were my creation. I wreaked havoc on Drum's command and someone—we don't know who—took the dispatches Drum was supposed to deliver. Whatever's going on here in the past, the plot of a book I've barely even thought about, much less written, has altered things, and we need to fix them. Oh, Tom," I cried, "can you ever believe me?"

Tom snorted. "I'm standing here with a sea captain who looks like me at a bad Halloween party. I had to listen to some sort of revolting hybrid of Admiral Nelson and the Marquis de Sade force Seph to engage in what amounted to soft-core porn. I've popped a minor historical figure. And not only is my girlfriend traipsing through Europe wearing shoes that could whip up frozen margaritas, she's emblazoned with two tattoos of which neither I nor disconcertingly *she* can name the origin. At this point, so long as someone doesn't turn me into a velociraptor or drop me in the *Millennium Falcon*, I think just about anything else goes."

He'd said "girlfriend." I smiled.

"*Two* tattoos?" Drum glanced at my ankle. "Where's the other?"

I cleared my throat and pointed discreetly to my breast.

Tom crossed his arms and gave Drum an eminently self-satisfied look.

"All right, guys." I felt like an art teacher trying to explain the finer points of pointillism to the varsity lacrosse team. "Here's what's important—"

"I'll tell you what's important," Tom interrupted. "Screw the dispatches. I don't give a damn about Captain Drummond's reputation. He's free. What he does next is up to him. What does matter is that we get to Admiral Leake in Portugal or to Barcelona before the French. I've had a taste of French hospitality tonight, and I've got no desire to see if an extra three hundred years of world domination improves their manners."

Drum lit a second lantern, and in the light I noticed for the first time the unhealthy gray cast to Tom's face.

"Oh, God, what did they do to you? What happened?" I yanked his jacket open to look for blood or a wound.

"Nothing." Tom stiffened under my touch. "Nothing you can see." In answer to my horrified look he added, "I was outside the wharfmaster's office, trying to steal a look at ship itineraries, when I saw a man coming out dressed in a turquoise jacket and a pair of blue trousers that would have done Elton John proud."

"I don't know who Elton John is," Drum said quietly, "but the man you describe is undoubtedly my friend Charles Davitch, a popinjay in the matter of clothing. Is he dead?"

A heavy pause. Tom nodded.

Drum's shoulders dropped.

"I wouldn't have paid much attention to him," Tom went on, "but he happened to mention your name, Captain, when he left the master's office. I watched him walk away, and was just about to hurry off myself, when I noticed two very questionable-looking gentlemen, including the one we left on the floor of the jail just now, standing across the street in front of a tavern. They stopped their conversation and began to follow him. Believe me, I had no desire to entangle myself in anything more, but by that time I had determined that the ship I wanted didn't sail until the tide went out, and your friend looked way out of his league."

Tom's fists were balled, knuckles white.

"I followed them down a narrow alley," he went on, "where they proceeded to pull a gun on your friend. I pulled out Basehart's pistol, which Seph had liberated from his cabin earlier, and told them to stop. Next thing I knew a garrote was around my neck. Apparently a third member of their party had followed behind me."

I opened Tom's collar. Below the dirty linen, a bright purple line circled his neck. His hand grasped mine as I pressed it gently against the wound.

"They didn't kill me," he said after a beat. "They had other plans. They took the pistol, tied me up and, while he pleaded for his life, shot Davitch in each knee, a cheek, a hand and then between the eyes. Then they left. The militia arrived a few minutes later and arrested me."

"Believing you'd killed a man while tied up?" I asked, incredulous.

"It wouldn't hold up in an American court, but apparently means is not a requirement for robust prosecution in England. Besides, the militiamen were not in the mood for debate. They had an eyewitness, a sailor of yours, Captain, who saw me follow Davitch into the alley. The sailor clearly assumed I was your cousin—which now, of course, doesn't surprise me—for they accused me of having a connection to you from the moment they arrived."

I felt the contents of my stomach begin to crawl up my throat. Davitch tortured and dead. Tom garroted. Drum bleeding.

"How did you get away?" I demanded.

"Interesting, that. They were not in the mood for a lengthy trial. I'm not sure a trial was even in the off-ing. But just as they were shoving me into a cell, a fight broke out among a gang of drunken sailors who'd been hauled in for putting two horses, a peacock, a herd of sheep and a dead swordfish in the upstairs parlor of the colonial governor while he was dining in town. Fists were flying, desks were being overturned, then all at once someone yelled "Plague rats!" and I nearly got trampled to death in the ensuing rush. I don't think there were any rats, but to keep the crowd from complete disappointment, one of the sailors dashed a lantern into a pile of papers on his way out. I gave the first militiaman I saw an upper right, lifted his pistol and purse, and ran. I hired a carriage, and here we are."

"And what made you run to us, counselor?" Drum asked.

I don't think he cared much for Drum's tone or his use of the word *us,* but Tom said, "Right before he put the barrel to Davitch's head, he asked who had the ship's inventory list. To his credit, Davitch never answered, but when he was dead, the man with Gabin said he'd seen a woman with Davitch earlier in the day and that another of their party had followed her to the jail."

Me. I paled, thinking of that chilling "Lie down, *ma petite.*"

Drum met Tom's gaze. If Tom was trying to stake his claim as my rightful suitor, his actions the last few hours had certainly earned him that place. The look on Drum's face showed not only burgeoning respect, but the changing calculation of the threat Tom posed as a rival.

"Please accept my heartfelt gratitude," Drum said. There was grudging appreciation in his voice. "I had no desire to end my life in that cell."

Tom nodded. Drum gave me a look. "I think we shall all rest a little easier knowing Gabin is dead, won't we, Persephone?"

"He's not," Tom said.

Drum's and my heads snapped up.

"Not the Gabin you're thinking of. That was Gabin's older brother," Tom explained. "Gabin—the French intelligence agent and the man who put the bullet in Davitch's brains—is on his way to the *Neuf Ouest*. To blow it up."

Chapter Twenty-two

We stood at the end of a narrow street that ran behind the carriage house. Ahead of us the harbor twinkled beneath the star-filled sky. Drum limped forward a step or two, wincing.

"I can see the *Neuf Ouest*," he said. "She's there, with her sails reefed."

Tom's face took on an admiring glow as he watched the red and green deck lanterns swing gently in the night breeze. "She's beautiful."

"Twelve knots on a high sea," Drum said with obvious pride. "As easy as anything."

"And you think Haverhill's in charge?" I said.

Drum nodded. "That's what Davitch told me. In any case, it makes sense. Haverhill would be next in line."

"Tell me this," Tom said to Drum, crossing his arms contemplatively. "If you were going to blow her up, what would you do?"

"Well, it's not as easy as you might think," Drum answered, equally as thoughtful. "A cannonball through her waist would claw her up dreadfully, and she might sink—but she wouldn't explode. There's nothing in her now but water, stores, ballast and whatever load she's taken on to deliver."

"You're right," Tom said, as the realization came over him. "There can't be an explosion without gunpowder."

"I did see the *Goodwill* lose half her quarterdeck and the mizzenmast once after their cook let a vat of molasses boil over," Drum said, "but in general, aye, one needs gunpowder. Even a fire, though, won't necessarily make her explode. Not unless she's taken on her gunpowder. And the *Neuf Ouest* won't take on her powder until she's on her way out of the harbor. At the powder hoy—there—to the southwest."

We looked in the direction of a large, octagonal-shaped floating structure about a quarter mile away.

"Harbormasters generally keep the powder as far from the docks as possible," Drum explained. "Too many careless captains."

I thought of poor Haverhill's navigational ability. If we didn't do something, the harbormaster was going to need some earplugs and a very long fire hose.

"How close are the ramparts to the powder hoy?" Tom asked.

"Ramparts?" I cocked my head.

Tom pointed to the line of gleaming cannons on a finger of land curled around the far end of the harbor.

"You don't think . . ." Understanding dawned on Drum's face. "No. Impossible. Gabin couldn't get to them. No one can touch the cannons but the English soldiers—"

"Or someone who's bribed or murdered one," Tom replied. "That's the only way I can imagine they'd be able to ignite the gunpowder."

I said, "But Gabin's associate said they were looking for rubies on board the *Neuf Ouest,* and couldn't find them. In that case, why would they blow it up?"

"Maybe there's something worse on board they want to get rid of."

"Something incriminating?"

Drum snapped his fingers. "The codebook! Remember I told you I'd captured a codebook from a French ship? Well, it's on board—hidden, of course—waiting for a time I could turn it over. Perhaps they know it's there."

"Maybe there's something else, something one of the passengers has."

"No. It has to be the codebook. Nothing else would make blowing up the ship worthwhile."

"How about revenge?" Tom said. The look on his face suggested he could easily imagine someone with an explosion-sized grudge against Drum. "Does Gabin have a daughter?"

"No," Drum growled. "Nor," he added pointedly, "does he have a woman he thinks he possesses but doesn't."

All-righty. This was getting us nowhere. "We need a plan, gentleman. And since none appears to be forthcoming from either of you, let me suggest this: each of you is wanted by the authorities—urgently wanted,

I might add—so you'll need to keep your heads down and carry pistols. Drum's got to get that leg iron off and his ankle treated. I'm sure he'll know a place that can help. Meanwhile, Tom, you think of a way to get us on the ship—"

"The one that's going to be blown up?"

"Not if we can convince them not to take on the powder."

"So we can just be sunk instead?"

"Okay, the plan has a few rough spots. But we have to get on. The only way for any of us to get back is to score some pink taffeta from the crazy Gypsy on board."

A vein in Tom's forehead jumped. "What?"

"Hey." I held up my hands. "No *Millennium Falcon*. Midnight's three hours away. Let's meet back here at eleven. Go."

"What, pray tell, is 'soft-core porn'?"

We were seated in the back office of Drum's friend Abdul, whose shuttered business resided in one of the more questionable districts of Gibraltar, when Drum asked this question.

I hesitated. How does one explain the difference between *Sex and the City* and *Lisa Does Liverpool* to an eighteenth-century sea captain? "Well . . ." I felt my cheeks begin to turn a bright Grateful Red. "Um . . ."

"Oh, for heaven's sake, I know it's something in the line of fornication. I could deduce that much from the context. I'm trying to ascertain if what Basehart did to you is a matter for murder, a duel, or mere envy."

"Er, let's stick with envy. Basehart did not distinguish himself in battle."

A gentlemanly attempt to suppress his curiosity ended in vain. "Churlish? Ungrateful? Ham-fisted?"

"Yes, yes and yes. Let us never speak of it again."

Abdul returned from his front office with alcohol and cotton wool in hand and bandaged Drum's ankle after mixing a stiff whiskey for me. Abdul appeared to be a man of many talents, most of which I pray never to have to avail myself of. His workshop table was covered with several identical jade Buddhas, an assortment of knives and needles, incense, dirty rags, a squat bejeweled wine decanter from which I expected at any moment to see the smoky materialization of Barbara Eden, oranges with pins stuck in them, several paint pots and a large, extremely scary-looking machete. Upstairs, I heard the sound of footsteps. Abdul said it was his family. I pictured an opium den.

"You're a Buddhist?" I said hopefully. Machetes don't mix with reincarnation.

He scratched his chest unrestrainedly with an ink-stained finger. "I no religion."

Darn.

"His ankle not broken," Abdul explained. "The flesh bad, though. Like kibbee. You change dressing every day. You understand?"

"We understand," Drum said.

"How much do we owe you?" I dug in my pocket.

"No money. Abdul not take money from Captain Drummond."

"Thank you." Drum struggled to his feet. He still

limped a little. "I'm going to check the street. Abdul, you check the alleyway."

Ignoring the implicit instruction to stay where I was, I followed Abdul's white-robed form into the darkness.

Abdul stopped by a triple-secured door. "Captain Drummond say you no wife—"

You'd get no argument from me on that one.

"—not even one-night wife."

Now there's a marketing idea. The one-night wife: four lasagnas into the freezer, sheets and underwear laundered, girlish approval of the tie your mother gave you, lap dance during half time, quick finish over the back of Barcalounger. Four-hour minimum; a hundred bucks an hour. Rapt attention during two "humorous" work stories—$50 extra.

Now there's the sort of marriage I might be able to manage.

"How *did* Captain Drummond explain me, Abdul?" I asked, curious.

Abdul slitted the blinds and scanned the alley. "He called you his compatriot."

Seph Pyle. Brand manager, writer, historical asskicker, compatriot. I liked it.

"Abdul, come take a look." Drum hobbled back from the front of the shop. "I thought I saw two men in the shadows."

"Stay back, both of you." Abdul grabbed a bucket of dirty water, lumbered through the front room and opened the door. Yawning, he flung the contents in the street. A shopkeeper at the end of a long day.

When he closed the door, he whispered, "They are

bad men. The sort that will do anything for a few pieces of gold. There are usually four of them. Their friends are in the alley even if we cannot see them. You must stay."

"No," I said. "We have to get back." The gilt clock on Abdul's shelf—stolen, I presume—read half past ten. We needed to meet Tom in thirty minutes; the ship sailed in ninety.

Drum met my eye. "We can't do anything foolish. If we're late, Tom can take care of himself."

"I'm certain he can," I said. "But I intend to be on that ship. I have an idea. Abdul, I'll need your help."

I squashed my eyes closed, trying to pretend I was not standing in Abdul's brightly lit upstairs bedroom wearing nothing but his oversized caftan and my chemise. Not that the yellow and orange gauze hung in gently swaying panels over the large round bed before me was unpleasant—the Moroccan look has always been one of my favorites on *Trading Spaces*—but I could have lived the rest of my life not knowing Abdul wore a hot pink caftan in private and that his bed offered room for four.

"Too breezy for you?" Drum asked.

"I'll live. The window has to be open or else this won't work."

"And you're sure this is an effective tactic?"

"Hey, variations of it have appeared in at least two romance novels I've read. In one, the painter uses a plaster model to make the imperious diplomat's daughter think he's focusing his artistic attentions on another woman, thereby driving her insane with jealousy. In the other, the baron's bastard son keeps the soldiers sent by the marquis from following the marquis's daughter, who must escape to Scotland so that she might marry the son of the baron, by making them think she's with him. Diversion of the finest sort."

"And to think I wasted my time on Caesar's *Gallic Wars*."

"C'mon, let's get going so we can get back to the ship."

Drum unfolded my arms and slipped his underneath. The shoes began to vibrate. He angled his head and examined me, instantly spot-welding something in my belly to my knees. He kissed me unhurriedly.

Dag! Come to think of it, we could probably spare five minutes for this. Drum's body felt as warm and welcoming as a feather bed.

His hands came to rest on my hips.

"Is that necessary?" I whispered.

"I felt the realistic details would help."

"Nothing below my neckline shows from the street."

"But consider the indirect effect on your face."

"How would you like to consider the indirect effect of a knee in your groin?"

"Now remove her caftan," Abdul instructed from where he sat cross-legged on the floor. "Slowly."

Drum's mouth rose appreciatively. "I wouldn't have it any other way."

The two women at Abdul's side—stolen, I presume—giggled.

"Not so loud," Abdul warned them. "They can hear it in the street. Are they still there, Captain?"

Drum turned me in profile to the window, skimming my neck with his mouth and slowly kissing the fabric off my shoulders. "Aye, I can see the two."

I lifted his chin up. "That's not the two Abdul was talking about."

"Two," Drum said through his teeth. "In the street, aye."

"The caftan." Abdul grinned. "Easy and slow."

It was clear Abdul found the role of director hugely entertaining.

Drum let the silk cascade through his fingers.

"Now her chemise," Abdul said. "Tell me, Drummond, have you unbuttoned a chemise before?"

"Never," he said. "Not a one."

The girls tittered.

Abdul said, "Ah, let me help. You must balance between too slow, the sin of old men and cowards, and too fast, the sin of boys and the self-absorbed."

"Oh, gosh," I said under my breath, "I can see where this one's going to net out."

"Quiet," Drum said, trying to work the first button. "I can barely manipulate the slippery devils, and Lord knows I'm not old."

After the third button I caught his hand. "That'll do. We only need to be able to drop it off my shoulders not all the way to the floor."

He pushed the straps off, one at a time, and took a step back. He did such a damn fine impression of a man taking in a work of art that I began to wonder exactly how much light the lantern at my back was throwing.

"Drink her in," Abdul called. "You must give our friends the impression of a night to end all nights."

"Abdul," Drum said without altering his face, "might you spare a pomegranate?"

"No time for food. This is the moment you have waited long for. Put the question in your eyes."

The top of the treasure map X peeked over the edge of my gown. Drum ran a thumb over it. The mischief disappeared from his face. In a voice so soft only I could hear, he said, "He has possessed you?"

"That's right," Abdul said. "Look as if everything depends on her answer."

I thought of that countertop in the hotel bathroom. Who knew the best water feature in Venice would be a sink? It wasn't possession in the fullest sense of the word, but it was more than the first step on the path there. "Yes."

"But still . . ." Drum looked deep into my eyes. "Your heart is not fully committed."

"Gee, are you going to guess what card I'm thinking of next?"

"You didn't answer."

"Was it a question? I thought you could read my thoughts?"

"At times I can. Not always, and hardly at all since you've arrived. Though to be truthful, one doesn't need to be much of a mind reader to see the answer."

"Meaning?"

"Meaning, I see enough to know even the most tempting kiss won't change your mind about Tom, though I'm more than willing to try."

His lips settling on mine for a moment. A man taking the first taste of an exquisite champagne. My knees turned to Brie.

"Eight of diamonds," he whispered.

"Hey!" I shoved him back. "Knock it off! How do you do that anyhow?"

"Your thoughts are like the aurora borealis at my horizon. A beautiful but unreadable miasma that occasionally offers great flashes of clarity."

"Action, please," one of Abdul's women demanded. "She fall asleep."

Abdul began, "Now I think—"

"I can take it from here." Drum lifted me into his arms, kissed me with abandon, then dropped us both on the feather bed hard enough to make the lanterns swing.

The women made silent cheers. One of them—the woman who'd demanded more action—crawled to a heavy chair and sat beside it. Abdul ducked into another upstairs room.

"I see no one in the alley," he whispered when he returned. "But let's be certain." He tiptoed to the other bedroom window and peeked. "All four are in the street, elbowing each other and pointing. Perfect! The alleyway is clear!"

He nodded to the women. The first scraped the chair across the floor. Back and forth, back and forth. At each 'forth' motion, the other woman let out an earthy gasp.

Drum and I slithered into the hall and stood. I slipped into my regular gown.

"How long should we keep this up, friend?" Abdul asked as Drum worked to close my buttons. "Your reputation is leonine, is it not?"

"Aren't lions like ten seconds?" I said under my breath.

Drum colored. "Er, a quarter of an hour should suffice."

Abdul shook his head sadly. "You Englishmen. At least I shall do your reputation the honor of a second campaign. And a third." The women giggled.

"It is her reputation you will honor, friend." Drum clasped my hand and began down the stairs. "Hers and hers alone."

"Good-bye, Drummond," Abdul said, waving. "Good-bye, Miss Pyle."

"Good-bye, and thank you."

"Don't thank me. I only provided the props." Abdul gave me a sly wink. "Keep an eye on your compatriot."

Chapter Twenty-three

With much relief, I saw Tom emerge from the shadows exactly at eleven. His gaze went to the competent bandaging on Drum's foot, but he asked no questions as to how, when, or where. A spyglass peeked from under his arm.

"Haverhill is captaining her," Tom said. He handed the glass to Drum, who put it to his eye.

"Good," Drum said. "There should be no problem getting on board then."

"The officers in town are looking for us. Sentries have been posted at the dock there"—Tom pointed— "there, and there."

"Small matter of maneuvering past them. Perhaps over the water in a small boat, then up—"

"Not so fast," Tom said. "Rumor has it Haverhill has taken on a pilot."

"A pilot—for this harbor? Even Haverhill should

be able to manage this one without too much hand-wringing."

I looked at the open bay. The docks were crowded with anchored ships, but I could see that less than a hundred yards out the moonlit waters were open. I looked at the fat moon above us with a soaring heart. But I was wrong. It wasn't the moon of before, when this story was under the full, if somewhat misguided, control of its author. It was a three-quarters moon, waxing or waning. I could never remember which was which.

"According to what I heard," Tom said, "the harbormaster required it. The pilot and his party boarded an hour ago. They are to stay on the ship until it takes on its powder stores, then debark on the far rampart."

"About a minute before an accidental cannon firing sends everything on board in a million different directions," I said. "Sounds like the harbormaster has some unsavory friends."

Drum nodded at Tom. "Good work, counselor. But how do we get on board?"

"Well, I've been watching the ships preparing for departure," Tom said. "Even if every hatch has been buttoned up and the anchor weighed, it seems there's always time for one last thing."

Drum met Tom's eyes and chuckled silently.

"What?" I demanded. "What last thing?"

"Tell me again where you got the wig." It itched like crazy, but my hands were too busy trying to keep the oars under control and the blasted boat pointed toward the *Neuf Ouest* to attack the lice I already imagined to be crawling across my head.

"You'll have to ask the captain," Tom's voice echoed from within one of the large wooden barrels sitting upright at my feet. The top lifted. "All I can say is that after I explained our predicament, she was most willing to do anything to accommodate—and I quote—'thems wot call themselves friends of Cap'n Drum.' Most willing."

"So I'm wearing the wig of a whore?" It was a ludicrous affair, with curls the color of Coke cans tumbling down my shoulders and halfway to my ass. I was reminded of the Ariel costume my niece Cameron picked out at Kmart, only that wig was more natural-looking. But every time I'd turned unexpectedly since putting it on, I'd caught one of my companions staring at me in lascivious slack-jawed wonder.

"She's not a whore," came Drum's muffled protest. The top of the second barrel lifted. "Nell's a woman of business, no different from you or me."

"I can tell you this," Tom said. "The boat we're in is named *The Bower of Venus*, and the larger one she transferred onto is *The Mount of Paris*. I doubt either was inspired by a lifelong study of mythology."

"The boats are hers, free and clear," Drum said with irritation. "Certainly she appreciates a convivial evening now and again. Which of us doesn't? But that hardly makes her a whore, counselor. Just because she's not the sort of starchy-spined harridan you're undoubtedly attracted to—"

"Starchy-spined harridans?" Tom said. "My women

may be too upright for their own good, but I know they could teach your Nell a thing or two about—"

"I'm sitting right here, boys."

They withdrew into sheepish silence.

I said, "So how does the wig fit into her business—pardon me, her conviviality? You said she had pretty blonde hair on her own."

Drum cleared his throat. "Well . . ." His voice trailed off.

"Well . . . ?"

"There are certain men who—"

"Okay, I was afraid that was going to be the answer."

I turned to Tom. His mouth snapped closed.

"So all it takes is red hair?"

He colored. "You have to admit it is rather exotic."

"How close are we?" Drum said.

"Five more minutes or when my back gives out, whichever comes first." I was going to be offering my barreled wares to the men of the *Neuf Ouest*. Drum and Tom, dressed in *Neuf Ouest* sailor togs and neckerchiefs, were my hidden wares. That would get us on board. In an hour we'd be safely out of Gibraltar, and then Drum would retake control of the ship and work his magic.

"Remember," Drum said. "A good fish woman negotiates. Don't accept the first offer."

In this wig, I was pretty sure I knew what the first offer was going to be. There didn't seem to be much danger of me accepting it.

"Oh, and don't mind a little tomfoolery at the

start," he warned. "The younger ones are rather high-spirited."

"We're almost there," I said. The lids snapped shut and were latched from inside.

The *Neuf Ouest* sailors hung out the hatches, staring down. "I'll take *two* of those." "Are ye selling by the mouthful?" "Does it come with a free taste?" "Do the cuffs match the collar?"

I heard Drum groan.

"Pickled cod, boys," I called sweetly. "Six shillings a barrel."

"You could pickle my cod anytime." "Cod? I've got just the skewer for it."

That last came from Simon Funkel. That boy should be ashamed of himself.

"Pickled cod," I called again. "Just the thing for a long voyage. Six shillings, or do I take it over to *The Ariadne?*"

We agreed on ten for both barrels, and two young sailors thumped down beside me. In an instant they had the boat anchored to the side of the ship and the barrels up and through the hatch.

"Do you mind if I board?" I asked as one of them counted out ten coins.

"Were it up to me, m'um, the answer'd be aye. But we weigh anchor in half a glass, and there's no women on board from supper on, not even whores, m'um. Them's the captain's orders."

We knew this was likely to be the most challenging part.

"But I am the captain's orders. I mean"—I gave

the young man a meaningful smile—"he ordered me."

I had to get to Haverhill, to convince him not to load on powder. And if the French pilot had been put on board by Gabin or one of his associates, I was the only face the pilot wouldn't recognize. Drum's—and therefore Tom's—was infamous at this point.

The lad protested, "But—"

"*Tut-tut.* Mustn't make the captain wait. I charge by the whole glass, you see, so if you're the captain and I don't get to you soon, the glass is definitely half empty, if you follow."

The young man wrestled with the logic. "I don't—"

"But your captain does. Take me to him."

He wilted. "Aye, m'um."

He pulled me up and escorted me to the outside of Haverhill's closed door before making his escape.

It had been Drum's door. I touched the wood sadly, then lifted my fist to knock. "Mr. Haverhill." Silence. "Mr. Haverhill, it's me—"

The door swung open.

Mr. Haverhill held the door. A slight pinched man with eyes that offered the warmth of chinks of coal stood behind him holding a pencil and compass. His long black coat nearly skimmed the floor. On the map before him was oval within oval of blue. The harbor.

"Good evening." The pilot's eyes strayed over me only long enough to reduce me to a three-shilling whore. Not that I had very far to go.

A palpable tension inhabited the room but I couldn't read its source or trajectory. Mr. Haverhill stared aghast at my face. "Miss Pyle?"

The pilot's black gaze cut back to me, standing my hair on end.

"How did you get on board?" Haverhill asked.

"A simple matter. I rowed out and asked for you." Not quite the truth, but I hoped to keep the barrel delivery as separate from my arrival as possible. The plan was for me to convince Haverhill to skip the powder load and, if that didn't work, for the dimple-chinned twins to move to the alternate plan they had assured me they'd formulated while I was wigging up.

Below us the screech of chains resonated through the floor.

"We've begun to weigh anchor, Miss Pyle," Haverhill said with obvious dismay. "You'll have to leave."

The Duke of Silverbridge didn't leave. His duchess had been about to sail away without him, but he held his ground, knowing that if he delayed long enough, a ship running out on the tide would be forced to take him along whether it wanted to do so or not. Who says you can't learn a trick or two from romance novels?

I tilted my head languidly toward the sea. "I hear you're heading for Portugal."

Remembering my little trick in the Mediterranean, Haverhill's eyes flew to the windows to look for the sun but found only the silvery darkness of the night. "How did you know?"

"A captain does not reveal his destination until he's at sea," the pilot remarked.

"That only applies to ships of war," I said. "This is a privateer."

"We are at war," the pilot said, "or haven't you heard?"

Without the anchor's massive weight to hold it in place, the ship strained at the ropes that remained, like a horse ready for a race. The din of the tide rushing along her sides grew in volume.

"Miss Pyle, you must go—"

"It's time, Captain," the pilot said impatiently. "They'll need you on deck."

Haverhill bowed to me, exited the room and disappeared up the stairs.

The ship gave a sudden jerk. We were free of the ropes.

The pilot eyed me disdainfully. "Looks like you've earned yourself a free voyage, Miss Pyle."

"Don't you have to go on deck as well?"

He brushed by me and took the steps two at a time.

Not one to miss the spectacle of a command Haverhill performance, I ascended on the pilot's heels, the sandals ably connecting with each stair like the bladed-toed shoes of a utility pole climber.

As he made his way to the helm, the pilot said something low to one of the sailors. Overhead, chaos reigned. Some sails strained like hot-air balloons and others flapped like clothes on a laundry line. Mr. Haverhill ran from one side to the other, shouting "Reef!" or "About!" and "Belay, belay!" to the legions of men awaiting his instruction. I threaded my arm around a taut piece of line and gratefully eyed the small boats hanging over the side. There was no telling where we were going to end up if this went on.

The dock let out a horrific squeal as the ship shaved ten years—literally—off its life.

"A shame there's no market for sawdust," a sailor near me muttered. Another added, "Did you hear the god-awful squeal when we pulled out yesterday? I thought we was going to have the copper ripped right off us. A fine sight we'd be, sinking in our own harbor."

The pilot waved Haverhill toward the helm and began to make some suggestions, which Haverhill eagerly repeated to the crew. At once the ship heeled, like a cat catching scent of a bird. For a quarter hour, the men worked in quiet harmony, displaying the expertise they'd developed under a far more practiced administration. Some ran the sails and some the ropes. A few toted heavy loads up through the hatch and onto the deck.

I paced to the front, then the rear, wondering what progress my partners were making. My eyes raked the ramparts, looking for a suspiciously busy cannon. I could see nothing. The powder hoy was growing closer and closer.

"You have an interest in gunpowder, Miss Pyle?"

I nearly jumped out of my wig. The pilot was seated now, one leg crossed languidly over the other. I hadn't seen him move into my path.

"No, not particularly." I dragged my eyes away from the hoy.

"There's enough powder in that little structure," he said, "to have completely provisioned every ship in the Battle of Gibraltar. Not that it did, of course, being entirely the property of the French when the battle started." He smiled.

I was beginning to worry. We were no more than a hundred yards from the hoy. Sixty more seconds and forget a hot cannon shot. A comb of fingers through my staticky hair would be all it would take to launch us into the stratosphere like some cheap Eastern European satellite.

"Look!" a sailor yelled. "There! A ship on fire." The men hurried to starboard—er, port—er, to my right to see.

A hundred or so feet to our side flames had begun to lick the sails of a small single-masted sailing ship. In half a minute, every inch of canvas was alight with flames.

"It's *The Mount of Paris*!" someone yelled, and I grinned. Drum, it seems, had paid dearly for this extravaganza.

The men of the *Neuf Ouest* gasped, and I saw what they saw. The deck of the ship was empty and without anyone to steer it toward the open sea, it was—like us—moving inexorably toward the powder hoy.

"We must turn away," Haverhill said, "go straight out of the harbor."

Leaving the harbor meant no turning back, not on this tide. Even I knew that.

The pilot, who had watched the flames with calculation, shook his head. "No. She'll miss the hoy. We can tack; that will slow us while she passes. You need to take on powder."

Our whole scheme rested on the *Neuf Ouest* giving

up and escaping. I prayed Haverhill had enough coward in him to not play dice with his life.

"I can get powder in Orvieto." A sweat broke out on Haverhill's forehead. "'Tis only a half day's sail. Less."

Good man!

"It is, of course, your ship," the pilot said, bowing, and I let out a sigh of relief. "But," he added ominously, "I wouldn't want to be in your shoes if the French attack this evening."

The sailboat lurched closer and closer to the hoy and so did we. We were close enough to the burning ship to lob a touchdown pass over its bobbing peak. I could smell the burning tar. Pale ashes like snow floated down over our deck. My heart started to hammer. This was no time for a game of Gibraltar chicken. The men waited for their command. Haverhill chewed the inside of his cheek.

"Turn," he commanded. "Toward the sea."

The men let out a collective sigh and flew to their posts.

With a groan like the morning wheeze of an old man, the ship began to turn. Slowly it progressed—10 degrees, 20 degrees, 45 degrees. The breeze was not so strong in this direction and it took some furious rearrangement of the sails to catch it.

The burning ship was not so lucky. Whoever had set her canvas—and I was beginning to admire Nell more and more—had known what she was doing.

The Mount of Paris moved closer and closer to the hoy until the hull made contact. Like a stole wrapping itself across a pair of welcoming shoulders, she seemed to stretch and hug herself against the hoy. The *Neuf Ouest* had not picked up much speed, and the stern felt more exposed than me in my first eighteenth-century dress. Damn Haverhill for his indecision.

The orange flames licked higher and higher. One flew like a bird and landed on the hoy. It died. Another flew in the air. With an ominous huff, the night air sucked in around our ears, and the world went up like a cherry bomb.

A huge roar filled the void, and flotsam and fire rained down on the deck like hailstones from hell. When the clatter ended, men ran with buckets, dousing flames or stamping them with their feet or bedrolls.

I took advantage of the madhouse scene to edge toward the hatch. Now that we were on board and irrevocably on our way out of port, I wanted to reconvene the team quickly.

At once a long black coat blocked the way.

"Off so soon, Miss Pyle?" the pilot asked.

"I'm certain I must be in the men's way."

"Not at all. Stay."

He lowered himself onto a nearby perch and stared out at the approaching rampart. The men in the sails were executing a delicate angle.

"*Très bon,*" he said to himself.

My stomach knotted. "You're French?"

"*Oui, mademoiselle.*"

"But you assist an English ship?"

"Ah, but my job is not to pilot English ships." He gave me a chilling grin. "It is to uncover and kill English spies."

A small, hot bomb went off in my gut. "P-pardon?"

He laughed—a vile laugh that curled my hair. "That's right, Miss Pyle. I refer to your . . . How would you describe him? Colleague? Lover? Co-conspirator?"

I took a step back.

"Take her," he said, returning to his flawless English. "She's a spy."

He said this as if he'd said "tighten that line," and the poor sailor to whom it had been uttered could hardly keep the look of horror from his face. But he obeyed.

The pilot stared at me, tapping the wood beneath him contemplatively. Then he stood—and the blood drained from my head.

The seat from which he had risen was a barrel—one of my pickled cod barrels. I could tell by the markings on the side. But now a row of neat nails circled the top.

My mind worked desperately to recall how the barrel had gotten on deck. Had I glimpsed it being carried up? Had it been carrying the weight of a hundred-eighty-pound man? And where was the other one?

By this time, Haverhill and the rest of the men were emerging from shock and beginning to stir.

"Mr. Haverhill," I said, "tell them I'm not a spy. He's a spy," I inclined my head toward the pilot. "He's French!"

Haverhill hesitated.

"Observe what I found in her possession." The pilot waved a sheet of paper in the air. When it came to rest in Haverhill's hand, I saw it was the ship's inventory. But the pilot hadn't gotten it from me. That had been in Tom's possession an hour ago. My heart threatened to choke me.

"Not Miss Pyle," one of the sailors said.

The pilot gave Haverhill a look. "Tell them the woman is under arrest."

Haverhill swallowed. "Don't move. Nobody move."

"Mr. Haverhill, you have to believe me!" I cried.

"The list." Haverhill held it limply in his hand. "Why would you have a list addressed to the admiral?"

"You two there." The pilot pointed to a pair of burly sailors by the ropes. "Assist me."

"Basehart gave me the list!" I said. "You can ask him yourself."

The sailors grabbed the barrel, and terror did a flat-out run through my body. "No!" I yelled, but it was too late. The men heaved the barrel over the side.

"Was it tight enough to float?" the pilot asked, not even bothering to look.

"Aye," one of the sailors replied.

"Too bad it shan't have that chance long." The pilot pulled a pistol out of his jacket, aimed and fired directly at the cask.

I heard the wood splinter and a sickening thud.

A part of me died. The other part of me decided I would live to see the pilot's death.

"Fucking bastard," I hissed.

The pilot chuckled. "Take her away."

"I'm not a spy, I tell you!" I struggled and kicked

against the arms that dragged me toward the hatchway. "He is!"

They tossed me unceremoniously into Haverhill's quarters and locked the door. I ran to the balcony, determined to find the barrel. It was there. A light speck in the distance. I was not a great swimmer, but I was good enough and the harbor was calm. I tore at my skirt. If I didn't ditch it, the weight would pull me under, Virginia Woolf–style.

A hand caught me and a familiar voice said, "Whoa."

It was Drum.

"Tom's overboard!" I cried. "The pilot's a French spy and Tom's overboard. We've got to get to him."

At that moment, the door reopened. It was the pilot. He looked at Drum, stupefied. I realized at that instant the pilot must be unaware of Drum's double. The pilot clearly thought he'd killed the only dark-haired adversary on board.

The pilot's face was the picture of confusion. His eyes flickered from Drum to the sea beyond the windows.

"What was in the barrel, Captain?" he said.

"Dried peas," Drum replied with a grim smile. "And a dozen Parma hams."

My heart lifted. If it were true, Tom was still alive. But Drum could as easily be lying.

The pilot reached for his pistol. At that moment, however, the ship made a violent lurch and he lost his footing. Drum body-slammed him and both crashed onto the floor. Praise God for Mr. Haverhill's sailing ability.

There was no contest. Drum outweighed the man by forty pounds and outmuscled him as well. But the pilot was a tenacious fighter and managed two or three particularly nasty blows before Drum pinned him and the man stilled.

"Don't move," I called. "I can tie his arms."

"Stay away." Drum's breathing was hard but his face was harder. He lifted a fist and brought it down on the man's cheek. I heard a solid crack, and the man howled.

"Stop," I said. "We can tie him up."

Drum didn't answer. He delivered a backhanded fist against the man's ear. A rivulet of blood streamed out. The man bit him bestially, and Drum yanked his wrist away. Drum's eyes turned a cold, murderous blue, and he began a brutal, rhythmic, two-fisted pummel of the man's face.

"Enough!" I cried, pulling at Drum's shoulders. "Enough!" Only one thing could have driven him to this frenzy. "Drum, it's the barrel, isn't it?" I said terrified. "It wasn't hams; it was—"

"*Quiet!*"

But the pilot was too far gone to have heard my question. He had stopped moving—and, I feared, breathing.

Drum stumbled to his feet like a drunk, blood on his hands. I stared at him, aghast.

"Is he dead?" I asked.

"If he is, no one will mourn. It's Gabin."

"I meant Tom."

Drum gathered the Frenchman's pistol and tucked it into his belt. "Tom's alive," he said, and left without another word.

Chapter Twenty-four

I finished tying Gabin to a post and stood. Not that he needed the bonds; he wouldn't be waking up for a while.

The ship made a long, sweeping turn—low to the water and as smooth as silk. The timbers purred like a 450 SL under my feet. That could only mean one thing. Drum was back at the helm. Good. He'd had to have gotten his head at least partway out of his ass to navigate. As I stepped out the door, the jingle of coins at the far end of the ship jerked me to attention.

"Hey!" I exclaimed. "I need to talk to you!"

Mrs. Kenney jumped like she'd taken a bullet between the shoulder blades. She bolted down a nearby ladder.

I flew down the rungs, turned and found myself face-to-face with a huge, steaming tub of water. A bellow of outrage rang out. Apparently I'd burst into the midst of the line for the cook staff's bath time—either that or the ugliest football huddle I'd ever seen. I hurried out with a hand over my eyes, praying that wasn't the soup base they'd be using later.

By the time I reached the passageway, Mrs. Kenney was nowhere to be seen.

Damn. But her day of reckoning would come. And then I'd find time to beat the tar—or at least a handful of pink fabric—out of her.

The last set of stairs deposited me back where I'd started—at the captain's quarters. I felt the tension drain out of me. Tom was there, crouched over our slowly stirring captive. For an instant I'd thought it was Drum, but the distaste at what he was seeing removed any question I might have had.

"Oh, Tom, thank God." I said, and meant it. "I thought you were dead. The barrel . . ."

"Hams." His mouth lifted briefly, but the emotion did not stretch as far as his eyes.

"Parma." I nodded.

An awkward silence overcame us. This was the first time we'd been alone since we'd parted outside Drum's jail. Before Tom had been tortured. Before Charles had been murdered. Before Drum had been shot. Before Tom saved Drum's life and mine.

I hardly recognized this man as the Tom of Pilgrim Pharmaceuticals. His hair, once neatly combed, now sprouted in untamed waves over his ears and forehead; his torso, normally hidden under conservative suits, had emerged sinewy and hard in his close-fitting sailor's garb; and his eyes, always intelligent and aware, shone with a wary, calculating sharpness, as if the next moment might require the sort of analysis one saves for battles, not balance sheets. But it was the unconscious ease with which he had assumed the role of chief architect of our destiny that seemed to throw everything I had known about him into question.

In truth, I felt a little unsteady around him, as if he were a tiger I had fed since birth, set free from its cage for the first time.

"Does Haverhill know about the pilot?" I asked.

"Yes. Drum's taken back command of the ship."

"I, ah, I can't thank you enough for coming back to the jail." An inexplicable heat flooded my cheeks. "Drum would have surely—"

"I didn't come for Drummond," he said flatly. "I came for you."

My breath jigged.

Tom held my eyes. "I don't care if you slept with him. I don't care if you *are* sleeping with him. I won't give you up."

Oh.

"And at some point," he added, "I intend for us to say a polite good-bye to our friend the captain and head back to the twenty-first century, where—I promise—I'll give you more to think about than a one-era stand with a ne'er-do-well ship jockey."

No much to argue with there—which was a good thing, since I felt like an athletic sock was stuck in my mouth.

Tom drew a finger across the plane of my face, leaving a trail of heat on my already warm skin. My wig had slipped crookedly over my ear. He finished the job, tugging it off my head and tossing it on the nearby table. He combed his fingers through my hasty topknot, drawing my hair down in gentle waves.

"Drummond claims he's the culmination of your ideal," he said. "And perhaps he is. But he was based on me, and in the end I have to believe no character, however three-dimensional, can compete with an imperfect, adoring, patient *man*. I'm counting on that."

"Oh, Tom."

"So sleep with him if you must. It won't change how the story ends."

Gabin began to move. The cuts on his face looked like grill lines on an overdone steak. Dried blood glazed his hair and ears, and the bruising that would swallow his face by morning was already beginning to color his chin, eyes and forehead.

"Well, you're more optimistic than I," I said. "I'm not sure I'd share a cup of coffee with him. Not after *that*." I pointed to Gabin

Tom stiffened. His eyes turned a cloudy gray. "I suspect he had his reasons."

"Gabin had been subdued. I could have tied him up."

"Perhaps submission wasn't his aim."

"Perhaps continuing to enjoy my respect wasn't either. Why are you defending him anyway?"

"I'm not. It's just . . ." Tom chewed the side of his mouth. "It's just that that's a reason for not sleeping with him tonight, Seph, not for never doing it again. Not if you care about him."

"Then I guess I don't. At least not as much as I

thought." I laid a hand on his arm. "Which is all I'm trying to tell you."

He drummed his thigh and nodded. "I'm glad."

Gabin jerked awake, rolled to the side and clutched his temples. He saw Tom and spit. "Pathetic English catchfart."

"You punch like a Frenchman, Gabin," Tom said, doing a remarkably fine imitation of Drum. "Shut your bloody mouth or I'll shut it with my boot."

I caught sight of Drum peering into the room. He gave Tom a questioning look.

Tom inclined his head toward the floor.

Drum's eyes raked the room. When he spotted Gabin, he started visibly.

Not even man enough to face up to his own work, I thought.

Drum gestured for Tom and me to step into the passageway. When we did, he closed the door and said quietly, "There's trouble."

"What sort?" Tom asked.

"A ship. Two points off our larboard bow. The lookout saw a light flash twice, then flash once more, then go out."

"A signal?"

"Aye. But not one I've seen before."

"Did they see us?"

"Can't be sure. Not in the dark. I've sent word for the men to extinguish the lights. It's a bloody mess out there though—rocks and outcroppings everywhere until we reach Sagres and turn north. Not a good time to be without our lanterns. I reset our course for the southwest. That will buy us some time and a clear sail for the night."

"Are you sure this is bad?" I asked. "Maybe it's an English ship. Can't you just wave a flag or shoot off a cannon or something to show you're friendly?"

The look on Drum's face suggested this was exactly the sort of help he expected from a twenty-first-century literature major.

A sailor flew down the stairs. "Captain, the wind has shifted—" He stopped dead at the sight of Drum and Tom. I realized almost no one on board had seen them together.

"Pick up that chin, Mr. Jones," Drum said. "Fly season starts early in this latitude. The man at whom you are openly gaping is my cousin."

Mr. Jones's eye went from Tom to me. "Another cousin, sir?"

"Aye."

"You are blessed to have so much family close at hand."

"Thank you, Mr. Jones. You were saying?"

"The wind has moved sou'-sou'west, and the topsails, well, . . ." He twisted the cap in his hand, looking for all the world like a small boy who did not wish to mention the overturned frog bucket in front of company.

Drum understood. "Tell Mr. Haverhill I'll be up shortly."

"Thank you, sir!" Jones fled up the stairs.

"The men seem to be glad you're back," I said to Drum.

"You'd be, too, if every tack sent your life passing before your eyes," Tom observed.

Drum did not reply. His eyes were fixed somewhere in the distance. "We'll know more at dawn," he said. "If the seas are clear, we'll turn northeast and have lost no more than ten or twelve hours. Counselor, what day do Leake and his battalions get word?"

"April twenty-fourth. What day is today?"

"April twenty-fourth. By half a glass."

Somewhere above us, a sail freed of its moorings flapped violently against a mast. We heard the scramble of a dozen feet. The ship shuddered, as if someone had tapped the brakes. I didn't bother to make such a comment. I am perfectly aware sailing ships have no brakes.

"Maybe a day here or there doesn't matter," I put in. "What day is Barcelona saved?"

Tom chewed the inside of his cheek. "April twenty-seventh."

"Well, see, that still gives us—"

"Three days," Drum said. "And it will take the battalions two days to get from Portugal to Barcelona—with the wind at their backs."

The impact of losing ten to twelve hours on such a schedule washed over us.

Drum made a long, troubled growl. "So much for room for error. I guess I'll see what I can do about resetting the sails."

"I'm going to look at a map," Tom said.

"And I'm going to find Mrs. Kenney if it's the last thing I do," I said, hoping it wouldn't actually be the last thing.

"Counselor," Drum said, catching Tom's sleeve, "allow me a moment."

Tom watched Seph disappear down the passageway, feeling the whiplash of his conscience with her every step. Her words had cut him deeply, though she would never know. He turned to find his companion's severe gaze upon him.

"What happened?" Drummond demanded fiercely. "You told me Gabin had been captured."

"He has been captured."

"What's he's 'been,' counselor, is beaten nearly to death."

Their eyes locked.

"He had a pistol," Tom said at last. "And he murdered Davitch."

"He's worth nothing to England dead."

"I wasn't thinking of England."

"Then it's bloody well time to start."

Chapter Twenty-five

"*Get* some sleep," Tom said when I appeared on deck. "We'll know nothing till dawn."

It was a good suggestion. I'd just spent the last quarter hour searching for Mrs. Kenney, to no avail.

We had cleared the harbor, and the great rock had disappeared in the distance. "Damnedest place for a supposed strategic piece of land," I thought. I wandered the length of the ship and peered out at the great swath of blackness before me.

"Hey," I said to a sailor repairing a net. "What are those lights out in the distance there? Gibraltar's in the opposite direction."

He gazed at me oddly, then spat a large plug of what I assumed to be tobacco into the sea. "That mass of land, m'um?" He was an Irishman, with a face like an old English bulldog.

I nodded.

"That's Africa," he said.

Africa? Africa as in Isak Dinesen? Africa as in Born
Free? "Africa, you say? You're telling me Spain is, like, a
mile from Africa?"

"Nine miles, m'um. And, no, I ain't telling you Spain
is that close. I'm telling you Gibraltar is. Gibraltar is
the closest Europe gets to Africa. It's the gatekeeper
to the entire Mediterranean. No ship passes through
to France or Greece or the Barbary Coast or even the
Levant without Gibraltar seeing it first."

Well, I suppose that could explain some of England's
interest in it.

I decided to cash in my chips for the evening. Tom
was busy, and I neither knew nor cared where Drum
was. I descended the narrow stairs and came to an
abrupt halt. Where was I to sleep anyway? I still hadn't
been in this godforsaken place long enough to be assigned a room.

I eyed the main cabin. No way, I thought. Not if it
meant Captain Asshole might think for an instant I was
there for him. I was spared further consideration when
a loud "*Pssst*" made me turn.

Peaches peered blearily out a doorway, clutching
a paisley dressing gown around her. She had a finger
to her lips, and unless Chanel makes rum-scented
perfume, I'm pretty sure she was tipsy. "*Pssst*," she
said again in what I believe is referred to as a stage
whisper.

"I think that's '*Shhh*,'" I said affably. "That is, if you
want me to be quiet. '*Pssst*' is to get me to pay attention."

"What if I want to get someone to pay attention *and* be quiet? '*Shhht*,' I guess." She exploded in sniggers of laughter. "*Shhht. Shhht. Shhht.*"

A prim-looking sailor heading for us stopped abruptly and turned around. I'm not sure if it was the language or Peaches's dressing gown.

"Perhaps we should withdraw?" I tilted my head toward her door.

Peaches waved me in, and in a moment I was seated on her cot with a goblet filled to the brim with rum in my hand. I noticed her eyes were puffy, and then I saw the pile of balled-up handkerchiefs.

"You heard about Charles," I said.

She snuffled but held strong. "Aye. Thomas told me."

"Did he?"

"He said Uncle Charles fought bravely. That he was trying to save a family being robbed. He said I should be very proud."

Bless that Tom. "You should be. Charles was a good man. Does he have any other family?"

"No, just me. Thomas said Charles told Drum I was his heir—which means I am part owner of this ship! Oh, Miss Pyle, do you think I can handle such a responsibility?" She had plopped on the cot beside me.

"Seph, please, and, yes, I'm sure you can. Think about it. Drum is a very experienced captain and, assuming we can get these spying charges dismissed, all you'll have to do is tell him your objective—catch two ships, catch three ships, that sort of thing—and let him do the rest."

"Hmmm." She rubbed her chin thoughtfully. "I've never tried that with a man before." Suddenly she sat up. "Does owning the ship mean I can order the sailors to do my bidding?"

"Well, er, there is that whole thing about captains at sea, highest authority and all, but I'm sure that when you're on land, they will conform to your every whim. And who knows where the captain–owner relationship might lead." I smiled, thinking of Drum's inevitable distress.

"Oh, Drum . . . he's not the man for me. I've come to see that. There's someone else I've been thinking of lately."

"Really, whom?"

"Thomas."

"What?" I jerked so hard a cubic foot of rum landed in my lap.

"He's like Drum, only nicer." Peaches plucked a clean handkerchief out of her drawer and passed it to me.

I mopped myself off. "B-but he's so . . ." Quick, Seph. Handsome? Nice? Smart? Funny? Taken? "American."

"But you're an American, Seph."

"Yes, but it's different on men, don't you think? So ill-fitting. Have you thought about Admiral Basehart?" I took a big gulp of rum.

Peaches smiled. "The admiral and I actually struck up something of a friendship in Gibraltar."

The rum nearly came out my nose. "Really?"

"He's got a charming sense of humor. You just have to dig a little."

Yeah, with a Payloader.

"Thomas says the admiral is my partner in the *Neuf Ouest*. I don't think I could fall in love with him, though—but who knows? Maybe for a little bit. I went to see him about Drum."

"You did?"

"I had an idea the navy should use him as a secret agent, just pretend they hanged him."

"Wow," I said, impressed. "That is a good idea."

She brightened.

"But first we have to save him now. Peaches, do you know anyone onboard with access to green ribbon?"

"Green ribbon?" Her brows knitted. "I'm sure I must. I've gotten more ribbons than you can imagine. They come on every love note."

She reached under her mattress and pulled out a huge wad of ribbons. One that looked exactly like the one that had been around the packet in Basehart's hands was on top.

"From who did you receive this one?" I asked.

"Oh, dear. I wish I could remember."

But she couldn't, even after I asked her to review the notes themselves.

"It was good of you to try," I said encouragingly when she finished, for it looked as if she was about to cry again.

"Thomas says I have a great capacity for kindess." She smiled.

"Really?" Dammit, Tom was *mine*. There are some things an author just shouldn't have to share. Fortunately I have a poker face.

"Seph, can I ask you a question?"

"Sure."

"You look like I hit you with a bucket of ice water. Are you in love with Thomas?"

The first notes of "The Theme from Love Story" rose from my shoes. "Er . . ."

"Because that's one rule I don't violate," she said as if there were a considerable number of others she did. "I don't steal my friends' lovers. That's why I never for a moment considered falling in love with Mr. Kenney."

"And none of the other men in the *Neuf Ouest* are married?"

"Married? What does that have to do with it? So all you have to do is tell me. Are you in love with Thomas?"

I looked at my shoes. I looked at Peaches. I thought of the recycling bin and the balcony of the Hotel al Ponte dei Sospiri. I thought of war movies and Cinco de Mayo and the French and Indian War. I thought of the kind, courageous man who let me go at the jail and still loved me enough to come back.

"Yes," I said quietly. "I think I do."

"Oh, Seph." She threw her arms around me. "Congratulations."

I felt a little like I couldn't breathe. Like I had this wonderful news and I had to share it with someone—a very specific someone. "Do you know where Tom is?"

"Isn't he in the cabin next to Mr. Haverhill? I think that's where they put him."

But he wasn't there, nor on deck, nor anywhere else I looked. I gave up. The cabin next to Peaches was deserted. I balled up my dress under my cheek and fell asleep before my head settled into the silk.

Chapter Twenty-six

Appreciative as I was for the rest, I was glad when my shoes gave me a shake just before sunrise.

I ran up to the top deck, hoping to find Tom alone. But he stood with Drum in the flat charcoal light of predawn.

"Have you spotted the ship?" I asked, remembering the excitement of the previous evening.

"No, but perhaps you should check with the officer of the watch." Drum closed his spyglass and smiled. "Tom relieved me after the second watch."

I turned to Tom in surprise.

"It's nothing," he said. "The sails had been set, and we had a good open sea in front of us."

Drum said, "Tom is too modest. He has a natural feel for the sea. The mechanics are somewhat lacking, but his strategy is sound. Dare I say that with a few years' experience, he might come to resemble a wholly adequate sailor."

"Thank you," Tom said. "I guess."

"Say, um, can I talk to you for a second?" I said to Tom. He looked so sexy with his windblown hair. I wanted to throw my arms around him and shout the news.

He nodded. "Sure. What's up?"

"Sir!" a voice called from above

Tom whipped the spyglass to his eye.

"What is it?" Drum boomed to the eagle's nest.

"Sorry, sir," the pubescent voice returned. "Nothing."

I stared at the shadowy sea churning behind us. In the darkness I could barely make out the color of the paint on our ship let alone the shape of anything in the distance.

Tom lowered his eyepiece reluctantly. "Sunrise is upon us. In a minute or two we'll know our fate. Now what was it you wanted to say?"

"Um, nothing. It can wait."

Tom and Drum scaled the rigging, spyglasses in hand. I was tempted to join them, but hanging above eighty sailors without underpants is not a prudent idea. I held my breath as the first glints of pink lit the sky.

"Blandcroft?" Drum yelled to the eagle's nest.

"Nothing, sir," the boy answered, cracking on the "sir."

A moment passed. The ocean glittered as the sun rose higher. A pair of seabirds wheeled and turned

in the breeze. Their calls were the only sound apart
from the rushing of the water and the pounding of our
hearts.

"Blandcroft?"

"Still nothing. Oh—" His voice stopped. I held my
breath. A beat. Two beats. Three.

"Blandcroft!"

"A ship, sir. Three masts. Directly on our larboard
beam. Three masts, white flag, Tourville Blue."

Drum slumped. "French. Ship of the line."

"How on earth did they know where to find us?" I
demanded when Tom and Drum reappeared on deck.
"It was pitch-black."

Drum said, "A seasoned sailor would know. 'Tis a
common trick, to sail south of your wind. Bypasses the
English naval shipping road. Damned handy if you have
something on board you'd prefer not to share."

"So this guy's pretty smart?" I said.

"Indeed he is, but that's not what's troubling me."

"What is?"

Drum and Tom exchanged a glance, and Tom answered for him. "It's one thing to be that smart, Seph.
It's something else to know the captain of the ship
you're chasing is that smart too. Haverhill would never
have ditched the regular road. Whoever's in charge
over there knows Drum's on board and in command."

The waves grew higher, like wolves around a lame
sheep, obscuring our view of the horizon. Once or
twice I opened my mouth to wonder if we'd lost our
pursuers, but both times I shut it again after seeing the

look on Drum's face. Whether by evidence or some inner knowledge, he knew they were still there.

Tom hovered at the helm, where the compass and the board tracking time, direction and speed stood. Each time a new measurement of the ship's speed was taken, Tom added the time since the last measurement and translated that into distance on the map. My father would have been happy; it was sort of the eighteenth-century equivalent of checking your miles per gallon on a road trip. A brief and bittersweet smile lifted my lips. I wondered if I'd ever see my father again.

To keep anyone from guessing the port to which we were headed, Tom was the only man allowed near the helm. Poor Drum. I know it pained him to think someone on board might be capable of betraying him.

I looked out to sea. "I don't see anything."

"She's there," Drum said. "I can feel her."

Tom scanned the horizon. "Oh, shit."

We turned. There she was on our right flank, twice as close as she'd been the last time we saw her.

"How far are we from Portugal?" I asked.

"Too far," Tom said.

Drum considered. "Maybe for the *Neuf Ouest.* But a small, fast sailboat, launched out of their sight . . ."

"Would never make it," Tom finished. "Look, I'm only a weekend sailor, but even with the shore in sight, this sea's far too rough for a light craft. And we're still fifty miles from Portugal. It would be a death sentence."

"Our only choice is to outrun her," Drum said, and added, disheartened, "At least for as long as we can."

"Then we'll fight." I hoped I sounded more certain than I felt.

"God, I'd love a fight." Drum slouched against the railing. "'Tis a bloody shame we left Gibraltar without an ounce of gunpowder."

For two hours, the other ship gained, slowly, steadily, like a distant thunderhead, turning when we turned, adding sail when we added sail. I was told she was *La Guêpe*—the wasp—a French warship. By lunch we could see her yellow portholes; an hour after that, the details of the men on her deck were visible.

Everything about the ship spoke of efficiency and speed, and she cut through our wake like a blade through paper. At this rate she'd be within shouting distance in a quarter hour. I doubted shouting was going to be her opening gambit.

"What will happen?" I asked.

Drum looked at me but did not answer. A rope flung loose and began beating the deck wildly. "Make fast with that!" he shouted. Men scurried to perform his bidding.

The mast above us creaked. Drum had every bit of rope and canvas screwed so tight it was a wonder we hadn't snapped something.

"Where's Tom?"

Drum hesitated. "Below, I think. Going through some papers."

A flash filled the sky and a sound like a 747 backfire shook me almost off my feet. My stomach sunk, partly out of fear, partly because Drum shoved me to the deck. A dark streak sent geysers of water skipping across the sea. Our friends had sent their regards in the form of a cannonball.

"Bloody French," he said. "In a lot of countries, that would be tantamount to war."

"We're at war."

"Assuming we're English," he said. "For all those bastards know, we're an Icelandic sea trawler chasing a mother lode of cod. We need to appear less English." He turned to the closest sailor, a thin, droopy-eyed youth knotting a rope. "Tell the flag officer to run a Martinique flag up the pole."

"Careful," I said. "They may be at war with Martinique too."

Drum laughed. "Your average Martiniquais might think so, but the French have owned Martinique for half a century." He added to the youth, "And call the men to their guns."

The youth paused, concern clouding his face. He was too well trained to point out we had nothing to shoot.

I, however, was not. "The Martinique flag—okay, maybe," I said. "But did the big boom knock you senseless? What's the point of getting the men to their guns?"

"The point is looking prepared. 'Tis often half the battle."

"That's not the half I'm worried about."

"I have good news for you then. There's no part of the battle you'll have to worry about. I'm sending you below."

I stiffened. "Like hell."

"Well, it may be a trifle warm, but I would hardly compare it with the underworld."

"*No.*"

He gave me a fiery eye. "You have two choices. Walk below like an obedient sailor or be carried below by the first four fo'c'sle men I can lay my hands on."

I had no idea what fo'c'sle men were but it sounded like keeping my gown from getting wrinkled was not going to be their top priority.

Several sailors on deck stopped what they were doing. I had the sneaking suspicion they were graduates of the London School of Fo'c'sle Management. Drum clasped his hands behind his back expectantly and waited.

I said nothing. He turned toward the men and began to speak.

"Understand this," I interrupted. "I am *choosing* to go below so that I may find Mrs. Kenney. This in no way represents any sort of accession to your command."

Drum gave a half-bow. "I acknowledge your disobedience."

"I'm going now." I made my way down the stairs, stopping at the bottom to shout, "But only to speak to Mrs. Kenney."

The hatch lid shut above me with a click.

Fortunately I *had* been planning to speak to Mrs. Kenney so my descent to the lower realm was truly of my own volition. I waited at the bottom of the stairs for a good five minutes, during which time the decks were cleared of gear and hammocks, the portholes opened and the cannons rolled into place, before Mr. Haverhill appeared, anxious and regretful.

"Nowhere, m'um," he said, wringing his hands. "I am sorry to have failed you but she is nowhere to be found. 'Tis the oddest thing."

"She could hardly have left the ship, Mr. Haverhill— or could she? Is there a boat missing?"

"No—and with the small tender we have, it would be a foolhardy thing in these seas."

"But did you look—"

"I looked everywhere, Miss Pyle. Everywhere."

I felt the pit in my stomach yawn wider. No Mrs. Kenney meant no fabric. No fabric meant no travel. I was stuck with a no-return ticket in a world of my own unconscious making. Worse, I had dragged an unwitting Tom here too. I thought of Tom's parents, blithely going about their business in North Dakota, unaware that they might never hear their son's voice again. The thought of Back-up Seph knitting my father intricate Nordic sweaters and cooking him gourmet meals should have brought me comfort, but it only depressed me more. Isn't it worse to have an imitation of what you're really meant to have?

A tremendous *boom* blew me off my feet. The port-hole to our right exploded in a shower of splinters and cannon pieces, and the gun crew scattered like bowling pins. Three were drenched in blood. Acrid smoke and powder filled the air. I crawled to my feet, ears ringing.

Haverhill ran to his nearest fallen comrade, a stout, redheaded man. "Don't move, McGinnis," he said. "We'll have you down to the surgeon in no time."

"They caught us on a tack," McGinnis said, clutching his arm. "Damned lucky shot."

No so lucky for him, I thought, and began to tend to the other two.

The ship took a turn and the latch clattered open. Drum vaulted down the handrails to the bottom step.

"Status, Mr. Haverhill?"

"Broken arm, a burn and a splinter," Haverhill answered promptly. "The cannon's ruined—not that that means much."

I took the hand of the young sailor with half his shirt and a good deal of the skin on his chest burned away.

"What happened with the Martinique flag?" he asked Drum.

Drum's mouth rose in an ironic twist. "They gave it a one-gun salute."

The sailor smiled.

"How long can we outrun them?" I asked.

"We can't," Drum said. "It's time to fight."

"The captain says it's time to fight!" a sailor shouted. The men cheered. "Fuck the bastards," one called.

"Fight, sir?" Haverhill was stunned.

"I have an idea," Drum said. "How much gunpowder do we have?"

"None, sir. You know—"

"You there," Drum called to a ringleted boy of ten or twelve. "Get me every grain of gunpowder in the ship. Sweep out the corners of the powder room. Comb the cracks between the floorboards. I want one full measure. And you—" He pointed to a group of sailors. "Begin to collect every bit of metal you can find.

Knives, nails, screws, forks, buckles. Hell, anything that can fit down the mouth of a cannon."

"Sir," Haverhill protested, "one cannon full of . . . cutlery is not going to get us anywhere."

Another cannon blast shook the air. This one fell just short of the ship. The absence of impact sounded like a sigh.

Drum fixed him with a careful look. "Can you think of any other way I can save this ship, Haverhill? Any other way at all?"

For a long moment nothing on Haverhill moved except the beating in the hollow of his throat. He hung his head. "No, sir."

"Then let's gather the metal, shall we?"

At once the ship was a hive of activity. Knives and cutlasses were tossed into a tub. Buckets of screws and nails followed. Belt buckles were hacked off their leather. One sailor dumped a jar of coins in, another a box of hinges. Peaches contributed several curiously sized rings. Two more blasts missed the ship—one to the left, one to the right. I slipped off my mother's garnet earrings, the ones my father had given her before I was born, and dropped them in too. If I'd gotten everyone into this, I was damned well going to be a part of getting everyone out.

Drum waited until the men were gathered around me. "My plan is this. Er, what is your name?" he asked the ringleted boy.

The boy squeaked, "Hawkins."

"Hawkins here"—he gave the boy a pat—"has found *three* measures of powder. We will load the stern chasers.

If we can take out a mast—or even set the mainsail on fire—we can outrun her. Who is the best shot on board?"

"Why, you, sir," the closest sailor replied, grinning.

"I?" Drum looked briefly uncertain. "Indeed. I shall aim the chasers at her. We shall have three chances to set things to right. Who here thinks any English ship would need more than that?"

The men stirred at once. "Not I," one called. "We shall overcome!" "Kick their bloody arses, sir!"

Renewed hope filled the room like a tide. My eyes searched the crowd for Tom but did not find him.

Drum marched into what had once been his quarters and I followed. The walls were still there, but every stick of furniture was gone. The chasers, I discovered, were a set of slim, shiny brass cannons with necks half as wide but half again as long as regular cannons. They had been pulled to the stern windows. The windows were gone, stored God only knows where, and there was little between us and the ship chasing us but our wake and a prayer.

"Their guns are starboard and larboard," Drum said. "They've nothing now in their bow. They can rake us when we turn, but we're safe so long as we stay directly in front."

The rest of us finished the thought: . . . *or until the three minutes it might take for their crew to move a cannon forward.*

Two sailors measured the powder with care. A third loaded the wadding and shot.

Drum took aim. I crossed my fingers, sending positive thoughts toward the cannon. A steady-armed man held a long match near the fuse. The sea lowered us and lifted us, lowered us and lifted us.

The muscles around Drum's eye tightened. He waved the hot, dusty air from his face. Every man held his breath.

"Now!" Drum called.

The light and the noise happened as one. The chaser shot back violently, shaking its bonds. A thick black smoke filled the room. When it dissipated, we could see the mainsail of the French ship was shredded, but the mast was standing. A few small fires burned on deck.

"Again," Drum said. "Hurry!"

The second gun was primed and adjusted. Drum hunched over it, sweat on his brow. The room was hot now, the smoke draining any hint of breeze from the air.

"Now!"

Another boom; another lungful of choking smoke. I waved the clouds away, desperate to see. The shot had hit its mark. The foremast was on fire.

A cheer rose up. "One more! One more! Knock it down!" Men slapped Drum on the back. I exhaled, thanking God.

The first gun was cleaned and filled. Drum wiped a towel over his face. Across the narrow belt of water, I could see the French sailors pulling a cannon toward the bow.

"Hurry, Drum, hurry," I said under my breath.

The winds had picked up; the *Neuf Ouest* was flying now. All we needed—*all* we needed—was for that one mast to be tilted. She didn't even need to fall, just become unsteady enough to make full speed impossible.

Drum took careful aim, calculating the exact second through one, two, three rises and falls of the ocean.

"Now!" he cried.

The last shot shook us to our bones. Again, the thick smoke enveloped us. Were we safe? Were we safe? The dark clouds parted.

The mast stood.

A hush fell over the *Neuf Ouest*.

The French ship began to aim its gun.

As if in slow motion, the sea of men around me moved away from the stern. There was nothing to do but stand back and watch. I don't remember if I fell down or was pushed. The boom was the loudest I'd heard. It seemed to howl right through me.

Men lay unmoving. Drum was beside me, his hand on my face, my neck. I heard his voice through the gauzy haze of a dream, calling to a sailor on deck. "What does the signal say? What does it say?"

"Surrender," a sorrowful voice replied.

"Haul down our flag," Drum said. "We are taken."

Chapter Twenty-seven

"Tom?" I caught Drum's hand. "Where is Tom?"

He crouched beside me. "For all of our sakes, don't mention him. He is hidden and will act when he can. We had a plan in the event this happened."

"Act?" I couldn't believe what I was hearing. "How?"

"Getting word to Leake in Portugal. I've briefed the men. They will keep the secret."

I let go of his hand. "That's not for our sakes. That's for yours."

The French swarmed the ship like hungry rats. The *Neuf Ouest*ers were herded into the lower decks by blue-coated sailors brandishing bayonets. The French flag was hauled up, unfurling itself into the blasting wind. They manacled Drum and frog-marched him into his quarters. Peaches and I were led to an empty cabin.

My ears strained for some hint of what was going on.

Apart from the raucous joy of the French victors and
the hammering and sawing that had already begun to
return the ship to seaworthiness, I could hear nothing.
The nothingness struck terror in me.

"Don't worry, Seph." Peaches patted my arm. "He
knows how to take care of himself."

"Which he?" I sank down on a shipping crate.

She gave me a dimpled smile. "You know who I
mean. I'm so glad you're in love."

In love. I thought of a picture of my parents as
young marrieds, sitting at the kitchen table in my
grandmother's house in Fargo. It was my grandfather's
sixtieth birthday, and the family was seated around my
grandmother's kitchen table, watching my grandfather
blow out the candles. My parents' backs were to the
camera, their eyes on my grandfather. But just under
the table, their hands were clasped. That, to me, will
always be the definition of love.

"It does feel like love," I said.

"Of course it does." She giggled. "The leap in your
chest when you see him, that tremble when he says
your name, that little wiggle in your belly when his
hand brushes yours."

"I have to admit I don't have a lot of experience." It
didn't feel like this with my ex, and the heroines in the
books I read always seemed absolutely sure. Would the
chest leaping, trembling and wiggle of the hotel bathroom sink with Tom translate into the chest leaping,
trembling and fulfillment of the kitchen table? "I hope
so, though."

"Vhy you say 'hope'?" the heavily accented shipping crate scolded. "Don't say 'hope,' say 'know.'"

What?

I jumped to my feet and flung open the box. Mrs. Kenney lay curled regally on her side.

"The French vill not have the satisfaction of taking me," she sniffed.

I suspected her hiding had more to do with me than the French, but I decided to let that pass. "What do you mean, 'Say "know"?'" Since Drum's revelation of how my cross-century travel pass got validated—namely, with a handful of Mrs. Kenney's supernatural silk—I had new-found respect for her powers.

"Da shoes." She straightened her head scarf, and Peaches and I rushed to help her to her feet. "Only vun person can take off your shoes. That person holds the key to your future. Happiness, love, pleasure. Eez all there."

I looked down at the shell pink taffeta, which crinkled in obvious pride. "All there, huh?"

"*Ja.* Find love, story over."

"Not quite over. As far as I know, love is not going to save our sorry asses. What I need to find this second is more of that fabric so that—"

A blood-curdling howl filled the air, the sound of a man who had done everything he could to swallow his pain and lost the battle. It was Drum, and I leaped to my feet.

As quickly as it started, it stopped. Quiet fell over the ship, a heartbreaking quiet that was immediately replaced by the angry rumblings of the captured *Neuf Ouest*ers.

Oh, God. Oh, God.

A French soldier yelled, "Silence!"

"Mrs. Kenney, I need that fabric," I said. "Drum told me how everything works. But he's out of his stash, and you're the source—like Lake Itasca and the Mississippi. So cough it up. I have to get Tom and Drum out of here."

She shook her head sadly. "Tom, maybe, if that eez his fate. Not Drummunt."

"Listen, babe. Deep-six the great-and-powerful-Oz routine. I need some answers, and I'm not averse to knocking around a few scarved heads to get them."

Mrs. Kenney's eyes widened. "It vill not work. Your plan vill not vork."

The door banged open. An Eiffel Tower–sized French soldier pointed his sword at me and sneered. "*Vous êtes* Persephone Pyle?"

I sneered back.

He delivered another sharply worded statement. He wasn't asking me what flavor crepe I wanted.

I shrugged. "*Didier est à la disco.*"

The soldier's eyes bulged. He jerked his sword at me and then toward the door. Crude, but requiring no translation.

I shook my head. He resheathed his sword, grabbed me by the hair and spun me around like a top.

"Hey, ever visit the German pavilion at Euro Disney?" I said as he dragged me toward the door. "Well, I hope you like Wiener schnitzel, 'cause there's a lot of it in your future come 1940. And don't think I've forgotten Princess Diana either." He shoved me into the corridor.

Peaches started after me but I held up a hand. I'd screwed up enough lives in the last two days. I wasn't going to drag anyone else down with me.

Another howl shook the hall.

"Why won't it work?" I looked Mrs. Kenney straight in the eye. "I need the truth."

Her gaze flickered to the soldier. "The captain," she said carefully, "can't travel."

"*Le capitaine.*" The French soldier snorted and uttered something scorching.

Peaches gasped.

"What?" I demanded. "What did he say?"

"He's taking you to Drum—to say good-bye."

Drum lay in a heap, barely moving. His shirt had been forcibly stripped from his back, and his skin glistened as if he were feverish. A large, sooty rag lay on his shoulder. I could smell smoke somewhere. I wondered if they were melting tar.

The soldier who'd brought me leaned against the door and crossed his arms. I got the impression I was being given some amount of time. How much, I didn't know.

When I got close enough to Drum to see his face, my stomach wrenched free of its moorings. It wasn't a rag on his back; it was a patch of burned and oozing skin. And what was left of the skin on his back hung in bleeding tatters. He'd been flogged.

"Drum!"

He opened his eyes blearily. "Damn. This isn't a dream, is it?"

"Sure wouldn't be one of mine. What happened?" I was relieved to hear him joke, but I knew the burn was bad. I scanned the room for first-aid supplies.

"They flogged me for a while, then beat the tar out of me—well, except the bit they dabbed on my shoulder. Rather an ironic flourish, that."

"Gabin, was it?"

"Actually that nice young man at the door. The opening act, it seems."

I gave the soldier my best "screw you" face and went to work. There wasn't much I could do for either the cuts or the burn, except keep it all loosely wrapped. They didn't have antibiotics in 1706.

"Why?" I asked, mostly to keep Drum talking. "They already have the ship and your men." A horrible thought struck me. "God, they're not looking for—" I was going to say "Tom" but stopped.

"No," Drum said firmly, then coughed and said quickly under his breath, "Check my breathing."

I leaned down, patting his chest.

"They're looking for the rubies," he whispered in my ear. "Tell me what the barometer reads. There, on the wall. How high is the water?"

I stole a glance upward. "High," I said, hiding the word in a cough. I leaned back to his ear. "*Rubies,* Drum? The ones you said you didn't have?" I was starting to wonder how much of this mess was my fault and how much was due to the unrestrained capriciousness of a piratical eighteenth-century privateer.

"I didn't have them—until today. I found them in the hold."

I pretended I was checking his arm for broken bones, though if I found one I was afraid I'd be tempted to twist it. "*Today?* You found them today?"

"Yes, Persephone. Today."

"So give them the damn things."

"No."

"Why?"

Drum looked at the soldier, who stood cleaning his nails with the tip of the blade, heedless of our English babbling.

"Because," Drum said slowly, "they represent enough money to outfit a small army. If they make it to Barcelona, the English cause is sunk. But also because so long as the French think the rubies exist and I've got them, they'll keep me alive. I find that rather comforting."

"Drum . . ."

The soldier had had enough of our whispers. He banged the wall with the blade and motioned for us to part.

"I can't help you, Drum," I said with deep regret.

"I hardly expect you to help me."

"I mean the bits of pink fabric. I talked to Mrs. Kenney. She says you can't travel." It wouldn't matter if the guard heard that, even if he could understand English. There was no question in anyone's mind that Drum was inescapably confined to his quarters.

Did his shoulders seem to deflate or was that a trick of the light?

"Ah," he said.

"Drum—"

"'Tis of no consequence. I would never have abandoned my duty." He struggled to his elbows. "Here, help me with my shirt."

"Odd time to be worrying about such a thing."

"You know me. I'm nothing if not proprietous."

I tied one tatter to another in the back so that at least his skin was covered.

Another blast rang out. I hit the floor instinctively.

Drum smiled and patted my hair. "That was thunder, Persephone." At once the hum of rain sheeted over us. "A storm is coming our way."

With an absorbed air, he turned his gaze toward the window—a gaze that sent a distinct unease through me.

"Drum," I said, "does the storm have anything to do with the situation you mentioned earlier? The one involving"—he gave me a sharp warning glance—"my colleague in commerce?"

He shifted, unwilling to respond.

"Drum?" I was growing irritated. I'd had enough of the tall, dark and secretive routine. I wanted some answers.

"Your friend is quite brave and determined," he said with maddening vagueness.

"Great platitudes. How about some specifics?"

Drum pressed his lips together. Whatever the plan

was, he was not going to share it—a bad sign if there ever was one. So I'd find out for myself.

I got to my feet. Drum gave me a look and coughed again—a sad, sorry, please-don't-make-me-tell-you cough. I leaned over as another crack of thunder shook the ship.

"There's a boat," he whispered into the fading echo, "being dragged behind the *Neuf Ouest*. Tom said he would cut it loose when night fell or a storm hit, whichever came first."

He saw the look of horror come over my face. I could only imagine Tom in the tiny boat in a storm at night, buried by a wave or crushed against Portugal's rocky coast. It was about the only escape plan I could think of where being discovered trying to escape would probably end up being less dangerous.

"I tried to stop him," Drum said defensively. "I did. He wouldn't listen. But he has help. My men have been briefed. They will provide him the assistance he needs, including a distraction when the time comes. When Tom frees the boat from its line, Blandcroft will call that he's spotted a signal on the other side of the ship. *La Guêpe* is south of us. If Tom guides the boat away . . ." Drum paused. "I'm sorry, Persephone. I did try to stop him."

Any sensible soul would have. I collapsed against the wall.

"How long?" I asked, staring out at the howling gray abyss beyond the stern windows. "How long would it take a boat like that to be out of . . ." I couldn't bring myself to say "range of the French cannons." ". . . sight?"

"In this weather, ten minutes."

The weather outside seemed to allow no demarcation between sea and sky. I could see only row after row of white-crowned waves as high as the ship.

I thought of Tom leaping over the balcony to hold me when I believed Drum had been hanged. It hadn't mattered to him that I was crying over another man. All that mattered was that I was crying and he could help.

"I never really slept with him, Drum. I should have, but I didn't."

Eyes still closed, Drum pursed his lips. "Ah, such comfort. You really must consider becoming a sister of mercy."

"It's different with you, why didn't I see that? I might have slept with you, but I would never have felt like this."

"I can assure you I don't care to hear this."

"It's not that you're not a great guy, Drum. As sea captains go, you're damned decent. But Tom understood things. He *knew* me I guess is the only way I can say it, and I always just took it for granted. He always teased me about my risk aversion." I smiled despite the worry. "Called me 'an insurance policy waiting to happen.' But he was so good to me. He visited my father when he was in the hospital, you know. They talked about some World War Two fighter plane called the Flying Fortress until I thought I'd fall asleep in my chair. I think he stayed at Pilgrim as long as he did just because he liked seeing me so happy." My eyes started to sting. "It was like Tom was two steps ahead of me—knowing my feelings better than I knew them myself—but always willing to wait for me to catch up. I just wish that I'd told him how I feel. I just wish I'd told him that—"

"Persephone, stop."

"C'mon, let me say it. It's making me feel better."

"No," he said sharply enough for the soldier to look over. "I don't want to hear it, Persephone. Not now."

I gave him a chilly look. "You know what? You can be a real prick."

Neither of us spoke, and even without understanding English, the guard could tell this *tete-à-tete* was over. He was just gesturing for me to stand when we heard a scuffle in the hall.

The door banged open. With two soldiers at his side, the pilot—the man I now knew to be Gabin—stepped in, clutching a cowering Mr. Haverhill by the arm. He flung Mr. Haverhill down beside us. Gabin's face had been stitched and he was holding his arm close to his side.

"A pistol has been stolen, *capitaine*," Gabin said in icy tones. "The gun room has been broken into, and a pistol, a compass and the ship's best spyglass are missing."

Drum shrugged. "Perhaps they're with the imaginary rubies. Feel free to search me again if you desire."

"*Merci, mon vieux.*" Gabin gave a deep, sarcastic bow. "I believe I shall. Let us see, then, do you have them here?" He gave Drum a brutal kick in the stomach.

Drum gasped and rolled into a ball.

"Stop it, you pig!" I flung myself at Gabin, but the guard thrust me violently to the side. Mr. Haverhill hunched over, his arms across his head, shaking.

"*Non,*" Gabin said sadly, gazing at Drum. "I did not hear any broken glass. *Tante pis.* Perhaps you have hidden the items here." He drove his heel into the burned spot on Drum's back.

Drum arched in pain, the cords on his neck straining with his effort not to scream. I wanted to scream for him—and thought I did—but no sound emerged.

Gabin brought his foot back again, but this time Drum was too quick. He caught the Frenchman's foot and jerked him off his feet.

Gabin hit the floor hard. He struggled to his feet, the fury of a bull on his face.

"You will know pain, you English cur. Hold him."

The soldiers hooked Drum's legs and turned him on his stomach, pinning him in place. Gabin grabbed Drum's arm and pulled it tautly up his back. Drum's face turned white, then green. Gabin smiled with the ecstasy of a lover. He heaved. With a sickening crack, Drum's arm bent in two.

I leaned over and vomited.

Breathing deeply, Gabin got to his feet and brushed the filth of the deed from his hands. "The initial rush of pain can mask too much of what follows," he said. "We shall have you sit for a while. I'll be back." Gabin and guards marched out, closing the door behind them.

I rushed to Drum's side, afraid to even look. His face was pasty white, and a sheen of perspiration covered it.

"Help me, Mr. Haverhill!" I commanded. "Try to sit him up. Carefully, now."

We brought Drum to sitting. I didn't need to feel his arm—there was no question it was broken—but when I tried to peel back his sleeve to look to see if the bone had broken through the skin, he resisted.

"Leave it," he croaked.

"Drum, I'm so sorry. He'll kill you."

"No. I have insurance. Don't forget."

"If you have those rubies, sir," Haverhill said, "you should give them up. Gabin's looked everywhere."

"Everywhere on this ship?" Drum guffawed. "Don't be a fool."

"Does that mean you know where they are?" Haverhill was stunned.

"You're assuming the rubies exist?" Drum said. "I personally think the entire French navy has had one fucking brandy too many."

"Aye, sir, I do think they exist," Haverhill admitted. "They must. Else why would they be tearing the ship apart?" Another roll of thunder shook the *Neuf Ouest* timbers.

"Oh, I don't know. Perhaps the person who was supposed to have smuggled them on board failed to receive them from the assigned contact? Perhaps the person who was supposed to have smuggled them on board decided to keep them for his- or herself?" Drum winced deeply as he wobbled himself to his knees. Then he thrust out his good arm, insistent I help him into the chair near the porthole.

Haverhill's face grew exponentially more agitated. "Please, sir. If you have the rubies, I implore you to give them up. I fear for your life—and the lady's as well."

"And you? Wouldn't they kill you too?"

"I am but a humble officer. Nonetheless, I suppose it's possible their anger would—"

"You're a goddamned liar," Drum said in a sudden

burst of fury. "They won't kill you. At least not so long as you can give them back their rubies. That's why they threw you in here, wasn't it? To try to extract information from me?"

Haverhill? I could barely believe it.

"No, sir." Shock covered Haverhill's face. "I don't know what you're talking about—"

"Don't bloody 'sir' me." If his arm hadn't been broken Drum would have probably wrapped it around Haverhill's throat. "The rubies were in your footlocker."

"But—"

"But maybe the same person who put them there also planted the stolen orders in my desk drawer? Is that what you were about to say?" Drum asked. "Aye, I think perhaps the same person did. You."

Haverhill shook his head wordlessly. It was starting to make sense to me.

"I didn't want to believe it," Drum said. "And didn't. I fought every intuition. But only you had access to the orders. Only you had seen where I keep them. You took them, read them and destroyed them. Then you created new ones. Only you assumed any color ribbon would do. You didn't know that Lord Dunwoody, the man who gave me the orders, always uses red to match his family crest."

Haverhill struggled against the emotion until he could struggle no more. "Aye, I took the orders. You and your bloody command. Never a chance for a promotion. Never a chance for my own ship."

"You haven't earned your own ship!"

"Damn you—and damn Basehart too. Telling me

I had one of the finest captains in the English navy and to learn from you! You can all go to the devil. The French were happy enough with me and the information I could provide. Happy enough to promise me my own command. Give me the rubies!"

"No."

Haverhill started to shake. "What about these? Would you do it for these?" He thrust out his palm and in it were two bits of pink taffeta.

My feet started to burn.

"I overheard the Gypsy give you her magic," Haverhill said. He looked at me. "I know these brought her here. The French found them in your pocket. And I used some to call her back yesterday."

"Why?"

"Insurance."

Drum's gaze fixed on the fabric like a laser. "Give them to me."

"Show me the rubies."

Drum's jaw flexed. He lifted his boot and smashed it on the edge of the table. The bottom of his heel snapped off, and a tiny gossamer bag fell out. Haverhill leaped for it, but I snatched it up before he could reach it and handed it to Drum.

"Heel, huh?" I had to smile.

"Old pirate trick." Drum held up the translucent bag, his face twisted in pain.

Even in the darkness of the storm, I could see the crimson. A thousand facets glinted in the light of the swinging lantern.

"Do you know the harm these stones will do?" Drum

shook the bag at Haverhill. "Do you know what you'll be funding? These jewels have more black magic in them than an entire ship full of pink fabric."

"I don't need a goddamned sermon—sir."

"You'll be pissing away the lives of thousands of English soldiers and sailors. Men you fought for. Men who fought for you. Is that what you want? Is that what a command is worth to you?"

Haverhill hesitated.

"It's not," Drum said. "You're not that man, Haverhill. I've fought with you. I've trusted you with my life. You are *not* that man. Let's hide the stones and figure out how to take the ship back. We can do it. Together."

Haverhill licked dry lips. His determination was beginning to falter.

The door opened, and an excited Peaches flew in. "Seph, Seph! I remembered whose note had the green ribbon! It was Thaddeus—" She stopped when she saw Haverhill. "Oh, Thaddeus, no . . ."

Haverhill grabbed her, brandishing a knife he'd pulled from his belt. He held it at her throat, and Peaches's hands flew to his wrist. "Give me the rubies," he said to Drum. "Now."

Drum shook his head. "Give Miss Pyle the fabric first."

"You're in no position to bargain."

"Forget the fabric," I commanded. "I don't need it."

"Give her the fabric," Drum growled. "First."

The unalloyed authority in his voice had a paralyzing effect. A telltale tremble ran down Haverhill's arm, and even clutching his wounded arm Drum seemed to quadruple in size. With a jerk that nearly stopped my heart, Haverhill thrust his free hand forward. He dropped two tiny bits of pink into my open palm.

The instant he did, Peaches flung herself free, and Drum threw the rubies out the porthole.

Haverhill's mouth fell open. "No," he wailed. "*No!*" He collapsed to his knees. "They'll kill me. Oh, God, they'll skin me alive."

"It's not too late," Drum said. "Join me in saving us—all of us. They think you're in league with them. We can use that against them."

"They'll kill us both." Haverhill's face had turned ghostly white. I could smell his terror, even above my own. "Don't you see? We are walking dead men."

A cry cut through the storm. "A signal!" Blandcroft's young voice called. "There, to the southwest!"

Drum's eyes met mine. That was the signal to cover Tom's escape. Shouts on deck mingled with the sounds of running feet. It was all I could do to keep from looking out the windows.

"It's too late . . ." Haverhill began to whimper.

"No! Listen to me. My cousin will help," Drum said. "He can get a message out. With time, he can save us."

Haverhill lifted his head. "Your cousin? The American? Impossible."

"No. It's quite possible."

Haverhill's face tensed as he considered the meaning behind this inexplicable promise.

Gabin reappeared in the doorway with a short whip in his hand. He was flanked by two French sailors. He pointed at Drum. "Tie him up."

"Wait."

Every eye turned to Haverhill. I saw the spark of sentiment ignite in his eyes, drawing life from a dozen years of shared memory. He looked at Drum as a brother looks on brother. Blood roared in my ears.

"Your brother's dead, Gabin," Haverhill said, and I felt all hope explode out of my heart. "Killed in the navy jail by Captain Drummond," he added. "That's two of your brothers he's killed, if you're keeping score. He has the rubies, but I don't know where."

Gabin's eyes glowed like a rabid dog. "Strip him! We'll know soon enough. And after we know, we'll watch him die."

"No!" I cried. "He doesn't have them! They're on the ship. He told me where."

"She's lying," Drum said. "Ignore her."

Two guards hauled him toward the wall and tore off his shirt.

Drum looked me straight in the eye. "Go to the lantern."

My heart sunk. "No."

"What lantern?" Gabin demanded. "What is he saying?"

"Do it for me," Drum said. "Do it for all of us."

That's when I saw it—or rather when I didn't see it. The tattoo of the hawk that I'd seen on Drum's shoulder, the one Gabin's brother had spotted on the man that ran him through in battle, was gone. I looked at the man before me.

The blue eyes turned clear, like a summer sky at twilight. I didn't need an affirmation to recognize him.

I knew it was Tom Fraser behind that bravado as surely as I knew my own heart. And he saw that I saw.

"Go to the lantern," he repeated.

"With you." With Tom in my arms I could save us both.

"Seph," Tom said slowly, "we need time."

At last it hit me. This whole charade was nothing more than a bid to allow the boat—captained by Drum—to slip over the horizon on its way to Admiral Leake in Portugal. It had been Tom all along! When had I last seen them together? On deck this morning, right before the rising sun showed us the French ship. Tom, not Drum, had been with me when the first cannonball hit. Tom, not Drum, had fired the *Neuf Ouest* cannon. Tom, not Drum, had been beaten and broken. Tom, not Drum, had been flogged and was about to be flogged again.

And now he wanted me to leave him so that he could sacrifice himself to save the land of the Spice Girls? I don't think so.

"You've made a mistake," I announced to Gabin. "This is not—"

"Persephone, no," Tom said.

"Peaches," I yelled. "Get Mrs. Kenney! As fast as you can!" Pleaches fled.

Without warning Haverhill jumped like a startled rabbit. He ran to the stern window, then pointed. "There! In a boat. He's in the boat."

At almost the same instant a French-accented shout went up on deck. "The boat! There, one point off the starboard bow. She's escaping!"

Gabin grabbed me by the arm and dragged me to the balcony. The rain pelted down in torrents. In my hand I clutched the tiny bits of pink fabric, trying to protect them from the elements. I could see a small boat in the middle distance.

"Is that one of your compatriots? Someone you've sent for help?" Gabin demanded.

I spit in his face and wrested myself free. In an instant I had my arms around Tom. The lantern was within arm's length. I reached for it.

Haverhill snatched it from my fingertips, threw open the porthole and launched it into the raging sea. "Tit for tat, Miss Pyle."

Gabin said, "Sentimental whore. You shall see how we deal with escapees. Leave them for now," he said to the guards. "Call the men to their battle stations."

They let Tom fall. The full weight of his upper body landed on his broken arm and he let out a piercing howl. His eyes fluttered closed as the room emptied.

"Tom," I said softly. I stroked his damp hair. His breathing was labored. I took his good hand and held it to my cheek. "Oh, Tom, how could I have done this to you?"

"You did nothing," he said hoarsely. "I chose. And I'm glad."

"Oh, aye," a slightly mocking voice said behind us, "'Tis a blessing to have the shit kicked out of you. Every captain's dream."

"Drum!" I squawked. "Where—"

"I hoisted myself over the railing. I've been in the

hold. Maneuvered around the outside of the ship with ropes. What have they done to him?"

"Shouldn't you be on that ship out there?"

"Boat." He knelt down by Tom. "And, aye—that's what Gabin's supposed to think, at least. Christ." He looked at Tom's arm and the burn on his shoulder. "I guess they really believed you were me. Bastards."

"Go," Tom croaked. "There's not much time."

The sound of a blast from the cannons above roared through the room.

"Aye, before the esteemed French figure out the boat's empty. Have no fear. I think they'll shoot at it all night. This was Tom's idea, actually," Drum said to me. "Said he got it from a book you gave him."

I looked again out the window. The boat was in the distance, angled against the current, sail taut against the wind, a spot of light at its stern.

Drum caught my gaze. "It's amazing," he said, "how much a swaying lantern can effect." He dug in the drawer and pulled out a flask. Then he got down on one knee, twisted off the top and held it to Tom's mouth.

"Drink."

The French unleashed another blast, but the ball passed neatly to the right of the little boat.

Tom took a deep draught. "Jesus," he sputtered. "That's the worst whiskey I've ever tasted. No wonder British cuisine is in the state it is." A smile formed briefly on his face. A moment later his eyes closed and his breathing eased.

Drum signaled for me to follow him to the balcony.

"You gave him whiskey?" I said.

"Laudanum." He began to unbutton his shirt.

"What are you doing?"

"I'm going to be swimming."

"Swimming?! It's miles from Portugal. You said so yourself."

"I'm not swimming to Portugal. We're in a shipping lane now. With that"—he pointed to a large piece of driftwood propped against the balcony wall—"and a little luck, I can last until an English ship passes."

"Look, I may not know much about sailing, but I know swimming. Look at those whitecaps. You won't last an hour."

Drum met my eyes. "Let us hope an hour will be enough."

It was suicide. "No."

"Dear me, not even willing to hope, are you?" He pulled off his shirt and chucked me on the chin. "Not after all we've shared?"

"Dammit, Drum, you know what I mean."

"We have no choice." He took a compass, watch and spyglass from his pocket and wrapped them carefully in the shirt, which he tied into a knot. Then he pulled a tiny knife with an odd silver handle from his pocket and cut away the extraneous fabric.

"What's that? There on the handle?"

"What? This? An egret. The woman who gave it to me said it was a symbol of fortune. I think it brought her more fortune than me, though, for she married the Earl of Donlevy not long after we parted."

A third blast rocked the ship.

In the cabin, Tom rolled onto his stomach and moaned.

"How long will the laudanum last?" I asked.

"Hardly matters," Drum said. "You need to take him home." He caught my fist and opened my fingers.

I gazed at the two tiny bits of silk. "How did you know?"

He jerked his thumb toward the far edge of the balcony. "I spent the last hour just under there."

"I don't want to leave you."

"Ah, if I had a crown for every time I've heard a woman say that."

"Drum," I said, agitated. "We have to think of a different plan."

The humor on his face evaporated. "They'll kill Tom. In two minutes, maybe three, they'll have either destroyed the boat or it will be out of range. Then they'll be back and they'll take Tom away. Is that what you want? You didn't eat the pomegranate seeds. Go."

"But you—"

"Will do my proper job. Persephone, this is my proper job. You have to see that."

"What about your crew? What about Elettra?"

"The crew will be unharmed. They can be exchanged for French prisoners. 'Tis a common practice. And Elettra will be taken care—one way or another."

"Come with me and Tom. I can hold both of you."

"You know I can't. Besides, there's only two pieces of silk. Two pieces, two people. You wouldn't want to end up with two halves of a man, would you?"

I swiped at an eye. "Depends on the halves."

"Well, Tom wouldn't care for it either way." He took my hand and kissed it. "And if I ever do take you to bed, I want a whole man to be there." His eyes gleamed like cerulean stars, and I fought for a breath.

"Drum, please. Stay here and hide. You know this ship inside and out. They'll never find you. Forget Barcelona."

"You know me as well as anyone could, Persephone. Do you think I could do that?"

Damn authorial understanding. No hero of mine worth his ink would hide.

"A ship will come," he said, "and I will get to Leake and Barcelona will be saved. You have to believe that. The Venetians have a phrase for it—*Ad ogni suo posto adeguato.* 'To each his proper place.' Get to yours."

Drum swung me around until I was facing the room, and I looked down at the bits of fabric in my hand. He opened a cabinet near his cot, pulled out a small lantern and lit it. "It's amazing what one lantern can effect," he said, handing it to me. He gave me a gentle push.

I knew he was right. Drum's entire life had been lived to reach this point. And as brave and self-sacrificing as Tom had been, he was the one who'd been blown off course. In helping Drum, I had wrenched Tom onto a collision course with history that was not his to run. This was not my brother's slot car set, after all, and I had no business merrily running the controls here. I owed these men their lives back. Who was I to take their proper fate from either of them?

"Wait," I said to Drum. "I have a crazy request."

"I may be fast, but two minutes is beyond even my capabilities."

"I'd like you to take off my shoe."

He cocked his head. "Your shoe?"

"Yes, that pink silky thing there, at the end of my foot."

He opened his mouth to question me, then shut it and shrugged. He dropped to one knee, and I closed my eyes. I loved Tom. I knew that now—though whether Tom loved me after all that had happened was another matter. But Drum . . . Drum had a place in my heart too. So as long as I had Drum right here, why not eliminate any doubt?

I felt a tug, then another, then another. The shoes burned so hot I squeaked.

"I'm afraid," he said, rising, "I cannot."

"I thought that might happen." I stamped my burning soles.

"I think I can tell you what the tattoo on your ankle says, though." Drum slipped his hands into his pockets. "I know only a little Arabic—Abdul is teaching me. But the words there translate as 'chase joy' or something close to it."

"Chase joy, huh? Me?"

"Maybe not once, perhaps." Drum smiled. "But now certainly."

"What about the other one?" If I was going to have an *X* hovering northwest of my nipple for the rest of my days, I'd like some insight into that as well.

Drum grunted grumpily. "I have not been so favored."

Oops. Wrong hero. I pulled the neckline of my gown down just far enough for him to view the mark.

"Ah, a cross," he said

"Like a treasure map."

"Fitting, indeed, given its placement over your heart. That one I cannot say. It is a mystery. Perhaps one day I'll help you solve that as well."

I held on to the vision of one day, pushing the next hour out of my head. "I'd like that."

"It's time we said good-bye."

I bit my lip. "You're very brave."

"Though foolish is what you think."

"Don't put words in my mouth."

"Then how about this?" He took me in his arms, bent me backward, and kissed me. The world turned a deep Wouldn't It Be Nice blue.

"There," he said when we parted. "Proof positive there's at least one good thing the French have given the world. Good-bye, Persephone. And always chase joy. That's the way I want to remember you."

I watched as his dark form disappeared over the side and heard the soft *plop* as he entered the water.

"Good-bye, Drum," I said softly. "Get to it."

The lantern's poetic light seemed to swell. I swear I saw roller coasters of sparkles zip Tinker Bell–like around its glass interior.

"As if," I said tartly, "I needed to prove I believe."

I heard the Frenchmen tromping down the stairs. With my heart thundering in my veins, I put the lantern on the floor and stretched out along Tom's length, conscious even in my fear of how natural it felt.

Fitting indeed. I hoped Tom felt it too.

I wrapped myself around him, careful not to jostle his broken arm, and with a heart pointed unremittingly toward home and, I hoped, both joy and indoor plumbing, I tossed the last of the silk into the flame.

Chapter Twenty-eight

"*How* do you say *chicken* in French?" Dana asked me.

Happily, her smirk disappeared as the cabbie took a hard right over what I presumed to be the Seine, and our bags thudded dangerously to the side of the backseat. When Tom and I had departed from the *Neuf Ouest*, he'd landed in Paris and I'd landed in Pittsburgh. Dana had gamely agreed to kick off her summer vacation as my chaperone on what was looking increasingly like an ill-considered trip to the land of soccer and crêpes.

"It's *vache*, I think. *Vache* or *bouche*," I said, "but I hardly think traveling three thousand miles from Pittsburgh without an invitation counts as chicken. Majestically stupid, perhaps, but not chicken."

"Did you bring condoms?"

I looked at the cabbie, but he was watching the road. Clearly we were just more gibberish-spouting Americans.

"I . . . well, no," I admitted. Since I'd hit the twenty-first century, I hadn't exactly felt like replenishing my paltry two-count supply.

Dana flapped her elbows, chicken-style. *"Brawk, brawk, brawk, brawk, brawk, brawk, brawk."*

The cabdriver met my eyes in the rearview mirror. *"Poulet,"* he said.

"Huh?"

"Vache, moooo," he said, lowing deeply. *"Brawk, brawk, brawk—c'est 'poulet.'"*

"Bouche?" I put in hopefully.

He pointed to his mouth.

Everyone's a critic.

Dana gave me a meaningful look. "Explain to me again why you didn't return Tom's call."

I shifted. Dana didn't know anything about my misadventure in 1706 or the conflicting feelings I'd had since I'd returned. "It isn't like he killed himself dialing either, you know. One call; that's it." I sighed. "I don't know. Venice ended up being really weird."

"Weird like lots of earthshaking sex and now you're too embarrassed to look him in the eye, or weird like there *could* have been lots of earthshaking sex but you held him at arm's length until the feeling passed?"

"Um."

"That's what I was afraid of. Girl, you need to get down to business. So you'll be bunking at his place, right?"

"He's in the hospital, remember? And I distinctly recall giving you my credit card number for our bed-and-breakfast reservation."

"Damned decent of you to help out a poor school-teacher like that. I'm sure Jacques can keep me company."

"Jacques?"

"The guy with the sexy voice who owns the place. Ditched the corporate world to write a novel—"

"Really? Has he ever shopped in Nine West?"

"—so be sure to take that overnight bag along."

"What? So I can split a bed with Tom's father? He's staying at Tom's apartment here, you know."

"But if you have the overnight bag with you, there's always the chance for an invitation, right? You said Tom was getting out soon, and old guys are hard of hearing anyhow. It pays to be prepared. Weren't you ever a Girl Scout?"

"My troop leader skipped over the finer points of nabbing a sex invitation. Too busy making those darn sit-upons."

"Your call, Seph. But if there's a beret on the door-knob of our room at the bed-and-breakfast, check back in the morning."

Perfect.

The cabbie pulled to a stop in front of an institutional gray building.

"No, no, let me get this," I said to Dana, handing the driver a bill. "The B and B's only a couple more blocks. I have the address. I'll be there in a couple of hours."

Dana put her hand on my arm. "Listen, Seph, I don't know why it took you three weeks to decide to come to Paris, and I don't know what happened in Venice, but Tom seems like a good guy. And I haven't seen you act this insane in a long time. Don't miss the opportunity to let him know how you feel."

"Thanks, Dana." But it wasn't *my* feelings I was worried about. I primped my hair. "Do I look like shit?"

"A little. But you also look like someone who hasn't had regular sex in a long time. That ought to make up for it."

I hoisted myself from the cab while the driver made change. He handed me a card. "Here's my number. If things don't work out, geev me a call. I can geev you ride."

"Thanks," I said, realizing far too late he'd understood every word Dana and I had said.

The cab pulled away, then squealed to a stop. My overnight bag shot out the back door and landed near the sidewalk. A foot of condoms flopped from the side pocket.

I gathered my bag and primly zipped the pocket. Walking toward the hospital's entrance, I passed beds of pansies and impatiens straining optimistically toward the late May sun. I stopped at the flower stand outside and chose a handful of sunflowers. They smelled faintly of water and chocolate, though I suspected it was the hint of Van Gogh insanity that spoke to me.

Flowers in hand, I took a deep breath and made my way to the reception desk.

"*Où est* Tom Fraser?"

I'm sure my masterful command of the French language impressed the ultraslim, ultrablonde hospital receptionist, which is undoubtedly why she gave my ass an openly disdainful look and said, "Hot chocolate? The café is next door."

Tom was right. Three hundred years hadn't improved their manners. Frenchwomen may not get fat, but they spend their whole lives screwing Frenchmen, so I guess in the end justice is served.

The lack of an answer didn't really matter. In the short conversation I'd had with Tom's father, he'd said Tom's room overlooked the street. And the hospital was only two stories tall.

I found the sign that read FRASER, T on the upper floor.

The blinds were drawn against the afternoon sun, giving the room and its bleak disinfectant smell a warm, suffocating feel. Tom lay on his side, asleep. I could barely make out his face in the long shadows.

Opposite the bed stood a chest upon which rested a vase of wilting carnations and another of wilting hydrangeas. I wheeled my suitcase to the corner and in the dark managed to find a half-empty water pitcher to hold the sunflowers. I was transferring some stems of still-vibrant greenery from the other two bouquets when I heard a rustle.

"Seph," Tom said. "It's good to see you."

My heart shook a little but I continued my arranging. "Back to the American accent, is it?"

"Americans don't have accents, remember?"

"They do when they're from Fargo." I wanted to throw myself into his arms, but the undertone of strain in his voice made me hesitate. "Where's your dad?"

"Back at the apartment. He's a little worried about

leaving his son in a city where a simple holdup turns into assault, battery and an inexplicable flogging."

"I know. France sucks. I think you should catch the first flight home."

Tom gave a weak chuckle.

"So that's what you told people?" I said. "You were held up?"

"Best I could do on short notice. Fortunately I wasn't conscious long enough to answer many questions. Open the blinds, will you?"

I found the cord and raised it. Persephone Pyle as Florence Nightingale, bringing light to the ill. A copy of *Le Monde* lay open on the guest chair. I busied myself neatening the sections.

"Afraid to look?" he asked.

"A little."

"Take your time. I'm enjoying the view."

I could delay no longer. I turned to see him in the light.

"Wow," he said, "if that's your reaction, I can understand why no one's offered me a mirror."

Tom's arm was in a cast held apart from his body by a metal brace. An ugly red scar snaked down his arm and a shorter one decorated his chin. His hair was clean and long and his pajamas fresh, but his sunken cheeks and the pallor of his skin made the depth of his ordeal apparent.

I went to him, horrified.

"It's not that bad, surely," he said.

He caught my hand and squeezed. His grip was strong and warm, but the weight he'd lost made the veins on the back of his hands look like some horrible Mapquest screen.

"You must be so sick," I said at last.

He sighed. "A bruised liver, lacerated kidney, compound fracture of the arm and a healthy infection from the whip. All somewhat tiresome. Hey, but the good news is, they've had me on so much medication since I arrived that half the time I didn't know who I was."

"That's kinda funny, considering."

"Kinda. The other half of the time I thought about you." His eyes glittered.

I was too scared to hold his gaze. I thought about the words he'd just spoken and the ones, more numerous, he hadn't. I thought about the back I doubted I'd ever have the courage to look at. I thought about all the thinking I'd done since I'd landed in Pittsburgh.

"Why did you do it, Tom?"

The glittering turned an innocent crystal clear. "Do what?"

"*Tom.*"

"Letting the bloody landlubber run my ship, do you mean?" he drawled in his pitch-perfect imitation of Drum. When I didn't smile he said, "I'm sorry, Seph. Drum and I thought it was our only choice. The crew was so good a monkey could have captained the damned thing. And someone had to get word to Portugal. Drum had a slim chance of getting on another ship and convincing them to help. I would have had none." His hand slipped distractedly from mine. "I-I hope he made it."

We'd never know for certain. Barcelona had been

saved—that much I'd checked almost immediately after I landed. But how, in fact, Admiral Leake got word and whether Drum played a role was a piece of minutiae lost to the sandstorm of time.

"You were sacrificing yourself," I said. "You knew Gabin would want to kill the man he thought was Drum."

"Drum's assignment was no cakewalk either," Tom replied. "Without even a boat in those waters . . . Did you see a ship pass?" he asked hesitantly. "I mean, how long did we stay there after I passed out?"

"Not long. A couple of moments." I shook my head. "I'm sorry. I didn't see anything."

"No, of course not. I didn't really expect . . ."

That dreadful last hour on the *Neuf Ouest* had been on my mind almost continuously since I'd returned. But one moment in particular stood out:

"*It was like Tom was two steps ahead of me,*" I'd said to Drum, "*knowing my feelings better than I knew them myself—but always willing to wait for me to catch up. I just wish that I'd told him how I feel. I just wish I'd told him that—*"

"*Persephone, stop.*"

"*C'mon, let me say it. It's making me feel better.*"

"*No,*" he said sharply enough for the soldier to look over. "*I don't want to hear it, Persephone. Not now.*"

I shifted from foot to foot and the sandals made a troubled noise. Drum's refusal to hear my confession had been understandable until I realized it hadn't been Drum at all—it had been Tom. His utter rejection of my feelings that day had kept me from flying to his side the minute I'd landed in Pittsburgh. In truth, it had nearly kept me from flying to Paris at all. Not that I blamed him, of course. I'd put him through a hell even true love couldn't survive, let alone simple collegial lust.

"Well," I said carefully, "I just wanted to tell you how brave I thought you were and how sorry I am about everything that happened."

"Hey, it makes a great story."

"Right." We looked at each other and smiled. As if there were anyone we could actually tell the story to.

"I tried to call," he said.

"Yeah, I was kinda busy with my dad for a bit. Then, once I decided I was coming, I sorta wanted to surprise you, I guess."

"Ah. And he's okay, your father?"

"Yes, thank you. He's doing great."

We fell silent. I tugged my cuff.

"You liking Paris so far?" I said.

"Great hospital food."

"Right. Sorry."

Suddenly he twitched and stole a glance at the clock.

"Oh, gosh, I'm sorry." I stood. "I'll come back tonight. You were napping and I just blew in like—"

"No, no, no. It's not that. Don't go. What time is it?"

"Two thirty-five."

"Oh, good." He settled back on the pillow, gingerly I noticed, and still on his side.

"Your back?"

He nodded.

"Can I . . . see?"

He met my eyes. "This is not your fault, Seph. I don't want it to be some sort of punishment for you."

"You can't change what I feel. I'm going to have to figure out on my own how to make up for things. I would like to see your back—I mean, if you're letting anyone see it."

He met my eye. "You're sure?"

"Yeah."

He struggled out of the pajama sleeve covering the good arm and let the fabric drop away. The wounds were in the initial stages of healing: angry, red and seeping. The burn on his shoulder was covered in a damp dressing.

"Will you need a graft?" I asked, pointing to the shoulder.

"Already had one."

"Shit." I placed my hand over my mouth and felt tears sting my eyes.

He caught me by the arm and pulled me down alongside him. "You didn't choose for me to take Drum's place," he said roughly. "I did. If you're looking for penance, let me choose it. I've got something considerably more satisfying on my mind."

Even with his injuries, his good arm was strong. "W-what?"

He kissed me slowly and insistently. Goose bumps exploded on every nerve ending.

"I have an idea that requires a certain accommodating here-ness," he said as he slipped a knee between my legs. "Kimberly had my new place stocked with the most wonderful French sheets." He ran the tip of his nose along the curve of my breast and took in the scent and texture with throaty delight. "Eight hundred threads per inch."

Per inch, I thought. What a wonderful way to look at things. "Sounds silky."

"They're called Porthault."

Port-o. I could barely watch his lips form the word without my favorite goose bump doing the Hokey-Pokey.

"They literally caress any part of you that's touching them when you move," he said. "Your back. Your shoulders. Your hips."

Oh, God.

"And someday very soon," he added, "I intend to introduce you to their pleasures. But for now, take off your pants."

"*Tom!*"

"One never knows the form penance will take, but in the state I'm in, I'd say it's going to be very slow and deeply felt."

"Tom Fraser! Your Sunday school teacher is going to turn you over her knee."

"We'll try that one another day. Is this a front-hook bra?"

"We're in a hospital room!"

"Look, if you think you're going to come in here waggling those fabulous hips—"

"I did *not* waggle anything!"

"—and not expect me to call you on it, you've got another thing coming."

"A fact you're foreshadowing quite nicely."

"You know me." He brought a leg over mine. "I don't believe in obscuring important plot points."

But as ready as I was to put this story to bed, I just couldn't. There are some men you can sleep with without knowing the truth. In fact, there are some men where the less talking they do of any sort is for the better. Tom wasn't either one of those. I moved my newly fabulous hips away from him. "Wait."

He sighed. "Please don't tell me this is going to turn out like that night on the recycling bin. I can't even look at the document-retention policy anymore."

"That day in Drum's cabin, when I thought you were Drum, I started to say something to you and you stopped me. Do you remember?"

His arm fell away. "Yes."

Uh, boy, I thought. This isn't going to have a happy ending, is it? Wrapping my arms around my knees and closing my ears to the howl of outrage from the lower half of my body, I said, "That day I started to tell you something about, well, you and me."

"Seph, c'mon. Let's not relive it."

The sharpness in his voice surprised me. "No, I'd like to finish this time. I'd started to say something about you and me that—"

"—I hadn't earned the right to hear," he said savagely. "And I still haven't. Christ, wasn't it bad enough I was lying to you about who I was? Do you really think

I wanted you to say something that you'd resent having said once you learned it was me?"

I felt as if a hundred pounds of helium had been pumped into me. "Oh, Tom."

"No, don't. Not yet." His eyes turned stormy. "I was the one who beat up Gabin. I found you in Drum's cabin starting to jump overboard, and you assumed I was Drum. Gabin walked in, and it was convenient to maintain the lie. "

I remembered Gabin's battered face. "Why . . . ?"

"Is there a reason that would excuse it? I doubt it. But I watched him butcher a man," he added more softly, "and I find I just can't apologize for how I repaid him."

I watched his heart beat in his throat as he waited for my response. This man had been willing to give his life to save England, and, likely, America. He'd saved Drum's life and mine in that jail. And he'd been willing to let me choose Drum if that's what I'd wanted. I hadn't been in that alleyway that day when Charles Davitch was killed. Who was I to judge?

"Tom—"

"But this I must apologize for: I left Gabin for dead and did nothing to correct your misconception. *That* was dishonorable."

"No one could lecture you on honor." I took his hand. "Certainly not me."

"A lecture on honor?" an elderly Italian voice said. "In bed? Oh, my dear Thomas, that is not an encouraging sign."

Professor Di Marvelo stood in the doorway with a

backpack in his hand, grinning. I leaped out of the bed and, with a face as red as Chianti, planted myself firmly in a guest chair.

Di Marvelo waved away my concern. "Am I not Italian? Do I not know the possibilities of a May afternoon?" He kissed me on the forehead and shook Tom's hand. "It is good to see you again, my young friends. I was very sorry to hear about Thomas's ill fortune."

"How did you know?" I asked.

"Did Thomas not tell you? He left me a message a week or so ago. Had a few more questions about the sea captain—though after all he's been through, I'm surprised his interest in history remains as strong." Di Marvelo dropped his pack on the radiator in front of the window. "Since I have business from time to time in Paris, I decided I would give him his answers in person."

He unzipped the bag, withdrew two books and took up residence in the chair at the foot of the bed.

"Thomas, you asked me if there was any mention of Captain George Drummond at or immediately before the Battle of Barcelona. Since the battle occurred after Drummond's hanging, it's fair to say I found the question an odd one. Nonetheless, it was no trouble to contact my colleague Alejandro Perez at the Universitat de Barcelona. If there's anything about the battle to be known, he knows it."

I found myself gripping the arms of my chair.

"Alejandro found nothing," Di Marvelo said. "In no source is there a mention of Captain Drummond."

I couldn't meet Tom's eye. Neither of us wanted to think about what that meant.

"Point number two. You asked me to reconfirm the hanging took place, the hanging that you and I read on the page, in black and white, in my office."

Tom nodded, solemn.

"As I had to assume you meant I should look for confirmation of the hanging in another source, I did a search. I found nothing. Nothing beyond the original source."

"But that original source?" Tom said. "Did you look at that again?"

Di Marvelo regarded Tom strangely. "I did," he said. "And I felt certain you would ask, so I brought it with me."

I held my breath. Di Marvelo handed me the book. The page in question had been marked with an index card. I opened to it. "Captain George Drummond, age 36," the words read, "lately of Portsmouth and formerly of Her Majesty's Royal Navy, was hanged today after being found guilty of treason."

Nothing had changed. Whatever we'd tried to accomplish in Gibraltar had been for naught. Barcelona had been saved. Drum had not.

I looked at Tom and shook my head. Two tears striped my cheeks.

Tom, as acutely aware of Di Marvelo's watchful gaze as I, said, "Seph had a dream that he'd been saved and thought—however improbably—that we'd misread the page. We must apologize for having taken up your time."

"Ah." Di Marvelo laced his fingers and looked at me sadly. "I thought as much. The time, it is nothing. *Per favore,* do not trouble yourself about it. I am sorry for you, Signorina Pyle. I wish I could have put your mind at ease."

"And there is nothing more?" I said. "Nothing at all of Captain Drummond in your books?"

"No, *signorina,* not of him. Of his ship, *sì.*"

I jerked my head up. "His ship?"

Di Marvelo shuffled through his notes. "It is not much. Let us see . . . ah, yes, the *Neuf Ouest* was captured by a French privateer within a day or so of Captain Drummond's hanging, though by that time it had been in the hands of another privateer captain for several weeks. The French renamed her *La Prix*—The Prize— and she appeared, ironically, at the Battle of Barcelona, though she did not distinguish herself in action there and earned little more than a mention in French ship lists. For two years, the French used her in almost every battle they fought in and around the Mediterranean. In 1708 she was captured by a ship owned by an American trader, a trader who coincidentally had a minor connection to the admiral you asked me about."

"Leake?"

"No, no. Basehart."

I sat up in my chair. Elettra Basehart's cover story was that she'd married an American trader, a man I knew to be pure fiction, if you'll pardon the expression, for if there's anything I've learned, it's that fiction is never pure. "What was the connection?"

"It is an interesting story," Di Marvelo said. "The stuff of great drama. You'll recall I told you it was rumored that Basehart's daughter . . . let me see . . ."

He reached for his glasses. "What was her name? Elora?"

"Elettra."

His brows rose significantly, and he turned to stare me full in the face. So did Tom.

"Yes, Elettra," Di Marvelo confirmed. "It seems Elettra had run off to marry a silk merchant. This was later found to be untrue. Let me see if I have this right—" He put his glasses on and checked a card in his hand. "Mrs. Mary Seltwhistle, a former and, may I say, not very kind, school friend of Elettra's, wrote a series of letters to her sister over a ten-year period beginning in 1707. Her sister was the wife of a Sir Richard Winslow, a naval captain who would eventually leave the dubious mark on history of foundering and sinking a ship called *The Otter* on her first day out of the shipyard. Winslow's letters—and therefore Mrs. Seltwhistle's—survived and were collected. They're at the British Library. When you mentioned Basehart, it struck a note in my memory."

Di Marvelo flipped the card over. "In a letter dated 11 July 1710 Mrs. Seltwhistle writes she'd found Elettra Basehart living alone in New York City—in, as Mrs. Seltwhistle wrote, 'an inordinately large home with a pudgy-faced daughter and far more servants than the immoral minx deserves.'"

I smiled. "Good for her. So Elettra never married?"

"No," Di Marvelo said. "She married a Frenchman."

"She married the Frenchman?!"

Di Marvelo stopped and gazed at me over the top of his glasses.

"Um." I felt the blood creeping across my cheeks. "It just seems odd to have married a Frenchman, don't you think? I mean, we were at war with them then."

I could feel Tom's interrogatory observation as well. He didn't know anything about Elettra or the Frenchman.

"According to Mrs. Seltwhistle," Di Marvelo said, "the marriage was an unhappy one, and the Frenchman was away for long periods."

Poor Elettra. The French have more to answer for than Peugeots.

"I don't understand then," I said. "What exactly was the connection between Admiral Basehart and this American merchant who took the *Neuf Ouest?*"

"Well, again Mrs. Seltwhistle is our authority here," Di Marvelo said. "She claims the merchant was known to spend long evenings at Elettra's home either alone with Elettra—"

"Oh dear."

"—or with Elettra and her father—"

"Her father the admiral?!"

"Her father the admiral." Di Marvelo had grown immune to my Tourette's-like interjections and barely paused. "And Mrs. Seltwhistle asserts this American was in fact the father of the child Elettra was carrying at the time."

"As if," I said indignantly, "Elettra would tell someone like Mary Seltwhistle who the father of her child was."

"Perhaps," Tom said under his breath, "she had 'Right of First Night Information.'"

"Indeed," Di Marvelo continued, "one would argue the lady was making a tawdry and baseless accusation. But thirty-six years later, in 1746, the American merchant's will was filed in a New York court. To whom do you suppose he left his fortune?"

My heart began to thump. "Elettra's children?"

"*Esattamente!* You are exactly right, *signorina.*"

Could Drum actually have survived to resurface as an American merchant? It seemed Elettra had reconciled with her father. If that had happened, couldn't anything? "What," I asked carefully, "was the American's name?"

Di Marvelo gave me a wry look. "What, *signorina?* You do not know?"

"*Professore.*"

"Thomas," he said.

"Thomas?" I nearly shouted. "Thomas *Fraser?*"

"Phillip," Di Marvelo corrected. "Phillip Thomas."

"Thomas" from Tom, Drum's American twin; "Phillip" from the name I'd bestowed on him. It seemed too much to be a coincidence, but there was no way to know for sure.

"That's all?" I said.

"*Sì.* No, wait. There is one more thing. To me it is insignificant, but the information about the American excited you so, I dare not judge, eh? After it was recaptured by the American merchant, the ship you know as the *Neuf Ouest* was mentioned a number of times in French naval papers as a potent 'commercial disrupter.'"

I stared at him blankly.

"Pirate ship," he said, smiling. "The French were quite bitter about it—I suppose because the ship had once been theirs and because they did not understand why an American merchant would involve himself in a war not his own."

Unless the war was his own. My eyes snapped to Tom, who saw the same thing. I felt so close to knowing.

"It was rumored,'" Di Marvelo added, "the merchant was an English spy."

Omigod. Just as Peaches had suggested. I wondered if she'd convinced Basehart.

"What did you mean," I asked, "when you said 'the ship you know as the *Neuf Ouest*'?"

"Ah," Di Marvelo said, "Thomas rechristened her. From the time he captured her until the day she was sold for scrap eighteen years later, she ran under the name *The Pomegranate Seed*."

I cheered and threw my arms around Tom's neck. He gripped me enthusiastically if somewhat confusedly.

When I turned, Di Marvelo was observing me with speculation.

"You see, um, that was in the dream too," I explained. "Captain Drummond had somehow managed to avoid being hanged and had lived on to become a spy. And now with what you've told us"—I made some complicated cross-referencing motions with my hand—"it's clear that's what happened."

"Perfectly clear." Di Marvelo gathered his books and returned them to his pack. "I am pleased I have made you happy again, *signorina*. I shall leave you to your May afternoon and even more happiness." He kissed me again and shook Tom's hand. "Be careful what she dreams, *sì?*"

Tom nodded. "I will. Thank you, *professore.*"

Di Marvelo shouldered his backpack, then stopped. "Oh, Thomas, before I go, I wanted to tell you the wounds on your back have a particular and, shall we say, historic naval look to them. You may want to alert the French police. It could be a clue."

Tom swallowed. "I will."

"I'm certain you will."

I walked Di Marvelo to the door. He gave me a benevolent smile. "You'll remember the importance of those in the present, won't you, Signorina Pyle?"

"*Sì, professore. Ad ogni suo posto adeguato.* To each his proper place."

He clapped his hands. "*Molto bene!* We'll make an Italian out of you yet. *Ciao,* my friends."

The instant he disappeared around the corner I cried, "Tom, he's alive!"

"I got that impression." Tom narrowed his eyes. "*The Pomegranate Seed?*"

I bit my lip. "Maybe he likes pomegranates?"

"Ha."

"Hey, I'm here with you, aren't I?"

Tom harrumphed. "I'd say the evidence was supportive but not entirely convincing. However"—he lifted his brow—"I am willing to consider an oral argument on the matter."

I sat down next to him and crossed my legs. "You

remember Typhoid Mary? Well, meet Heart Attack Seph. I'm afraid your system isn't up to the challenge."

"What better place to test your theory than a hospital?"

"Uh-uh."

"Maybe a second one would restart my heart—like a defibrillator."

"Gosh, sounds like a real breakthrough in resuscitational medicine."

He smiled, and our fingers laced.

Was I fated to end up with Tom? I didn't need a tug at my sandal laces to answer that one. One look at the way those thin cotton pajamas slid over the deeply fascinating terrain of his lower torso, and I was pretty sure I was. In fact, if my body was a Magic 8 Ball, I'm pretty sure you could turn me over and my ass would read ALL SIGNS POINT TO YES.

I smoothed a stray lock over his ear, and he caught my hand and kissed it.

"I don't suppose I could convince you to come to Paris," he said.

"And leave Pittsburgh?"

We both laughed.

"Yet," he said wisely, "you didn't say yes."

My eyes met his. In that sparkling blue danced both invitation and understanding. He would welcome me into his life—I knew he would—but he saw the obstacles as well. The ending was mine to write.

"It's not that easy," I said, shifting. "I like my job. I really like what we do at Pilgrim. My dad's sick. There's

a lot of things. Heck, I don't even know if they let se-
quoias into France."

His hand tightened around mine. "Not to mention
the fact you've got a book to write."

"Oh, cripes, that too."

"But I could count on you to visit a lot?"

I traced the ridge of his knuckles. "How much is a
lot?"

"Mondays, Thursdays and Saturdays."

I laughed. "Well, I have two weeks of vacation
scheduled for November, but I was hoping for someplace hot."

Tom pulled my ear to his mouth and made a colorful
suggestion.

"Okay," I said as my shoes did an energetic *chinga-
ching*. "That would be hot."

He peered over the edge of the bed. "Still no 'ET
phone home' for the sandals?"

"Nah." I stretched out a leg. "I've sorta grown used
to them anyhow."

His eyes ran from my Mrs. Robinson Red toenails to
the edge of my black cotton miniskirt. "Magnificent."

I didn't ask him to untie the bow. I decided I did
not need to know. One of the things the last few weeks
taught me was, trust your heart, not your shoes. I was
livin' life Laurie Partridge–style now.

"Two weeks in November it is then," he declared.
"But I'm taking a week off when I get out of here and
I'll absolutely need you then or . . . or . . ."

"Or what?"

"I'll die."

"Really?" I crossed my arms.

"I'm an officer of the court. I cannot lie about such matters. A week in June; it's settled."

"Hmmm. I suppose I owe it to medical science—"

"Don't forget that resuscitational research."

"—not to mention your father—to keep you alive."

"And don't forget my requirements."

"Requirements?"

"White, cotton and a tiny pink bow."

"Oh, those." I made a dismissive gesture. "I'd totally forgotten."

Tom hooked a finger into my waistband and fished out a small length of panty that looked suspiciously like it met every one of his requirements.

Somewhere in the hallway a clock chimed three times.

"Oh, Christ!" Tom jerked to attention, nearly knocking me off the bed. "Suddenly I'm exhausted. Can you come back tomorrow?"

"Well, sure, but—"

"Your stuff's over there."

"Gosh, okay. I get the message." I crossed to my suitcase and knelt. "Is there anything I can bring you when I return?" I asked, trying to extract my purse from the side pocket.

"Um."

"Um?" I repeated. "'Fraid I don't know 'um.'" I pulled out the brochure for the bed-and-breakfast and the cabbie's card. "Is there anything I can bring you for which you can provide slightly more detail?"

This time I got no answer at all.

"Tom," a contralto voice chided, "are you going to answer her or just sit there gaping at me?"

I turned to find Kimberly Jacobs standing in the doorway.

"Steph, darling," she cried. "So good to see you." She swanned over and gave me a pair of French smoochie-smoochies. "Tom didn't mention you were coming."

"It's Seph, actually," I said, "and Tom didn't know. I wasn't quite sure myself until the last minute."

Kimberly wore a white linen sundress cut so close I could see her entire lack of imagination. Think Grace Kelly with a hefty dose of Gwen Stefani. Dangling from one hand was a bunch of pink roses large enough to support a tree house, and from the other, a two-thousand-dollar Chanel clutch. Does anything scream "Pay attention to me" more than roses and Chanel? I hugged my Isaac Mizrahi for Target purse to my side.

She inclined her head toward Tom. "Dreadful, isn't it?"

"More than you know," I said.

With unstudied elegance, she flung her clutch on the bed and gave Tom a proprietary kiss. She curled up beside him, roses in hand. I eyed Tom narrowly.

"So," I said, "is this the big surprise you were just about to tell me about, Tom?"

Kimberly spread her arms and nodded, grinning. "You're standing beside it."

I felt like I was standing in it and nearly lifted my foot to check.

"Tom and I sort of found each other." Kimberly flushed demurely.

"Gosh, I wish I had known you were missing," I said. "I'd have pitched in."

"You'd have to call it whirlwind," Tom said through the abject horror on his face. "Kimberly was so helpful during the job-change process, I guess it just sort of happened when I arrived. Then the attack occurred, and Kimberly was there when I woke up. A surprise, I tell you," he said carefully. "An unexpected surprise."

Like a bad case of ass eczema. "I see." I reached again for my bag. "Well, I suppose—"

"Oh, don't let me interrupt." Kimberly jumped to her feet. "I just came in to drop these off." She swept the carnations, hydrangeas and my sunflowers into the trash and installed her roses in the largest vase. "I told Tom's father I'd take him to the Louvre today. What were you two talking about?"

Since her back was turned, I slid a surreptitious finger along the waistband of my underpants and snagged the bow, offering it to Tom as a suggested response. He shook his head in terror.

"Tom's so happy with his work at the new company," I said. "He was just trying to convince me to do a rotation on his staff."

Kimberly's forehead wrinkled—actually, with all that Botox it just sort of wavered around the edges like an albino manta ray.

"I don't understand," she said to Tom. "Are you hiring?"

I waved away her concern. "Not to worry. I said no thanks. I've seen what a rotation on Tom's staff can do to a girl."

Tom harrumphed. "In any case, there is a matter I left unresolved at Pilgrim, something Seph's been good enough to remind me of. I'm afraid it will necessitate a quick trip back to Pittsburgh the minute I'm released."

Kimberly tousled the same lock of hair I'd smoothed and smiled. "So long as we don't rush things. I want you to get well first." She kissed his cheek. Even her lips didn't wrinkle. They looked like two banana halves. "See you later, love. I'll be back around dinner. I'm bringing your favorite—Brie and *jambon*."

She grabbed her purse and hurried out, giving us both a final Grace Kelly wave.

I pursed my lips. "No wonder you like the hospital food."

He held up his palms. "My twin! My twin! Not me!"

"Gee, what was it—a whole twenty-four hours after the last time you saw me?"

"He appears to be fairly unsentimental."

"Untangle yourself before you get out of here—and buy more sheets."

"You're beautiful when you're mad, you know."

"You're lucky you're a charming bastard. Are you really coming to Pittsburgh?"

He gave me a crooked smile. "I think it's pretty clear I need to get back to the Golden Triangle as soon as possible."

I leaned back and put my feet on the bed. "Looks like we have a few hours before the *jambon* arrives. What shall we discuss?"

"*Discuss?*"

"Discuss."

"The cautious approach?"

"*C'est moi.*"

He picked up his water glass. "To caution."

I picked up a plastic pill cup. "Long may it reign."

And as we clicked glasses, I noticed half a dozen tiny triangles of fabric cut from the tie of one of my shoes, triangles that could only have been made by the blade of a silver egret-handled knife.

"Um, Tom. How many days did you say you have off in June?"

POCKET BOOKS
PROUDLY PRESENTS

Seducing Mr. Darcy

Gwyn Cready

Available August 2008
from Pocket Books

Turn the page for an excerpt of
Seducing Mr. Darcy. . . .

"_YOU_ vill stretch out on the table, ja?" Madame K the masseuse commanded. "And clear your head."

But what Flip wanted to clear was her nose. The mellow orange-y scent wafting from the candle was making her a little woozy. Madame K tucked her in on the table, covered her with a warm sheet and snapped off the towel like a magician doing a tablecloth trick.

She worked in small circles, from Flip's shoulder blades to her hips, folding back the sheet as necessary to ensure every muscle got its proper workout. Flip felt like a tube of recalcitrant toothpaste.

"You work at the Aviary here in Pittsburgh?" the woman said.

"Yes."

"How eez your work there?"

"Usually great, but today—ugh. Don't ask."

The woman made a sympathetic clucking noise and continued her Nobel Prize–worthy kneading. Flip felt the tension begin to trickle out her fingers and toes.

"Are you clearing your head?" Madame K asked.

"Mmmm-mmm."

Flip considered the flowered carpet visible through the table's porthole, and watched the suede tassels of Madame K's odd little booties flop as she worked. But then her eyes grew heavy and her lids began to flutter in time to the rhythmic rearrangement of her muscles.

Clearing her head was not easy. Whatever Madame K was releasing in her back seemed to come pouring up her neck into her brain in a soft focus, home-movie sort of way: her girlfriends and their over-the-top fascination with Darcy, *Pride and Prejudice,* and that whole weird historical romance thing; her loathsome ex-husband, Jed, jogging up the stairs of the Cornell Ornithology building like Rocky as he stole the birding fellowship from her; a black-and-white ivory-billed woodpecker soaring through the forest top; Jed's painful and all-too-frequent indiscretions during their marriage; that asshole Brit professor from the café today with the interesting topaz eyes; that asshole Brit professor from the café today in a pair of ivory breeches and an open linen shirt, turning her over his knee—

What?? Flip started. *No.*

Darcy in a pair of ivory breeches and an open linen shirt, tugging the laces of her chemise. There we go. Or even better: the hero in the romance she was reading, who'd been only too happy to serve his heroine on his knees in that Venice hotel bathroom, his shiny, dark head of curls bobbing between her—

"Hey." Flip, who had gone two years without any head bobbing, shiny, dark or otherwise, lifted herself on an elbow. "What about the imagining yourself in your favorite book part? That's part of your advertisement for the massage, right?"

Madame K gave her the fish-eye. "Indeed it is. Have you cleared your head?"

"Oh yeah, absolutely."

"Very vell. There are two very important rules. You cannot imagine something that vould not naturally happen in the book. King Lear, for example, cannot fly a plane."

King Lear. Flip snorted. Like that's what she'd be imagining. "And?"

"And you cannot imagine the same book twice. Both rules observed or big trouble."

Flip waited. "That's it? That's the value-added favorite book service? You don't hypnotize me, or play the book on tape, or give me a crown and princess dress or anything?"

The woman slitted a frosted blue lid. "Our clients are very happy."

Well, this I could've done that in my own bed, Flip thought, and the only rule there would have been D-cells give out in about thirty minutes.

"Okay. Sure." Flip rested her head again.

Madame K's palms continued their efforts, bringing warm, healing heat to Flip's shoulders and neck. Her thoughts tried to drift to the sexy scene atop the bathroom vanity, but the tile marks, the steam, even the cool, hard marble under the hips of the heroine kept slipping away from her mind's eye, like sand through open fingers. She wondered for a long moment if Darcy had topaz eyes too, then slowly drifted off.

An instant later—had she fallen asleep?—the scent had changed, from citrus to a heavy floral—roses or honeysuckle. *Like my Grandma Thompson's powder room. God-awful.*

Flip drew her eyes open, a momentous effort, to say as much to Madame K, and stopped, shocked.

The massage tables were gone. The room was gone. At least *that* room was gone. The room Flip found herself alone in was easily eight times its size. And the quaint Georgian furniture of the massage studio was now enormous, expensive Georgian furniture. Brocade sofas as long as an Airstream. Curlique table legs. Impediment-topped sideboards, and silk-tasseled drawer pulls. She was resting on a chaise, her head inclined.

Oh, I get it. I'm dreaming. This must be the lobby of the hotel in the romance novel. Very Room With a View.

Flip smiled. At the point she'd reached in the book, there hadn't been any scenes in the lobby, but, hey, she thought, one's sexual escapades had to start somewhere. But if this was Venice and Mr. Iron Knees was about to whisk her up to the bathroom, why was she feeling a strange niggle of unease?

She looked down, eager to see what sort of slinky outfit she'd provided herself for this dreamy adventure, only to discover her skirt covered her knees. In fact, her skirt reached to the floor, and the bra she was wearing was so uncomfortable, it felt like she was wrapped in a picket fence.

God, I hope the honor bar has wire cutters, she thought.

Flip grabbed an armload of the voluminous fabric and pulled it up before her eyes, examining the stiff violet satin and heavily beaded hem.

Cripes, no wonder I'm uneasy. I'm a freakin' bridesmaid!

She dropped the skirt and found herself looking straight into the embarrassed gaze of a bald servant in tails. Definitely not her Venice hero.

He cleared his throat. "Lady Quillan?"

"Yes?" Flip answered.

Isn't it strange, she thought, how you automatically accept what happens in a dream: you're a one-legged avocado designer from Tunisia; the sky turns paisley at sunset; an English butler addresses you as Lady Quillan, and, boom, you're Lady Quillan. Weird.

"A messenger has arrived." He tilted his head toward the hall.

The words hit her like a two-by-four. There was something in his tone, or perhaps it was the uncomfortable look on his face, that made all hope of an evening rendezvous disappear.

"He's been instructed to give the note to you directly, m'um."

"Thank you." Flip stood, feeling like a heavy weight had been dropped on her shoulders. Whoever she was, Lady Quillan was not looking forward to this message.

"You look unwell," the man said. "May I call for something?"

"A bathroom vanity?"

His forehead creased. "Bathroom?"

And then Flip saw it. Outside the room's intricately paned window. A carriage and horses at the top of the long treed drive that led to the house.

Oh, hell. There wasn't a bathroom vanity in the house because there wasn't even a damned bathroom. It was freakin' England, before freakin' plumbing! She was absolutely not paying anything extra for this massage.

"Nothing, Samuel."

Samuel, is it? Things were coming to her in bits and pieces—and the oddest bits and pieces. She knew Samuel's name, just as she knew her right slipper was missing its second button, just as she knew this wasn't her house, just as she knew her hostess and her hostess's sister were in the room next door. But why this as-of-yet unseen note was making her feel like she'd taken a belly punch she didn't know.

Samuel bowed and gestured toward the door. Flip stepped tentatively into the cavernous hall. Tall and square and built to showcase the looming double door entrance, the hall housed a staircase that curved elegantly to the upper floor, a massive silver chandelier, and doors leading in every direction.

"There you are, Francie," a concerned voice said as she rounded the corner.

The man who had spoken was tall and expensively dressed, in a midnight blue coat, cream waistcoat and breeches, and gleaming black boots. Despite a disappointing lack of curls, his striking brown eyes, dark hair, and strong patrician profile were oddly familiar.

A footman stood next to him holding a top hat and pair of riding gloves. *Was the blue-coated man the owner of the carriage?* The man accepted the items, but his eyes stayed on her.

"Has Jared arrived at last?" he asked.

"No," she said. "A messenger, it seems." Embarrassment throbbed in her like a fresh bruise. But why?

Samuel called, and a dusty-faced youth fiddling with a pouch emerged from a doorway. He scratched his nose unselfconsciously and extended the note. Flip accepted it with unsteady fingers.

The note was written in a neat, masculine hand.

"Clearly I have not made the supper. Nonetheless, I had thought I would be able to arrive in time to accompany you to Abbot House, but I find my business keeps me longer than I expected. Secure an invitation for the night from Louisa. I feel certain she would be pleased to keep you. I shall fetch you in the morning, and we can arrive at Abbot House as our servants do, which shall be more convenient in any case. — Q"

Flip felt a black stone settle in her gut.

"Bad news?" the gentleman asked, oblivious to the footman who stood poised, waiting for the signal that would prompt him to open the double doors.

"No," she said. "Not at all."

Across from them, beyond another door, where the sound of indistinct female talk had been apparent for the past moments, a clear snippet rose. "Business, my foot," said a bemused woman's voice. "Quillan's with his whore in Stourton." Another woman tittered. "Ah, the poor, oblivious girl. Do you suppose she even knows?"

Flip stood rigid, drowning in the all-too-familiar waves of shame and humiliation. Husbands hadn't changed much in two hundred years.

The youth was the first to break the uncomfortable silence. "Is there a reply, m'um?"

"No." Her voice was barely a whisper.

The gentleman pulled a coin from his pocket and placed it in the hand of the boy, who immediately trotted to the back of the house.

Interpreting this as closure, the footman placed his hand on the knob.

"Sir, your phaeton—" Samuel began, but received an unspoken signal from the phaeton's owner and stopped.

The hall was silent now, save the pounding in Flip's ears.

"Has Jared been held up?" The gentleman held his tone even, as if he hadn't heard the women, giving Flip every opportunity to collect herself, though it was clear from the mild disgust in his eyes the women were not people whose claim on him was strong.

"Yes." Flip folded the note carefully. "My husband will not be arriving until tomorrow. I-I must ask Louisa if I might stay. I am a bit of trouble," she added with a forced laugh. "I'm sure Louisa didn't expect a simple supper invitation to stretch into an overnight stay."

"Is there anyone else in Wiltshire to whom you owe a visit?" the man asked carefully. "A cousin, perhaps? You have so many. I should be happy to drive you anywhere you'd like to go."

The footman waited, motionless.

"No," she said. "No one." Wiltshire felt like a vast, lonely place.

The man nodded, understanding. There was no more to be said. He placed his top hat on his head and bowed a regretful good-bye. The footman clicked his heels and opened the door.

Flip gathered her skirts, full of dread. Sadly, it looked as if the only person on his knees tonight would be her, deep in humiliation, asking the Wicked Witch of Wiltshire for an extra bed.

She took a deep breath and entered the room. The

women were seated at a table playing cards. The first was reed thin and brunette, too recessive to be the owner of this home. The other was horsy, plump and blond. That one, Flip knew, was Louisa. Though her face bore the mask of polite concern, Louisa's eyes were lit with the spark of recently shared amusement.

"Oh, Lady Quillan, you look hardly more rested than when you laid down. Pray, do not fear. I was just saying to Caroline I'm sure your husband is merely detained and—"

"I have heard from my husband," Flip said. "And I shall have to beg your indulgence. It seems—"

"It seems," interrupted the blue-coated gentleman who had appeared unnoticed at Flip's side, "my phaeton shall require an extra cushion, Louisa. My old friend Lord Quillan sent his man just now to ask me to give her ladyship a ride to Abbot House."

The man pressed his elbow very lightly against Flip's, a gesture invisible to their hosts.

"Abbot House," he went on, "is quite close to my destination, after all, and Quillan has arrived in Wiltshire more tired than he expected."

"Quillan is in Wiltshire?" Louisa repeated, unbelieving. "At Abbot House?"

The gentleman's eyes flashed cold, hard iron. "Without a doubt."

For a moment, the women sat silent under his chilly gaze, then Caroline broke into a coquettish giggle. "Oh, Darcy, will you be always the knight who rescues the fair maiden?"

Darcy! Flip's gaze shot to her savior, and her knees began to buckle.